WHITE RUSSIAN ON THE ROCKS

Yuri turned quickly. With horror, he saw a massive head rise from the crevice near the rover, its eyes fixed on the two humans near the cliff-edge. A powerful hand swung upward, grasping for a handhold. Leonid broke first and ran for the rover, shouting a warning.

The alien caught Leonid in two long strides, knocking him to the ground with a blow of its fist. Leonid bounced hard on the broken stone, his rifle skittering out of his hands. He screamed as the alien pounced again and lifted him high in the air, then dashed him downward onto the rocks.

RINN'S STAR

Paula E. Downing

A Del Rey Book

BALLANTINE BOOKS • NEW YORK

A Del Rey Book
Published by Ballantine Books

Library of Congress Catalog Card Number: 90-91851

ISBN 0-345-36919-X

Manufactured in the United States of America

First Edition: December 1990

Cover Art by Barclay Shaw

ACKNOWLEDGMENTS

My special thanks to Jacqueline Lichtenberg for her wonderful encouragement and enthusiasm; to Marti Steussy and Kara Anne Schreiber for their friendship and help with *Rinn's Star*; to my editor at Del Rey, Shelly Shapiro; and especially to my husband and best friend, T. Jackson King, whom I love in all the ways.

Chapter 1

RINN McCREA CROUCHED IN THE SHIP'S AFTER-hold, listening to the jumbled thoughts of the aliens outside. They were strange creatures, darkly hostile now that they had revealed themselves in the sudden massacre of *Sing Fa*'s crew.

She listened, cradling her unconscious crewmate in her arms, as the alien warriors searched the area near the ship, looking for the two humans who had escaped into the surrounding swamp: Ma Ching and Hseuh Jo, also her shipmates. She sensed the color of Ching's thoughts, panicked, now unable to comprehend her coming death. The two fled through the stagnant pools of Delta Bootis, away from the ship and the aliens beating the brush behind them.

Rinn cradled Mei-lan more tightly, without response: Mei-lan had found her own escape, however temporary, in oblivion. Rinn had guessed the weakness that lay beneath the other woman's hard speech and conduct. Mei-lan was the most fervent of the crew's revolutionaries, the first to accept criticism in *Sing Fa*'s weekly political-correction meetings—and the first to pronounce it, even daring to edge on Captain Hung's own authority. She had a strange nobility in her fanaticism, a singleness of purpose typical of Xin Tian's elite colonists chosen from Greater Asia's billions on Earth. But Rinn had also heard the fear-color deep in Mei-lan's secret mind, a terror of space that she could not fully conceal from an adept. In the strange way Normals

1

had, Mei-lan had guessed Rinn's awareness—and had hated Rinn the more for it.

Odd that Rinn and Mei-lan might be the only two to escape the death of *Sing Fa*. It was an irony Mei-lan would not enjoy.

She sensed Mei-lan slipping still deeper into unconsciousness, away from the disaster that had struck their ship. Of their crew of twelve, six had died in the initial attack, when Captain Hung had unwisely opened the ship to the natives come to trade. Two others had died quickly as they ran from the ship; two others were, at that very moment, fleeing through the swamp surrounding them—and two, herself and Mei-lan, remained cowering in the small hold near the engine room, waiting for the horror to end.

Not wanting to quest farther, Rinn focused her thought on the natives nearest the ship. She did not want to hear the deaths of her remaining crewmates, did not want a repetition of the intense rage-pleasure of the aliens who made the kill. She gathered in her perception, building a barrier around herself, key-patterned only to the immediate threat of those who might yet discover her hiding place. A telepath learned early to guard the mind from unpleasant perceptions; Rinn had an uncommon skill in the guarding from hard experience. The crew of *Sing Fa* had not liked her presence aboard.

She gently shifted her grip on Mei-lan and lowered her to the metal deck. Mei-lan's narrow face was pale and drawn, her short black hair fanned into a fringe against the deck. Rinn studied her companion for several moments, then tiredly pushed back her own dark hair and rubbed her eyes. She felt within the breast of her blue cotton-padded tunic to the inner pocket; her fingers touched her Star and she drew it out. It winked and shimmered in the half-light of the hold telltales, emblem of what she was— badge of shame and horror to some, badge of great honor to herself. She was a Starfarer, one of the few telepaths who had left Ikanos for another destiny than Group-Mind.

Two centuries earlier, humanity had risen beyond its Earth cradle and found new homes on other worlds. The radiation of alien environments and the harsh particle-storms of space had caused mutations, some of feeble body and short lives, others threatening new and superior breeds of human that might supplant the old. Some governments had hunted down and murdered the strange; others had passed ghetto laws to the same end, calling it merciful. For a time, all had overlooked the possibility of mutation of mind in an unchanged body—until, eighty years ago, a new people had subverted a Chinese research station at 44 Bootis and claimed it as their own.

They called it Ikanos, an ancient word for mind.

The Treaty of 2298 had divided Near Space among the major nations of Earth into broad quadrants of exclusive exploitation: the Soviets had taken most of Bootes, the Chinese the nearby constellations of Corona Borealis and Hercules. 44 Bootis lay squarely astride the boundary radiant, on an uneasy border afflicted by poaching on both sides. Among a series of more important outrages, each vigorously protested by the colonial legates on Earth, 44 Bootis had remained a minor squabble over station rights on a single airless moon. Until Ikanos.

As the Normals debated, the telepaths hid children in secret enclaves on every colony in Hercules/Bootes, guarding themselves against a preemptive strike on Ikanos' fragile bubbledome by fearful governments. Then, to complicate still further, Xin Tian abruptly claimed Ikanos as a protectorate and dared the Soviets to intervene. The Soviets hesitated, waiting for guidance from a divided Earth government, and lost the point through inaction. Instead, they retaliated ruthlessly against the enclaves on Novy Strana and Rodina, hunting down the telepaths in unswerving determination, executing all prisoners after much publicized trials. Few in their enclaves had escaped, and Soviet law still proscribed any contact with Ikanos on pain of execution.

Nor had the Soviets forgotten the humiliation. In colonial politics, ancient grievances had a long life.

After its political coup, Xin Tian preened in the councils of Earth, then exacted its price from Ikanos. From each generation of telepaths, Xin Tian demanded a corps of contract employees—the Starfarers—to undertake the risky exploration of new worlds, and earned valuable credits by lending Starfarers to other Chinese colonies for a heavy fee. Other telepaths assisted the guards in enforcing Xin Tian's policies of revolutionary and racial purity; still others worked in the hospitals and labs, using the Gift as their Chinese superiors directed.

For three years I have tried to serve them, she thought, watching Mei-lan's face. Never as a friend, not quite as a slave. And in the end I failed them all—except one. She slipped the Star into her pocket: emblems could not help her now.

It was turning dark outside; she turned her mind outward and felt the coolness of the twilight air against an alien skin, felt the alert-sense take hold of its owner as night senses stirred in response to the setting sun. She waited, listening.

* * *

His name was Isen-glov-amar, son to the chief of the Lily People, destined to be chief in his own right. Long-bodied, multilegged, yellow-skinned, the young warrior prowled the perimeter of the clearing, his unease about the tall bulking Devil-house lessening with familiarity. He kept the house in his side vision, his second brain studying it carefully while his first gave commands to his warriors and listened for the death-cry from the swamp. It had been a clean attack, Isen-glov-amar's first leading, and his third brain felt the pleasure of anticipation. There would be a procession through the coraal of his village, a dance to celebrate his victory, and then the ancient ceremony of strength-for-strength. He glanced over at the bodies near the edge of the clearing: enough to give all his warriors their portion of the curious flesh that made up the Star-Devils' brains.

His snout lifted as a cry echoed in the distance, followed by the muffled hooting of a victorious kill. Isen-glov-amar's neck fur ruffled in response, his third brain responding automatically to the passion of the hunt. But he repressed his urge to follow the chase and continued pacing the clearing, his eyes watching both the Devil-house and the swamp surrounding it.

The door to the ship still gaped open, half-concealing the bulk of the warrior he had posted to guard it. Isen-glov-amar paused, considering. He counted eight bodies at the side of the clearing, and he knew that two more Devils had escaped into the swamp. He wondered if more Devils lurked within, despite the previous search. He would see for himself.

As he turned toward the shipdoor, his stride sank into a prey-stalk, signalling his intention to the nearby warriors. Maret and Belos, by rank his side-guards on any hunt, promptly followed him. He stepped up the short ladder to the shipdoor and dropped the strap of his fire-weapon off his broad shoulder, cradling the weapon in his powerful hands. Then he linked his first and third minds and crept silently past the door-guard into the darkened interior of the Devil-house.

Rinn rose to her feet and quickly examined their small sanctuary. The ceiling arced downward in a low curve, following the shape of the domed floor of the engine room above. The walls bent in at odd angles, constrained by the bulk of the engines on either side. It was a catchspace created solely by the engine design and adaptable to many uses. *Sing Fa* used it as a hold for little-used supplies.

Rinn bent down and grasped Mei-lan's body by the arms, then dragged her into shelter behind a stack of cartons. Moving quietly, she built up a wall around her shipmate with other nearby cartons, then uncrated a small deckplate from a box standing against the far wall. The alloy plate lifted easily, and she built a roof over the cartons, then stacked others on top of it to conceal the plate. The sharp smell of the packing material drifted upward as the plate crushed their borders, perhaps enough to hide their human scent from the searchers.

Two levels above, the three aliens moved silently through the ruined control room. Rinn paused, listening to the intense focus of their thoughts, careful not to touch their minds with her own. She was aware of the aliens' third brain and felt wary of its hunter-senses that might respond to her own conscious Gift. But she caught no awareness of herself in that searching and continued her preparations.

She had no weapons—there had been no time during the speed of the attack, and weapons had not helped the rest of the crew. The aliens were hunters, laser-armed and key-sensed for the kill. Her chosen answer, right or wrong, was in concealment and stealth. She tugged the last of the cartons into place and crouched down next to Mei-lan in the confined space. It was a waiting game, one she knew well.

She listened to Isen-glov-amar and his guards as they worked their way down through the ship. As they approached her hold, Rinn slipped into other-mind, controlling her breathing and emotions by strength of will. Mei-lan lay insensible beside her; Rinn slipped her fingers to the pulse at Mei-lan's throat, ready to choke off blood to her brain if she stirred, sending her deep into her coma again for the sake of their lives. She sat crosslegged in their enclosed space and made a like enclosure of her mind.

The hold door opened, and the aliens padded into the room. They paused, sniffing, seeking the scent of their prey. Then, after a few minutes, they withdrew, swinging the door shut behind them. Rinn sat motionless, deep in the other-mind, as Isen-glov-amar searched other levels, finding nothing.

Two hours later, the aliens left the clearing, bearing their grisly burdens with them. Rinn waited another hour, then moved slightly. She blinked and stirred her muscles, wincing at the pain of a body held too long in one position and now forced to move. Then slowly, like a swimmer through water, Rinn thought of new plans.

She sent out her thought, a single strand looping toward the shipbase far up the peninsula. *I am Rinn, Starfarer. Help us, help us.* Distantly she heard a blur of uncomprehending thoughts from another trader ship, a Soviet ship.

I am Rinn, Starfarer. Help us. She heard no answer. The other ship, then, did not carry a telepath among its crew. She had expected as much. After eighty years, few telepaths, perhaps none, still survived on the Soviet worlds. She was alone.

She looked down at her unconscious companion, a shadow half-drawn in a fetal curl on the deck. The control room was in ruins, the radio smashed beyond repair. There could be no rescue by that means, either. They would have to walk.

And if they reached the Soviet ship . . . The Near Space Treaty mandated rescue for shipwrecked crewmen, no matter what the circumstances. They would take Mei-lan aboard—they had to—and give her medical care and transport back home. But would they take a Starfarer? She did not know. There were no precedents.

And who, in the councils of Earth, would protest if they would not? Xin Tian? Perhaps. If it suited the politics of the moment— and perhaps it might and save some future Starfarer wrecked on a Soviet world, however too late for Rinn.

Later, she told herself. I'll think about it later.

Rinn pushed at the carton nearest her, shoving it aside to clear a crawlspace out of her shelter. On hands and knees, she crawled into the dimly lit hold, then stood to stretch. Pain seized her calves as blood circulated into the oxygen-starved muscles. The Gift respected its owner's life but sometimes gave little heed to lesser bodily wants. She winced and repressed a groan as she walked in a circle, slowly exercising her legs.

The pain subsided. Rinn paused a moment, listening for alien thoughts, then dismantled the wall of the shelter to reach her companion.

"Mei-lan, wake up," she said, shaking her.

"Uhhhhh . . . " Mei-lan's eyelids fluttered.

"Mei-lan!"

Rinn shook her again, but Mei-lan only batted away her hand, muttering querulously. Rinn dipped lightly into Mei-lan's mind to judge her nearness to consciousness, and felt her reflexively slip away into deeper coma. Mei-lan could not yet face the loss of the ship.

Rinn left her in the shelter of the cartons and stepped into the corridor. On either side of the hold door, the massive metal-shod shapes of the engines bowed into the corridor; to the left, the ship corridor stretched several meters to a riser of steps that led to a wide receiving bay and the ship's exterior airlock. She looked to the right, seeking another access in case the airlock was being watched.

She remembered a service port to the lower engines, used for repair. Did it have an interior access? She tried to remember the vague schematic *Sing Fa*'s engineer always carried in his inner mind: she thought it might. But first she moved swiftly to a nearby ladder and climbed upward. They would need clothing, food, weapons, and a light. Already the night had settled its darkness on the swamp surrounding the ship.

She packed two carryalls with supplies from storage, then stepped into Captain Hung's office. The furnishings of the office reflected the severe but competent character of its occupant. Poaching on another colony's trade route was a delicate task, well-measured to the talents of Xin Tian's most subtle captains. A week before, Hung had chosen his new landing site with exquisite care, seeking advantage of the Soviets' established trade with the peninsula natives on Delta's sole inhabited continent, yet not so close to the Soviet base that *Sing Fa*'s landing provoked a confrontation. He had chosen deftly: aside from a spluttering reproof, the other ship had not acted.

Later there would be angry protests and yet another fierce debate on Earth. Both ships were a long way from home, and damage inflicted risked damage received. The Soviet captain had made the prudent choice.

Perhaps Hung's satisfaction with his coup had caused his resistance to Rinn's warnings—though the roots of their conflict were far older. He did not *like* her fair skin, her Caucasian blood. He did not *like* her telepathy, though Xin Tian's extended experience with telepaths had blurred some of that instinctive prejudice. And Mei-lan's bitter diatribes about Rinn's political errors—though by contract Starfarers were exempt from the usual correction—had only hardened his attitude. Rinn did not fit, risked distraction at a key moment, could not always be predicted, did not *belong*.

"Give me *specific* data, Starfarer," he had demanded, his expression sour with irritation and dislike. "Not this vague 'I sense trouble, Captain,' or 'Be careful, Captain.' *What* trouble? *Why* careful?" He waved his hand at the peaceful marsh surrounding the ship. "I see nothing to alarm. Nothing!"

"But, sir . . ."

"The Novy Strana ships have traded successfully here for two years. Give me a reason why we won't do the same."

"I can't," she said helplessly. "But something's wrong, something . . ."

"Faugh!" Hung spat disgustedly and stamped away. Only later, in the sudden shock of the attack, had Rinn found the reason for her unease. She had learned too late the significance of the Deltean third brain, its deep drives of violent intention, its compulsions that could not be resisted—too late for Captain Hung, too late for *Sing Fa*.

My fault, my fault, she berated herself. But would he have listened even if I'd known?

She glanced around the spare office which was littered with trade reports and memorabilia, and drew in a sharp breath of pain. *Sing Fa* had paid the price of their mutual failure.

She keyed the site map on Hung's desk computer and printed a fresh copy, then bent forward under the yellow glare of the lamp to study the route to the Soviet base. The orbital resolution of the map was not good, nor did it extend much farther north than the interior mountains fronting the piedmont—Captain Hung had interested himself only in poaching on an established trade. The map showed few details of the trackless salt marsh to the south, then a featureless wide sea beyond stretching half the planet to an ice-laden and barren continent on the pole. A small circle marked the Soviet base near the peninsula tip. Twenty kilometers. She considered the distance and felt a jab of worry and despair. Her muscles already ached with fatigue and stress—later, the ache would not be so easy to ignore.

When she returned to the afterhold, she found Mei-lan sitting groggily in the tumble of cartons. As Rinn stepped into the darkened room, the Chinese woman started violently, shying from the Starfarer's looming shadow.

"Who's there?" she cried.

"It's Rinn. Be at peace, Mei-lan." Rinn dropped her burden on the floor and crossed quickly to the stricken woman, reaching out to comfort her with a touch—but Mei-lan struck out wildly.

"Go away!"

"Mei-lan, be sensible." Rinn tried to touch her again, but Mei-lan shrank away, her eyes staring in white-rimmed terror. Rinn sank back onto her heels, watching. The retreat seemed to calm the hysteria. After a moment, Mei-lan looked around the small hold, examining its contents and walls as if they were utterly strange.

"What place is this?" she asked. She pushed back her disheveled hair with a trembling hand. The shuddering spread to her whole body; her teeth chattered with it. Fear filled her mind, an amalgam of unnamed terrors and personal dissolution, the loss of self and belief, an endless pursuit by monstrous evils of unknown form. Rinn shuddered in response to Mei-lan's unconscious projection.

"*Sing Fa*, Mei-lan," she said soothingly. "Don't you remember?"

"Remember? Remember?" Mei-lan jabbered, then abruptly stood up. She blundered into the stack of cartons, crashing them to the metal floor, then turned in panic from the sound and ran full-stride into the rear wall. Rinn caught her as she fell, and Mei-lan clung to her, blood running thickly from a cut above her brow. Rinn staunched the wound with her pocket-cloth, then smoothed antiseptic from her med-kit across the cut and applied a bandage. Mei-lan shivered again, more from Rinn's touch than from the pain.

"Mei-lan," Rinn began once again, and then contented herself with holding the woman close, rocking her slowly back and forth.

"Ahhhh . . ." Mei-lan cried, her voice rising to a thin wail. "Ahhh . . ."

Mei-lan's fear flowed in shuddering waves, beating at Rinn's mind. For a moment she felt tempted to assert the subversive mind-control she had learned as a child—and had rejected as an adult—to escape the roiling terror that struck at her mind and emotions. Rinn gritted her teeth, resisting both the fear and the temptation.

Mei-lan's hysteria rose still higher, threatening both herself and Rinn with a fear-driven dissolution into madness. Rinn quickly fumbled for a sedative in the kit; Mei-lan scarcely felt the prick of the injector. After a minute, her fear began to ebb, calmed by the false security of the drug.

"Come, Mei-lan. Come with me."

Rinn pulled Mei-lan to her feet and held her upright, then guided the woman's staggering feet toward the hold door. Mei-lan sagged against her, forcing Rinn to drag her limp body the last few meters to the access hatch. Rinn quickly retrieved their supplies, then bent over the hatch.

She cracked the seal and entered the man-height access through the hull. She dangled a moment, then released her grip and fell the short distance to the lower port, her boots ringing hollowly on the metal hatch. She shifted her feet to the rim of the hatch and fumbled for the release lever; the lower hatch opened with a clang. The warm, humid air of the swamp, redolent with strange scents, gushed into the ship.

Quietly, Rinn lowered herself to the ground beneath the ship and crouched, listening with her ears and mind.

An animal coursed through the dank water far to her right, seeking the small crustaceans that clung to submerged weeds or buried themselves in the mud. Alert, feral, quick-moving, the predator relished the night and its own active appetite. It dove into the blood-warm water, hunting. Beyond it, a night flyer swept over the reed-beds, the warm air a silky flow over its naked skin. It beat its frilled wings lazily, patrolling its territory for interlopers of its own kind, vaguely aware of an urge to mate: the two instincts warred in its consciousness as it entered its cyclic estrus. Beneath its effortless flight, smaller creatures felt their half-aware impulses of hunger and need and responded to the touch of reed and water, the sounds of the night, and the scents that drifted on the water and air.

Rinn sent her perception farther and touched the watcher a hundred meters beyond the northern edge of the glade. She knew that watcher from Captain Hung's meetings with the aliens: Maret, bodyguard to the Lord Isen-glov-amar, and he had heard the clang of the opening hatch. Rinn sensed his sudden alertness, then the small shock of joining as Maret linked his first and third brains for the stalk. Silently, he crept through the tall reeds toward the looming shadow of the Devil-house.

Rinn immediately climbed back through the port-access and closed the upper hatch door behind her, then fumbled for the stunner in the side pocket of her carryall. She wrapped her slim fingers around the barrel, hefting its weight. *Sing Fa*'s stunners had failed to halt the earlier attack, either inadequate against the bulk of the warriors' bodies, or ill-suited to their nervous system—but she had no other weapon. The key to the laser-rifle cabinet had left with Hung's body.

She crouched by the sedated Mei-lan and the supplies, the stunner cradled in one hand, as Maret stealthily approached the ship. The alien circled the clearing, his three-lobed mind focused on the hunt. When he sensed nothing in the clearing, he approached the ship, close enough to touch its sleek metal sides. Within a minute, he found the dangling port-access and peered upward into the dark tunnel. Rinn waited above, hardly breathing, her hand again on Mei-lan's throat to choke off any revealing sound.

Go away, she wished desperately at the alien below. She closed her eyes, trying to still any thought that Maret might detect, but again her wish whispered in her mind: *Go away.*

Maret considered as he touched the metal port and pushed it into a lazy swing. The hinged lid rocked back and forth in decreasing arcs, then became still again. He heard the *plop* of a fish in the nearby pond and felt the moving air on his body, awash with familiar scents that partly masked the Devil-smell of the ship.

He again touched the cold metal of the hatch, saw how it joined to the underbelly of the ship, and flicked the prong of the latch. It gave easily beneath his fingers—too easily? Who knew the ways of a Star-Devil's possessions? Maret looked around, listening to the night. Then, satisfied, he unlinked his third mind and returned to his northward post.

Rinn bowed her head over her arms a moment, her heart thudding, then rose determinedly to her feet. The night was waning, past midnight; they would have to be far away before dawn. She lowered the supply bags down the access-chute, careful to make no sound, then lifted Mei-lan into a shoulder carry and climbed down the port, her feet reaching blindly for the narrow rungs set into the access walls. Outside she bent awkwardly for the carryalls, Mei-lan's deadweight dragging at her, then left the concealing bulk of the ship.

She reached the reeds at the edge of the clearing and slipped among them, then eased herself into the protecting pool beyond. An insect shurred by her face, singing its faint whine. The warm night air sighed against her face, carrying her scent away from the alien who kept guard in the darkness, but that benefit would last only as long as the night blew its breezes from land to sea.

Sheltered among the shadowy reeds, Rinn breathed deeply of the night air, then listened for any alarm given by their escape. Maret still patrolled to the north, his night-senses alert but unaware. That could not last; perhaps, in its deepest convolutions, Maret's third brain already sensed her. She hoped for an hour's grace, enough time to lose herself among the trackless pools.

Rinn shifted Mei-lan's awkward weight to a better grip, then turned south toward the distant murmur of human minds.

Chapter 2

MARET BREATHED IN THE REDOLENT NIGHT AIR, gathering its scents. He stood easily on the edge of the Devilhouse clearing, legs splayed, laser-rifle shouldered across his broad back, keeping the night watch. A warrior several years into manhood, Maret was accustomed to the night watch and knew his value in his able senses. Few among the Lily People could equal his awareness of the night air, and that skill lay among his Names of Honor. He gathered the night to him, aware of the whiff of camp fire smoke from the north where his coral lay in somnolent contentment, of the lingering taste of blood in the clearing where the Star-Devils had died, of the murky scents of water and dying vegetation to the south.

He kept alert, his second brain classifying the information brought to him by his senses, while his first brain studied a faint disturbance within him. Something . . . something he had overlooked. Although all seemed silent and undisturbed, he felt the steady signals of alarm from his third brain. He scanned the surroundings again, peering through the darkness with night-widened eyes, then opened his broad mouth to draw in the tastes of the air. All seemed quiet. The land breeze sighed across the marshes, barely stirring the tops of the reed-beds. Some meters away, a marsh-hunter called alarm against an intruder, then engaged in a furious splashing as it drove off its rival. Nothing to cause alarm. Maret paced in slight agitation, stirred by the instincts of his deepest mind.

He reviewed the hours of his watch and thought again of the strange clang from the Devil-house. There had been nothing there except a swinging hatch. He knew the Devil-house was partly alive: he had seen its lights and heard the hum of machinery. The warriors had silenced most of the lights as part of their attack, a prudence ordered by Isen-glov-amar. Perhaps the crippled Devil-house sensed its own emptiness and signalled to its dead crew. Who could understand the ways of Devils? Or perhaps . . .

Maret stiffened. The Devil-house still reeked of the smell of the Star-Devils, but was not that smell especially strong at the hatch? As if a Star-Devil had placed its foot to the ground, hands to metal? Perhaps . . .

Linking his first and third brains, Maret loped into the clearing. He circled the Devil-house warily, senses alert, until he reached the open hatch. The Star-Devil reek assaulted his nose, and he grimaced in disgust. A Star-Devil had walked there, and recently. He quested farther away from the hatch and found the scent-trail leading toward the distant reeds. He followed, third brain thrumming with the need to hunt that trail.

He stopped at the reed-bed, and for a moment discipline warred against instinct. He swayed back and forth in his need, then forced himself away from the trail. He could abandon his post and hunt alone, but a warrior met his own fault bravely and knew the purposes of his watch. Like a black shadow, Maret fled northward to the tribal coraal.

Two kilometers to the south, Rinn stopped to rest on a wide mud-pan surrounded by concealing reeds. As she emerged from the blood-warm water, the night breeze plucked at her sodden clothing and sent an unhealthy chill across her sweat-drenched shoulders. She clamped her mouth against her chattering teeth and climbed onto the shelf of firm mud. Wearily she lowered Mei-lan's limp body from her shoulder, dropped the carryalls, and collapsed. The planet's light gravity had made the carry easier, probably even possible, but she was near exhaustion now. She breathed heavily, the fatigue poisons coursing through her body, dragging at her.

She wrapped her arms around herself against the chill and slipped into other-mind for whatever refreshment it could bring. Blessed other-mind. Of all the skills of Ikanos, she valued it the most. She felt her tired muscles relax as she floated, only semi-aware. The dampness of the mud seeped into the fabric of her trousers, chilling her buttocks until the cold shivered up her spine. The night breeze moved against her body, bringing its feather touch to her skin, its strange odors and distant sounds to her dulled senses. The sensations of cold and air prickled at the edges of her mind, not unpleasantly. Dimly she sensed the presence of other minds, feral and limited; they shifted across the mists of her perception, like half-seen shadows in the distance. She breathed deeply, at peace.

As Rinn sank deeper into the sheltering trance, other presences rose into her consciousness, unwelcome shapes of old memories, memories she wanted to forget. She stirred restlessly, unwilling to leave other-mind to escape them.

"Create a womb for your conscious mind," Master Tolan had said years before, his mental voice resonating with the many echoes of Group-Mind. "The fetal memory is deep in the id; you must draw it upward and create a shell for the other-mind. Johanssen, will you demonstrate?"

Tolan pointed at the girl seated next to Rinn on the front bench. Marla tried, her sly face tense with effort. A minute passed, and Marla's half-created shape wavered, then dissolved. Tolan snorted, the lines near his mouth accentuated by his displeasure.

"Mind your skills, girl," he warned, "or I'll know the reason why not. Anyone else want to try? Yes, McAllister." He pointed his instructor's rod at another student.

Rinn bowed her head, hunching her shoulders forward to study her fine-boned, delicate hands. A week before, on her sixteenth birthday, she had asked for travel-rights to the Starfarer enclave on Xin Tian. It was her right as a citizen to seek Starfarer service, a choice rigorously guarded by protectorate law; any complaint about Contract denial to the local Xin Tian legate prompted immediate and severe action. A bubble-colony dependent on a fragile shield and imports had many vulnerabilities; the Group-Mind reacted predictably to any threat to its continued existence. Better to let the miscreant go than risk another "example" by the legate.

Even so, she thought it best to keep her decision strictly to herself and hope the school administrator respected its confidentiality, however useless such a wish among the Group-Mind. She wondered briefly if Tolan knew, then carefully hid the question away in her deepest mind.

"McCrea!" Her head jerked up reflexively, and she felt the prickle of her classmates' unfriendly eyes on her back. Perhaps they all knew; she could drive herself mad wondering who knew. Already several in her class had entered the Group-Mind, and what one knew, all knew. Her stomach began a slow panicked twitching, laced by the familiar sharp pain in her side that always reacted to stress.

"Sir?"

"You weren't paying attention," Tolan said. His rod snapped down smartly for her hand. She shifted her fingers quickly before it struck, reacting instinctively to the intention before the movement began. Tolan looked surprised, then lashed out again—for her face. The rod cut into her cheek, slicing it open. Rinn cried out, her hand lifting involuntarily to her cheek. She sensed Tolan's jab of pleasure at her outcry; she fled that sick pleasure into the grayness of other-mind.

Tolan chuckled. "Excellent. Class, observe Rinn's mental configuration . . . ." Rinn escaped Tolan by fleeing even deeper into herself, conscious only of the pain and the blood seeping through her fingers from her cut cheek: she would later carry its scar to Xin Tian.

Images of older memories floated into her mind, unwelcome overtones of her sluggish thoughts. The children of her crèche, herself among them, walking in lockstep, eyes blank, following the instructions of their nursery teacher. The frightening wrongness of mass sex in the sensoriums, overheard as she lay in her crib at night, as the Group-Mind greedily magnified its pleasure with too many arms and mouths and thrustings. Her mother's distorted, terrified face in the Assimilation chamber as she and others were absorbed into the Group-Mind—and the aftermath, even more terrifying to the six-year-old Rinn, when an alien presence supplanted everything Rinn had known in her mother's mental presence. The loss of self . . .

"No! No! Mother!" She had flung herself at the window, screaming, only to be dragged away by the adults. She had fought them furiously but quickly lost the struggle, then had fled away deep into her own mind. A disgrace, they had said, shameful! They had lectured her afterward, impressing on her the magnitude of her conduct. She watched them dully from other-mind, apathetic and empty, until finally they went away. When they returned, they found a different child, one who watched warily and denied them access to her mind.

Be one with us, the Group-Mind cajoled. *Share our thoughts.* And grew angry when she still refused them.

In the colony's beginning, safe from the pressures of Normal minds, the telepaths of Ikanos had joyfully experimented with shared thought, creating patterns of merged identity that enlightened and magnified its recipients in an ever-ascending gestalt. They linked dozens of minds, then hundreds, then a thousand, eventually passing a threshold only the most cautious had suspected. A new mentality, the Group-Mind, formed among the inhabitants of Ikanos, one that had needs quite apart from its individual members. It grew quietly among them, first as an entertainment, then as an addiction, then as a Person in its own right, a god that demanded surrender of all self into its own totality. Barriers into the id were broken, the subconscious trained into obedience, a destiny created for the New Humans of Ikanos.

But always a few children resisted, even after years of indoctrination and constant exposure to the Group-Mind, rarely knowing why they fought dissolution. Reluctantly, the Group-Mind recognized the continuing necessity of losing some children to the Contract, and so allowed the rebels to survive in its midst. It damaged them, accepting no possibility of rivals later; it cajoled and tormented and punished, but it permitted.

Rinn had drifted the next ten years, quietly desperate, waiting for her escape from Ikanos. And everywhere, the Group-Mind pursued her, calling its siren voice to the deepest levels of her mind, pretending itself as her mother's voice, promising unity and completion, love.

Rinn shuddered and wrenched herself out of other-mind. She had too many ghosts tonight. Ikanos still pursued her through invisible scars that matched the visible scarring on her face. Even among the Starfarers, she often hid herself away—causing doubt among the leaders, and new pain to those who offered comfort. The enclave had openly debated her assignment to *Sing Fa*, placing new pressures and new guilts upon her shoulders. If Rinn could not find a place among her own kind, some argued, how could she find a place among Normals?

How indeed? Perhaps *Sing Fa* had died because of it, all but the sleeping woman who lay beside her.

She raised her head and listened. She heard only the sighing of the night air, Mei-lan's labored breathing, and the dim thoughts of the animals moving through the reeds. The night was quiet, a concealing damp cloak of darkness. She had heard Maret's shock of discovery an hour before, knew he returned to the coraal to gather the hunt. To the south, the other ship's crew slept, unaware. For the moment, such threats seemed distant— her immediate concern was her growing exhaustion.

She could not carry Mei-lan any further. Rinn pulled a shield-lamp from her pack and activated it, creating a small sphere of yellowish illumination around them, then unpacked a small parcel of food and water. They would camp awhile longer, then push on. Rinn bent over her shipmate and shook her shoulder.

"Mei-lan! Wake up."

Mei-lan muttered groggily and turned away, drawing up her knees into a self-sheltering oblivion. Irritated, Rinn shook harder, then yanked upward, forcing Mei-lan into a sitting position.

"Mei-lan!"

Mei-lan blinked, her eyes shadowed by the night. Rinn felt growing awareness, then shock and distaste for Rinn's touch. The Chinese woman hated to be touched, an aversion Rinn now drew upon. Mei-lan shoved at her, forcing her away.

"Get away from me!"

Rinn shifted backward and spread both hands to placate her. "I have. Wake up, Mei-lan. I need your help."

Mei-lan rubbed her face with a muddy hand, then fingered the bandage on her forehead in confusion. After a moment, the hand dropped limply into her lap. She examined the reeds and water surrounding them, then looked upward at the clouded sky. Somehow the darkness overhead, bare of stars, reassured her, as if it were a cocoon surrounding the small globe of light in which they sat. Rinn sensed her panic recede at last, allowing some degree of a reasoned awareness.

"Where are we?" Mei-lan asked.

"Two kilometers south. The ship is lost, Mei-lan. Our only hope is the Soviet ship." She pointed to the south. "About eighteen kilometers toward the sea, if we can make it."

"But where are the others?" Mei-lan asked, avoiding her eyes. She looked around in bewilderment. "Why are we alone? Where's Captain Hung? He should be here."

"They died, Mei-lan," Rinn said gently, disturbed by the childlike reaction. She suspected that Mei-lan had found a new emotional sanctuary, one far older than the identity she had found in adulthood. "We're the only two left. Look: I brought food and water with us, clothing, a light." Rinn offered a food-pack, then set it on the mud when it was not accepted. "You need strength. Eat."

Mei-lan grew more agitated. "That's not right. Captain Hung

should be here. Captain! Captain!" Mei-lan called loudly into the darkness, then tried to stand up, as if to begin a search. Rinn yanked at her sleeve, unbalancing her, and Mei-lan sat down with a thud.

"Stop that!" Mei-lan said crossly. "I need to find Captain Hung. Our duty—"

"Our duty is to survive. Eat."

Mei-lan's lips quirked slyly, and her black eyes turned mocking. "Always the pragmatist. Go here. Do that. Eat." She wrapped her arms around herself. "There's more to life than the practical, Starfarer. Some of us believe in a greater good than self-aggrandizement."

"Since when is survival self-aggrandizing?"

"When it supersedes the ideals of which you are sadly ignorant." Mei-lan looked at her coolly, eyebrows arched, waiting for Rinn to take the bait. She was well-practiced in the quick verbal games of *Sing Fa*'s criticism sessions, usually carrying off every contest. Mei-lan, the fervent revolutionary—it was her best role.

Rinn unsealed her own food-pack and ladled out a bit of stew. "I've heard about your revolution many times, Mei-lan. I don't need more right now."

Mei-lan's black eyes flashed angrily. "Reactionary!"

Rinn replied calmly. "As I've said, also many times, I am *not* a reactionary. I'm your Contract Starfarer and currently your only guide in this swamp." She pushed the other food-pack closer to Mei-lan, who made no move to pick it up. "Consider that while you eat."

"You're a degenerate reactionary and a mutant freak!"

"Mutant, yes; degenerate reactionary, no. Eat your food."

Rinn ate more of her stew, watching Mei-lan from the corner of her eye. The other woman sputtered, poised to storm off in a rage, hesitated, thought to throw the food-pack into the nearby water, then realized she was hungry. Again, Rinn felt tempted to exert control, just a nudge to Mei-lan's will to steady her. She bit her lip: no.

Mei-lan picked up the food-pack and yanked open the seal.

Rinn relaxed a little, still watching Mei-lan. Her companion ate neatly, without wasted motion by her small elegant hands, her lovely mouth, pearl teeth. Short dark hair gleamed above the white bandage, a tight cap to her narrow head. Mei-lan seemed a sleek ferret, lean and small, quick-moving and ferocious, tearing apart her prey with sharp white teeth. Rinn closed her eyes a moment, banishing the over-image.

She finished her own meal and repacked the empty container in the carryall. She heard a splash behind her as Mei-lan disposed of her own food tin. Wearily Rinn waded into the warm pool and retrieved the pack.

"Why so neat, Rinn?" Mei-lan asked. She waved a slender hand at the swamp. "This is hardly Xin Tian—no compliance officers to watch for littering. Or is there?" Mei-lan made a show of bending apart a nearby stand of reeds and peering into their interior. "Not here. Maybe over in those reeds. Shall I look?"

"Are you done with your joke?"

"Always so serious, our Rinn." Mei-lan's teeth gleamed in the yellowish light of the lantern.

"The Lily warriors are tracking us. Do you still want to toss that for them to find?"

Mei-lan laughed. "Tracking us? Who?" Her eyes danced in merriment, and she waved a chiding finger. "Rinn, Rinn. You always were an alarmist. So bourgeois. There's no danger here. Look around you." She laughed again, her voice tinged with an eerie madness that sent a tingle up Rinn's spine; then she smiled upward at Rinn, hugging herself. "Captain Hung will be here soon, and everything will be all right."

Rinn set her jaw. "Get up, Mei-lan. We have to move on."

"Don't be silly. Why?"

"Because Captain Hung is waiting for us," Rinn lied. She pointed southward. "Over there. He's set up another trade base and needs us to talk to the natives for him. It's very important that we get there as soon as we can."

"He's waiting for us?"

"Yes, Mei-lan. Let's go."

Mei-lan jumped to her feet and strapped on one of the carryalls. "Why didn't you say so? You just let us sit here, wasting time, while you moon about trivia like always. When will you ever understand what's important, Rinn?" She splashed into the pool, heading for the nearby reed-bed.

"Wait! Let me lead the way."

"Hurry up! Captain Hung is waiting!"

Rinn shouldered her own bag and hurriedly scuffed out their marks on the mud. In the distant north, she heard the vague fury of the gathering warriors and knew they had begun the hunt. In the east, the false dawn had lightened the darkness to a dim

gray-black. To the south, a ship still slept. She splashed toward
Mei-lan. "This way."

The two women pushed forward, Mei-lan leading. She
seemed to have a manic energy as she walked, forcing her way
through the waist-high water, impatiently pushing aside reeds
as she hurried forward. Rinn tried to keep up with her, although
her muscles protested the pace. After an hour of the rushed pace,
Mei-lan finally slowed, panting.

"How far is it?" she asked, her voice a childish whine.

"Quite a way, Mei-lan. Conserve your strength."

Mei-lan grunted and slogged onward.

The morning sun slowly lifted out of the low mist covering
the swamp, a dull reddish ball that quickly banished the remaining mist. Before them stretched a seemingly endless plain of
reed-beds and open water, dotted with the white fronds of
blooming marsh-lilies in far-scattered stands. The reek of the
swamp blew into their faces as the sea breeze shifted the air
currents inland, raising Rinn's anxieties. She glanced backward,
listening for the pursuit, but heard only a distant murmur of
angry thoughts, nothing yet focused. The Lily tribe still cast for
the scent. If they followed their general course, the breeze would
give them the trail they needed. They had to hurry. She picked
up the pace again, wading as fast as she could.

"I'm tired, Rinn," Mei-lan said petulantly. "Perhaps we
should rest awhile." Her fervor had dimmed during the long
trek.

"No, Mei-lan. Captain Hung wants us as soon as we can get
there."

"But how far is it?" Mei-lan asked. Her narrow face looked
flushed with exertion, and she irritably wiped sweat from her
eyes. The moist air of the swamp oppressed them, accentuated
by the rising heat of the morning sun. Rinn sensed the fatigue
in Mei-lan's muscles as a faint overtone of her own twitches and
pains. She repressed a yawn, then blinked her aching eyes.

"A way yet. Be patient, Mei-lan."

"But I don't want to be patient," Mei-lan whined. "Why are
we here? Where are we going?"

"I told you. Captain Hung wants us at the new base."

"But it doesn't make sense." Mei-lan stopped abruptly, her
thoughts tinged with suspicion. "Where are you taking me?
What are you up to?" She looked around at the murky water
and reeds, then slapped at an insect on her neck. "What *is* this
place?"

Rinn bit her lip. Mei-lan's inherent suspicion could undermine whatever fragile accord they had achieved. But perhaps . . .

"I know it's hard, Mei-lan, but a revolutionary is often tested. Haven't you said as much in the correction meetings? Captain Hung wants us to set an example for the others, to show how true revolutionary spirit can surmount any obstacle."

"A testing?" Mei-lan was dubious.

"Yes."

It was enough—for the moment. Mei-lan's chin lifted. "My apologies, comrade. I will do my best."

Rinn nodded. "Good. Let's hurry."

"Yes. We must hurry." Rinn again let Mei-lan lead the way, correcting her direction only when she drifted off course. Rinn sensed the human thoughts of the other ship like a beacon to the south; behind her, a dark cloud of anger pursued them, coming fast. Rinn looked skyward and mentally cursed the breeze.

By midday, they had walked nearly eight kilometers, a wearying routine of wet clothes, face-slapping reeds, and sticky mud that clung to their sodden boots and skin. Mei-lan had borne it more patiently than Rinn had expected, showing a core of strength powered solely by determination. Rinn watched her, trying to keep her attention on the path ahead and Mei-lan's state of mind. She endured, but a deep weariness was growing dangerously near the deepest levels of her mind; she pushed it away, drawing upon the Gift for a new reserve of strength. It was risky to rely too much on the Gift, for it could savage the body—but she had no choice.

Perhaps the clinging mud had masked their scent, for the aliens behind them had grown uncertain. As she and Mei-lan plodded forward, Rinn listened, tracking the warriors by their thoughts as they bore slightly westward, away from the direct trail. But not enough—they still followed, and at the speed with which they were moving, they could overtake the women. At midmorning, the warriors had been five kilometers behind them; that gap had narrowed to three, with the treacherous breeze blowing steadily toward them.

She sensed the dark thought of another predator ahead of them as it crouched in its lair. Twice they had shot at charging marsh-hunters, the large wolf-sized marauders that defended the marsh with uncanny ferocity. Day-blinded, this one had not yet sensed them. She touched Mei-lan's arm and tugged her to the left. "This way."

Mei-lan stopped short. "Why that way? You said the base was straight ahead."

"It is, but I hear another predator. We have to go around it."

Mei-lan's black eyes glinted with renewed suspicion. "A predator? Where?"

"In front of us, about two hundred meters," Rinn said, swaying with fatigue. She blinked at Mei-lan, trying to marshal her sluggish mind for another argument. Somehow, she had to keep Mei-lan moving; there would be time enough for explanations later at the safety of the Soviet base—if the Soviets would help. She pushed away that anxiety. "Come, Mei-lan. Come with me."

"Why?" Mei-lan's voice was shrill. "Where are you taking me?" Rinn reached for her, and Mei-lan retreated a step. "Stay away!"

"Come with me, Mei-lan." She tried to touch Mei-lan's mind, to reassure, to compel if necessary. As she invaded the other's thoughts, Mei-lan staggered backward.

"Stop it! Stop!" Mei-lan pulled her stunner from her carryall pocket and pointed it directly at Rinn. "Get away!"

"Mei-lan! Don't!"

Rinn saw Mei-lan's thumb move on the trigger, and she threw herself sideways into a clump of reeds. The warning hum of the discharge whizzed over her head, achingly close. She rose to one knee and raised the carryall as a shield, blocking the next shot, then staggered toward a nearby pool.

"Freak!" Mei-lan cried, her voice distorted by hatred.

Mei-lan's next shot hit Rinn squarely in the back. As she felt her body convulse into racking tremors, she cried out wordlessly, *I am Rinn* . . . but the blackness swept down upon her, extinguishing all thought and need.

She awoke facedown in a stand of reeds, her legs trailing into a muddy pool. Dizzily, Rinn pushed herself to a sitting position, then threw up her head in panic. Five meters away, two pairs of glowing eyes watched her from deep shadow. The marshhunter hesitated. Rinn grabbed her carryall and fumbled for her stunner. At her sudden movement, the eyes vanished as the animal retreated to its lair, wary of her alien smell. Rinn swallowed, her heart still pounding from fear.

Mei-lan. Rinn cast for Mei-lan's thought, stretching outward in an expanding circle. Finally she touched the edges of the other's mind, half a kilometer east. Mei-lan was already lost, confused by shock and the trackless swamp, and in growing panic. Rinn shuddered as the woman's fear echoed in her own mind.

She stood up and swayed, then looked longingly to the south. Another half-day and she might reach the Soviet base. Maybe if she pretended she was Normal, they might accept her. Greater Asia had a few Caucasian minorities—perhaps this ship did not know about the emigration ban against non-Asiatics. It might work, at least until—when? The only destination for that ship was Novy Strana or Rodina, where possession of her Star meant a death sentence.

Throw away the Star? It would be so easy to drop it in a deep muddy pool, never to be found among the reeds. Her hand moved toward her breast pocket, then stopped short of the deed.

Perhaps that ship won't know its mèaning, she thought desperately. She could keep the Star and explain it as something else, an item of jewelry, a personal memento, something innocuous. She looked east again.

Give it up, she told herself. You can't save her. So easy to choose that. So easy. She rubbed her muddy hand across her face, lingering at the rough scar on one cheek. So easy.

No, I can't. I can't lose all of them.

Wearily, she turned east to follow Mei-lan.

Chapter 3

THE AIR TURNED COOL AS THE SUN SANK TOWARD the distant horizon, stirring the life that hunted in the early evening. Rinn avoided another marsh-hunter lair and repeatedly chased off the smaller predators who investigated her intrusion into their territories. She blundered into a cloud of gnatlike insects that bit and stung painfully, then floundered through a near-quagmire.

Mei-lan, she sent out, but her shipmate could not—or would not—hear.

As she neared the sea margin, her progress became even more difficult, and Rinn sensed Mei-lan's even greater troubles. Gnat stings had swollen her shipmate's face, puffing the flesh near her eyes until Mei-lan was nearly blind. Muscles ached with every wrenching step in the muddy pools; reeds slapped at reddened and water-poisoned hands. An hour before, Mei-lan had fallen and dropped her carryall, leaving it behind. She was possessed by a paralyzing fear that blunted all thought. Pursued by nameless terrors, Mei-lan veered north, back toward the Lily tribe's territory.

Rinn hurried, trying to overtake her shipmate before she blundered into Isen-glov-amar's path. Like points on an interior map, she saw Mei-lan's flight inexorably converging with their pursuers; soon the sea breeze, though failing, would carry Mei-lan's scent to the hunters, and Mei-lan would truly be lost. Rinn pushed forward desperately but could not match Mei-lan's fear-driven strength. She fell steadily behind, the gap widening to nearly a kilometer, then more.

Mei-lan!

The treacherous breeze sighed against her face and body, chilling her sweat-drenched skin. The strap of the carryall bit into her shoulder, and its weight grew steadily heavier as she exhausted her strength. She drew upon the Gift, demanding still greater effort from her legs and back, careless of the toll on her body. She staggered forward, lost in her own miasma of pain and exhaustion.

Mei-lan!

A Lily warrior, questing to the north, lifted his head suddenly as he caught a scent on the breeze. His booming call rang out over the marsh, summoning the other hunters. Rinn sobbed as she threw herself forward, vainly trying to bridge the distance between herself and her shipmate. Helplessly, she witnessed the gathering hunt, the swift descent, Mei-lan's mental shriek of terror as a trio of warriors burst upon her from the reeds. The warriors' kill-passion flared, overwhelming all trace of Mei-lan's thought, then ebbed into fierce repletion. Rinn shuddered as Maret cracked Mei-lan's skull and tore free a handful of her brains.

She stopped, chest heaving, and stared in anguish across the sodden marsh. Water dripped from her clothing into the shallow pool, smearing the encrusted mud on her body. Her frequent falls had intruded water into her carryall, damaging her stunner and seeping past the sprung tabs of several food tins. Her legs trembled, and she felt the deep muscle-ache of overextended tendons and torn muscle. She had thrown away her own means of survival in desperation, for nothing. She swayed with exhaustion as the clammy breeze sent shivers along her sweat-drenched back.

An alien snout lifted, scenting the air. Maret slowly rose from his crouch over Mei-lan's body and turned toward Rinn, his third brain thrumming, then cried out triumphantly to sound the hunt. Others answered from a distance, rushing forward across the reed-beds to join him.

Rinn threw down her carryall and fled southward. Behind her, Maret ran effortlessly over the mud-pans, leaping the pools and crashing through the reed-beds, his companions following in swift pursuit. Desperately, Rinn turned aside and plunged into a large stand of marsh-lilies, beating at the flowers with her hands to lift a cloud of pollen to cover her own scent. The pollen settled on her head and clothes, and she coughed rackingly against the cloying, acrid dust. Far behind her, she heard a second hooting call as other warriors joined Maret in the hunt.

She continued to veer left, off the direct line of the airborne scent trail, then reached a string of muddy pools bearing southeast. She splashed into the dark water and waded forward, her breath coming in ragged gasps. Her vision blurred, then grayed out, as she exhausted her remaining strength. She slowed, unable to flag herself further, a growing terror in her mind as her body finally failed her. She pushed forward, each step an agonizing effort.

A marsh-hunter stirred in its poolside lair several meters ahead, roused from its sleep by her noisy approach. It bared serrated fangs, its fur rising, and scrabbled forward to investigate. Rinn sensed its threat and instinctively threw her panic at the animal barring her path.

Go away! Kill! Kill! I'll kill you!

The marsh-hunter squealed in fright as the threat-image, driven by the full force of Rinn's terror, crashed into its mind. It thrashed out of its den and fled southward through the pool, frantic in its own fear. It jumped and leaped, snapping at the empty air, then disassociated completely as it slashed at its own underbody with its claws, disembowelling itself. The animal shrieked in pain and convulsed, then sank, still thrashing, beneath the surface of the water. The water stilled, broken only by trailing air bubbles that popped slowly on the surface.

Rinn stopped short in the open pool, appalled at what she had done. To kill with the Gift, even a nonsentient animal, was a violation of everything the Starfarers believed, everything she had sought to escape on Ikanos. She shuddered, deeply shocked by the creature's death, then saw the tunnel-opening to its den.

The Gift chooses where it will. On Ikanos the maxim justified too many evils. She swallowed painfully, not knowing whether to accept the bounty to which the Gift had impelled her.

Beneath the water, the marsh-hunter moved weakly on the mud bottom, its lungs still vainly struggling for air, for life. Rinn sensed the hovering blackness of its death, then heard it die. Anguished, she covered her face with her muddy hands.

Damn you, damn you, she shrieked at the Gift-source deep within her mind. She perceived it as a glowing coil-shape, floating in the dark unknowing of her unconscious—unhearing, unseeing, inexorable in its demands, rich in its gifts. She clenched her fists, driving her nails deep into her palms. The Gift, possessed and possessing, caring only that her life continued, whatever the price to herself. *Damn you!* she cried.

Behind her, the dark mind-cloud of the warriors swept nearer. Rinn sobbed and drew her hand across her face. Survival . . . but what survived, what self?

She drew a shuddering breath, then crept into the marsh-hunter's lair.

The Star-Devil's scent wavered, then blew itself to fragments on the breeze. Isen-glov-amar snarled in frustration and gestured angrily at his warriors to cast wide across the marsh, hunting for a better trail. A few minutes later, Belos found the broken stand of lilies where the Star-Devil had forced through, and they followed the visible groundtrail until it vanished into an open pool.

[Beat the reed-stands], Isen-glov-amar ordered, his gesture choppy with his anger. Near him, Maret stood uncertainly, his eyes downcast on the mud. Isen-glov-amar approached him, his tensed body-crouch signalling his threat. [Your fault, Maret].

[Lord, forgive me], Maret replied humbly, his body trembling with humiliation.

[Where is the Star-Devil, Maret]? Isen-glov-amar stopped two paces away and raised his fire-weapon.

[Lord] . . . Maret lifted his head and looked back, a start of fear in his dark eyes. Brave Maret, whose manhood honors surpassed even those of the son of the chief. Isen-glov-amar hesitated, tempted to accept that fear in reparation, then snapped his jaws once, twice, as his third brain insisted on the kill. He surrendered to its impulse. The ruby fire of the laser leaped the space between them, burning deep into Maret's flesh, through skin and muscle to the beating heart. Maret's dead body leaped backward in a last reflex, to crash smoking into the reeds.

The other warriors stopped, looking back, and Isen-glov-amar swung toward them, his weapon raised. [Beat the reed-beds], he gestured with his other hand. [Find the Star-Devil and redeem this warrior's fault]. As one, his warriors crouched in deference, their heads low to acknowledge his power, then they quickly scattered among the pools. Only Belos, shield-brother to Maret, looked back once again, emotion simmering in his deep-set eyes.

I will watch him, Isen-glov-amar thought. He looked at Maret's blackened body and wondered briefly if he had acted in too much haste. The Star-Devil might still be found, Maret's error removed. Then he shook himself angrily. A chief did not doubt his own judgment—had not his father told him so? And Maret had failed the Tribe, for all his honors. He deserved the penalty.

Deep in his third brain, Isen-glov-amar's jealousy simmered—and eased. He stepped into the pool and waded forward, then sank into a prey-stalk. The water chattered as it swirled around his legs and abdomen, reminding him of other stalks, other raids, when he was still a youth bound to his father's side. The Lily People had not ventured south into other territories for ten years and had little need to do so—the peninsula tribes knew their lesson and paid ample tribute in gems and victims for Lily ceremonies. Matters had been quiet—too quiet for a young warrior seeking to establish his right to be chief.

Isen-glov-amar stopped, his eyes fixed on the distant south, and considered a wider purpose for their journey.

Five meters away, Rinn lay curled within the safety of the marsh-hunter's den. The dried reeds made a yielding bed and a comfortable warmth; she relaxed into their crackling embrace and wrapped herself in other-mind. Her chest rose and fell in slow exhalations, a steady rhythm that paced her fall inward into herself. A muscle slowly twitched in her thigh, protesting its overuse. She focused on the muscle and stilled it, then sank deeper into the trance, deeper than she had ever reached. She trembled on the very edge of self-dissolution, where the Gift touched the autonomic need of breath and heartbeat. If they found her, she had the means to make an instant death: let them rip apart an emptied body, for whatever satisfaction it would give them.

Dimly, she had sensed the passing of the warriors through the nearby pools, each seeking a mud-slid footprint, a broken reed, a faint scent on the water, any trace of the prey. A darker shadow had passed, Belos, his predator instincts overlaid by grief and a dull wondering, the first trickle of doubt pricking at his mind. He had brushed against the reeds that overshadowed the lair entrance—her scent lay there, but he passed by, unalerted. Now Isen-glov-amar stood nearby, deep in his ambitions of glory and murder. She retreated still further, until she hovered at the edge of consciousness itself. The alien moved on.

Rinn slept and awoke to deep night. She cast her thought outward, seeking threat, but heard nothing. Then she stirred, stretching her aching muscles, and uncurled her body in the narrow confines of the den. The dried reeds crackled under her weight, shifting uneasily on the undermatting of waterlogged vegetation. She blinked her eyes, trying to rouse herself from the dull headache that throbbed at her temples. She crawled down the short tunnel of the lair exit and stood up in the hip-deep pool. I am alive, she thought with exhausted wonder. She breathed deeply, gathering in her perceptions of the night and the marsh.

The land breeze sighed over the marshes, bending the flexible stalks of the marsh-lilies, whispering through the reeds, ruffling the surface of the ponds. Animals stirred in the darkness, obeying primal drives for food, territory, a mate. A marsh-hunter pounced on a marsh-rat, rending it with sharp teeth. A night-flyer slipped through the cool air, its wings barely moving as it swooped into a glide over the black pools. The marsh spoke in their several voices, its sound underlaid by the steady shurring of the reeds.

She cast farther until she touched the dark thoughts of Isen-glov-amar, far to the south. Diverted from his fruitless search for a Star-Devil, he was creeping toward the sleeping coraal of another tribe, his third brain pulsing with the excitement of the hunt-stalk. Beyond him, she sensed the somnolence of the coraal guard at his post, the sleep-thoughts of the warriors and females within the camp. A child lay awake, listening to the quiet breathing of her mother beside her, wrinkling her nose at the acrid scent of smoke confined in the small house. Then she sighed, content in her mother's warmth, and drifted back to sleep. A pet marsh-hunter, tethered in the open space between the huts, growled uneasily and paced the length of its chain, its back fur erect.

Rinn closed her eyes, concentrating on the marsh-hunter. *Alarm! Alarm!* The animal snarled nervously but did not hear her thought. She tried again, her hands clasped tightly at her waist, pressure on flesh to help her concentration. *Alarm! Danger!* The Lily warriors crept steadily closer to the sleeping co-raal, and Isen-glov-amar trembled, poised for the attack.

No! Rinn focused on her need to repay him for a murdered crew, her blighted duty, and Mei-lan's death. *Alarm! Alarm!* She fed her emotion into her thought, sending wave after wave toward the marsh-hunter's primitive mind. *Alarm!* She strained toward it, needing, needing—and touched it at last, infecting it with her deliberate fear. The animal scrabbled backward onto its haunches, gibbering, then let out a terrified howl. It cried out again, and Rinn promptly withdrew her sending, remembering the other she had killed.

It was enough. A warrior threw back his coverlet and snatched up his weapons, calling out to others in nearby huts. The mother clutched her child to her, listening with pounding heart to the marsh-hunter's wail. The coraal guard snapped to attention from his doze, then spotted the darker shadow among the reeds that was Isen-glov-amar. He cast his spear too hastily and knew instantly he had missed, then reached for the *amtla*-globe on his waist thong. The tiny sphere arced through the air and exploded among the reeds, splattering its corrosive fluid in every direction. Isen-glov-amar threw himself aside, barely escaping the acid's bite, then flinched as the *amtla* ignited the reeds. He heard the guard's cry of sure discovery and saw him lunge for a second spear. With a curse, Isen-glov-amar called out the retreat and fled back into the marsh, the roused camp in an uproar behind him.

Rinn laughed and spread her arms wide. Thank you, Gift. Thank you. She hugged herself, laughing again as she heard Isen-glov-amar's dark anger, his perplexity at the aborted attack, and she exulted in both. *I am Rinn, Starfarer!* she shouted her thought. She flung her arms wide toward the dark sky and danced in a circle on the shifting reeds, head lifted, arms outstretched, in conscious imitation of Isen-glov-amar's earlier ecstatic dance around her shipmates' laser-blackened bodies. *I can do anything! Yaaa!*

Then her muscles cramped a sober warning, reminding her of the damage she had done to her body. She stopped, panting, and looked down at her ruined clothes, stiff with dried mud, and remembered that she had thrown away her carryall. In filthy clothes, still exhausted, without food or weapons, and half-crazed with recent fear, she was hardly a model of the super-human.

She waded forward into the pool, heading southward for the human base.

"Anything," she whispered stubbornly. "Anything at all."

Several hours later, her triumph had ebbed into a miasma of pain and renewed exhaustion. The dawn slowly spread its waxing light across the marsh, touching the lily-fronds with a sparkling sheen and shedding its reds and ambers in broad sheets across the open pools. Rinn stopped near a large stand of marsh-lilies, oblivious to a cloud of gnats and the stink of the brackish mud. She crept forward and lay down on the yielding reeds, her feet dangling into a pool.

I'll stop for a while, she told herself, and relaxed against the reeds, conscious of the razored pain of torn muscles in her shoulders and legs. Only a little while. She stared upward, dazed, and wondered if she had found her grave on this bed of reeds. Death hovered behind the pain in her muscles and the sluggishness of her thoughts. *No!* She turned on her side and tried to relax, hoping her stillness would put new strength into a body that was progressively failing her. As the dim coolness of othermind brought its comfort, her mind slipped again into memories.

"The Gift is governed by the will," the Ikanos teacher had instructed. A group of young children sat arrayed behind her as she drew a pattern of trapezoid and intersecting circle on the wall-screen. "And we train the will with mind-patterns, until each pattern—and thus each level of the Gift—is as easy as breathing. This is the first level." She turned to face the primary class. "When you think this pattern, and only this pattern, you will hear the Gift within you. Close your eyes and think of this pattern."

Rinn closed her eyes obediently and imagined the trapezoid and circle. She felt the teacher gently enter her mind and draw her pattern *downward*. Against the darkness of her closed eyes, a tiny coiled shape emerged, spinning idly, then dancing, a bright toy-thing that wanted to play. Rinn reached toward it.

No, Rinn, her teacher said from within her mind. *Don't touch it yet; merely see it. Isn't it pretty?*

Yes.

The teacher drew her upward again; she opened her eyes. She felt her mother's wash of pleasure and turned to look at her in the back of the room. Her mother made a turning movement with her finger as she smiled. *Pay attention to the teacher, my darling. This is very important.*

Please, Mrs. McCrea, the teacher said irritably. *You are disrupting the class.*

Rinn's mother flushed. Then, in a mental whisper, a breath of thought almost too slight to catch: *We'll practice later; I love you!*

Mother, Rinn mourned and covered her eyes.

See the pattern, Conner said to her, *and allow the Gift to open the world.* The harsh light of Xin Tian's sun, only partially muted by the polarized windows, streamed into the common room, casting her enclave tutor's face into half-shadow.

What do you hear? Connor asked patiently.

I hear . . . anger.

And? he asked, his expression quizzical, as if her answer surprised him. She looked down at her hands.

Only anger.

You must try, Rinn; you cannot hide forever.

I'm not hiding, she protested.

Oh? What do you hear, Rinn? The inner or outer world? Who is angry?

Anger is . . . dangerous.

Not here. There is no danger here, not with us. He lifted his holo-slate and tapped the glass, bringing the mind-pattern lines into sharper relief. *See the pattern and live the Gift. Be what you are, all that you are. What do you hear?*

I hear . . . She shook her head helplessly.

Connor sighed and lowered the slate. *Little one, I admit your shields are formidable; the Group-Mind must have sought you avidly, given your potential. But a singer must use her voice, an artist his brush or wheel. Until you will hear, I can't help you.*

I hear . . . you, Connor.

What do you hear?

Sadness.

Connor smiled. *Yes, that. We all have scars, we of the enclave . . .*

See the pattern . . .

As she lay on the reeds, her mind imagined one key-pattern after another, each a set of three lines shifting at neat angles, a sequence practiced since childhood and amplified by her adult training in the enclave. Her perception expanded and retracted at random, following the patterns dutifully. Stop, she thought, bewildered by the kaleidoscope of half-sensed, too rapid impressions. Stop.

She escaped into another memory.

See the pattern . . .

"McCrea!"

Phan Tha stalked angrily toward her, his guard baton rapping his heavy thigh in agitation. "Not that way!" He tore the flask from her hands, splashing some of the chemical on her tunic. She grabbed for a rag and hastily sponged the cloth before the poison seeped through to her skin.

"Please be careful, sir," she said and bowed, a shade too

obsequiously. Tha, not the most subtle of men, missed the sarcasm.

Careful, Moira warned from behind her. *He's unpredictable. I see the pattern.*

"You stupid!" Tha raged. "I'll report you to the lab supervisor if you don't do better." He slammed the flask onto the counter and stamped off.

"Yes, sir," she murmured.

Why are the Thai so touchy? she asked Moira.

Because they aren't Japanese—and the Japanese are angry because they aren't Han Chinese. Even the Han have their rankings, by both birth and politics. In a racist society, many things reduce to that one fundamental. And you really shouldn't mix that noxious potion with oxygen. Moira's thought rippled with amusement. *Can't you read a label?*

Oh.

See the pattern . . .

The reed-mat swayed with the incoming tide, rocking her gently with its slow undulation. As she rested, the colors of the dawn changed from red to gold to greenish gray, colored by the reflection of sea and marsh against the clouds. Too green, her human senses told her, reminding her of the alienness of this world. She ached for the familiar corridors of Xin Tian, even the dark jumbled plains beyond the city dome of Ikanos; in a deeper instinctive level, she ached, too, for the blueness of an Earth sky she had never seen.

What is this place? she wondered confusedly, her thoughts sluggish with exhaustion. *Why am I here?*

She shifted again, then lay inert with arms flung backward, conscious of the slow rocking of the reeds. A fish nudged her foot, its dull thought little more than shadow and instinct, before it slid away into the deeper pool; nearby a night-flyer huddled asleep in its nest. She listened to the marsh around her, aware of too many things to return into the rest she needed. Her perceptions shuddered against her mind.

Gift, she pleaded, not sure of what she asked of it. Then, again, she queried, *What is this place?* In her thought she heard the echo of another voice tightened by madness and fear. She pursued the memory and matched it to a face: Mei-lan. With a convulsive shudder, Rinn rolled over and hid her face against the reeds. She remembered the crew she had failed, the companion she had allowed to die.

I am Rinn, Starfarer, she thought, and wept with her exhaustion and grief. Then, finally, she slept.

A series of dark shadows moved along the edge of her perception, becoming stronger as the aliens approached her shelter. Rinn lifted her head, trying to sense their direction and distance. The shapes wavered and grew thin, then shifted into stark clarity a half-kilometer away, heading north. She listened, only half-awake, confused by the strangeness of their three-lobed minds.

Who? she called, as she had once called to Moira and Connor when abroad in the city. There was no answer, but she jerked awake, suddenly aware of her danger in that careless greeting. Other memories crashed in: the assault on the ship, Mei-lan's death, her own flight. She burrowed forward into the yielding reeds, concealing herself.

In the distance, she sensed Belos stop and look around him, alert sounding in his third brain. Something . . . *Who?* he answered, seeking the source of the thrum-note that still reverberated through his senses. But he heard no repetition. *Who?* he sent again, not knowing what he attempted, save that someone had called him as if from the air. A spirit? What spirit? The weak but benign spirits who guarded the Lily People spoke only to the shaman; the evil swamp-demons who dwelt beneath pool and reed attacked the unwary without outcry, killing in stealth and malice. Or so he had been taught since childhood. He looked around again, his neck fur ruffling in agitation. What magic was this? He quickly signed himself against evil.

Yet still . . .

Who? he sent again, curious.

Isen-glov-amar looked back irritably and gestured a sharp summons. [Belos]! Belos hurried forward, offering deference to the chief's son whom he now despised.

[We have circled long enough], Isen-glov-amar said curtly. [What do you advise]? He looked petulant.

As Belos crouched, secret questions pricked at his mind, distracting him from the strange alert. Whose fault that the coral attack had failed? he wondered. Whose fault that Star-Devils escaped our first attack? Maret's? I think not.

But Isen-glov-amar was asking advice, as he should have asked the night before but had not. That youth remembered his father's teaching only when it suited his arrogance.

[Approach them openly], Belos replied, his hands moving with sharp and decisive strokes. [We are the Lily People. Sunstone bows to us, gives us tribute as we demand. Our night attack was unneeded, as any of your senior warriors would have told you—had you asked].

Isen-glov-amar's snout lifted, but he accepted the rebuke without comment. Belos regarded him sourly. Perhaps he might yet learn some prudence, he thought.

[Very well. We will approach them]. Isen-glov-amar shouldered his weapon-strap and turned south.

Whose failure? Belos thought again, watching Isen-glov-amar's arrogant profile, but he kept his thoughts hidden. Shield-brother . . . he keened to himself, and reluctantly put away thoughts of other murder.

Isen-glov-amar headed south, his warriors following in his wake. The morning sun beat strongly upon their backs, threatening a dangerous overheating of their leg-joints if borne too long. As one, the warriors shifted into a line of pools, wading deep into the water. The coolness spread like fragrant oil through their bloodstream, strengthening, reassuring. On the air, a dozen scents drifted enticingly, filling the world with a thrumming of the senses, a joy of the physical body.

We are the Lily, Belos thought as he walked beside the leader he disfavored. He focused on that thought, remembering honors given and duty owed. We are triumphant . . . But the familiar chant struggled against the memory of Maret's blackened body.

Rinn dissolved the mind-pattern, breaking the gnosis, too weak to follow Belos farther. She rested awhile, snug in her shelter of reeds, then forced herself to struggle forward to open water. At the edge of the reed-bed, she stood upright, blinking against the bright sky.

Too much, she thought. Can I go on? She focused on the single task of putting one foot before the other and turned again toward the Soviet base, only three kilometers away. To her right, the dark mental shadows of the Lily warriors wavered and faded, moving eastward. Let them find me if they can, she thought dully, and told herself she no longer cared. She floundered into the water.

She made slow progress, hindered by the muddy pools and stands of reeds. The sun rose higher, heating the air as it sighed over the marsh. She panted in the oppressive heat, her vision blurring. She stooped for a drink, then spat out the brackish water. Her walk focused to the single effort of movement, bearing south.

I am Rinn, Starfarer, she thought groggily, drawing what comfort she could from that identity. It mocked her as she staggered forward, as her exhausted mind created flickering illusions of a domed city to the right, of Connor and the blackened bodies of *Sing Fa*'s crew to the left. She bit her lip and refused to follow the illusions, holding to her steady course.

I am Rinn . . .

Chapter 4

CAPTAIN YURI IVANOVICH SELENKOV EXCHANGED final greetings with Ba-rao-som, the trade chieftain for the local natives, with a series of polite bows and grimaces more Deltean than human, then watched the alien party leave the ship-clearing. Yuri still had to repress an instinctive revulsion for an insectoid form with too many legs, an eerily blank-featured face, and six-fingered hands. *No doubt he has a similar problem with me,* he thought wryly as he watched the aliens vanish around the trail bend.

Yuri was a tall, brown-haired young man, new to his captaincy and anxious for its success. Novy Strana offered its young star captains great opportunity, far more than the straitened and oligarchic mother-state on Earth ever offered, but imposed an equivalent penalty for failures. Earth, with all its wealth, could waste its ships on incompetents; Novy Strana could not, and punished accordingly. Yuri did not intend to fail.

At thirty-two, Yuri had spent most of his adult life in the fascinating puzzle of geological surveys, first in university-sponsored studies on his home planet, then as second officer on the *Aryol.* When the captain's post opened on *Zvezda,* Captain Brodsky had recommended him for the promotion. Somehow personally conducting the Delta trades had a different quality than watching through the airlock, but he thought he had made progress. *There's more to life than rocks,* he told himself, and felt almost persuaded of that geologist heresy.

Beside him lay several bales of delicate *sevena*-herbs and four packets of distillate gems, the rare produce of Delta Bootis and the chief financial lure for trade. The herbs had promise as a life-extension drug, and the gems, called "three-finger stones" by the aliens, had unique fluorescent qualities that excited even the sour-faced Trade Commissar. Already the Bureau labs were modifying a certain ship-engine relay switch into new efficiency, timed to the flawless twinkling of the new stones. Attempts to duplicate the three-finger stones' crystalline structure had less success, a puzzle still not understood. Four weeks of trade had garnered a small fortune in each for Novy Strana's coffers. Galina Kirillovna Sakharova, blond and plain-faced, bent over the bales, cataloging the contents. She ran her hand gently through the bulbate fronds of the herbs, testing their quality, then lifted one of the gems to the sunlight.

"Pretty," she said, smiling.

"Valuable," he responded. "I just hope that Ba-rao-som brings more tomorrow." He frowned and looked toward the gap in the surrounding reeds that marked the trail to the nearby alien coraal, mentally tabulating the bales of synthetic cloth and metal culinary left in *Zvezda*'s hold for continued trade. He heard Galina chuckle.

"Worrying again, Yuri?" she asked, her smile broadening with a genuine affection.

Yuri shrugged and then grinned reluctantly. "It's not proper to notice your captain worrying," he said with mock gruffness. Galina laughed.

Of all *Zvezda*'s crew, Yuri felt most comfortable with Galina. Middle-aged, she had an unshakable calmness and acceptance of life's misfortunes that he envied—and tried to copy. Sometimes Galina caught him copying and seemed amused. Somehow he didn't mind the amusement, not from Galina.

He looked up at the sky, judging the time. The aliens always came at two hours past dawn, then disappeared again until the following day. Twice Yuri had suggested a reciprocal visit to the Sunstone coraal, but his suggestions had been either ignored or misunderstood. *In all matters, the locals have first initiative.* The Trade Commissar's orders were specific, but one could maneuver within their restrictions. Sometimes.

Delta Bootis was the only planet in the Soviet Hegemony of Worlds with an intelligent alien life form. Perhaps there might be others farther out in Bootes—where? he wondered idly—but in the meantime Novy Strana proceeded most carefully, mindful of United America's disastrous mistake on Canopus. The Americans had tried to hush it up, but all Earth eventually heard the rumors of the genocide of an alien culture. Too many American scientists had heard the mission tapes, and Americans had a habit of talking too much.

And so the commissars proceeded carefully with First Contact on Delta—so carefully that its trade captain felt like a Deltean snail inching along a sagging reed. In two days, *Zvezda* was scheduled to leave for her next stop at Seguinus, with time ticking on an appointment with an ice drill at Mu Bootis twenty days later. The latter could not be delayed long; even three ships rotating through the Delta/Seguinus run stretched out the ice drill maintenance to dangerous intervals.

I wish the Bureau would give us more time here, he thought. Maybe we can stretch that appointment on Mu Bootis a little.

"Where's Oleg?" he asked Galina. Any delay in lift-off required a consultation with the second officer, a restriction that irked Yuri on this bright morning.

"Collating the trade reports with Tatiana. Or so he *said*." Galina's voice carried a definite reproof. Yuri grunted, not commenting. Oleg Andreivich Konstantin was a supercilious, ambitious man, bland in his subtlety except for one area, his passion for Trade Officer Tatiana Nikolaevna Kirova. Not that Yuri blamed him; Tatiana managed to invest everything with a simmering sexuality. It was one of her weapons for her own ambitions, and somehow she considered Oleg more a stair-step to her career than Yuri. He scowled.

As usual, the Space Bureau had decided the crew's sexual pairings before *Zvezda* launched, choosing for psychological balance without consulting the parties involved. But Tatiana had family connections inside the Bureau and could arrange the choice she preferred—and no doubt had. It vaguely bothered him. Tatiana had a way to make a man wonder what was wrong with him if she looked elsewhere.

Yuri's own ship wife, Natalya, had died unexpectedly during their flight to Delta Bootis. It had created an imbalance in the crew and tinged his own thoughts with envy. He missed Natalya, and for more than the sexual release they enjoyed with each other. She had had a gentleness he valued, a depth of personality that Tatiana lacked, for all Tatiana's brilliance of intellect and body. But, still, lately he spent too much time thinking about Tatiana, and he suspected that she deliberately invited the attention to plague him. Captains had been disranked for psychological instability based on far less, and Viktor Roblev was always watching.

He toed his boot in the soft dirt of the ship-clearing, wondering what the psychologist really saw with those clever eyes of his. Viktor watched with reason, of course. Such tensions were dangerous among a small crew. During the initial wave of colonization into Hercules/Bootes, there had been incidents, murders, lost ships. Perhaps the old terror had led to the American destructions on Canopus—who could tell? Earlier Soviet experiments with larger crews and more expensive ships had shown that the difficulties only magnified with more personalities. The Chinese controlled their starship crews with revolutionary fanaticism, the Americans with ship rules and careful committee decisions by command vote; the Hindus and Shiites used religion. The Soviet Hegemony relied on its state psychologists, men and women of even temper and careful training who might bend even a political point to keep a ship in balance. And so Viktor watched over *Zvezda*, counselling here, warning there, mediating, advising, skillfully manipulating the emotions and tensions that naturally arose in any human group.

So far it had worked well. He wished, however, that Viktor could bottle Tatiana until *Zvezda* returned home.

Or Oleg. A second officer should know when the captain wanted to talk to him—by osmosis? What's wrong with you? he asked himself.

Galina dusted her hands on her trousers and looked up, an eyebrow raised. "Will you stand there all morning?" she asked pointedly.

"I could. I'm the captain."

Galina snorted scornfully and threw him an empty sack. He helped her carry the new trade goods into the ship and stow them safely in the hold, then climbed to the crew-quarters level to find Oleg. A discreet tap at Tatiana's door did not get a response. He stood in front of the door, frowning at it, tempted to barge in. Then he turned away and walked the several steps to his own quarters four doors away. The narrow confines of his room—bunk, shelves, com station—were comfortingly familiar. Natalya's perfume seem to drift on the air still, and he felt a small jab of regret and loss that was becoming just as familiar.

On a side shelf stood Natalya's small collection of perfumes and cosmetics, neatly ordered. He touched the array gently. The glass chimed, a gentle clinking, another sound associated with her. Then he withdrew his hand and sat down at his com to compose his summary of the morning trade.

TO: TRADE COMMISSAR, NOVY STRANA
        BUREAU 67YB2, SECTION 5
FROM: YURI SELENKOV, CAPTAIN
        BOOTES TRADE SHIP *ZVEZDA*
DATE: JUNE 12, 2386

Sir: At our twenty-third trade meeting with the local Sunstone chief, we obtained 12 kiloweight of Deltean herbs and 15 three-finger stones, a five percent increase to cargo. As noted in previous reports, the two prior trade meetings also yielded new product after a hiatus of several days. Ba-rao-som did not explain the earlier failure to produce new goods, but I suspect our current mission has exhausted local supply, necessitating additional interior trade by the locals with the upper peninsula tribes.

I again pursued your order to identify the source of the three-finger stones. With some reluctance, the chief indicated a direction north-northeast, toward the interior mountains. He would not answer any further inquiry. Orbital scans confirm the presence of surface clays containing two trace elements found in several three-finger stones currently in storage; a productive vein is quite probable. I will try to gain more specific information on the location, with the aim of establishing a second trade base closer to the original source of supply.

Yuri paused, scowling at the words on the screen. The Trade Commissar who supervised *Zvezda*, a dour balding man run to fat, rarely invited suggestions. Yuri's idea about a second base might be considered impertinent. Reports to the Space Bureau had an unpleasant tendency to end up a ghastly error: words could get twisted into strange meanings, never-intended ambitions, or subtle threat. He shrugged. He was a geologist by training; he had geologist ideas. He resumed his typing.

Our challenges to the intruder Xin Tian ship remain unanswered. Engineer Usu has identified the ship from transponder and radiometric data as *Sing Fa*, a Class Four cruiser previously assigned to the Kornephoros trade run. Her intentions are apparently nonmilitary and directed toward intrusion into our Bootean market—"

He heard a tap at his door.

"Come in!"

The door swished open, and Galina put her head into the room. "Ba-rao-som is waiting in the clearing. You should come, Captain."

"Ba-rao-som? Now?" Yuri glanced up at the wall clock, surprised. "But—never mind. I'm coming."

Galina stepped aside as he emerged into the corridor, then followed him to the stairs, her expression anxious. She knew as well as Yuri that Ba-rao-som's reappearance that day was unusual—and any unusual development threatened their fragile accord with the local natives.

Near the exterior lock he slowed down and gathered his thoughts. He took a deep breath, then stepped onto the upper platform overlooking the sunny glade. Below him waited a group of four natives—Ba-rao-som, two assistants, and another native Yuri had not seen before. He approached them in the free-swinging stride recommended by First Contact, indicating his friendly intentions with his body posture. He stopped four paces away.

[Greetings, trade-friend], Yuri signalled.

[Greetings], Ba-rao-som replied curtly, omitting the after-gesture of friendliness. [It is after midday].

Yuri signalled agreement, wondering why the aliens had come. The aides ruffled their fringe of neck fur—agitation? impatience?—and sidled quietly to the left and right, presenting a coequal front of their four to Yuri's two of himself and Galina.

"Get Tatiana," Yuri muttered to Galina. Galina bowed gracefully, gestured her regret at temporary departure, and quickly reentered the ship.

[Where go]? Ba-rao-som signalled.

[My trade party is incomplete. A moment of time, no more].

Ba-rao-som grunted assent and politely stared upward. The fourth of his party kept his eyes fixed on Yuri, his forward arms raised in a curious conformation, upper digits touching, first joint angled at a careful degree. Yuri had not seen the gesture before. He sorted through the carefully memorized pictographs from earlier trades but found nothing similar. Gestures had high importance among the natives, comprising eighty percent of their language—Yuri had the uneasy feeling that particular gesture was not friendly.

He heard a clatter behind him as Tatiana bounced down the steps, but he did not turn toward her. A moment later she joined him to take the customary position of second official on his left. Galina matched her on the right.

Ba-rao-som's three companions drifted another pace outward, creating a line to outpoint the three humans. Yuri did not like it—somehow it seemed hostile. He felt an emotion adrift on the air. Little as he knew the aliens, their current behavior differed from all previous contacts—and difference meant threat.

[I repeat greetings], Yuri said, restarting the meeting.

Ba-rao-som lowered his eyes and shifted his stance slightly. [Greetings, Star-man. I see the midday. I see your house-ship]. At each of Ba-rao-som's gestures, the fourth native shifted his upper arms into new configurations, an eerie counterpoint to the trade chief's words.

[I see your party, trade-friend], Yuri answered.

The fourth native hissed, and the two aides promptly retreated a step, their neck fur rippling. Ba-rao-som trembled and gestured vehemently. [Silence]!

Yuri froze, alarm pricking his scalp. After a moment, the natives quieted.

[I see words from the north], Ba-rao-som resumed, [where the //// abides, of displeasure with you, Star-man. I see //// before me, a //// of the ////. Because of this, we must //// and seek ////. I am sorry]. Ba-rao-som turned to leave.

[Wait]! Yuri signalled. [I don't understand].

[Good-bye, trade-friend], Ba-rao-som replied, and led his two aides toward the exit to the clearing. The fourth native then began a strange dance, shuffling from side to side, his upper arms waving gracefully. He saluted the cloud-covered sky with grave dignity, then carefully wove a pattern against Yuri and the ship. Finally, he drew a small bag from his body-pouch and threw it on the ground between them. A noxious odor swirled up, and Yuri stepped back, grimacing. The native seemed satisfied by the human's disgust; with a final chopping gesture, he turned and stamped out of the clearing.

Tatiana set her hands on her slim hips. "Well!"

"Yes, but what does it mean?" Yuri had a sinking feeling of a just-occurred disaster. "Your opinion?"

Tatiana scowled, obviously as perplexed as Yuri. "The trade went well this morning? He brought more gems?"

"Nothing unusual at all. Galina can tell you."

Tatiana huffed, flipping back her dark hair. "I assure you, Captain, my absence this morning was necessary. I was occupied with ship's business."

Yuri frowned at her distractedly. "I didn't mean any reproof, Tatiana Nikolaevna, only an answer to your question. We all have duties, both inside and outside the ship. Do you have an opinion?"

Galina spoke up softly. "Judging from all appearances, I think we were cursed." She nudged the still-smoking herb bag with her foot. "The First Survey report said Ba-rao-som's people practice sympathetic magic. I think we just saw one of their sorcerers in action. But why? What did we do wrong?"

"That's a good question," Tatiana said. Yuri caught a strange nuance in her voice and looked at her sharply. Would he ever understand that woman's mind?

"We'll review this thoroughly," he said. "Meet me in the conference lounge in ten minutes, Tatiana, and bring Oleg with you. Galina and I will inform the other crew members."

"Yes, Captain." Tatiana's eyes glinted with sly pleasure, and she walked away, deliberately accentuating the roll of her hips. Yuri scowled again.

"Don't let her upset you, Yurushka," Galina said unexpectedly. "Whatever her ambitions, it'll take more than that to get the rank she wants."

"Oh? I can think of a few commissars who found sex highly useful for their ambitions."

"A few," Galina agreed, "and some of them male. Patronage cuts both ways across sexual lines. But only a few. Once you have the rank, you also have the responsibilities—and the blame. Tatiana forgets that."

"Tatiana never forgets anything."

"Don't be so sure. I find that she consistently forgets your abilities as captain. May it be her lasting error, as I fully expect it to be."

Yuri smiled. "Thanks, Galinka."

"You are most welcome."

Yuri pointed at the smoking herb bag. "Put that in a container to stop the smell and bring it to the conference. We'll have Khina analyze it later." He looked around the empty clearing and then beyond to the distant line of surf. The familiar surroundings suddenly seemed threatening, as if unknown forces were moving behind the screen of water-reeds and pond, stalking his ship.

Yuri shuddered with a sudden prescience, then stamped toward the open airlock.

Three hours later, the mystery still remained. Khina Termez, the ship biologist, reported that the smoke-pouch contained only herbs, a few unfamiliar to *Zvezda*'s data from previous bio-surveys, but obviously local vegetation that stank badly when burned, nothing more. An hour's conference about the aliens had produced few ideas; the others were as mystified as Yuri. They reviewed each contact during *Zvezda*'s stay, then consulted the databanks. But nothing was found, save a vague reference to a shaman at an early meeting. Nothing about any other tribes to the north, nothing similar to the gestures Yuri sketched from memory. Nothing.

And so *Zvezda* waited, her crew occupying themselves with the usual routine checks of a survey ship at station. Galina had pressed Viktor into helping with an inventory of ship supplies, despite his humorous protests. Yuri could hear their muffled voices below, a pleasant counterpoint of bass and contralto, as Galina poked and prodded into *Zvezda*'s stores. Yuri sat at Natalya's computerman screens, running an environment-systems check with Khina's help. On the other side of the control room, *Zvezda*'s engineer, Hara Usu, checked the ship's propulsion system, his broad Kazakh face intent on his instruments. From time to time, Khina found a reason to walk over to his station, a desertion Yuri tolerantly allowed her. During the six weeks of *Zvezda*'s journey, the relationship between Khina and Hara had become a genuine love, one of those rare ship-pairings that confounded the Bureau's interest in mere sexual balance. Yuri enjoyed watching them together, his liking for Khina's quick infectious laughter and Hara's quiet competence having ripened into the smugness of an old matchmaker uncle.

Not that I had anything to do with it, of course, he reminded himself. He heard Khina's murmuring laugh as she bent over Hara's chair, then an answering dry chuckle from Hara, and felt another pang of loss for his dead ship wife, Natalya. Resolutely, he concentrated on the screen before him and tried to banish his envy. They suit each other, he thought.

Oleg and Tatiana had again busied themselves in their cabin, emerging once or twice to inspect the ship-clearing from the open airlock, a silent comment Yuri resented. He continued with his computer checks, ignoring their passages to and fro on the deck-level below Command. The day stretched—and still Ba-rao-som did not come back.

Yuri caught a quick late lunch with Khina in the dining room and then joined Oleg and Tatiana as the two again lounged at the shipdoor. He allowed them the grace of genuine concern—the breakdown of Deltean trade could affect Tatiana's trade career as much as his own—but still suspected both of their ambitions. He wondered fleetingly if the Bureau had chosen Oleg with just that edge in mind, merely to keep *Zvezda*'s captain on his toes. Probably they had—it would match Psychological's devious approach to almost everything.

I could chase myself in circles wondering about those doors behind doors, he mused. Great Lenin save me from mind-managers.

"Any sign?" he asked Oleg.

"Nothing," Oleg said unpleasantly, "as you can see for yourself."

"Hmmm."

Oleg slipped his arm around Tatiana's slim waist, and she relaxed against him like a cat, smiling slightly. Oleg Andreivich was tall and blond, with a military leanness imposed by his Academy training; Tatiana was darkly beautiful in her sensuality. They also suit each other, Yuri thought sourly, like models in a Bureau recruiting poster: *Join our comrade heroes in exploration of the stars!* Above the logo would be the handsome captain and his competent and beautiful trade officer, smiling blankly outward, with an artistic array of flaming ships and alien landscapes behind them.

Yuri looked past Oleg to the empty clearing and wondered what *Zvezda*'s "comrade heroes" were supposed to do now.

An uninvited trip to the Sunstone village? On her last visit, the *Nauka* had spent several days smoothing over bent alien feelings after two crewmen took an unannounced tourist jaunt to the aliens' coraal. Captain Shemilkin was still raging about it when he left a satellite report for *Aryol*, and he narrowly escaped disranking when *Nauka* got home. The three Delta/Seguinus ships had later received a sharply worded addition to their standing orders. Reluctantly Yuri abandoned the idea. Orders notwithstanding, the result was too unpredictable, likely to make a bad situation worse.

"I don't understand," he said, more to himself than his two companions. "What did we do?"

"Yes, what did we do?" Tatiana echoed sharply. "The Bureau won't be happy about losing Delta Bootis."

"We haven't lost Delta yet."

"Oh?" Tatiana swept her arm at the empty clearing. "Then where's the trading party?"

"I asked for suggestions this morning, Trade Officer. You didn't have any, except to sit."

"Inaction never solves anything," she said impatiently.

"Not true. Inaction often solves problems, one way or the other. It's the standard trade precept of waiting for the other side to act. Not always effective, not always an advantage, but standard. Unfortunately for *Zvezda*, it got included in ship's orders as a directive, too. So we have no choice."

"There are always choices. If Oleg Andreivich were captain—" She stopped abruptly.

"Ah, yes," Yuri said sarcastically. "If Oleg Andreivich were captain. Always that. Would a different captain get more useful advice? I didn't know you matched your expertise to fit your preferences."

Tatiana's jaw dropped. She spluttered a moment, her mouth flapping impotently, then pushed herself away from Oleg and flounced into the ship. Yuri smiled grimly.

"I don't encourage her in that, Captain." Oleg looked upset, and Yuri felt inclined to believe him—partly.

"Don't worry about it," he said with a shrug.

Oleg hesitated, then grimaced and stepped past Yuri to follow Tatiana into the ship. Yuri stood in the bright sunshine, blinking wearily at the marshland that surrounded his ship. Why had Barao-som broken off trade? Again, he reviewed the last few weeks' contacts with the Sunstone chief but found nothing.

Perhaps he was looking at the wrong end of the equation, he thought. A change in pattern needed only one changed fact— like a poacher ship up-peninsula. His eyes narrowed. Aside from a dry acknowledgment of *Zvezda*'s challenge upon landing and several irritating minutes of Xin Tian patriotic music, *Sing Fa* had ignored them. In time, he had tabled the problem, then had forgotten *Sing Fa* in the surprise of Ba-rao-som's actions.

Yuri looked northward and wondered what the Chinese might have brewed. Ba-rao-som had mentioned the north.

He turned and reentered the ship, walking quickly through the wide access bay to the control-deck ladder.

"Khina!" he called.

"Yes?"

"Come down here. I have something for us to do."

Khina's delicate face, framed by a complex intertwining of heavy braids, appeared in the access hatch above his head. She grinned down at him. "Something to *do*? Really?"

"Oh, shut up," he muttered. Khina laughed and scrambled onto the ladder, then leaped off the rungs two meters above the floor. She landed with an impact that sent a ringing shudder through the hold; Yuri hastily stuck out a hand to steady her. "You can break an ankle that way," he chided. "Seventy-Standard is hardly bouncing-level gravity."

"Yes, Captain." Her black Kazakh eyes were merry and quite unabashed.

" 'Yes, Captain,' " he mimicked. "I need your help with the satellite relay. I want some drone pictures." According to the tech report, the Delta satellite had a few observation drones left over from the initial survey, enough to send one over *Sing Fa*'s landing site.

"Of the coraal?" Khina asked, eyes widening. "Won't that just make things worse?"

"Not of the coraal. Of *Sing Fa*."

"Hmmm." He saw the thought catch hold in Khina's expression. "You think the Chinese have meddled somehow?"

"Maybe. In any event, it's time we looked them over. I don't like being ignored."

He crossed the hold to the open airlock and descended the exterior stairway, Khina bouncing down the steps behind him. The satellite relay stood fifty meters from the ship, a permanent structure of the base. Its four pylons were sunk deep into the mud to form a stable platform for the web of metal guides that supported and maneuvered the small focus dish. A control station sat within its lockable bunker nearby. Yuri activated the bunker's palm-lock, then had Khina read off position numbers from the other operator station as he programmed the fly-by. Then they closed up the bunker.

"The drone may not get anything useful," Khina commented.

"True. But still . . ."

His eye caught a movement along the coraal path, and he turned toward it with sudden hope, then stood shocked in astonishment. The figure who staggered into view was not the aliens he expected, but a human woman dressed in the blue quilted pajamas affected by the Xin Tian Chinese. He heard Khina draw in a sharp breath of surprise. They both stared.

The woman stopped as she saw them, weaving slightly on uncertain legs. Her short dark hair was cut straight at the jawline, framing a thin face marred by a long scar on one cheek. Caucasian, Yuri realized, again surprised. He had not heard that Xin Tian allowed non-Asiatics to serve on their survey ships. Unless . . . His spine chilled as he thought of another possibility.

The woman grimaced strangely and seemed to shrink within herself, then wiped a soggy sleeve across her face, smearing the traces of swamp mud. Slowly she reached into her breast pocket and held up an emblem. The afternoon sun winked on the metal star.

"I—am Starfarer," she said in a hoarse voice. "I seek—sanctuary." She swayed, then sank to one knee, her dark head bowed forward. "Help . . ."

Yuri stared as the woman slowly collapsed onto the damp ground, a slim hand stretched out toward him.

"Please . . ."

Chapter 5

"PLEASE . . ."

Had he heard that anguished word with his ears?

Impulsively, Yuri ran forward and knelt beside the stranger. He turned her over gently, then stared down at her face. He felt another apprehensive chill run down his spine: he wanted nothing to do with telepaths. The long-standing proscription fitted too well his wariness of a mutant who knew every secret, every weakness; and there were tales of worse things—wills subverted, personalities warped, puppets moving to a mentalist's fingered strings. Xin Tian denied the tales, boasting of their safeguards, but the Soviet Hegemony kept to a wiser rule. Let the Chinese take the risks.

"Please . . ." The *need* behind the word . . .

He touched the scarring on her cheek, wondering. Her narrow face was deathly pale—surprisingly young, he realized, and vulnerable in its exhaustion. Had she walked twenty kilometers from *Sing Fa*? Obviously she must have. He gently traced the well-healed scar with a finger, again wondering how and where, then looked up as Khina knelt beside them.

"The Chinese ship?" she asked.

"Apparently. Help me get her inside."

Khina looked shocked. "A Starfarer? You must be joking. We can't have one of those on *Zvezda*." She drew back fearfully. "Why isn't she with her ship? She must have done something to them, something awful."

50

"You don't know that."

"But she's—"

"Khina!"

"Yes, sir." Reluctantly Khina helped lift the unconscious stranger and carry her into the ship. By the time Yuri had installed the telepath in a spare cabin, all the crew had clustered in the corridor outside. A few brief words by Khina alerted them, and their expressions made their mutual thought quite clear.

"Damn," he muttered, wondering if he had lost all sense. He beckoned Galina into the room and dismissed the others with a nod. They left reluctantly, though he knew he would hear their opinions later.

Stupid, stupid, he berated himself. Already he regretted his impulse and rued the new disaster he had brought down on *Zvezda*. Belatedly, he remembered the penalty for contact with a telepath. First I somehow wreck our Delta trade, and now I've racked up a firing squad for us all. He looked distractedly at the unconscious woman on the bed. What had he done?

And what do I do now?

Galina lifted her eyes to his, calm as always. As ship services officer, Galina provided *Zvezda*'s crew its medical care. It was a role well-suited to her skills and person.

"You don't mind?" he asked, nodding at the Starfarer on the bed.

"No, though I do wonder at your decision."

So do I, he thought. He looked down at the woman again. I could carry her back out again, dump her in the swamp, somehow pretend it never happened . . . And what then, Yuri? Who helps you forget?

He took a deep breath. "Get your medical kit, please, to give her the care she needs."

"Yes, sir." Yuri stood by the woman's bed, looking down at her, until Galina returned a minute later. As Galina prepared a hypodermic, the woman's eyes fluttered open in alarm.

"No . . . drugs," she whispered. "Can't . . ." She seemed to grope for the word. "Tolerate. Please."

Yuri touched Galina's arm, and she slipped the hypo back into her kit. The woman's eyes fluttered shut again and she sighed, relaxing bonelessly into the soft mattress of the bunk. Yuri bent over her.

"Who are you?" he asked. Her eyes opened again, and he looked into the deep blue, almost black, of her eyes. His head swam slightly at their hypnotic pull; he started backward, alarmed. He had heard tales . . .

The woman grimaced. "Everyone . . . hears tales," she whispered. "No harm . . . no harm to you . . . promise." Again, she struggled for the words. Her eyes closed again wearily. "Sleep . . ."

He reached for her arm and gripped it firmly. "I need information first. Who are you? What happened to *Sing Fa*?"

She sighed deeply, her breath fluttering with weakness. "Lily People . . . attacked. All dead . . . follow." Her hand stirred on the mattress, then fell back. "Tribe out there . . . Warn . . ." Her breath escaped in another sigh, and she sagged into unconsciousness. He shook her, but she did not respond. He looked at Galina.

"Do what you can for her."

"Yes, sir."

Yuri moved aside and stepped toward the door.

"Yurushka?"

"Yes?"

Galina looked at him soberly. "Don't doubt yourself. As mad as it is, it's the right choice."

"Why do you think so?" he asked, surprised.

"I thought as much. May I remind you that impulse is a command prerogative?" Galina smiled knowingly and busied herself by smoothing the covers on the bed. "She has walked a long way on a difficult journey. That shows strength. She didn't conceal her nature from us, though she could have, but surrendered herself to our choosing of death or life. That shows honesty." She studied the woman's exhausted face, then straightened a final corner of the blanket. "Or perhaps the last defiant challenge in a hard life. Have you ever wondered what it's like for them on Xin Tian?"

Yuri shook his head, bemused. He had thought Galina would rarely surprise him.

"I have. My brother is with our embassy there and brings stories home on his leaves. They live in a walled enclosure surrounded by robot laser-mounts; Xin Tian doesn't chance a guard of human soldiers. Wherever they go, two guards, never one, walk beside them, watching, arguing, berating. The Chinese regulate the food they eat, the air they breathe, the children they bear. And everywhere they are watched, even in their warren. I wonder how they tolerate it—why they even leave Ikanos for that." She sighed. "They work in the hospitals, too, you know; I've often wondered what I might heal with such a gift."

She turned and smiled up at him. "You see, I'm biased. Envy is always a useful rationale."

"As is compassion, my gentle Galinka."

Her smile widened. "I will tend your Starfarer, Captain. That is *my* gift; yours is explaining to the others why it's a good idea."

He hesitated, imagining the reception that awaited him in the conference room. "Uh, any suggestions?"

"The obvious, which has no doubt occurred to you. She knows what happened on *Sing Fa*, something we must know, too. Start with that—it will hold Tatiana, at least until the Starfarer can be interrogated. But have you considered what she might know about the Sunstone—or could find out? She can hear our minds—what might she know of theirs? Xin Tian is still looking for a sentient race in Hercules; picture how they'll use the Starfarers when they find one."

"Hmmm."

"You have a new resource, Yuri Ivanovich," Galina said earnestly, "one we've never had a chance to use. Imagine what we could discover here, what knowledge we might have of an alien people. What do the Sunstone know? How do they see us? Themselves? What is their character, their loves, their beliefs, their knowledge of their world?" She pointed at the woman on the bed. "And *she* can find out, merely by willing it. We poke and prod at herbs and three-finger stones, tiptoeing around our ship-clearing, waving our arms in pidgin at Ba-rao-som; *she* holds the key to aliens who might become brothers."

"The Delteans?" Yuri asked, astonished.

"Why not?" Galina said defiantly. "Because they're primitive? Because they don't look like us, talk like us, *think* like us? Believe me, if anyone would understand that gap, it's the Starfarers. And perhaps, just perhaps, accepting the Delteans might make humanity more tolerant of its own." She crossed her arms and glared at him fiercely. "Just once, Yuri, try to think of something beyond your precious rocks."

Yuri laughed uncomfortably. "I was just thinking of explaining all that to the commissar."

The corner of Galina's mouth quirked upward. "So why tell him at all? Haven't you realized yet, Yuri, how things are *really* done?"

Yuri studied her for a long moment and abruptly settled his mind on a half-suspected possibility. It saddened him a little.

"Enough to know wheels within wheels, Galina. Who assigned you to watch *Zvezda*? Kirova? I had assumed that Tatiana . . ."

Galina looked away. "No, not that one; she's too focused on succeeding her aunt as commissar. And you know I'm not supposed to tell you that. But I happen to agree with Commissar Kirova's policies."

"About what? Delteans as brothers, or Starfarers as a personal tool?"

Galina said nothing, her expression placid.

"They can have many uses," Yuri added softly, "and some are as obvious as others."

"If the Starfarer cooperates," she countered.

"Oh, they'll cooperate. Look at Xin Tian. All you do is enslave them and they'll spy on anybody."

She smiled then. "Are you so sure? And are you as certain of what Kirova really wants?"

"What do *you* want, Galina?"

"Your regard, your friendship. I would hope that's assumed. And a way to take the Starfarer home to Novy Strana."

"I'll consider it." He turned toward the door.

"Thank you."

The others of *Zvezda*'s crew awaited him in the conference room. The faces that greeted him were impassive and noncommittal. Command decision, he thought, and hoped the decision ended up the right one. Right—but for whom?

He briefed them on Rinn's warning, but the unspoken question still hovered in the air.

"I reviewed the statute," Tatiana said, launching the common attack. "You know the penalty."

"It's an old law," he countered. "Ship survival can have precedence, even over statute."

"And how does *her* presence aboard relate to survival?"

"She has knowledge we need. Knowledge *is* survival, especially when we haven't much time. Our ship schedule requires us to leave in two days; we might delay an extra forty-eight hours and take a risk on the ice drill. We could skip Seguinus and gain three weeks—I'll leave the explanations of *that* to you, Tatiana. But, maybe, after poking around in the swamp-grass that long, we could figure out things. And *then* we have to decide what to do.''

He shrugged. "*Zvezda* is not in danger, not from a primitive tribe with spears—though, I point out, *Sing Fa* no doubt thought the same. Our practical danger, comrades, is the consequence of failure, as I'm sure you appreciate. Personally, I might consider quick execution a better fate than Sirov's labor camps—the result is the same, only longer.''

Tatiana flipped her head. "I hardly think we're in that kind of trouble.''

"Oh?" He stared her down. "Where are the Sunstone, Tatiana?" he threw at her. "Why did they break off trade? What do they plan? How do we change their minds? Give me some answers, Trade Officer.''

"Yes, I have answers," Tatiana hissed. "*She* did it. Whatever her purpose in coming here, she managed to wreck our trade with the Delteans. Two years of careful work—phttt!" She waved her hand imperiously. "You allowed her aboard, and look at the result!''

"Ba-rao-som broke off trade hours ago; she's been aboard thirty minutes. At least have some time-logic in your arguments.''

"Very clever, Captain. You know what I mean. Who are these Lily People? What did *Sing Fa* do to offend them? We're obviously paying the price of their ineptitude, thanks to your Starfarer.''

"She's not 'my' Starfarer, Trade Officer." He paused, struggling to keep his temper. "As I said before, what is your alternative?''

"Give her back to them! Let her pay for her own fault, whatever it was, for the sake of our trade. She's not one of us. What do we owe to her?''

The others murmured, whether in assent or protest, Yuri could not tell. He surveyed their faces, hesitating. "It is my command prerogative," he said slowly, "to make this decision. I will account for it, however it falls, but I'm willing to listen to your arguments, since we'll all bear the consequences. Tatiana has expressed hers. Who else? Viktor Fedorovich?''

The psychologist looked pensive as he tugged on his long chin. He said nothing for a moment. "I see another consideration, one of particular concern to my expertise. The law prohibits all contact with telepaths for the obvious reasons. That rule is strictly enforced on Novy Strana and our ships. On the other hand—though some experts may argue—the Central Soviets haven't yet declared the telepaths unhuman. To eject her is tantamount to murder, if her tale of a hostile tribe is true. Where is the balance, Captain? To protect the ship against her telepathy, or to abandon another human who has asked sanctuary? That conflict has entered the ship—either choice will have its consequences.''

"The good of the ship—" Tatiana began.

Viktor looked up at her, his expression stern. "Is not served by murder," he said. "On the other hand—"

"In short," Yuri interrupted impatiently, "You haven't any real opinion."

Viktor shrugged. "Baldly, no. I see problems whatever we do, and we have two more trade-points to complete, time enough for the conflicts to threaten the balance of our ship."

"Hara?"

"I think she warned us," Hara said slowly, "even if she brought the trouble in the first place—if she did. I don't like turning over another human to savages. Besides, if we refuse Treaty sanctuary once, Xin Tian may retaliate when *we* have the need. Who will save us then? What knowledge might be lost with us? If anyone in this crew appreciates how fragile *Zvezda* can be, it's an engineer. I know the systems, the warp-drive, the machinery that keeps us alive in the void; I know the razor-edge we skate. If we must set a precedent, I'd rather accept the telepath."

"Oleg Andreivich?"

Oleg glanced at Tatiana, then grimaced. "I agree with Tatiana Nikolaevna."

"Naturally," Yuri said sarcastically. Oleg glared at him, and Yuri promptly regretted the remark. He turned toward Khina. Her small face was troubled.

"Khina?"

Khina pushed back her fine dark hair, then shrugged. "I think only that I might be in her place. We Kazakhs understand exclusion and"—her glance darted angrily toward Tatiana—"the blame for unwelcome events we haven't caused."

"Those riots are history," Tatiana said dismissingly.

"Not to us. It didn't help our dead to have apologies later, after the mobs destroyed our warrens out of fear of a plague we never started, merely caught first. Nor the testimonials and reforms that followed, however Hara and I have benefited from the official regret. I say we should accept her. I don't understand her gift, and I don't like having a telepath aboard, but I don't see any alternative. If we have any chance of salvaging Delta, it lies through her.''

"If we can salvage Delta—" Viktor began.

"And argue a conflict in the statutes—" Hara added.

"Maybe we can scrape by, somehow," Yuri finished. Hara chuckled.

"You fools!" Tatiana hissed.

"You're outvoted, Trade Officer. Thank you, comrades. For the record, your opinion is evenly divided and my decision will stand.'' He let a silence fall, then stood up. "To your stations, *Zvezda*."

The Starfarer continued to sleep. Mindful of her warning, Yuri posted Khina as a guard outside the ship, but nothing stirred, neither friendly nor hostile. He could see the apprehension of the crew, and it troubled him. Viktor could worry about his incipient space-madness; Yuri worried only about the ship. Why *was* the Starfarer here? What had happened to *Sing Fa*? He prowled the control room restlessly, anxious for the photo report from the drone. Information—he thirsted for it like a sun-parched man in a desert.

"Satellite report coming in, Captain," Hara said at last.

Twenty kilometers away, the drone swept low over the Chinese ship, its cameras patiently transmitting images to its mother satellite overhead. The satellite caught the video signals, converted them to binary signals for pixel packing, and retransmitted to the relay station at the base.

"What does it see?" Yuri asked as he leaned over Hara's shoulder. In the engineer's small analysis screen, the computer began reassembling the pixel lines, one by one, from the satellite's transmission.

"Freeze that," he ordered, conscious of others crowding behind him. "Post it to the main screen so we can all look."

He straightened and turned toward the forward screen. Within the wide frame of the monitor, almost life-size, a ship's door stood open, the black scorching of laser-fire apparent on its metal frame. In the shadowy interior of the lock, he glimpsed the broken debris and twisted metal of a wrecked ship.

"Lasers?" Oleg asked. He turned toward Tatiana in surprise. "I thought Delta had a nontechnic culture."

"It does." Tatiana looked just as puzzled. "At least we thought so. The First Contact report mentioned only primitive spears and slings. We've never seen the Sunstone carrying any-thing more than that. What did *Sing Fa* blunder into?''

''That's the question,'' Yuri said grimly, ''and maybe our answer for the break in trade. The Starfarer said, 'tribe follows.' '' He waved his hand at the screen. ''Whoever did that must be coming south—toward the Sunstone coraal.''

''And us,'' Viktor said softly.

''Yes. And us.''

The computer displayed another photo, showing more of the ravaged ship. Beneath the broad shape of one engine, a hatch dangled open, the ground beneath scuffed and marked with foot-prints. A line of tracks led away toward a nearby reed-bed, then disappeared into the marsh.

''Can you get any more resolution on those tracks, Hara?''

''That's the best at that angle. The drone was already past the base of its curve.''

''Well,'' Tatiana said, ''we know how she got out. What if the aliens want her back?''

Yuri scowled at Tatiana's unspoken suggestion. ''As I decided earlier, I'm not throwing her back like a bone to a dog. She's human, Starfarer or not.''

''Maybe they won't kill her,'' Oleg suggested.

''They killed everybody else. She said so.''

''You've only her word for that,'' Tatiana argued.

''I believe her. Why would she lie?''

Tatiana shrugged. ''But why would the natives attack a ship?''

''I don't know. With her help, maybe we can find out.''

Tatiana scowled at him, unappeased.

''In any event,'' he continued, ''we'll keep proper security. Hara, set out the ward-beacons around the clearing. Oleg, we'll keep a double-watch on the screens. If the Delteans do attack, I want some advance warning. Maybe we can defuse it.'' He swept his glance across his crew. ''Keep alert, comrades. It could be a long night.''

Chapter 6

RINN LAY ON HER BACK IN THE COMFORTABLE bed, her body relaxed into the yielding mattress. She felt her body as a sagging weight, pricked by occasional pain in the muscles of her legs, her shoulders, her left hand, like a darkness touched by isolated flashes of light. The fatigue liberated her mind, depriving it of the normal sensations of body and movement; she floated, semiaware. The blond-haired woman had returned to the others, darkening the room as she left. Rinn felt grateful for her kindness, whatever its motives.

She lay unmoving, then stretched her mind outward, curious. She heard the dulled mental voices of the ship's crew as they prepared for the night's watch. The captain had taken her warning; she felt relief at that, though she knew the problems she had created for him. But what other choice? She was as bound in her choice to live as he was bound by his instinct to shield her. Uncommon, that, to choose so easily, nonetheless. He was an uncommon man—she had sensed his strength, liked him instinctively. She rarely liked Normals. Odd, she thought.

Her mind drifted out of the ship toward the gathering tribes, skipping lightly from mind to mind until she found the one she sought. Isen-glov-amar had approached the Sunstone coraal in all his arrogance, his warriors at his back. The Sunstone chief had grovelled before him, terrified for his people, eager to consent. Sunstone would not deny the Lily—such stupidity was generations in the past, and Isen-glov-amar's appearance had brought instant obedience.

Why? she wondered. In the alien's mind, she caught the shadows of terrible wars and the unspeakable ferocity of a Lily chief who accepted no limits in his carnage. In that cataclysm had been born the Lily ceremonies of cannibalism and sacrifice, the dark testimony of an oppression that had persisted for generations. The Lily had taken an ancient technology, too, its reasons now forgotten, and kept it afterward from all peninsula tribes. In time, the Lily influence had spread even beyond the interior mountains, where other tribes dwelt and had learned cause to fear the Lily. And so the power survived unchallenged.

Perhaps the Sunstone had hoped for an opportunity in a new power, bargained from gods who claimed a home among the stars—a chance lost now. In his terror, hoping to placate the raging Isen-glov-amar, the Sunstone chief had told him about *Zvezda*. The Lily chieftain's reaction had been swift.

In the center of the coraal, the Sunstone chief stood bound to a high stake, his upper-limb joints slashed to prevent any further insult in unwelcome news. His tribe grovelled before Isen-glov-amar, heads bowed, hands pressed to silence against their bodies. A child whimpered, quickly silenced. The sea breeze swirled over the coraal walls, ruffling neck fur, teasing at the tender cartilage of leg-joints, cool in the spreading dusk of sunset.

Isen-glov-amar's eyes swept the villagers, daring any challenge. [We are the Lily People], he declared. [Who will speak for the Sunstone]? He waited a moment, watching the villagers, as his third brain thrummed, exciting him to the rage-lust of strength-for-strength. [Who will speak]?

A Sunstone warrior straightened and proudly stepped forward, his fear confined to a slight weakness in his stride, a slight hesitation as he approached Isen-glov-amar. [I will speak], he gestured. Belos stepped forward and held high the ceremonial lance, ready for the strike.

The Sunstone warrior trembled, then gestured in sharp quick motions. [Kill me, Lord, and take my strength].

Belos' spear arched forward, thrusting deep into his heart, then wrenched downward, ripping open his abdomen. The spear spun and crushed his skull with a blow of the spear-butt. As the warrior crumpled forward, a low moan arose from the watching Sunstone.

Isen-glov-amar paced in front of them a moment, then halted, his legs splayed wide. [Who will speak for the Sunstone]? he gestured curtly, and another warrior stepped forward and died. And another, to lie crumpled on the well-tramped soil of the coraal, their blood mingling with that of their dying chief's.

[Who will speak]? Isen-glov-amar again demanded, his third brain incited by the smell of blood and the sight of the warriors' glistening brains.

He sensed a stir from the Lily warriors behind him. Even for defiant insurrection, now distant in memory, the penalty required only three victims; Isen-glov-amar remembered that now. His warriors looked at each other, and Isen-glov-amar saw their doubt. It infuriated him.

[I am the son of the Lily chief], he raged. [And I ask who will speak]?

An elder stepped forth, his neck fur bleached with age, his walk painful with the joint-disease. He walked toward the Lily warriors and stood in front of Isen-glov-amar, his head raised proudly. [I am Ba-rao-som, trade chief, and I will speak].

[You are not a warrior].

[You have three warriors], Ba-rao-som said calmly. [Take our strength, Lord of the Lily, and be satisfied].

[Belos, take him], Isen-glov-amar gestured angrily.

[Lord, it is not custom], Belos objected. Isen-glov-amar whirled toward him and raised his fire-weapon in threat.

[Obey me, Belos], he warned.

[And do you murder me, too]? Belos asked coolly. [And the next who takes up this lance? And the next? Until you have all our own warriors to feed your strength, son of the chief]?

Isen-glov-amar's hand tightened on the rifle-guard, his vision misted with a haze of blood-lust pounding from his third brain. *Kill, kill,* it thrummed at him. Belos straightened from his prey-stalk and stood before him, head high, cold anger in his gaze—and an unmasked contempt. Behind them, the ranked Lily warriors shuffled in agitation, their eyes wide with alarm—and a dangerous excitement.

[Take me, Lord], Belos gestured defiantly, [and feed on your own people]. The obscenity lay on the air for a heartbeat.

Isen-glov-amar trembled with his need, then slowly lowered his weapon. Belos would die for this humiliation, he promised himself, but—not yet. Not in front of the Sunstone, with his warriors near hysteria. But he would die. The intention soothed his third brain's lust but prompted another idea of different violence. Isen-glov-amar drew himself up proudly and turned toward Ba-rao-som.

[You have spoken with Star-Devils. You will help me take *their* strength].

[Lord]! Ba-rao-som protested.

[Obey me]!

Ba-rao-som's head sagged. [I will obey].

[My Lily, feed of their strength], Isen-glov-amar ordered.

One by one the Lily warriors strode forward to eat of Sunstone brains, then sank into a prey-stalk facing the tribe, a line of darkness against the coraal timbers. [We are the Lily], Isen-glov-amar threatened, and blasted the stump-bound Sunstone chief to a stinking ruin. The Sunstone wailed aloud and crumpled, hiding their eyes behind their hands. Isen-glov-amar roughly pulled a Sunstone warrior to his feet and forced a fragment of dead brain between his jaws.

[Eat of the strength], he commanded, then moved toward others. Two retched, only to be clubbed to the ground by the butt of a rifle and kicked aside. Others cooperated more readily, their eyes wide with terror.

As he fed his new warriors, the air reeked with the scents of the Sunstone shaman. [Go forward in strength], the shaman pranced, shaking his herb bag and rattles. [Cleanse the world of this evil. O Lily, guide us]!

[I will], Isen-glov-amar told him. Then, as the last of the sunlight disappeared into the distant sea, Isen-glov-amar led his warriors toward the Devil-house.

Rinn swept her perception back to the ship, then reached upward toward the minds aboard it, touching each to gather names and reasons. The medico sat at her station, calm and resigned. Near her, a woman's agitation and discontent—Tatiana Nikolaevna; beside her, smug disbelief and a calculation of chances in her lover. She swept over the two Asians in the crew, a fearful Khina, a phlegmatic engineer, and avoided the subtlety of the psychologist who watched all too earnestly, then reached the clear determination of the captain. She lingered there, sensing the shape of his mind but not penetrating, and found comfort in it.

Odd, she thought again.

She was intrigued by the captain—perhaps too intrigued. *The Gifted are pariah* went the enclave maxim; she clung to that belief a moment, protecting herself against her own weaknesses, then set it aside to reach out again to the strange, new ship.

Zvezda. The shape of the word lay in every mind as the comfort of home-port, the place-to-be-defended. Other words lay beyond; she gathered them to her, taking in their language in gestalt leaps through the Gift, as she had adopted the Han language four years before. Words, images, syntax, inflection—she became a sponge for the words that poured down upon her. If the ship survived the alien attack, she would have to live among these people—at least until they returned her to Xin Tian and whatever awaited there for a Starfarer with a murdered crew. She must know *Zvezda's* reasons, and for that she must have their words.

In the distance, she sensed the darkening shadow of the Lily's approach. As Isen-glov-amar moved closer to the ship, he paused to send out scouts. Four Lily warriors crept ahead, testing the marsh wind for any scent, wary of the counterattack. Rinn heard the kill-lust in their mind and shuddered.

Not again!

She tried to stir her apathetic muscles but fell back, panting from her weakness. Her body was long abused by the fears and exertion of her escape from *Sing Fa*; it demanded tending. She tried again, only to collapse weakly upon the mattress, unable to override those demands. So tired . . . Her eyelids fluttered and closed.

No!

She relaxed and opened herself to the essence of the ship, binding herself to it. She felt the smooth curve of metal and the still air in the contained spaces, the steady ticking of machinery, the beating heart of the nuclear engines beneath her. She tasted the emotions that lived aboard the ship, touched the purpose of its crew, drew in again their words. *Zvezda* . . . the Star. She thought of her own emblem and bound its significance to the ship that shielded her.

She paused and wondered if it were better to be cautious, to keep to her own spaces, until *Zvezda* returned her home to Xin Tian. Better to choose isolation, nonbinding—it was the safer course. *Zvezda's* crew had never known a Starfarer; Novy Strana banned all telepaths from its cities and its ships. To bind to people who distrusted, who could not be turned . . .

I am a Starfarer, she thought fiercely. If that means anything, I can't fail again. She focused her will on that thought and reached toward the Gift-coil deep in her mind. *Help me,* she demanded. *Help me move!*

She lifted her head and rolled painfully onto her side, then slipped her legs off the edge of the bunk. Gravity aided her movement as her feet swung toward the floor. She pushed with her arms and sat up, balanced precariously on the edge of the bed. Her head swam unpleasantly at the change in elevation, and she shook it vigorously. *Move!*

She pushed herself forward with her arms and wavered to her feet, one hand clutching the mattress for balance. She slid one foot forward in a shuffle, then the other, and walked slowly toward the door, holding onto the bunk railing, then the dresser and wall. At the door, she stopped and leaned against its smooth surface a moment, then lifted her heavy arm to the key-lock. The door sighed open in its automatic track, revealing the corridor beyond.

She heard a voice above her, accompaniment to a melange of thoughts from the crew. She walked toward the ladder at the end of the corridor, seeking a way upward. It was the right ladder: she could see a lighted space above that led to the control room, and the voices sounded clearly.

"Anything stirring, Hara?"

"Nothing, sir."

Rinn set her hand on the ladder-rung and began climbing upward, pausing at each step to pace her strength. As her head appeared in the well of the floor above, she saw several crewmen at their stations, their backs toward her. Khina and the engineer—Hara?—sat to the right near the engine panels; another woman and a blond man lounged nearby, their expressions openly bored. She matched the several faces to her earlier mental impressions, naming them. Tatiana Nikolaevna Kirova, Oleg Andreivich Konstantin. The syllables rolled in her mind, joining the other words that still poured into her gestalt from their minds.

An older man—Viktor Fedorovich Roblev, she named him—sat in a chair to the left, watching the captain as he sat in mid-room behind another control panel, Galina Kirillovna standing behind him, their attention focused on the readouts on the screen before them.

Rinn reached up for the railing above her head and pulled herself upward to step off the ladder. Roblev's quick eyes immediately caught the movement and focused on her.

"Well, well," he said. "We meet you at last."

The captain swivelled in his chair and looked at her in surprise. Rinn walked toward an empty chair nearby and sank into it gratefully. She spent a moment catching her breath, conscious of the eyes upon her. Then she lifted her head.

"Comrades, you should be warned. The Lily warriors want— to attack this ship tonight." She stopped, trying to concentrate on the language that still frustrated her. "They have talked to the Sunstone—threaten if not help."

"Lily warriors?" the captain asked, confused.

"Tribe up-peninsula—killed all of *Sing Fa*. Want to kill you, too. Please—must listen." She pleaded with him, watching his face. "Please . . ." Then her shoulders sagged, and her eyes unaccountably filled with tears. I am alone, she thought, and ached for the familiar touch of another mind, one like her own. "So tired," she mumbled, and sensed Galina's answering pang of concern. "Forgive."

"How do you know these things?" Oleg demanded.

She shook her head, pushing away his hostility. "They approach from the north. Isen-glov-amar, the Lily—chief, has sent four scouts toward the ship." She reached out with her mind automatically to gather in the words, growing more practiced as she spoke. "One is in that direction." She pointed past Hara. "The others are there, there, and there."

Her hand swung in an arc, jabbing toward each of the scouts stalking the ship. Then she pointed past Khina's station and closed her eyes a moment, listening.

"The main body of warriors is there, behind the third scout in the center. I count—um, fifty Sunstone, plus the ten Lily warriors who pursued me from the north. They are armed with laser-rifles and a larger weapon—of some kind. Their chief will attack two hours after sunset, circling from the south."

She let her hand fall limply into her lap. "He wants to murder you all, just like *Sing Fa*. Then the Lily warriors will eat your brains and take your strength and clean the world of your evil. They will dance around your bodies, slicing them apart with ceremonial spears, and then eat your bodies, too. And every tribe on the peninsula will hear of it, and know that the same fate awaits any other Star-Devil who dares to land here."

They stared at her, saying nothing.

Tatiana scowled. "An interesting hypothesis, Starfarer." Rinn heard the speculation in Tatiana's mind as she questioned the Starfarer's motives and looked for possible advantage. Gifted in intrigue, Tatiana always rejected the obvious. Rinn stared at Tatiana, challenging her.

"Not hypothesis—only fact," she said. "I listened to Isenglov-amar as he murdered my crewmates and as he followed me through the marsh. I know his mind and know his influence here. And I know he wants to attack this ship." She looked at the captain and spread her hands in entreaty. "My own crew is dead—I couldn't save them. Don't add your ship to my—failures."

They heard a faint chime at Hara's board. The dour man studied the display. "An alien two points left of north—your third spy, Starfarer. Approaching slowly. Ah, he just struck one of the wards." Other telltales lit on the boards, signalling the alarm.

"Do you detect others?" the captain asked, his eyes on Rinn.

"A second scout to the right, exactly where she placed him. She knows, Captain."

"I don't doubt that. A fascinating ability, Starfarer, this Gift of yours." Rinn nodded her acknowledgment of the compliment. "Why did the Lily tribe attack *Sing Fa*?"

"The Lily won't tolerate intruders—we landed in their territory. But they think *everywhere* is their territory, too. I doubt if your Sunstone ever told them about you."

"Well, they know now."

"Yes."

"Thanks to you," Oleg growled.

Rinn looked at him coolly. "My fault, Second Officer, to prefer life over your trade fortunes. At least you are warned—the Lily would have heard of you in time and tried to kill your trade-ship as they killed ours."

"A point," Oleg conceded, shrugging. "A definite point. But even so, *Sing Fa* paid the price of its poaching."

Rinn scowled and felt a stab of anger. She lifted her chin proudly. "My crewmate, Mei-lan, would call that an imperialistic comment. But, of course, the Soviet system is ever imperialist. It carves trade routes everywhere to build more of—the *Rodina* that others cross at their peril. And God himself, or whatever you substitute as God—Lenin, isn't it?—punishes any intruders." She smiled thinly. "My crew died because the Lily warriors killed them. Let's avoid the metaphysical."

Oleg scowled in return, but whatever rejoinder he intended was smoothly interrupted by Roblev. The psychologist flicked invisible dust from his tunic as he drawled, "Politics are always interesting, but another time, Oleg. Tell me, Starfarer—um, you do have another name?"

Rinn clenched her hands in her lap, trying to not react to her suspicions of this man. He reminded her unpleasantly of Tolan. "McCrea. Rinn McCrea."

"Well, then, Rinn McCrea, tell me why we should trust you? You know that Novy Strana bans your kind from all contact with our citizens—we are in violation of that code right now, merely in your presence on this ship." A rush of emotions breathed over the crew, tantalizing at the edge of Rinn's perception. She blocked them out to focus on the psychologist.

"Those who resist change often make such rules," she said. "I'm not a threat to your ship."

"So you say," Viktor muttered. They eyed each other warily.

"A party of natives now approaching from the north, Captain," Hara said in the silence that followed.

"They are the Sunstone trade chief and two aides," Rinn said. "Isen-glov-amar has ordered them to bring you out of the ship. Then his war party will attack from the south. The trade chief knows that he and his aides will also die as they stand with you, but accepts punishment for making friendship with Star-Devils. He is accursed now—but hurts more for the lives of his aides, whom he loves."

"I see," the captain said noncommittally. "You are certain of this?"

"Yes."

"Then, thank you, Starfarer. I'll take your report into account."

"But, Captain!" Tatiana protested. "You're not going to listen to—to—"

Selenkov swung toward her. "To what? As I told you before, when it comes to the safety of the ship, I'll listen to any source. Oleg Andreivich, you and I will meet Ba-rao-som in body armor with laser-rifles. All others will remain inside the ship. And don't say, Tatiana, that weapons violate our trade protocol—we're beyond trade protocol right now. Is that understood?"

"You'll destroy our Deltean trade!"

"If Rinn is correct, that trade is already gone," the captain said firmly. "Your orders, *Zvezda*. Let's move."

His eyes swept back to Rinn and lingered there. "I want you at the airlock too. Can you manage that?"

Rinn nodded. The captain stood and strode by her chair, headed for the ladder, Oleg following reluctantly. Rinn endured the second officer's suspicious glance, then locked eyes with a simmering Tatiana. Uncaring of the psychologist's too-clever eyes, she smiled grimly.

I will serve this ship, Tatiana Nikolaevna, she thought. She sagged slightly as a new wave of fatigue swept over her. In the distance the gathering dark cloud of the Lily crept nearer to *Zvezda*, intending assault, murder, rage, the end of threat, the triumph of victory. A little longer, she told herself. Hold on just a little longer. Her vision blurred as the Gift again wavered, clicking relentlessly through its automatic patterns, bringing too much, too little. She steadied herself by digging her nails into her palm, welcoming the slight pain for its strength.

Hold on.

Chapter 7

IN THE ACCESS BAY, YURI UNPACKED THE LIGHT-weight armor from storage. Less than a spacesuit but more than protective cloth, the armor could deflect most radiation including, he remembered grimly, laser-fire. Its breathing gear would also protect them from atmospheric contaminants, should the natives have more lethal versions of the smoke-charm used to curse them. The armor fit their bodies like a sheath, glimmering in the muted telltales of the storage hold.

"Are you sure this is necessary?" Oleg asked, still resistant. "All we have is her—"

"Word, I know. But it's a useful precaution." Yuri wondered tiredly if his second officer had any capacity left for independent thought. He snapped on his helmet. "I'd rather be overly alive than stupidly dead."

Oleg shrugged. "Well, so would I."

"Then come along."

Yuri lifted a laser-rifle from the weapons rack, then handed a second to Oleg. The telepath joined them and propped herself against the wall by the lock, her blue-black eyes vacant and unfocused. As they approached the door, she jerked slightly and looked at them.

Yuri leaned past her and pulled a cordless microphone from the lock control. "You can speak to us with this. Clip it on." He glanced upward inside his helmet to check the frequency, then reached to adjust the panel com-control. Then he looked down into her strange eyes.

"I'm going to take a risk, Starfarer—for the sake of my ship. I'm going to trust you, and that only because I can't see any advantage for you if you've lied."

"I understand."

Yuri keyed open the lock and stepped inside, Oleg following. The inner door cycled shut, momentarily entombing them. Yuri keyed open the outer door, then stepped outside on the stair. The shiplights illuminated a wide circle around the ship, reaching almost to the reeds at the edge of the clearing. Yuri studied the shadowed entrance to the coraal trail, then swept his eyes to either side. He motioned to Oleg to take position halfway around the ship.

"She said they'd attack from the south. Go see what you can see, if anything."

"Right."

The two men cautiously padded down the stair, then walked in opposite directions around the looming bulk of the ship. Yuri paused by one of the massive engine-pods to peer into the darkness beyond. He touched his collar-control and polarized his faceplate to infrared sight. Through the exterior mike of his helmet, he could hear the innocuous calls of the night animals and the shurring of the reeds, but he saw nothing in the strange reddish gloom.

"They see you, Captain." Rinn's light voice spoke next to his ear. "They haven't noticed the body armor, but they wonder about the weapons. The scout is thinking about them." Yuri stood still, his eyes still scanning the reeds. He felt a prickle along his spine from the unseen eyes—imagination? truth?—but pretended unawareness as he turned slowly.

"What has he decided?" Oleg asked, his voice tinged with apprehension. Perhaps the eerie shadows of the clearing had sobered the second officer—his tone was oddly respectful.

"He thinks maybe the rifles are a variation, perhaps wards against night-demons; that perhaps you are a more suspicious breed of Star-Devil than those aboard *Sing Fa*." She paused, and Yuri again listened to the faint noises of the marsh. He wished this planet had a moon to throw some light into the shadowy reeds. Then Rinn spoke again. "He sees no reason for a change of plan—you are not alerted."

A low whistle shuddered over the marsh, a cry of a night animal—or a signal. A moment later Rinn's voice again sounded in his ear. "The trade chief is approaching the clearing, Captain."

"Thank you. Meet me at the lock-stair, Oleg."

"Yes, sir."

Yuri retreated toward the ship-lock and faced the coraal trail, Oleg by his side. Both men held their laser-rifles loosely in their hands, without overt display, as they waited. Within a minute, Ba-rao-som emerged into the clearing, three other aliens closely behind him. They walked slowly forward toward the two men, then stopped several meters away.

[Greetings], Ba-rao-som signalled.

Yuri shifted his rifle to the crook of his arm, and raised his hands to reply. [Greetings. It is late].

[Yes]. Ba-rao-som gestured assent, then paused. Yuri watched him in the brilliant glow of *Zvezda*'s lights, looking for any trace of hesitation. The alien looked back impassively, impossible to read.

[Trade-friend], Ba-rao-som began, then stopped again. [Trade-friend] . . .

[Yes]? Yuri prompted. [How may we help you, chief]?

Ba-rao-som closed his several eyes and seemed to shrink within himself. His aides stirred nervously. [It is late], the chief repeated lamely. [I] . . .

The ship mike crackled in his ear. "The attack party is moving up now, Captain," Rinn said. "The advance scouts are about a hundred meters from the clearing edge."

"Your opinion, Starfarer," Yuri said quietly, watching Ba-rao-som's blank face. "What if I took Ba-rao-som into the ship to protect him?"

Oleg's helmet swung toward him. "Into the ship?" he asked unbelievingly.

"Unknown," Rinn said. "He's suicidal now—and he's been persuaded that you're evil. I advise against it."

"I hate to lose our trade contact here."

"You may have already lost him, even if he survives the attack. You brought down the Lily People on his tribe once again; the young people will pay the price in new sacrifices—he grieves for them and blames you."

[Trade-friend] . . . Ba-rao-som said again, oblivious to their spoken conversation, and again fell silent.

"Is he stalling?" Yuri asked Rinn. If accurate, she was invaluable help in understanding the risks—no mere guesses or human extrapolation, but reliable knowledge. No wonder Xin

Tian had set aside its racism and own distaste for Ikanos. What we could do here—and elsewhere, if we find other aliens . . . Galina is right. "Is he stalling?" he repeated urgently.

"No . . . he only regrets the betrayal, despite your fault."

"Hmmm. Can any of the others see my gestures?"

She paused. "Not yet. The light blinds them."

Yuri made up his mind quickly. [Chief, you must leave the clearing], he said. [We know of the danger and are prepared. Save your own life].

Ba-rao-som's head jerked upward, his eyes wide.

[We have had a disagreement], Yuri continued quickly. [I will drive you off with my weapon, and you will flee to your coraal]. Yuri swung up his laser and aimed it at the aliens. Ba-rao-som backed a step in alarm.

[No]! he signalled. [You must accept] . . . Yuri aimed the laser at the ground a meter in front of the alien party. The rifle ignited in a burst of ruby flame, glancing off the hard reflective ground to the marsh-grass beyond. Yuri swung the laser to the right, firing a swath of the dry vegetation. The cloud of smoke swirled up, obscuring his view of the aliens, then cleared in patches to show Ba-rao-som's aides running for the coraal trail.

[Trade-friend] . . .

A laser-bolt flashed into the clearing, striking Ba-rao-som in the heavy muscles of his neck. He screamed, a high-pitched wailing, his hands clutching at the wound, danced awkwardly on his stilted legs, then sagged forward. An eerie hooting rose from surrounding dark grasses—to the front, to the left, to the right. Yuri whirled in a half-circle. How do they move so damn fast? he wondered.

"Back into the ship!" he ordered.

"No!" Rinn shouted in his headphones. "Bring the body! Strength-for-strength! You mustn't leave it behind!"

"What in the devil?"

"Take it!" The words shuddered through his mind, amplified by an irresistible command. Yuri was shocked into immobility, his senses reeling from the mental impact.

"Whaaa—" he said stupidly, then shook his head, trying to clear his senses. Oleg grabbed him roughly and dragged at him.

"Come on, Yuri!"

"No!" Yuri shouted, pushing him off. He pounced on Ba-rao-som's body and tugged it backward several yards with a mad energy, then heaved again as laser-bolts flashed uselessly off his armor. Oleg cursed and took hold of the alien's back legs, swinging the body into a carry between them. Together they staggered toward the ship. They pounded up the stairway and fell into the open lock, the smoldering corpse at their feet. An eerie wail echoed out of the swamps, followed by a cacophony of high-pitched screams and shouts. He heard bodies crashing through the reeds, rushing the ship; the outer door sighed shut. There was a sudden silence.

"This is utterly crazy," Oleg said.

Yuri grinned and started to laugh; Oleg joined him helplessly, both cackling in near-hysteria. Then the airlock door boomed as a heavy body hit it from outside. The sound sobered them, and Yuri looked down at the dead body of Ba-rao-som. Already the chief's large eyes had glazed with a milky film, his body rent by laser-burns, his fur smoldering. What kind of people would do this . . . and for what? he thought.

"Trade-friend," Yuri murmured sadly, and stroked the blackened silky fur of the alien's mane.

"Captain?" Khina's anxious voice reverberated from the airlock interior com.

"It's all right. We're safe."

The inner-door sighed open, and he stepped out. Rinn looked exhausted, her eyes deeply shadowed and her face drawn. The others clustered in the access bay, all save Hara, who was still watching the screens above.

"I did not need the compulsion, Starfarer," he said tightly.

"I'm sorry—I didn't mean it, but you didn't have time . . ." She trailed off in confusion and looked away. "I'm sorry." He saw her eyes fill with tears. With a sudden empathy, he suspected that the visible signs showed only part of the reality, that the Starfarer had pushed herself dangerously close to the edge—for his ship. He felt gratitude for that effort—and respect. Whatever she might be, she had earned his sanctuary. Gently he removed the com-mike from her collar, then slipped a hand under her elbow.

"You're tired, Starfarer. Come with me."

"But they're attacking!" she cried, her mouth distorted with horror. She twisted away from him. "Ching! Jo! Run, run, run, run . . ." Another body boomed against the outer door, and Rinn screamed piercingly.

Yuri shook her, trying to break her hysteria. "Our ship has a thick skin—and we are fully warned, thanks to you."

Rinn covered her face with her hands. "He has killed Ba-rao-som." She moaned. "They are killing the others, too. I hear

their cries. Mei-lan! Mei-lan! Pain . . . oh, the darkness . . .''
She sagged forward, and Yuri caught her in his arms. She yielded
against him, limp-bodied as she fainted at last.

Yuri hoisted her over his shoulder and carried her below to
her quarters. As he lowered her body onto the mattress, a vibration shook the ship. Mortar fire? Yuri looked up in alarm, anxious for his ship, and moved aside for Galina. The ship services
officer leaned over Rinn, testing her body responses.

"What happened?" she asked.

"I tried to save Ba-rao-som. It didn't work. Do what you can
for her, Galinka."

"How? This isn't a normal faint."

"You can at least tend her body!" The ship shuddered again,
and he nearly danced in his anxiety to go above to Command.
"She's still human, despite the rest!"

"True," Galina said calmly. "Be careful, Yuri," she added
in obscure warning. Yuri stared at her a moment, then ran from
the room. He bounded up the ladder to the control room, nearly
losing his stride as *Zvezda* shuddered violently for a third time.

"What is it?" he demanded as he burst into the control room.
"Hara?"

"Exterior sensors indicate laser-fire directed against the ship.
No hull damage, of course. The others are projectiles of some
kind. One exploded near the nav-radar housing, causing minor
damage. It must be that 'larger device' she mentioned."

"Yes. Where are the aliens now?"

"Still gathered near the ship. One party is manning that mortar of theirs; the others are attacking each other."

"Yes. She said that."

" 'She' being the Starfarer, of course," Hara said dubiously.
"Captain . . ."

"You have a comment, Engineer?"

"Nothing, sir." The engineer turned back to his sensor board.
"Still out there, but no new explosions. Quieting now. A party
is moving back north."

"Establish a two-person watch for the night on the sensors.
We'll see what we can do in the morning, if anything."

"If anything," Tatiana echoed. "And when you have to tell
the Bureau that we've lost our trade stand on Delta?"

"I'll deal with that at the proper time, Trade Officer," Yuri
said angrily. "If you're lucky, maybe they'll let you watch. For
the present, however, I command this ship and you will follow
orders."

Tatiana glared. "Sir," she spat.

"Yes, exactly that. To your stations, *Zvezda*."

He stayed in Control until every alien had withdrawn out of sensor range. The attack was not renewed. With the Starfarer unconscious, Yuri again lacked information he needed: what was happening at the Sunstone coraal? He tapped his knee impatiently, watching the crew at their posts, acknowledging Hara's reports as they were offered. "Inaction solves nothing," Tatiana had said. He felt restless to be again forced into waiting.

He suspected that *Zvezda* could now wait until Doomsday before any alien approached her, offering trade.

The following day proved him right in his suspicion. *Zvezda* waited throughout the day, watching the empty clearing. Twice Yuri went below to check on the Starfarer, hoping vainly she might awaken to give him news. In the night, when the sea air again sighed over the empty marsh, stirring the reeds, he acknowledged their defeat and gave the orders to lift for Seguinus.

Zvezda rose in a cloud of flame and dust, then streaked skyward through the heavy cloud-cover of Delta Bootis. As the ship made orbit, Yuri sent his report to the waiting satellite, warning *Nauka* of the Lily hostility waiting below—and by-the-by gifting the Space Bureau with all the evidence it needed to destroy one Yuri Selenkov. The telepath aboard *Zvezda* would only be a delicious tidbit to finish off the feast.

Maybe, he thought desperately. Realizing how essential Rinn could be to a solution, he smiled at the irony of using one disaster to solve another. But perhaps a solution, nonetheless. For himself . . . and for the Delteans. "Think beyond your precious rocks," Galina had said. If the Lily would not come to terms, Novy Strana might wreak another Canopus, wiping out an alien race for a few baubles of organics and crystal. Would we? he wondered. No doubt the Americans had considered it impossible, too. For all their faults, the Americans merely substituted different errors for the weaknesses in the human-fallible workings of Lenin's ideal.

He thought of Ba-rao-som, whose corpse lay below in storage, and remembered their tentative friendship, a fragile thing built of hand gestures and mutual interest in the strange. *Perhaps a solution for both of us, my friend.*

If she'll cooperate, he reminded himself. How much could— would—she offer?

"But what is human?" Yuri had asked Viktor earlier after the others had finished dinner and departed to their ship duties.

"By the majority definition, nontelepath." Viktor Fedorovich delicately speared a peach from its container and plopped it in his mouth, then gestured with his fork to emphasize his point. "Humanity is always defined by the majority, economics by class will."

"And politics?" Yuri asked skeptically.

The psychologist looked at him, unsmiling. "By power, of course. And power comes from the majority—so we come full circle in our definition of Truth."

"A neat reasoning, Viktor Fedorovich."

Viktor popped another peach slice into his mouth. "Leninist."

"Naturally," Yuri retorted, earning himself a sharp look.

But what is human? Yuri thought, pausing by the door to the Starfarer's cabin. What is it like to know too much of those around you?

And then: Can we ever know too much?

He hesitated a moment, then passed on to his own cabin. The corridor deck vibrated with a faint rhythm as *Zvezda* arced outward, gaining distance for the leap into nonspace—and Seguinus. And beyond that? Should they have stayed? Inside his room, he stopped by Natalya's bureau, again wistful, then stretched out on his bunk, not bothering to undress. He turned over the decision in his mind. Had he chosen correctly? Like Viktor, he could see potential problems in the conflict among the crew, emotions that, if not checked, could simmer and explode during their long voyage. Tatiana could be counted upon not to let matters be.

Easy for you to second-guess, too easy, he thought, mentally addressing the ranked and disapproving faces of the Bureau commissars. I chose the best I could, as I saw it, he argued to them, knowing good intention never outweighed error, not in the convoluted politics of the Bureau, not in a contest between a young ship captain and the powerful authorities of the Bureau.

As he relaxed into the comfort of his bed, drowsing, he remembered the hypnotic depth of her blue-black eyes—such strange eyes—and her exhaustion, as if she had pressed herself far beyond her strength. Why? For *Zvezda*'s sake? Or merely for survival? Who *was* this Starfarer?

He lay awake and thought of her, and wondered if she already controlled him.

Chapter 8

RINN AWOKE TO THE WHISPER OF SPACE. SHE sensed the emptiness beyond the hull of the ship that enclosed her, perceptibly turned aside from itself in the strange distortion of reality generated by warp-drive. She lay inert, listening to the currents of the void, then gradually roused herself from her somnolence.

Where?

She felt momentarily confused, believing herself aboard *Sing Fa*, her home for the past three years. Instinctively she reached out toward the minds near her, seeking the comfort of her familiar companions—and touched a stranger. She shied away from that unknown touch, and memories rushed back into her mind: the massacre, Mei-lan, the Soviet ship—the last blurred by the mists of her exhaustion. She stirred, and felt the lancing pain of her healing muscles.

She felt a slight tug at her temple and raised her left hand to finger the monitor-lead fastened to her forehead. Other leads led to her chest and right wrist; she became aware of an IV slowly dripping into her vein, her right arm wrapped into a restraining board, and the faint discomfort of a catheter.

She turned her head slowly to examine the room. Utilitarian yet comfortable, with bunk and dresser, a comset desk in the far corner, and a large photograph of a building on the nearer wall. She studied the building, seeking its significance but finding none. *Sing Fa* had forgone all room decoration, preferring the simplicity of a true revolutionary spirit—Rinn had never understood the connection between the two, but had accepted the stark restraint. She was accustomed to unadorned walls.

She decided she liked the building, stolid and unimaginative as it was. She was vaguely aware of the sluggishness of her thoughts but did not feel unduly alarmed. She turned her head and saw another picture on the wall above her bunk, one of flowers in a vase. She reached up her left arm, trying to touch the frame.

"Pretty," she murmured. Her head swam with her movement, and she lowered her arm weakly. "Nice flowers."

The childishness of her own voice startled her, jerking her out of her fog. Where? What had happened?

The room door opened with a swish beyond her head, and she heard footsteps approaching her bed.

"So! You're awake," she heard, and she craned her neck to see her visitor. Galina Kirillovna stepped to her bedside and smiled down at her as she adjusted the coverlet. "How are you feeling?"

"Where . . ." Rinn asked.

"Two days on our way to Seguinus, our next trade-point. You slept a long time—you'll have to tell me if that's normal." A frownline appeared between Galina's eyes, mirroring her healer's concern. Rinn tried to smile, but gave up any effort to answer the unspoken question. Later, when she knew this place and what threats it might hold. She closed her eyes wearily.

"Seguinus?" she asked after a moment.

"Yes. We had to abandon Delta for now. Not your worry, though Captain Selenkov will have questions. Again, how do you feel?" Galina's voice had a forced heartiness, and Rinn sensed the war between Galina's apprehension and her healer's compassion.

"I feel quite well," Rinn said, "although I'm still, uh . . ." She struggled a moment, too drained to focus on the new language, then picked up the word as Galina completed the thought in her own mind: "Tired. I used the Gift too much, and it affected my body . . ." She saw confusion in Galina's eyes as Rinn's words set off a torrent of alarmed speculation. Superrace, freak—the words drifted between them. "Thank you for your care, Galina Kirillovna," Rinn ended lamely.

Galina shook herself slightly, then smiled again. "You're welcome. Push that call-button if you need anything." The medico hastily left the room.

Rinn looked at the ceiling angrily. Would it never end? She had left Ikanos because of her difference, only to find it endlessly repeated in the service she had chosen.

Why the protest? she asked herself. You are what you are. She reached for the pride she had learned as a Starfarer, but found it badly diminished. Starfarer . . . it had not saved *Sing Fa*.

I am Rinn, Starfarer. The thought tasted of ashes. She closed her eyes and wished for oblivion, then found a partial release in other-mind. She floated, turning into herself.

"It may be a coma brought on by shock." Words jangled over her head, striking unpleasantly at the cocoon she had created for her mind. She cringed away from them, trying to ignore their noise and meaning. "Or perhaps a healing trance."

"Can the Ikanos telepaths do that?" rumbled a lower voice, one Rinn vaguely recognized as Selenkov's.

"I don't know, Yurushka," Galina said with some asperity. "That's the problem with enforced noncontact—it shuts off information. How much is fanciful rumor and how much is fact? Novy Strana hasn't had willing contact with Ikanos for eighty years. If it's shock, I should treat it; if it's a trance, my treatment might block her self-healing. I don't know which applies."

Rinn turned her mind away from them, retreating deeper into herself. She touched the Gift and warmed herself at its glowing spiral deep in her mind. I am Rinn. The Gift expanded, absorbing all of herself in its warmth, until it obliterated all perception, even of herself. I am Rinn . . .

The thought wavered, then broke into drifting strands as she lost herself in other-mind.

I am Rinn . . .

She gradually became aware of her body again as she awoke, then stretched languorously, enjoying the tension-pull on her muscles. Her arm was still bound in its IV restraint; the monitor-lead was still at her temple. She stared at the picture of the building on the opposite wall, trying to focus her attention on the here-and-now, then shifted to the flowers above her bunk. Pictures. Even Ikanos had preferred the stark lines of nonadornment—the smooth curve of white walls, the unbroken expanse of poured-rock floors—as a constant reminder of the oneness of the Group-Mind to which all should aspire. She followed the gentle whorl-edges of the roses with her eyes, liking their symmetry.

How long had she slept?

As her mind shed the fogs of her long rest, she sensed the drifting emotions of other minds gathered nearby. The muted sound of voices filtered through her closed door, the clatter and brisk laughter of a common meal. Anxious to be freed of her bed, she thought to summon Galina with the call-button, then decided to wait. Patience: time enough to meet the new stresses of the personalities on ship, and no real reason to disturb Galina at her meal. She stretched again to limber her stiffened muscles, then turned on her side toward the wall.

How long?

She drowsed, limp in her relaxation. So comfortable—lie here forever. Safe, safe . . .

She remembered another time of safety, when the tensions accumulated during her short life had abruptly uncoiled with a shock as intense as pain. She had walked across the enclosed space-dock to the Xin Tian freighter, the weight of her instructors' disapproval heavy upon her shoulders. She could feel Tolan's eyes boring into her back, willing her to return. The school administrator, a city official, and the Chinese legate stood with him, two aware of the surreptitious command, the third oblivious. Rinn clenched her teeth and continued walking, Tolan's compulsion beating at the surface of her mind.

A man met her at the top of the ship-ramp, of later years, tall, gray-haired, and deeply tanned. He thrust out his hand, smiling. "I'm Connor Matthieu. Welcome, Rinn." His brown eyes swept past her toward the official party, and he frowned irritably. After a moment, Tolan's compulsion abruptly fell away, as completely as lamplight extinguished in a room. Rinn staggered, and Connor hastily caught her elbow.

"Careful there," he said kindly. *They always try. It's the last gauntlet, Rinn—you're safe now.*

She had looked up into his face and studied it, trying to comprehend his words. For ten years she had waited for this one chance, focusing all her hopes on this one choice to endure present torment. Yet for all her hopes, she had never truly believed she could escape Ikanos; her tormenters seemed all-knowing, all-powerful, able to manipulate and persuade until a disapproved intention wavered into nothingness.

Safe? she asked.

He lightly traced the half-healed scar on her cheek. *Safe, Rinn. Truly.*

The he reached within his breast-pocket and drew out a small metal emblem, a seven-pointed star that winked and flashed in the docklights. He held it up before her face a moment in ceremony, then laid it in her hand.

"Welcome, Starfarer. Be one of us, by your free choice."

"Yes," she had answered, and her joy had swept through them both.

Safe . . .

She heard her door open, and Galina bustled into the room, her arms full of fresh linen. Rinn shifted onto her back and saw Galina's smile.

"Good morning," the medico said cheerfully.

"Is it?" Rinn's voice cracked from disuse, and she cleared her throat. "Morning, I mean."

Galina deposited the linen on the dresser top, then straightened the foot of Rinn's coverlet. "By shiptime, of course," she said, and straightened to look at her patient. "So you decided to wake up at last; I'm pleased."

The smile broadened, and Rinn sensed Galina's genuine pleasure at her awaking, a healer's unique satisfaction colored by both professional detachment and an emotion almost motherly in its intensity. Rinn returned Galina's smile.

"When may I get up?"

Galina Kirillovna checked her pulse and touched her forehead briefly. Then her hand fluttered away as she laughed. "Well, I'm afraid you know more about this than I do."

"Actually, no, though I've heard of certain techniques . . ." Rinn's words trailed off awkwardly. She wanted Galina's empathy and interest to last awhile longer before it slid again into apprehension. She had missed that compassionate touch aboard *Sing Fa*. She had missed many things on her ship, after too brief a time in Xin Tian's labs and the Starfarer enclave.

"I look forward," Galina said firmly, "to discussing your Gift and its wonders in detail. You should be aware that your heartbeat dropped to almost nothing as you slept. I've never seen the like. But, then, I've never met a Starfarer, much less tended one." The smile had returned, before Galina became brisk again. "For now, you seem fully recovered, and I see no reason to keep you abed. Are you hungry?"

"Yes."

"Good. An excellent symptom. Let me help you sit up, and I'll bring you a tray."

As Galina propped her up on pillows, the room tipped and grayed a moment, then steadied.

"Dizzy?" Galina asked.

"A little. Thank you, Galina Kirillovna."

"As I said before, you're most welcome. You sit there and rest a bit; I'll be right back." She bustled out of the room, and Rinn smiled after her, then sighed. Safe. It might not last, but she had found another of those unexpected times when she indeed felt safe. She stretched her legs again under the coverlet, then relaxed backward into the soft pillows.

She was eating breakfast when the psychologist entered the room. She tensed immediately and wondered a moment at the cause. The man was not Tolan, whatever her instinctive fears. Roblev smiled at her pleasantly as he seated himself at the end of the bunk, but she distrusted the smile—he reminded her too much of Tolan. Be reasonable, she told herself.

"How are you feeling?" Roblev asked.

"Much better, thank you," Rinn said cautiously.

"I am Viktor Fedorovich Roblev, the ship's psychologist. May I speak with you for a while?"

"If you wish."

Roblev ran a hand through his thinning hair, a gesture of hesitation she sensed was calculated, a kind of offered empathy more act than real. She grew more wary.

"You present quite a problem to us, Rinn—may I call you Rinn?"

She nodded, watching him.

"As you may know, some of the crew opposed taking you aboard, and even I had my doubts. Novy Strana does not accept association with your people; our ship may be in difficulty when we return to base, solely because you are aboard *Zvezda*."

"I understand."

"You will ease matters for our ship if you do not practice your depravities while aboard this ship."

"Depravities?" Rinn asked sharply.

Roblev shrugged, then laughed shortly. "Perhaps I mischose my word. We have heard rumors of certain practices—particularly against non-telepaths but also among the telepaths themselves . . ."

So the Soviets had not been entirely indifferent, not enough to ignore diplomatic gossip.

"I know," she said. "I've encountered those rumors—and rejected their reality when I left Ikanos. We Starfarers share your opinion on many points, though the greater cause for our flight you wouldn't understand. Only a telepath truly knows the Group-Mind, and the Group-Mind pursues only telepaths with dedication. Normals are irrelevant, an evolutionary dead-end, perhaps useful as inferior tools, usually not."

"Normals?"

"Every people has its labels for outsiders. The Chinese once used 'barbarian' but have politer words now, at least in your hearing; *Sing Fa* called me 'freak.' "

"Group-Mind?" Roblev struggled with the concept. She wondered what half-twisted information he had, if he even comprehended at all.

"You needn't fear for your crew, Doctor."

"Good, good," Roblev said, but she knew he disbelieved her. "I fear, however, that you have already practiced some objectionable actions—this matter of mentally influencing Captain Selenkov to give you sanctuary . . ."

"I did not influence him, sir," she said firmly. "He chose that freely. He is a decent man, to whom I'm most grateful for my life and safety. I did, however, overstep during the aliens' attack, a combination of my own emotion and lack of control. I have apologized to him; I will do so again."

Roblev laughed again as if embarrassed, although he was not. Rinn was aware of the keen scrutiny behind the affable mask. The man feared her, not only for her potential disruption of the psychological balance he so carefully tended, but personally. Roblev's belief in the integrity of his mind and its subtle gifts was a self-identity as fundamental as Mei-lan's revolutionary fervor. Rinn felt a touch of despair and closed her eyes.

"Just checking, my dear," Roblev said and chuckled again, inviting her into a pleasant—and vulnerable—ease with him. He shifted more of himself onto the bed and leaned back comfortably, his arms crossed. "Why don't you tell me something about yourself?"

"What do you want to know?"

"Your life, how you regard yourself, how you see your role on this ship—things like that." He waved his hand airily.

Rinn abruptly tired of his games. She shrugged. "I was born on Ikanos and at sixteen joined the Starfarer enclave on Xin Tian. I later took berth aboard *Sing Fa*. I regard myself as a telepath. And I see no role for myself aboard this ship."

She stopped and took a bite of her cooling breakfast, then looked at him as she chewed. Roblev waited expectantly for a moment and, when she remained silent, allowed himself to look annoyed. For once, the exterior quite matched the interior, and Rinn felt a small touch of satisfaction. Jousting with the ship's psychologist was probably unwise, but she was feeling reckless.

"That's all?" Roblev asked irritably.

"It answered your questions." Rinn donned her best innocent look and took another bite of her food, chewing busily. "There's little else to say, Doctor."

Roblev scowled, openly displeased and not bothering to hide it. "You wish to play games, then. I would advise against it."

"You started the games, Doctor. I offer the same advice." She put down her fork and looked at him squarely. "Doctor Roblev, you recognize my Gift, yet you haven't thought through its implications. You visit me—highly suspicious, worried about my effect on the crew, if I am even now tampering with your mind—yet you expect me to relax into your camaraderie and good humor, hearing nothing of your true emotions, revealing my secrets, allowing myself to be manipulated by you."

She shrugged. "It won't work. I left Ikanos to escape such manipulation—of a far higher degree than you could ever attain. My teachers, most of whom had joined the Group-Mind, were experts at tricking, persuading, and especially dominating. I fought them for nearly ten years before I won my freedom—fought then with my Gift, just as I will use my Gift to fight the lesser domination you attempt now. But that use is only defensive—I have no interest in controlling your unwilling mind."

"Indeed?" Roblev said with some surprise but still partly unconvinced. Behind his thoughts, she sensed the memory of institute lectures twenty years before, when a political officer had railed at his class, his hand chopping, his face contorted, as he blatted out the evils of Ikanos. The younger Roblev had accepted without question, his skin crawling at the officer's descriptions. The years had tempered him, making even politics less than black and white—perhaps he might be persuaded, if she were honest.

"We Starfarers, Doctor," she said, "are the Gifted who reject all you've heard of Ikanos, yet we bear the burden of your fear and distrust. Novy Strana has guarded itself against a nonexistent threat—the Ikanos telepaths do not leave Ikanos. The Starfarers practice a different code, one that turns the Gift to service and respects the essential mind. Or at least we try. Our

Xin Tian masters rarely appreciate or even interest themselves in the effort." She shrugged. "You have only my word, of course—and it does not solve *Zvezda*'s problem." She continued eating, aware of the struggle in Roblev's mind.

Roblev stroked his chin reflectively, his eyes bland. "I see," he said at last. "You have a refreshing honesty, Rinn."

"Honesty is always refreshing."

Roblev smiled then, genuinely amused. "I can see why you think so. Interesting. I will think about it; we may still end up adversaries, but perhaps not. I still have my suspicions."

"As I'm very aware. The perception of emotions is the foundation level of telepathic awareness." Think about that when you review your data-tapes, Doctor.

"Umm, yes. I suppose so. We'll talk again—after I reconsider my manipulations."

"Your other manipulations won't work, either," she challenged him. "I've defeated experts—or at least denied them a victory by getting out of range. I'll eventually get out of your range, too."

"There are many methods," he retorted, unperturbed. "Honesty itself can be a method, can't it?"

"You have a subtle mind, Doctor."

"It suits both our professions, my dear. In the meantime, recover your strength." He stood up and regarded her a moment, his emotions a complex of calculated advantage and deficit, then caught himself with alarm. She smiled ruefully.

"Don't worry about it," she assured him. "It is only another form of communication, one that can bind more than it rends."

"Indeed," he said. "I'll consider that, too."

Chapter 9

RINN REMAINED IN BED THROUGH THE NEXT DAY until Galina finally gave her permission to rise and dress. Galina provided her with the simple brown coverall worn by *Zvezda*'s crew, and Rinn zippered herself in, admiring the smoothness of its fabric on her body. *Sing Fa* had copied the traditional dress of Old China—a loose tunic, baggy trousers—despite its unsuitability to ship life. It was another instance of Xin Tian's determination to prove itself the pure revolutionary state, one that might surpass even the mother-state on Earth. Rinn liked the practicality of her new clothing, and her pleasure mirrored an optimism about her new berth that blithely ignored all problems.

Careful, she thought.

Opening her door and looking out into the empty corridor, she heard the muted sounds of the ship—the slam of a cabinet door, footsteps above her head, the ticking of machinery—and felt the palpable vibration from the engines below through the soles of her boots. They were familiar sounds after her three years aboard *Sing Fa*, accompanied by her telepathic sensations of enclosed space, the unending emptiness outside the hull, and a gestalt impression of the crew's thoughts. She paused to brush the edges of each mind, seeking renewed impressions of the people aboard her new ship.

A calmness filled one mind as Galina Kirillovna patiently checked her medical stores on the level below; it permeated the woman's sense of self to the foundations of her identity. A prick of anxiety about Rinn, for Rinn's health, for the ship's balance: that concern about psychological balance lay in every mind, and mostly in Galina's and Viktor's, enhanced by the sexual bond between them. Rinn sensed dormant memories of conversations, confidences, shared concerns, a mutual task of tending *Zvezda*'s crew that bound the couple together.

Another binding, in the simmering passions that possessed the second officer's mind: ambition, a raging desire for the beautiful Tatiana that could extinguish all thought. Oleg Konstantin knew he lacked control but no longer cared in his satiated and self-renewing passion; dimly, he recognized Tatiana's manipulations and knew her faults, but still he no longer cared. And with his passion for Tatiana Nikolaevna came an avarice for *Zvezda* as his own command, fueled by the trade officer's whispered compliments.

Trouble there, Rinn thought, and growing worse.

She brushed by the two Kazakhs, Engineer Usu and Biologist Termez, who were preoccupied with their duties on the control deck. She sensed their satisfactions with their ship and its captain, and their joy in each other, but she chose not to intrude. Minorities under pressure quickly acquired a wariness to their emotions and thoughts, curiously more sensitive to an adept's probing. I wonder why, she thought, but the enclave had few answers for its common experience with the Japanese and Thai. To be honest, few of the enclave's leaders felt much interest; they only noted the fact and warned accordingly. She drew a parallel to Mei-lan's own awareness and puzzled over it, then thought of other rare examples among the Chinese. A personality under fundamental threat in identity? A Normal who could not accept the basics of life as certain? Was that how the first telepaths had found each other in Earth's Old Europe, among the children of the early voyagers? After all, the telepaths had arisen from Normal stock; perhaps that human awareness of one's difference, of the majority's demand to conform against nature, had laid the earliest foundations of the Gift.

She felt an interest in Hara and Khina, wondering about their perceptions in a society that granted token equality, then laid upon them its subtle pressures—a disdainful glance, a lost ship berth to the "more qualified," a host of customs and memories that characterized home and yet of which one's companions were wholly ignorant, the mark of being set apart. All colonies had similar peoples, even Xin Tian's rigorous commonality— some marks one bore from birth, and the dominant Chinese still carried their centuries of conscious superiority over the lesser Asian peoples they had absorbed into their empire. Ikanos had erased such barriers as it created new ones in its hierarchy of mind. Still, she should be careful with the Kazakhs.

She smiled ironically: I guard myself against those whom I guard.

She lifted her chin to look upward and touched the captain's mind. Yuri Ivanovich Selenkov . . . she drank in his presence, attracted despite herself. Strange, she thought. It's almost as if—

"What are you doing?" a voice demanded. Rinn jerked her head toward the sound and saw Tatiana leaning against the corridor wall, her arms crossed across her breasts. The Starfarer felt irritated at not noticing Tatiana's approach. The trade officer's hostile gaze was accentuated by Rinn's perception of a matching interior hostility. And you, Tatiana Nikolaevna? she asked silently. What do you fear? Me? And why?

Rinn smiled thinly and raised her hand, her fingers crooked into a menacing claw. "Good morning. Threats to you."

Tatiana blinked, then hesitated in momentary confusion. But the old pattern was too strong; her mouth pulled downward in her habitual irritation.

"Clever, my dear," she said sarcastically. "We can no doubt expect other fancies to suit."

"If you wish." She is beautiful, Rinn thought, but she sees her beauty as a tool, a means to her ambition. "I intended a pleasantry, nothing more."

"I see." Tatiana tipped her head archly, eyeing Rinn from head to toe in an overt inspection. She tapped a slender finger to her lips, raised an eyebrow.

Games, Rinn thought. On Ikanos you'd be a novice, Trade Officer. They play real games there.

"You have a question?" she asked aloud.

Tatiana shook her head. "Oh, nothing," she said, tossing back her hair. She smiled. "Truly nothing."

"Meaning, I'll find out later." Rinn crossed her arms and leaned against the doorjamb, smiling in return. "But perhaps I already know. I know many things, Tatiana Nikolaevna, more than you realize. My Starfarer rank is often a burden, but it has its compensations."

"So I've heard. You may have impressed Viktor Federovich with your frankness, but I'm not so gullible."

So she had made an impression on the psychologist; that was useful information.

"I know you, Starfarer," Tatiana continued. "I know all about your kind."

"You know nothing."

"Oh? Novy Strana proscribes your kind as unclean."

"Unclean?" Rinn felt amused and showed it. "On *Sing Fa*, I was only 'reactionary.' You carry older traditions in your prejudice, Trade Officer. It does not, however, change the fact that I am here, on your ship, and now part of your crew."

"Not of *my* crew," the woman hissed. "In fact, you just might be surprised—" Tatiana stopped abruptly, staring beyond Rinn at Captain Selenkov as he stood on the stairwell. Rinn refrained from turning to look. There, she thought, now you didn't notice, and we're even.

"You were saying, Trade Officer?" Selenkov said coldly.

Tatiana disdained an answer and strode past Rinn to her own suite; the door hissed shut behind her.

Selenkov walked up to Rinn and looked down at her a moment, as if he sought some words he could not find. Rinn closed her eyes momentarily, absorbing the sense of him—capable, strong, determined, laced by a pricking anxiety about his ship, his crew, and herself. She drew in a deep breath, listening.

"Starfarer?" he asked, his tone puzzled.

She opened her eyes quickly. "Sorry." She cleared her throat, slightly embarrassed by her own preoccupation. "You carry a strong presence, Captain. I was relishing it."

He reacted uncomfortably, shifting his weight to his other foot as he thought of a way to leave her. She touched his sleeve gently, then as quickly withdrew her hand, regretting her words. "Forgive me my mysterious comments, Captain Selenkov. On Ikanos I spoke in a language of exalted words; it is a habit continued in the Starfarer enclaves and best abandoned."

"Some realities need appropriate words," Selenkov said judiciously. Then he smiled and seemed to relax slightly—if this man ever truly relaxed. Rinn wondered about the places he had seen, the pressures he had faced.

"I've been wondering about the telepaths," he said, oddly echoing her thoughts. He bowed ironically. "For obvious reasons. You must perceive reality differently than we; I've wondered what you might see."

"As I wondered how Normals might see. I have an advantage, however: I can find the perception in Normal minds and at least glimpse it. To you, I can give only exalted words, some of which escape me in my ignorance of your language."

"You speak Russian very well."

"Thank you. I will improve the longer I am exposed to this ship. In the meantime, do you have duties for me, Captain? I prefer to earn my way, even without the obligation of the sanctuary you granted me."

Selenkov looked uncomfortable as he hesitated. "That sanctuary is temporary—you understand that?"

"Yes. I expect only to rejoin my enclave after you return to Novy Strana. Do you agree?" She felt regret at the offering—and wondered at it. Of course she would go back! Yet still . . .

"Yes," he said, nodding. "But I hadn't considered the interim." He frowned thoughtfully. "I want you at Ba-rao-som's autopsy, and later we can talk about the Delteans in detail. Hmm . . . Do you have computer skills? We lost our computerman in transit to Delta."

She sensed a brief pang of grief and guessed at the connection. *Natalya* . . . The name sighed between them. She had heard that the Soviets practiced ship-pairing in place of the sexual abstinence imposed on Xin Tian's ships, with both colonies convinced of the necessity of their method. But the captain's emotion hinted at more than a loss of a convenience, approaching a genuine grief. It was a bond between them.

"Enough to be of assistance," she offered softly. "I was assistant trade officer on *Sing Fa*."

Selenkov glanced toward Tatiana's door with a sudden grin. "I doubt that position is available on *Zvezda*."

"I would think not. Will her opposition create trouble for you, Captain?"

"Yuri," he said suddenly. "Call me Yuri."

"Then I am Rinn. Will she be trouble for you, Yuri?"

"Tatiana doesn't need an excuse to be trouble," he said sourly. "But don't worry about it. Come this way. I'll show you the computer station."

"Thank you."

Rinn followed him up the stairway to the command deck, then sat in the chair he indicated near the viewscreen. He leaned one hand on the back of her chair as he bent forward, indicating the series of controls, his dark head close to her own. Then he left her for his own chair in midroom, where he began a low conversation with the engineer. Rinn turned her attention to her station and slowly began learning the controls.

The new language again frustrated her, for the machine could not supply the thought necessary to complete the words, but she soon located a dictionary within the computer banks and drew upon it heavily. After two hours of work, she had learned the essentials of the system, then began on the backlog data entry she found stored in the wait-disc. Apparently the *Zvezda* crew had worked on the update materials as they found time, but even a ship of *Zvezda*'s small size needed a full-time computerman. Survey reports, research, ship-status entries—she worked steadily and added the information to her gestalt in understanding the new ship and its crew.

"Well, you learn fast," said a voice immediately behind her chair. Rinn started violently at the sound, half-rising from her chair in the abrupt shock of the interruption. Yuri took a step backward in surprise, then shrugged his apology with a wry grin. "I'm sorry."

"That's all right."

He grimaced. "A curious aspect of manners, to exaggerate to inanity. But I'll accept the fiction of 'all right' while your heart slows its pounding and the blood returns to your face." He raised his hand and gently traced the scar on her cheek. "How?" he asked softly.

"An Ikanos instructor who resented my decision for enclave," she said as softly. She smiled. "Thank you for your courtesy."

"You are graciously welcome. I'd like to hear more of Ikanos and your enclave, if you will tell us."

"I may."

Yuri turned away. Rinn was suddenly aware of the sharp attention of Dr. Roblev, who had just entered the room from the stair. She glanced quickly at the psychologist, then changed pattern to brush the edges of his mind—speculation, a slight worry, a comparison of options. The man was always thinking, driven by his hidden fears of a crew lost to madness. Rinn turned back to her station.

To worry too much about instability invites an unstable mind. Another homily from Ikanos, one Rinn distrusted more than the others; it seemed more excuse than assurance. But she wondered if Roblev had ever considered it.

Perhaps I will tell him, she thought, with a brief impulse of empathy—but that would involve her in the psychological controls aboard the ship. She had known too many manipulators to wish herself one, and the enclave warned against psychological advising. The Normals feared Starfarer insights, Starfarer mental control, too much. I wish . . . she thought, and was not sure what she wished. She continued her programming, aware of Roblev's troubled attention like a prickling sweat on her back.

Of course I'll return to Xin Tian, she told herself. I haven't any real place here, not on this ship, not on their world. She pushed away the strange sense of loss in that choice and regretted the binding she had made to rouse her abused body on Delta. *The Gifted are pariah*. She must remember that, and resist her own weakness.

Yet still . . .

She tried to focus on her work, wondering at the need that tampered with her choices. Stay with your own kind. On that, she and Tatiana could be of one resolution.

I am Rinn, Starfarer . . .

For the first time in her life, she was tempted to wish away that identity. I am Rinn, she told herself angrily. I am Rinn . . .

"Tatiana!" Yuri called. Rinn watched as the captain rapped at the trade officer's door. "Are you coming or not?"

A muffled snarl filtered through the closed metal door. Khina gave Rinn an amused glance, inviting; Rinn tentatively returned her smile.

"Marsh-hunters keep to their dens," she offered.

"Marsh-hunters?"

"A Delta predator. I met several during my trek."

"An able description," Yuri said with exasperation, and turned toward the two women. "I'll get Viktor to talk to her. Perhaps he has more threat potential than I do. Come on."

He led the way to the small lab beneath the access bay, a pleasant room with serried ranks of glassware on shelves, the neat bulk of analytical machines, and bright lighting. On the wide table in the room's center, the body of Ba-rao-som lay prepped for dissection. Yuri paused by the corpse and caressed the neck fur a moment, then turned away. He brought two stools from the corner and gestured to Rinn to sit. Khina collected her implements from a cabinet and neatly arranged them on the shelf beneath the table.

"What I don't understand," the biologist said, "is why a primitive race has laser-weapons. I doubt if physical structure can answer that kind of question."

"It's an ancient technology," Rinn offered. "Only the Lily have the weapons now—and I don't think Isen-glov-amar knew how they worked." She thought back a moment. "Yes, I'm sure of that. To him it was a 'weapon of power,' a magical thing guarded and maintained by the Lily shaman."

"Hmm," Yuri said. "I wish I had one of their rifles to take apart."

"At least we have one of the aliens to take apart," Khina said brightly.

Yuri looked pained. "Please, Khina. I liked him—he was a gentle and wise old man."

"Sorry," she murmured, abashed. "I know that; I did, too. Sometimes I make stupid jokes." She repositioned the recording camera above the table and switched on its voice-recorder, then picked up a laser-scalpel.

"Beginning autopsy of Deltean corpse," she told the camera. "Initial cut begun in the thorax through ligamentous plates, continuing downward through the abdomen to the anterior legs. The body is badly damaged by laser burns, two of which have penetrated to the interior organs." She pointed to the blackened flesh for the camera's benefit. "I see analogues of lungs, heart, digestive tract, and interior gonads, plus several structures of unknown function. Taking samples." She cut several fragments of tissue and transferred them to vacuum slides, labelling them neatly. Rinn and Yuri watched silently.

"Hemoglobin blood chemistry," Khina commented, "from the reddish color."

"Delta's geosphere is a close analogue to Earth," Yuri said. "It would encourage a similar evolution, however much the Delteans look like insects. Is he a mammal? He has fur."

"Earth taxonomy doesn't apply here, Yuri Ivanovich. Fur does not an alien mammal make."

"So I'm an ignorant geologist," Yuri retorted. "Educate me."

"That would take *far* too long." Khina's scalpel moved to Ba-rao-som's head, slicing it open neatly to reveal the brain. Rinn winced slightly and looked away, remembering too much, then forced herself to watch as Khina finished the initial dissection of the face. "Well-developed sinus cavity with a very complex structure." Khina bent lower to examine the delicate webbing, then took more samples for analysis.

"They have exquisite senses," Rinn interjected, "especially smell. And a three-lobed brain, each with its own function."

"Yes, I can see the cerebral divisions. Curious."

"What functions?" Yuri asked Rinn.

"It's hard to tell," she said. "I'm only guessing from what

I heard telepathically. They can link and unlink the segments of the brain; the third brain controls emotion and instinct and seems to overpower the other two. Most of the violence comes from the third brain.'' She closed her eyes and shuddered, remembering. She wished she could leave.

"Rinn?" Yuri asked. She caught an impression of his concern and changed pattern to block him out.

"It's nothing."

"Hardly—you're pale as death. Are you feeling all right? Would you like to rest?"

"No." She summoned a smile for him. "Please continue. I'd like to help."

"You have," he assured her. "Tell me more about this third brain."

As calmly as she could, Rinn told him about the massacre of *Sing Fa*, the pursuit through the swamp, and the murders at the Sunstone coraal. Khina continued to work on the dissection, occasionally looking wide-eyed at Rinn.

"They're cannibals?" she asked at the end, her expression shocked.

"Strength-for-strength," Rinn corrected. "It's a ritual, one of great power and meaning to the Delteans. The Lily People use it to assert their authority and to take away magic from the other tribes, if magic is an analogue."

"A working analogue," Yuri said thoughtfully, "until we have something better. Is that why you told me to take Ba-raosom into the ship?"

"I'm not sure." She rubbed her face tiredly. "It just seemed right—or, rather, it felt *wrong* to let the Lily have the body. Telepathy isn't an exact science, Captain. I try to explain as best I can."

"I'm not complaining," he said gently. She wondered at his consideration, so different from Captain Hung's suspicious resistance. Her spirits lifted a little.

"In any event," she said, "I think the cultural order here is very ancient, enough so that the initial wars are now almost mythic, more legend than memory. The Lily have controlled the Sunstone for a long time."

Yuri looked at the corpse. "And the Lily have laser-rifles and some kind of explosives. Odd. How do you reconcile a primitive tribal culture and that kind of weaponry?"

"A degenerated technology?" Khina suggested.

Yuri shrugged. "We'd see other signs of the older technology, I'd think. Our orbital scans didn't pick up any metal concentrations—steel, machinery, ruined buildings. How can you have a technic-culture without steel?"

"Maybe the mud buried everything," Rinn suggested.

Yuri shook his head. "The magnetometer penetrates soft soil to several feet. Look, the Sunstone live in a mud-and-reed coraal, do occasional primitive farming and aquaculture, and cook in sun-dried pottery. Where are the other artifacts? Surely they'd keep something besides weapons. But, then, maybe not." He shook his head, puzzled. "Perhaps we shouldn't even look to Earth equivalents."

"What other guide do we have?" Khina asked, her eyebrow raised.

"True."

As Yuri pulled a plastic covering over Ba-rao-som's body and prepared it for frozen storage, Khina dried her tissue-slides at the side counter, then wheeled over a portable electron microscope, angling the small screen so all three could see.

"Could you adjust the camera, Captain?" she asked, jerking her chin at the overhead recorder. Yuri stretched up and repositioned the camera lens toward the 'scope, then settled back on his stool.

"Since we're interested in the third brain," Khina suggested, "let's look at the brain-tissue slides first. This is a slide from tissue near the forebrain." Khina inserted a vacuum-dried slide into the port, then bent forward to examine the screen for several moments. "See the configuration of the neurons," she said, pointing to the long filaments in the screen. "Very complex, with more connections than we have, perhaps more sensory efficiency. I'd like to activate a few neurons and see what readings I get."

"They are very aware of their environment," Rinn said. "They revere the physical senses as Names of Honor, and they can move very fast, react very fast. It's hard to distinguish more about a sensed thought, but I remember that feeling of the air, the way they can move. It's very important to them."

"Are their minds different?" Yuri asked.

"In most essentials, I've been told, Mind is fundamental—but, then, I've had training only in human mentality. Aside from the Gift, your mind is identical to my own, at least in the essentials of the human gestalt. When I hear the Delteans, I may 'translate' something alien into quite different human terms. Like

I said earlier, nothing is exact.'' She spread her hands helplessly.

"Well, it can get close," he said. "You know, you could pretend certainty," he drawled, "and look like a wizard when you're right."

"*When* I'm right," she amended.

"And *when* you're not . . ." he said.

Rinn dimpled. "Everybody knows telepathy is impossible."

"Well, of course."

"Children, your attention . . ." Khina reproved, rapping a slide against the metal casing of the 'scope. They both looked at her obediently.

"That's better." Khina took a slide of other brain tissue and slipped it into the microscope's vacuum port, studied it a moment, then changed slides again. "Strange," she muttered.

"What?" Yuri asked.

"Just a moment." She jumped up and went to a nearby cabinet for a long tray of other slides, found the one she wanted, and arranged the three slides to display together on the screen. "Look at these," she told Yuri, who obligingly leaned forward.

"So?"

"Stretch a little, Yuri," Khina said with some exasperation. "If you must, think of them as crystal microstructures. Life is more than rocks."

"So I've been told. Sorry—really. What am I looking at?"

"On the left is a sample I took from the local vegetation; it includes a plant virus common in the local reed-stems." Yuri peered again at the screen. "The center slide is the tissue from the brain stem; the last a slide from a higher site in the brain. What do you see?"

"A virus in the brain stem?"

"Exactly. It looks like another parasitic virus, only this one feeds on Delteans. See the physical damage to the brain tissue? And it's seated in the most primitive part of the Deltean brain."

"The third brain," Rinn said. "Instincts and emotions."

"Yes."

Yuri straightened. "And violence, perhaps even territoriality. Isn't that an instinct, too?"

Khina shrugged. "Well, it's debatable—a chicken-and-egg problem, like heredity and environment. Tatiana would know."

"Tatiana isn't here," Yuri said irritably, shrugging off the suggestion. "And Rinn says the Lily tribe regularly eats Deltean brains."

"Which increases their infection," Khina said, "and thus worsens the physical damage to the brain stem, and thus their violence. It fits, Yuri, it all fits."

"Maybe," he said cautiously. "Let's take more samples from the brain stem and run a DNA-genetic analysis. Find out how the virus works, if you can. It seems the most promising lead."

"Yes, sir."

He turned to Rinn. "Thank you for your help, Starfarer. We may have found one piece to our puzzle."

"And the solution?" she asked.

"That may take more thought—assuming the Bureau gives us a second try at the problem."

"Yes, there is that."

"Always that."

Chapter 10

THE PASSAGE TO SEGUINUS, THE SECOND TRADE-point on *Zvezda*'s run, required several days. The eighth planet in the system, New Prague, was still enshrouded by a primitive methane/hydrogen atmosphere not yet noticeably changed by the out-gassing of oxygen and other plutonic gases from the planet's many volcanoes. It was a young world in distant orbit around a hot young A7 star and unlikely to finish its planetary evolution in the short life of its brilliant primary. Even so, it promised a mineralogical bounty for centuries to come.

In a packet drawn from stores, Yuri had shown Rinn a sample of the tectonic minerals discovered by the First Survey team. Of particular interest was a variant of tourmaline, a piezoelectric crystal enriched by boron and aluminum. He held the Seguinus stone to the light, showing her the shifts of light within its depths—a dozen shades of blue that reflected its scale of multi-sonic frequencies.

"Stones," she murmured bemusedly as he handed it to her.

"Treasure," he corrected. "On Earth, tourmaline is brown or gray even in its gemstones, with limited piezoelectric conductivity. These beauties resonate at frequencies far beyond normal scale."

"Like Delta's three-finger stones?"

"Those are different. We can't decipher the natural process that creates them on Delta—one reason the Bureau wants to find the source." He paused suddenly. "I wonder . . ."

"If they're manufactured?" she said, completing his thought.

He gave her a mock scowl. "One problem at a time—we're still working on the Lily tribe's laser-rifles. Look, crystalline structure can be as varied and random as combinant protein. To make new proteins, we just have to try a few million combinations in a test tube. Unfortunately, crystal needs the temperatures and pressure of a magma chamber, with maybe ten thousand years to precipitate a few kilograms." He shrugged. "With sufficient power, we can duplicate the conditions in the lab, but even we find it easier—and cheaper—to go prospecting elsewhere. If Delta had a technic-culture that could manufacture plutonic crystal, where are the traces? The orbital scans showed nothing."

"Need they be metal?"

He slowly repacked the tourmaline gem in its case, then glanced at her appreciatively. "That's a very good question. A nonmetal culture? Based on what?"

"Are there enough equivalents to steel?"

"Maybe. We use several, though our technology still depends heavily on ferric metals. Nonmetallic crystal, ceramics, graphite, other carbon compounds, superconductors, plasmas. And the transuranics, though the scans would have picked those up, too. But a completely nonferrous technology? Or is the real question our own technological bias for iron?" He smiled. "You have good ideas."

She looked down at her hands and flushed. "I've learned to think in nonstandard patterns, having a nonstandard nature."

"Sometimes standard is boring." He offered her a hand off her chair. "Come. That's the warning chime. Let's go prospecting."

She followed him to the control deck and sat down at her computer station, then occupied herself with data-entry as *Zvezda* swooped into the Seguinus system from high over the ecliptic. Within a few hours, the ship tipped her nose into the planet's upper atmosphere and began the long spiral downward through the buffeting weather of a world in transition. Rinn turned to watch, fascinated. Captain Hung had never allowed her in Command during *Sing Fa*'s ship maneuvers, another of Xin Tian's illogical constraints against the Starfarers who took ship.

Sometimes we cannot see the bars of our own prison, she thought, looking around with delight. This is fun! She smiled at her own reaction, then shook away her own automatic reproof at such an unsober, unrevolutionary thought. She sensed the slight tension of the Command crew, a pleasant blend of excitement and confidence as *Zvezda* descended into another world. They think it's fun, too, she realized. Amazing. On *Sing Fa*, anything of moment had been inevitably grim.

I like this ship.

"Descending to two hundred fifty kilometers," Hara reported. "Winds at fifty knots, cross-pattern to prevailing currents."

"Thank you," Yuri said quietly. "Have you found the trade beacon?"

"No—uh, yes. Passing over it now. We should land on the return flypass."

"Very well."

They waited the next forty minutes as *Zvezda* orbited one last time, then steadily descended toward the surface and the radar beacon at the base. Rinn watched her crewmates as each bent to his or her tasks: the reflection of Hara's calm Asiatic face in his radar screens; Khina's quick movements of hand and arm as she keyed successive displays on sensors; Yuri's absorbed concentration at the pilot's monitor a few meters from her own computer station. She glanced at the steady patterns of hull and basic ship-systems on her own monitor: all well.

"Readout on atmosphere?" Yuri asked Khina.

"Methane-ammonia, some carbon dioxide, traces of sulfur and noble gases," she responded. "Sir, scanners show new volcanic activity approximately four kilometers from the base. *Nauka* may find the beacon isn't there anymore."

"Or the base," Hara amended and reached aside to key another display on Khina's sensors. "And maybe not next time, either." He turned his chair toward the captain. "We see extensive infrared readings across several square kilometers northwest of the beacon, with three major vents and a major flow heading directly for our landing site. Isn't the tourmaline mine northwest of the base?"

Yuri scowled. "Yes. Continue flight pattern." The elation of the crew quietly dimmed. *Not again!* Rinn caught Yuri's anguished thought as he faced another setback, yet another problem to explain to his Bureau.

"Entering injection pattern," Hara intoned. *Zvezda* shuddered as she descended the final kilometer to the surface, buffeted by the winds. Rinn braced herself in her chair, her heart pounding faster as *Zvezda* lurched abruptly, then resumed its steady descent.

"Heavy infrared beneath us, Captain," Khina reported. "Activating exterior monitors."

The wide screen above Khina's station flared, revealing a vision of damnation. Methane mists swirled around the ship as it hovered on its engine flares, a swirling yellowish smoke back-lit by the eerie glow of chemical interactions and the illumination from the nearby eruption. Above them, Seguinus burned with a penetrating white light, its vapors streaming as it sent its energetic firestorm of particles outward. It seemed to dance and weave as it shone through the turbulent atmosphere, sometimes disappearing behind opaque clouds of sulfur and frozen carbon-dioxide crystals, then emerging to cast its glare on the planet surface.

"Let's look northwest," Yuri said quietly.

The scene changed, and several volcanoes along a tall range gleamed redly through the murk, the nearest a fountain of explosive gas clouds and white-hot lava running furiously from the vent onto the plain. The river of molten rock spread a kilometer wide, pulsing white-hot in a rapidly moving flow. Already the lava river coursed beneath the hovering ship, dividing itself into the frozen rifts and pits of the broken rock, retracing the frozen convolutions of earlier flows. There was no sign of a base.

"The beacon is still signalling," Hara murmured. "Infrared indicates a temperature of eleven hundred degrees. The casing alloy could last for weeks."

"Metal is useful," Yuri said, glancing wryly at Rinn. He sat a moment, staring at the screen, then seemed to shake himself. "What kind of geological surveys do we have for this area?" He stood and crossed the few steps to Rinn's station.

"A new base?" Hara asked as he joined them.

"Why not? We can hardly do anything here."

"I'm not arguing, Captain," Hara reproved mildly. "Just trying out the idea."

"Sorry."

Rinn found the index to Records and keyed in the entry display. Yuri leaned closer, studying the design of color and curving lines, meaningless to Rinn. She instinctively reached out to his mind, seeking knowledge; the display seemed to shift subtly as its data acquired his meanings, his words: olivine, triclinic, pyroxene, feldspar . . . She changed pattern and the bands of color acquired yet another substance, one built of his memories—the heft of each ore, the quick strike of a hand-pick on the rock, the echoing stamp of a comrade's booted foot nearby, and the faint scrabble of dislodged stone.

Sunlight washed the memory, when Yuri had admired the oddly neat angles of the crystal's surface and turned the rock facets to the sunlight—stilbite, he had named it, and had thought of the tetrahedral structure, loose, three-dimensional, bound tightly by oxygen's grip on the silica cores. He had loved the touch of stone, the use of his muscles as he tramped, each turn in a gulley a chance for new discovery, every height a wide vista of the mountains that contained his beloved rocks.

Hara's voice abruptly jarred her from the gnosis. "Standard survey, sir, with detail to ten-meter squares."

Rinn glanced at the captain's absorbed face. In his rocks, he finds the order in things, she thought; an elegant order drawn from chance combination and variable cooling, Nature's random violence caught in crystal's frozen beauty. In the exterior monitor, volcanoes lit the horizon with their fury. She watched the image a moment. Yes, you are beautiful—but you could have waited past one more ship's landing.

The two men studied the map, then Yuri reached to key the screen wider.

"Ground survey would be prudent," Hara offered.

"We don't have time."

"If *Zvezda* lands on uneven ground, she could tip over. We don't have gyro power beyond thirty degrees, nor the pod extenders to compensate."

"Yes, I know." Yuri studied the screen and then tapped one loop of a ringed pattern in the lower left. "Let's try for that site twenty kilometers away. It looks fairly even."

"A lot can hide beneath ten-meter resolution," Hara warned.

"True, but we'll try it anyway. Orders to lift ship, Engineer. Khina, please call the others to Command."

"Yes, sir."

The captain turned to Rinn then and smiled. "Thank you."

"You're welcome."

His hand grasped her shoulder briefly, then slipped away as he turned from her. The other crew members appeared on the deck at Khina's summons and walked quickly to their stations—Oleg, Galina, Tatiana. Roblev seated himself beside Rinn to watch. She glanced aside at the psychologist, but he was looking elsewhere, his lips pursed thoughtfully.

Yuri waved at the hellish scene in the monitors, "Comrades, as you can see, we need to find a new base—and then hope to find more tourmaline near it. Standard procedure, please. The computer should handle most of it, but I need your several eyes to react to unpredictable conditions it might not recognize.''

"Yes, sir," Khina murmured, her eyes alight with suppressed excitement. Her eyes met Rinn's across the control room, and Rinn felt a surge of friendship from the slender biologist. She has forgotten her fear of me, Rinn wondered. Something expanded within her, a sense of bonding to an outsider too long denied.

Odd . . . And how long will it seem odd, I wonder? First the captain, now Khina—others? She glanced at Galina, then Oleg. She felt a sudden longing for the time when it would no longer seem odd—and wondered how she had survived without the bonding. More bars of my prison, she thought.

"Begin ascent," Yuri ordered quietly.

"Captain, I'm not so sure . . . ." Tatiana began.

"Shut up."

Tatiana's eyes flashed, but she clamped her lips and turned back to her board. Rinn saw a glance exchanged with Oleg, seated at the pilot chair vacated by Yuri earlier. She caught Tatiana's simmering fury and Oleg's irritated indifference. Trouble between those two? Rinn bit her lip and turned to her own screen.

She felt a slight tug of acceleration downward, pressing her into her chair, as *Zvezda* rose upward, then edged sideways on her jets for a long lateral glide.

"Give us some room for a long descent," Yuri said. "I want time to look at what we're landing on."

"Yes, sir."

The ground receded in the forward screen, a cracked expanse of tortured rock broken by narrow rifts. As *Zvezda* outran the advancing lava flood, the terrain worsened markedly. The First Survey ship had likely searched for some time to find its landing site. Now *Zvezda* made a similar search, farther from the volcano that stripped her of a safe footing. The ship drifted through the turbulent methane clouds, the vision in the forward screen often obscured by yellow sulfur mists and the deeper purple of methane-dioxide. Beneath flowed a speed-blurred expanse of black basalt, cracked and tumbled in primordial disorder.

"Beginning descent," Hara said a minute later. "Looks good."

"Visuality?"

"Declining to sixty percent," Oleg said. "Resolution to three meters."

"That ought to be enough. Pick us a place, Oleg Andreivich."

"Yes, Captain." Oleg keyed in his manual override. *Zvezda* sank downward on a controlled glide, riding her underjets and the more powerful energy of her main engines. "Eight hundred meters," he said, his hands steady on the controls. Rinn watched the flow of engine power, checking the computer readings against standard program. All well.

"Six hundred meters. Looks good."

"Do you have a site, Khina?"

"It's rough. Visuality still decreasing."

"We'll chance it. Continue descent."

"Yes, sir."

The view of the ground in the forward screen abruptly cleared as *Zvezda* emerged from cloud cover. Beneath her gaped a wide fissure bracketed by smooth ground on either side. "Side-jets," Yuri ordered. The ship drifted sideways across the rift, still descending. "Take that lava pan at thirty degrees, Oleg."

The ground seemed to rush up in the final hundred meters, and the forward screen filled with a ferocious cloud of pumice dust as *Zvezda* touched down. The ship swayed, then tipped alarmingly to the left.

"Gyros!" Yuri yelled.

"Compensating." At Hara's deft touch, *Zvezda* righted herself on her pods. The engine vibrations quieted, then died into silence. "Well, it's a postage stamp," Hara said judiciously, "but we made it." The swirling dust subsided, revealing a near-duplicate of the terrain at the first base. A half-kilometer away, the level ground rose into jagged hills, climbing steadily toward another volcanic range on the horizon, thankfully quiescent.

"We'll survey the surrounding area," Yuri said. "That nearby rockface looks good for another mine."

"Not likely," Tatiana murmured.

"We'll see," Yuri retorted. "A survey, anyway. Thank you, comrades," he said to all, and his glance swept toward Rinn a moment, then away. "Run your systems checks, then we'll go see what we've dealt ourselves in this card game. Out-ship survey in one hour." He sounded ebullient. "I'll take Hara and Oleg on the survey and . . ." He looked at Rinn.

"I have suit training; Kornephoros Four isn't much different," she said. She gestured at the monitor and smiled. "Colder—with fewer volcanoes, practically none at all."

"Sounds like a definite improvement. Well, come along then. We can use your extra hands." He ignored Tatiana's outraged glare, and Rinn's skin prickled from the hostility.

She will not give it up, she thought. Why?

An hour later, the four prepared for the out-ship survey. Hara loaded a motorized cart with sensor equipment and a small laser-drill, then activated the robot brain. It trundled across the bay floor, heading singlemindedly for the airlock. Lights flickered across the lock controls as Yuri programmed a sequence of complicated fail-safes of the lock to protect the ship from any accidental atmospheric penetration. The cart rolled into the airlock and they crowded in after, facing outward toward the exterior door. The outer lock cracked at its left edge, then slid smoothly aside.

"Be careful of your footing," Yuri told them as they maneuvered the motorized cart down the metal stair. "Raw lava plain can have some nasty surprises. We'll hope for a pleasant surprise—more tourmaline to reestablish this trade-point."

"A little slim, Captain," Oleg said dubiously.

"Maybe so, but we'll look. Keep your sensors keyed to the robo-carry monitor; the computer can sort the readings on the radio link with *Zvezda*."

"Yes, sir."

"Let's go." The party set out toward the south and a nearby ridge. Rinn again felt a faint tremor through the soles of her insulated boots, a warning from the now-distant volcano. The lava field stretched endlessly into the distance, encrusted with the deposits from the atmospheric gases—purple, yellow, blood-red, white. Nearby gaped a huge rift, fifty meters across. They walked single file along the edge of the rift, Yuri and Oleg in the lead, Hara bringing up the rear beside the lumbering robo-carry. Twenty minutes later they reached the ridge. It towered over their heads in frozen black sculpture, marked with deep cracks and the sparkle of mineralized veins.

Oleg nodded toward a particular thin vein that winked blue in their suitlights. "Might not be that unfeasible—that looks like tourmaline."

Yuri inspected the vein judiciously as Rinn and Hara crowded behind him, craning to look. "Not much of it."

"Might be more inside the geodome."

"Might. Let's take a core sample, Hara."

Hara lifted the portable drill from the robo-carry and together the two men cut a hand-sized hole into the rock, exploring the depth of the vein. The crystal deposit proved only a few centimeters deep, with basalt beyond.

"Well, let's spread out and look for more crystal sign. Here, Rinn—the controls for your polarized lamp are set in your neck collar."

"Polarized light?" she asked as he bent his helmet near her, his gloved hand making a delicate adjustment at her collar ring.

"Standard mineralogical analysis, one we've suit-adapted for survey. Each silicate structure reflects a different frequency in polarized light. Your suit broadcasts the readings to the cart's monitor while you watch for the tourmaline numbers in your helmet display. The cart sends the readings to *Zvezda* for recording and later analysis. That way we can survey and search at the same time."

"I see."

He made a final adjustment, and a small bar-dial lit on her interior helmet display. "The number on the left is the search reading," he instructed. "On the right is whatever you're looking at now."

"Forty-three point two-five-two."

Yuri grunted. "Olivine. Lots of that around here." He turned back to Hara. "Complete the set-up at this site, Hara. We hope to have something more for you in a few minutes."

"Yes, sir."

Yuri walked to the right along the ridge, his helmet craning upward as he swept his headlamp up and down its black face. Oleg headed in the other direction. Rinn hesitated, saw Hara start to move after Yuri, and decided to follow Oleg. After a few dozen meters, Oleg turned toward her, an unpleasant expression on his face, distinct unwelcome in his mind.

"I don't need you, Starfarer."

She changed pattern and blocked out his hostility like cloth across a slate. She was not in the mood for this Tatiana clone. "Nonetheless, I am here," she answered coolly. "And my name is Rinn. Shall we continue the work?"

Oleg scowled, then turned away. They both turned their headlamps upward, quartering the ridge above them. Beyond them, the ridge rose higher, mounting the flank of a small fumerole several hundred meters ahead. Slowly they worked their way along the ridge, watching the number display in their helmets.

She relaxed her guard and sensed Oleg's irritation at her presence fade into his absorption with the work.

As the ridge rose, their light-passes became more difficult, the effect of the beams fading with the greater distance to the upper shelves of rock. Oleg slowed, then tried backing away from the ridge, his head craned backward. Rinn concentrated on the lower shelves of rock and saw a pink flash as her lamp passed over another kind of deposit, then the subtle amber of gold, the metallic shimmer of mica and a copper ore named stannite. As the right-side number in her helmet display shifted steadily, flicking from one reading to another as her headlamp played over the rock, she borrowed their significance from the memorized list in Oleg's mind. *See the pattern.* She smiled, her spirits lifting despite her dour companion. The numbers changed again to another copper ore, yellow, named chalcopyrite, then to argentite, dark-gray flashing with the pale sheen of silver.

"Treasure trove here," Oleg murmured. "Like a foundry planetwide." His blue eyes swept after the beam of his light, seeking eagerly for the revealing shimmer and flash of mineral deposits embedded in the basalt. "I see garnet, siderite, other ores . . ." He stepped backward, trying to direct his beam still higher.

Oleg's boot pierced the shallow basalt of a lava tube, unbalancing him. He waved his arms wildly, unable to stop another step backward.

"Watch out!" Rinn cried.

His other foot cracked through the brittle surface, and he fell backward, crashing through the roof of the tube. His shout stopped abruptly as he disappeared into the ground, cutting radio contact.

Rinn ran the few steps to the edge of the gaping hole in the ground, then checked herself as the broken rock cracked beneath her own boot. *Careful.* She knelt and crept forward on her belly, careful to spread her weight as much as possible on the thin stone. At the edge, she put her head over the jagged lip of stone, directing her helmet-light downward. Oleg lay five meters below on the floor of the tube, sprawling helplessly. She could hear his labored breathing in her headphones.

"Oleg! Are y   all right?"

"Rinn!" The captain's voice blared in her helmet-mike. "What happened?"

"The lava tube collapsed!" She inched forward another foot. "Oleg!" she shouted at the man below.

"Mmmmph," he grunted, only half-aware. His thoughts shifted vaguely as he lay stunned, pricked by fear and a growing panic. Rinn saw the fabric of his suit, normally smooth with interior pressure, begin to wrinkle as his precious air leaked to the outside. Recklessly, she scrabbled over the edge of the rift and dangled by her hands, then released.

She fell heavily to the rift floor, then flung herself on Oleg, searching for the leak in the suit. Oleg's eyes eyes looked up at her through his faceplate, terrified as he realized the injury to his suit; his mouth gaped open as he struggled to breathe. Rinn found the tear near his boot-heel and ripped open her repair kit, then slapped on a patch.

"Open your tank-valve to full aperture," she ordered.

Oleg responded groggily, graying out with lack of oxygen, but fumbled at his neck-ring to open the linkage to the air tanks on his back. Rinn quickly inspected his suit for more leaks, turning first one foot, then the other, into the glare of her helmet light. She found another, smaller, leak near the first and patched it also. After the repairs, Oleg's suit slowly reinflated, smoothing its deadly creases. His breath came easier, although he coughed from the alien methane inside his suit. She felt his consciousness begin to slip away as he surrendered to his shock.

"Oleg! Don't pass out on me now! I need your perceptions." Rinn shook him roughly and earned herself a weak glare from the injured man. "Good. Where is your pain? Think of that, Oleg Andreivich." She shook him again, more gently, trying to recover him from the blackness edging his mind.

"Arm . . ." Oleg's head lolled weakly against her chest. She held him closely to her a moment, automatically comforting him as she responded to his mental projection of pain and shock. Oleg looked upward into her face, his expression one of dull wonderment.

Rinn double-checked Oleg's atmospheric controls and talked to him quietly to keep him awake. He responded indistinctly, but she cared only that he remained aware. Carefully she probed with the Gift for the signs of a head injury, either random bursts of thought from damaged nerve tissue or a spreading blackness in the deeper parts of the mind, where the brain drove the heart and lungs. Oleg stirred uncomfortably but did not resist her intrusion, his eyes still fixed upward on her face.

"What . . . are you doing?" he whispered.

"Rest easy, comrade," she said gently. "I mean no harm to you, only good."

"I know . . . that. I . . ." His eyelids fluttered. "Rinn?"

"What?"

Oleg murmured indistinctly, his thoughts scattered into an undercurrent of gratitude and ebbing fear. She felt him slip away from her again; she looked upward, anxious for help from the others. After a short wait, Yuri's helmet appeared overhead.

"Rinn!"

"His arm is broken. Concussion, I think."

Yuri cursed. "Hold on. I'll throw you a line." A moment later, several loops of a light cable slithered over the edge of the break. She snatched it as it swung, then quickly tied the rope around her body, with an end through the waist-ring on Oleg's suit. She raised him awkwardly into a half-carry, her arm around his waist, and tugged on the taut line. The rope lifted them, swinging them toward the side of the tube. Rinn quickly lifted her feet to catch their swing, then braced herself against the curving wall. As the rope was pulled slowly upward, she walked up the side of the tube, holding Oleg's suit away from the sharp edges. Near the top, Yuri reached down and pulled on them, then snagged Oleg's suit-belt. Together they maneuvered the unconscious officer over the sharp edge of the break and onto firmer ground.

"Which arm is broken?" Yuri asked as he ran his own check of Oleg's suit. Hara knelt beside them, his face anxious.

"Left, I think," Rinn said. "It aches like a broken bone, but he was too shocked to confirm it. I don't detect any head trauma, but he's obviously been jarred."

The captain's helmet swung toward her. "Is he conscious?"

"Half-aware but slipping, Captain. Probably a concussion."

"Let's get him back to Galina."

As she followed Yuri and Hara back to *Zvezda*, Oleg supported between them, she wondered angrily what else could go wrong for Yuri and his ship on this benighted world.

Chapter 11

A DAY LATER, RINN SAT QUIETLY IN A CORNER OF Oleg's room, watching Galina's sickbed nursing. The ship services officer neatly changed the sheets without overly disturbing her patient, checked Oleg's reflexes and pulse, then murmured to the injured man. He responded groggily, still affected by a bad concussion, but Rinn did not detect any worsening of the head injury. She sensed his pain, a collection of sharp bruises and a deep bone-ache in his left arm, and a pounding headache Galina did not dare ease with opiates. Her own head ached in sympathy as she maintained her mental rapport, but she kept the watch without resentment.

"Anything?" Galina Kirillovna asked again and turned toward her.

"He has a very hard head."

Galina smiled with relief. "I keep asking you that, but how often do I have such a reliable guide? A wonderful help, this Gift of yours. I envy Xin Tian."

"Thank you."

"Did you work in the hospitals there?" Galina asked as she folded the discarded linen. Rinn sensed her friendly interest and something deeper she could not quite define. A complicated woman, Galina, accustomed to many layers of intention. Behind the thoughts she glimpsed a stern-faced but beautiful woman, another Kirova, long accustomed to power and trusting no one.

"Only the labs," she answered, "but health-sensing is part of my training. Unfortunately, it came too close to mind-probing for Captain Hung's taste; it wasn't encouraged on *Sing Fa*.''

"Personally, I think your Captain Hung was an idiot."

"Just a cautious man. I am a dangerous person."

"Very dangerous, to Oleg's good fortune." Her expression changed subtly. "And I hope to ours. In case you don't know, I'll do everything I can for you on Novy Strana—you have a powerful advocate there, though she hasn't yet heard of you. Some commissars can see further than others."

"Tatiana's aunt?"

Galina stared a moment, then laughed nervously. "It *does* take some getting used to, doesn't it?"

"I'm sorry," Rinn said and looked down at her hands. "It's a matter of perception level. To listen to him, I also hear you." She twisted her fingers in her lap. "I'm sorry," she repeated.

"Perhaps someday, Starfarer, you can leave off with apologies for something that should need none."

Rinn looked away. "I have learned to keep my hopes more modest." Though she heard the comfort, she finally identified the hidden intention in Galina's mind—an avarice for the Gift, to use and control for Soviet purposes. Is a tool ever human? she asked Galina silently as the woman moved around the small room, and felt her own wariness revive.

But what if I choose to be more than a tool?

Two days later, *Zvezda*'s crew discovered its new vein of tourmaline. Yuri tramped back to the ship, elated, and promptly set out ordering a party to begin drilling. He found Tatiana in the lock bay, preparing the spacesuits. She grunted absently as he entered the bay, preoccupied with her struggle with a balky connection on one helmet.

"Can I help?" he asked.

"No thanks," she replied curtly as she bent over the suit. "How long until we leave?"

"Less than an hour." His eyes swept over the suits she had prepared. "There'll be four in the party; you should break out another suit."

"Four? Standard procedure is for three."

"I'm taking McCrea with us."

Tatiana's head jerked up. "You can't be serious! Hasn't she done enough already?"

Yuri scowled. "What do you mean? Galina says Oleg's awake and doing well." He knew that Rinn's presence in Oleg's sick-room had grated badly on Tatiana; Galina had reported sparks every time Tatiana went to visit. "And he's alive because of Rinn's prompt action, Tatiana. Can't you give her that?"

"In solving a problem *she* created," Tatiana threw back, her eyes blazing. "Don't be so blind, Yuri. Oleg has had years of spacesuit training, just like us; he knows the risks on a Class Four world. Yet the first time he goes out with her, he nearly dies. Oh, brave Rinn, running to the rescue." Her voice shrilled with loathing. "How do you know she didn't make him forget the danger, just so she could 'rescue' him?"

"That's ridiculous," Yuri said calmly, disturbed by the hatred in Tatiana's eyes. "It's true that your opposition has become legendary in only two weeks, Trade Officer, but there are limits. She is an asset—" He raised his hand warningly "—and the subject is not open to discussion. Prepare a fourth suit."

Tatiana shut her mouth with a snap and glared, then quickly schooled her expression. "Yes, sir," she said demurely.

Yuri gave her a sharp look and hesitated, then gave up the half-formed intent of trying to reason with her. Any accord he had had earlier with Tatiana was gone, and he doubted if even Viktor had much influence left. Why? he wondered. Why did she hate Rinn so much?

He left Tatiana to return to the bridge and check on the weather, then met the drill-party in the access bay thirty minutes later. Tatiana helped Khina suit up, then offered assistance to Rinn as well. After a startled look, Rinn assented. Yuri put on his own suit and snapped down the helmet.

"Testing com," he said.

"Sir," came Tatiana's voice, tinny through his headset. The other two women echoed her, their faces obscured by the glare of the ceiling lights on their faceplates.

"Do you all know the procedure?" Yuri asked.

Again an affirmative chorus, with repressed excitement from Khina, a calmness from Rinn, and an edged voice from Tatiana.

"Then let's go." Yuri depressed the intercom button to the bridge. "Departing from anterior lock."

"Yes, sir," Hara responded. "Good luck." Lights flickered across the lock controls. As Yuri stepped out on the lock platform, he craned his head to right and left, analyzing conditions. "Within parameters," as Hara would say, but the parameters included swirling methane winds, frozen rock, and a steady ground-trembling from the continuing eruption far to the north. He wanted a quick journey to the new mine before the world's perils again gathered to strike; New Prague resembled Hell a little too much for comfort.

At least Oleg is alive, he thought. It was close, too close.

"We'll need the robo-carry," he said.

"Already loaded, Captain," Tatiana said, pointing downward to the left. Yuri scrambled down the ladder and walked to the small cart half-concealed by the bulk of the ship. Tatiana had packed supplies and extra air canisters in the rear compartment, their hedge against delay and accident. The laser-drill occupied most of the front compartment; they would load that compartment with tourmaline and carry the drill back.

"Very good. I'll take the point; Khina, take the rear," he said, ordering their small expedition.

"Yes, sir," Khina murmured.

Yuri activated the robot controls of the cart and programmed its course, then moved aside as the machine rolled forward at a walking pace. "Let's go."

As they walked toward the nearby ridge of hills, Yuri noted wide bands of feldspars and augite in the surrounding basalt, as well as other plutonic minerals: an occasional flash of mica and zircon, a few rare tumbled outcrops of quartz, several winding veins of an unknown mineral variant—rose, green, dark blue— swirling with the patterns of sulfur and methane deposits. He repressed his instinct to stop for a sample and slogged ahead beside the robo-carry.

Steadily they made their way toward the rockface and the small rift that led to the crystal mine. To their right, he could see the distant eruption that had destroyed the first base, a line of tiny mountains spouting fire, half-veiled by the shifting methane crystals whipping by on the wind. A gust staggered him, and he hunched his shoulders, careful of his footing on the broken ground.

He glanced behind at the others, checking, then followed the robo-carry up the gentle slope to the dark slash of the mine entrance. At the rift, he glanced around and called Hara for a report on conditions. All well. *Zvezda* seemed almost toylike in the distance, a tiny sliver of metal that gleamed as brightly as her namesake. Then, careful not to scrape his suit against the jagged rocks, he climbed into the rift.

His helmet light struck the rock of the narrow walls, lighting the brilliant blue of the tourmaline, then other colors of several gemstones, other crystal, a thin line of gold, all contained by the sober black of basalt. It was a Hell demon's treasure trove, crafted miles deep in a volcanic vent as raw magma cooled and made its distillery from the fundamentals of atomic weight, crystal bonding, and variant temperature. He played his helmet light onto the opposite wall and saw the answer of other crystal-flash, suspecting the new site might be even richer than the old. It better be, he thought grimly. His luck had to turn sometime, and a rich deposit would help certain other explanations.

He paced forward, tracking the tourmaline vein to a wider deposit where they could start the drill-face.

As Yuri disappeared into the rift, Rinn looked toward the volcanoes to the north, then quickly scanned their surroundings. No threat yet. Absently she listened to the autonomic awareness of her companions, monitoring heartbeat and breathing, listening for any sensation of physical distress. For this she had been trained at the enclave, a valuable use of the Gift as guard that she continued . . . She felt grateful to Yuri for including her again.

The ground trembled more violently beneath their feet, and a faint sifting of dust fell across the rift opening. Rinn reached out to the supporting rock, testing for weakness, but rock had no awareness. She heard only blankness, no more than a sense of enclosing and weight. Some at the enclave were Gifted in planet-sensing; her own Gift reached out to living things. She touched each of her companions again and reached out to the captain as she probed her way into the darkness of the mind. All safe . . .

The bottled air of her suit felt raw in her throat, and she coughed slightly. She looked north again, wondering how much longer Yuri would stay in the rift. She coughed a second time and imagined she could almost smell the reek of sulfur, the bloated scent of other erupting gases. *Mountain*, she sent wistfully, looking north again, *do you hear me?* She coughed again from a raw pain in her chest.

"Suit check, Rinn," Khina said abruptly.

"What?"

A thrum of hostility touched the surface of Rinn's mind, an attention so pointed that Rinn glanced at Tatiana. She heard Tatiana try clumsily to guard her thoughts, in the process attracting the very interest she was trying to avoid. As Khina moved toward Rinn, the Starfarer caught a brief image of a suit regulator valve, of Tatiana's fingers adjusting the control to a dangerous weakness. Could her hostility have reached such a point?

Rinn probed deliberately and felt the trade officer shy violently away from a touch she vaguely sensed as alien and exterior.

"Freak! Mutant!" Mei-lan had cried, ages ago.

Rinn glanced down quickly at the suit valve at her waist and saw it set well below the red warning line. If left at the lower pressure setting, the suit admitted infinitesimal amounts of methane into the enclosed atmosphere of the suit, tainting the breathing mixture. Already she had enough methane in her suit to irritate her throat membranes. She wrenched the setting upward, choking off the poisons. Khina saw the movement and whirled toward Tatiana.

"I thought you checked these suits, Tatiana . . ." Her voice trailed off; then, harshly, she added, "I see, oh so well. Isn't it enough to be a total and unalloyed bitch, Tatiana? Must you add murder, too?"

Tatiana's mouth gaped. "Khina! I never intended . . ."

"Oh, sure. Put on the act. Lie. Bat your pretty eyes. You're so good at that." Khina's voice trembled with rage.

"What's the problem?" Yuri asked as he emerged from the narrow rift of the mine entrance.

Khina tossed her head. "Oh, nothing. Just a little case of convenient murder. Tatiana sabotaged Rinn's pressure gauge."

"I did not!" Tatiana shrieked.

"Lies," Khina spat back contemptuously. "It's just like you, Tatiana, you Russki bitch."

"That's enough!" Yuri ordered. He scrambled down the broken rock in front of the rift, walking gingerly on the unsteady footing. "Khina, help Rinn through a biosystems check of her air supply. Tatiana . . ."

"I did *not* sabotage the suit," Tatiana raged. "Khina's as paranoid as that Starfarer, but you always listen to *them*, not to me. You just bumble around, Yuri, seeing what you want to see and risking us all. If you'd only listen to me!"

Yuri stopped a pace away, facing her. "I am listening," he said calmly. "Tell me why Rinn has a contaminated suit."

"I don't know. Maybe the suit's defective. Maybe she did it herself."

"Why would she tamper with her own suit?" he asked reasonably, but Rinn sensed his baffled and weary frustration, laced by fear for her own safety. She'll try again, was his thought. He was convinced of it.

"Why would I?"

"Yes, why would you? I gave a direct order about Rinn, one

sanctioned by the majority aboard this ship. You responded by withdrawing your help at Ba-rao-som's autopsy, challenging my every order, raving idiotic accusations about Rinn. And now Rinn has suit problems. You draw the connection, Tatiana Nikolaevna.''

''I deny that I tampered with her suit.''

''Fine. We'll let a board of inquiry decide if you did.''

''A board? You're crazy. She doesn't have ship-rights.''

''Oh, yes, she does, Trade Officer. Go read your precious statutes and look it up; you can start now. You're confined to quarters.''

''You can't mean that! Over *her*?''

''Return to the ship,'' Yuri ordered inexorably.

Tatiana hesitated, then whirled and stamped down the slope. The captain turned toward Khina. ''How's her air?''

''Tainted but breathable. I've adjusted the oxygen flow; the filters should handle most of the rest. Within safe parameters, sir.''

''Good.'' Yuri took a deep breath and looked back longingly toward the rift.

''I'd rather continue,'' Rinn said. ''Wouldn't three be better than two?''

''Quicker, and thank you.'' He handed carryalls to both women and lifted the portable laser-drill from the robo-carry. ''The vein is twenty meters beyond the entrance on the left side.'' They followed him into the dark crevasse and waited as he braced the drill against the rift wall. Yuri braced himself, keyed on the brilliant ruby pencil-beam of the drill, and guided it back and forth across the crystal vein. Through her exterior headphones, Rinn could hear the shrieking crackle as the rock yielded to the laser. A faint dust sifted downward inside the shaft, set loose by the steady trembling of the ground.

Several minutes later, Yuri shut down the laser. Rinn loaded her carryall from the tumble of rock, bending awkwardly in her suit, as he shifted the drill to a new angle. The harsh helmet lights made the narrow space inside the rift a semblance of strobe lighting as the team moved back and forth—first a blinding glare off the smooth fabric of a suit, then a flash of sparkling stone as a light beam passed across a wall, each counterpointed by the dark moving shadows that followed the team as they moved.

Rinn made her way out of the rift to dump the ore into the robo-carry, stifling a cough from still-sore lungs, then squeezed by Khina as she emerged with her own burden. She reentered the shaft and bent again at the drillsite to refill her carryall.

"Careful, Rinn," Yuri said. "I'm drilling lower now."

"Yes, Captain." Rinn backed away as Yuri sliced downward to the bottom edge of the vein. She could sense the strain in his arms and back from working the heavy power pack of the drill, and saw a faint sheen of perspiration on his face through the ruby glare on his faceplate. She leaned forward slightly to read his wrist monitors, and he noticed the movement.

"Hot in here," he said.

"Don't overload your suit."

"I won't." He grunted slightly as he again maneuvered the drill to begin a new pattern upward. "Is that what Starfarers do?" he asked. "Shepherd anybody within range?"

Rinn smiled. "Basically."

"An interesting vocation."

"Oh, it's not that much different from captain."

Yuri chuckled.

The drill bit into the naked rock, surrounding him with a veiled plume of gases released by the molten rock. Again Rinn sensed the drag at his muscles as he struggled to hold the drill in position. After another minute, he keyed the drill control and the rock-face blaze faded to the narrow illumination of their suit helmets.

"A rather primitive way to harvest mineral," she suggested tentatively.

"Good for starting the drill-face. Later we can mount the drill on a robot, providing its carriage fits through that doorway." He looked down the rift toward the entrance, measuring the width with his eyes. He grunted. "May have to enlarge that, but that's typical. What do the Chinese do at Kornephoros?"

Rinn bent to shove more chunks of ore into her carryall. "I wasn't involved in that much. Something similar, I think, but for different reasons. Greater Asia is accustomed to mass labor."

"Hmmph. They didn't take you out-ship?"

"Not often."

"Idiots." He raised the drill and maneuvered to another angle farther up the vein. "I appreciate you, Rinn—you and your Gift. And you *are* welcome on my ship."

"I know." She smiled.

"Yes, you would."

To him I am not a tool, she thought as Yuri reignited the drill. Or do I deceive myself, merely because I wish it so?

An hour later, Rinn emerged from the rift and again dumped her carryall into the nearly filled bin. She straightened and looked north toward the volcanoes. She watched the shifting colors, mesmerized by the sensory display made safe by distance, then lifted her hand toward the raging mountains.

Do you hear me? she sent. *Mountain . . .*

Khina dumped her own load into the robo-carry compartment, then stretched awkwardly within the confines of her suit. The ground shook violently, jarring them off their balance and sending a sheet of dust over the rift entrance. Both women heard the click of the ship circuit.

"Increasing ground tremors, Captain," Hara said. "Computer predicts a rolling series for the next hour, some of two point four temblor range."

"Acknowledged," Khina said. "We're almost done here."

"I respectfully suggest that you not wait, my love," Hara's usual calmness seemed strained.

"Coming now." Khina bent over the robo-carry to program the reverse course, then headed for the rift to warn the captain. Rinn struggled with the flexible cover and managed to snap it down just as the motorized cart lurched away from them, heading down the long slope to the ship. Khina and Yuri appeared a moment later in the rift opening, carrying the drill between them. As Yuri stumbled, nearly exhausted from the long hour of manhandling the drill, Rinn smoothly intercepted them and took the handle from him.

"Thanks," Yuri said, breathing heavily. "How's your air?"

"Fine. How's your back?"

"I hope in worse condition than your air. Are you sure you're all right?"

"You've only asked that a dozen times, Yuri."

"So I worry about you. Enjoy it a little, Starfarer, however strange it seems. Let's get back to the ship."

A half-hour later, Rinn entered the cabin assigned to her and sat down heavily on the bed. Her throat still ached and longer muscles sent their own pain, matching the tired confusion of her mind. She looked at the pictures on her walls—a building, some flowers—and found no meaning in them. On *Sing Fa*, crew rooms had no distinction, no difference except the subtle presence of the personality, if that. At least they had been familiar, a complex of association with the crew that had occupied them.

She tried to remember the sense of grief that had possessed her in the marsh, when she wept in her exhaustion, but it eluded her. One by one, she imaged the faces of *Sing Fa*'s crew. I feel nothing for them, she told herself. Why?

She sat, studying her narrow hands, wondering if she had any emotion in common with Normals. The enclave had recommended keeping a careful distance from the Normal crew, a means of survival among intense prejudice. But somehow, however prudent, however cautious, it had left Rinn bereft of an essential. *Zvezda* promised—what? Anything? Could a Starfarer ever find that essential among Normals?

A tap at her door interrupted her thoughts, startling her. She jerked up her head, then sensed Yuri waiting in the corridor.

"Come in," she said and walled away her emotions.

The captain entered the room and hesitated awkwardly, then sat down in the chair. She said nothing.

"I was concerned," he began, then shifted uncomfortably in the chair. She sensed his discomfort and looked away, hating the divisions between them. Both human, but divided by her Gift, and by his captaincy for a distant Space Bureau that despised her kind.

"Rinn?"

"Yes, Captain."

"I . . ."

"Yes?" Rinn looked at the floor, keeping a careful barrier against her own perception. Her emotion aided her, until her sensing of him wavered and extinguished into grayness. *I refuse you, Gift.*

Yuri rose from his chair and crossed the few steps between them. Rinn looked up in surprise as his hand caressed her face, then her hair. She held herself motionless under his touch, not knowing how to react. After a long moment, he reached down and pulled her upward into his arms, his expression questioning. She sighed, perplexed beyond imagining.

He smiled down at her, amused by her expression. "Don't look so startled, Rinn."

"I don't understand," she said. "Why?"

"I think," he said, "we both ask too many questions." He cupped her chin in one palm and kissed her. She jerked in surprise at the touch of his lips on her mouth, then leaned tentatively into his kiss. After a long moment, he broke it off, and she felt his rumble of pleased laughter.

"Nice," he murmured, then pressed his lips to her neck, exploring the touch and scent of her skin there. Rinn relaxed still more, dropping the barriers to his mind, and felt his temptation to take the embrace further. She smiled at his automatic balancing of debits and advantages as he wondered how she might respond. Perhaps some things never changed, a fundamental between man and woman despite other barriers.

"What's so funny?" he asked gruffly, noticing her smile.

"You. Must everything be a command decision?"

Yuri looked startled a moment, then almost abashed. "I'll have to get used to this; I'm accustomed to my hidden maneuvers." He looked at her speculatively. "Uh . . . speaking of that—well, never mind."

Rinn laughed up at him and pulled down his head for a second kiss, then released him. "I'm afraid *that*," she said, "should be discussed with Doctor Roblev, like everything else of importance. And there are other consequences to discuss before we rashly—"

"Why?"

"It's not that simple, Yuri."

"Why not?" Yuri asked stubbornly, and pulled her closer to him.

Rinn pushed him away. "Oh, give me room, please?" she cried in anguish. "I have been so alone . . ."

He backed up hastily. A heartbeat stood between then, then her took her hand and raised it to his lips, turning it to kiss her palm. "Of course," he said simply. Then he smiled again, his eyes sparkling. "Any room, Rinn, and endless discussions—well, not endless, we must have a conclusion, the obvious end to—"

"You're a bold one," she said, embarrassed by her outburst.

"Certainly. And reckless and calculating and a number of other opposites."

"As am I."

"Yes. You never have told me much about Ikanos and your enclave."

"Ikanos was a long time ago, the enclave almost as much."

"Still, I would like to hear about it, when we have time to talk about such things. I can tell you about Novy Strana—you need some preparation. We can tell each other all sorts of things."

His voice had an ingenuous quality, as if he, too, felt apart
at times. She wondered at the nuance, then smiled again at the
subtle empathy between them. Strange, to feel so attuned with
the nonGifted. But perhaps not so strange.

"Yes," she said. "I would like that."

Chapter 12

DURING THE NEXT WEEK, *ZVEZDA* REAPED THE products of the new mine. Besides the precious tourmaline, the vein yielded a new mineral, pale yellow and unknown, that excited the robo-carry's sensors with odd piezoelectric readings. Yuri decided to collect a sample for testing at Novy Strana, then gathered other minerals at the drillsite and elsewhere, some easily recognizable, others strangely distorted by the unique tectonic forces that had created them. Rinn tramped around with him, helping him collect samples from every likely rock, both amused by and sharing his enthusiasm.

Tatiana remained confined to her quarters, occasionally visited by Dr. Roblev. The psychologist emerged unhappy and dissatisfied, and she sensed his worry about the polarization of the crew. Murder, madness: the specter haunted his mind constantly. His disquiet added an unwelcome nuance to the nightly crew conferences; however unfairly, Roblev blamed Rinn for the trouble aboard the ship. It divided him from Rinn, edging any words he spoke to her. And so she retreated from him, guarding her face and voice, to avoid the very controversy he would put to her credit. Yet still he watched her with uneasy suspicion.

On the third evening, *Zvezda*'s crew again gathered in the crew lounge to examine the new minerals of the day and to continue their ongoing discussions about Delta. The Seguinus samples, some dun-colored, others brightly faceted, still others glinting from the recessed crannies of common ores, made a visible symbol of the ship's newest successes; the crew's frustration about Delta signalled its unsolved disaster. Yuri pressed his crew for ideas, secretly hoping in the free-for-all for a proposal, an analysis, something to present the bureaucrats of Novy Strana when *Zvezda* returned home. Time was growing short, with only a brief visit to an ice planet separating them from that accounting.

"Think, comrades!" Yuri urged again. The others looked at him blankly—Roblev, Galina, a pale Oleg, Khina and Hara with fingers entwined. From her chair at Yuri's left, Rinn watched their faces, aware of the subtle interplay of emotions and intention among her shipmates. Yuri turned to the slender biologist. "Khina, have you finished your DNA analysis of the virus?"

Khina shrugged. "As much as I can with our limited ship resources. As best as I can tell, the virus mimics a Deltean's proteins but varies in a single receptor enzyme—an enzyme not found in other Delta proteins, by the way. This enzyme allows the virus to penetrate other neurons, but attracts an immune reaction, which in turns leads to the brain infection and damage. The closest Earth analogue is an artificial virus like N37-X, a germ warfare agent developed in pre-Treaty India. It did nasty things to neurons, too. A parallel? How can we tell?"

Roblev stared at her. "Artificial? Are you sure?"

"No, I'm not sure. The enzyme could be a simple variation within normal permutations—but it looks, sort of, like the virus might be manufactured." She wrinkled her nose, irritated with the scientific vagueness of her analysis. "But if it is artificial, why would the maker build so ineptly? Anyone who can gene-splice with that delicacy could predict the inevitable infection. It's almost as if the infectious damage was deliberate."

Yuri rolled his eyes. "A deliberate infection?"

Khina shrugged back at him "So put it up on the shelf by your laser-rifle, Yuri. That's as far as I can go with *Zvezda*'s equipment. I've frozen a number of samples, and, of course, the university will have the rest of Ba-rao-som, too, but a final answer won't be available until its megabrain computer can run a permutation analysis."

"And if it confirms your suspicion?" Rinn asked her.

"Yes—what then? Why would a people deliberately infect itself with a plague? Germ warfare? A mad Deltean scientist scuttling around his lab? His nasty beastie that got loose? Lab? Where?"

"And when?" Yuri added thoughtfully. "How does it fit?"

"Beats me," Khina said. "Too bad we can't raise the dead and ask our friend in the freezer, assuming he even knew."

Yuri scowled. "That doesn't help much, Khina."

"So *you* go in, Captain, and ask *Zvezda*'s computer questions it can't answer. That's all I have."

"Okay, okay." They looked at each other, frustration etched on their faces.

"Are you sure the answer is only biological?" Rinn asked, earning herself a sharp look from Roblev. Whenever she spoke up, the psychologist eyed her suspiciously. That he knew his suspicions unfair only rankled the more. She tried to ignore him. "We've been looking at differences, at pieces that don't fit. What is similar?"

"To the Delteans?" Hara asked incredulously. "They're a primitive tribe."

"People are people," she retorted. "A race organizes itself on cooperative lines, fulfills basic needs, reacts according to its cultural imperatives. How are the Delteans like us? Why do the Lily seek to dominate other tribes?" She looked around at the faces.

"Population pressure?" Galina asked. "Delta doesn't have much habitable territory."

Khina shook her head. "I doubt it. We've never seen a Deltean tribe-woman with more than one child at a time. That suggests a low birthrate, either biological or cultural, and thus either a negative birth strategy or a positive survival tactic. Both would look the same from outside. Are the Delteans a low-birth species, and thus less flexible in adapting to environmental change? If so, the slow climactic and tectonic changes now underway could be drawing them down to extinction. Or is the limitation strictly a cultural choice? Among the early Amerindians in North America, the mother refrained from sex for several years after a child's birth, both as a survival device to nurture the child but also an inhibition against rapid population growth that would overtax the local biological resources. A few of our marginal colonies have attempted the same restriction of births—for the same reasons."

"Perhaps the Lily tribe wants more of the available births," Oleg hazarded, "and so they sacrifice members of nearby tribes."

Khina shook her head again. "Our orbital scans don't show that the Lily coraal population is any larger than the others. In fact, we chose the Sunstone partly because their grouping had the higher numbers."

"High death rate?" Hara ventured. "What about the other end? Perhaps the viral plague kills a significant number of tribe members, especially in infancy. Perhaps that's the reason for the low births. Add injuries and tribal violence, with only herbal medicine to heal . . ."

"Herbal medicine can be quite effective," Galina said.

"Not against constant violence, my dear," Roblev interjected. "Traumatic internal injuries can't be healed by herbs—you need surgery. And the Delteans are apparently unaware, if Rinn is accurate, of their endemic viral infection—which means they have no immunological or serological techniques, no concept of the vectors of microbiological disease. In the Middle Ages, our culture looked to religion for answers, not science. Perhaps so do they—on a shamanistic level, of course."

"Perhaps." Galina looked unconvinced.

Yuri frowned and tapped his fingers on the table. Rinn again sensed his dissatisfaction, pricked by a secret fear that Zvezda might not find a solution. She bit her lip, watching his face.

"Earth analogues again," he said.

Khina shook her braids impatiently. "And, again, what else do we have as a model? Like Rinn said, perhaps we should be looking at similarities. Life does repeat itself, Yuri. We see the same patterns again and again in Earth biology—certain strategies work, others may work in some situations but not in others. The result is extinction, followed by radiation of the surviving species into the empty niches. The indigenous life on Novy Strana, though rudimentary, has shown several analogues to Earth patterns. The main difference is Arcturus doesn't have a dwarf companion to rain down comets and wipe out life forms en masse every sixty million years. So things are slower, with a greater emphasis on the patterns of natural extinction by tectonic climate change."

"Delta has a dwarf companion," Oleg pointed out, "and tectonic change is now diminishing habitable space. As the sea rises, even more land disappears."

"On a geological time scale, and the companion is farther out," Yuri countered. "Nearly five thousand AU, and about half as massive as Nemesis. The effects on the Oort plane would be much less." He thought a moment. "But I suppose you're right. It's like a scale—Novy Strana very slow, Earth faster, Delta slower but not as slow as Novy Strana. But how does it fit?"

Roblev yawned and stretched hugely, then recurled his fingers around his coffee cup. "So, Oleg Andreivich and Khinà suggest evolutionary pressures; Rinn argues for cultural change. What about the psychological? The emotions, the primal drives? Life drives are basic, all focused on survival of the genotype: territoriality, sexual drives to breed, protection of the helpless infant, basic instincts of hunger, thirst, sex. A society cannot survive if their emotions and cultural patterns don't advance survival. Perhaps theirs does not. If they are a degenerate society, they may be on the downswing and irrecoverable."

Khina scowled. "Let's cure the viral infection before you write them off, Viktor Fedorovich. Did the Renaissance Italians check out when birthrates fell off from lead poisoning? Did we become extinct when Europe lost a third of its population from bubonic plague? And what about the typhoid that followed the Yellow River's floods through four thousand years of ancient Chinese history? Sometimes half of Old China was submerged when the Yellow broke the dikes. They rebuilt, they survived."

Roblev shook his head impatiently. "And smallpox wiped out half the Amerindian population of North America?"

"That was an infection from the outside. Whenever you separate populations for long periods, immunities change. There's no sign that this infection is recent—Rinn says the strength-for-strength ceremony has gone on for generations."

"She says," Viktor argued, glancing aside unpleasantly at Rinn. "There's no other sign it isn't recent—nor can we analyze how rapidly the Delteans are degenerating."

"We don't know that they're degenerating," Yuri said. "Look at the Sunstone. They find food, raise their young, maintain their culture, trade with the interior tribes—"

"—and are subservient to the Lily cannibals."

"That's cultural, Viktor, not biological," Khina said. "And don't sneer at cannibals—they can be quite effective. Reciprocal cannibalism maintained a dynamic balance in New Guinea for two thousand years."

"So." Roblev said, again summing up. "We've considered the biological, the cultural, the primal. What's left?"

"We're just arguing in circles," Oleg complained.

"Not necessarily," Yuri said firmly. "The answer's there somewhere."

Roblev shrugged. "I tend to agree with Oleg, Captain. This discussion is going nowhere."

"So we just give up?" Yuri demanded.

"I say that we don't have the expertise. We need Tatiana Nikolaevna—she has the training." The psychologist glowered at Rinn.

Rinn stared back at him a moment. "So let Tatiana out of isolation," she suggested. She sensed Roblev's surprise and smiled at him thinly. "You persist in blaming me as victim, Doctor, instead of looking to the perpetrator. Why not continue the thought and wish the entire event away?"

"I'm not blaming . . ."

"Oh?"

Roblev had the grace to smile, however insincerely. Games again, she thought, Do they ever stop?

"Well, I suppose I am, somewhat," Roblev said. "You are an inconvenience, Starfarer."

"So are laser-rifles, artificial plagues, and a native tribe that doesn't like Star-Devils, Doctor Roblev."

Roblev chuckled. "That, too. Still it would have been easier if you hadn't—"

"Yes, that." Rinn stood up, highly irritated. "I cannot change my nature. I am what I am, however you disapprove. Good evening, comrades." She turned and stalked out of the conference.

Different, different. The rhythm of the words seemed to time the thud of her steps on the stairs. Feel nothing, she told herself, and you can lose nothing. She remembered that Connor had said as much during her remaining enclave days before she joined *Sing Fa.*

"Normals have different needs," he had said, "and will use a tool to its full potential. If you identify with their needs, you may be tempted to go beyond our code. Don't give too much of your loyalty, Rinn—you make yourself vulnerable by coming too close to them, by caring too much for the outcome."

Connor had shrugged, the filtered light through the windows making his face a pattern of light and shadow. "We live a narrow life, at the sufferance of Normals. The Chinese do not often ask us to abuse the Gift; in this, their suspicion is our safeguard. Use it to preserve what we are."

Yes, but so easily said, Rinn thought angrily, torn between what *Zvezda* offered and what *Zvezda* denied. She flung herself on her bed and escaped into other-mind, its other places, its other griefs.

* * *

"Rinn." Yuri stood in the doorway of her room.

"Yes, Captain," she said, her expression carefully schooled.

"I—" He stopped and looked at her helplessly. "Where do you go when you wear that face, Rinn? Is it a face you learned on Ikanos? I know Viktor's been unbearable, but . . ."

She shrugged, then looked down, unwilling to meet his eyes. "I don't know what you want of me."

He took both her hands in his. "I want many things, if you are willing—but mostly I want to spare you any need to escape into that safe place."

She lifted her eyes, looking at him sharply. "I have no safety. The Gift makes all things unsafe."

"Not so! Or, it doesn't have to be that way. You haven't asked what happened after you left," he said hurriedly. "Khina told Viktor he stank."

Rinn smiled. "That's like Khina."

"Hara and I agreed, and I told Vicktor I wanted you as a permanent member of the crew, with petitions filed at Novy Strana, and—as my ship wife, if you—uh . . ."

Rinn stared at him. "What did he say?"

"Well, he doesn't approve much, which is an understatement. Do you?"

"What? Approve?"

"I'm not explaining this well," Yuri said in frustration, then released her hands to run them through his hair. He looked strained, with newly grown lines in his young face. He touched her cheek, tracing her scar with one finger. "I don't know where you go. I can't reach you there."

Rinn reached up to take his hand, then moved it to her lips. She sighed. "Perhaps it only takes persistence, Yuri Ivanovich." Her shoulders sagged. "But the Bureau would never allow it. Novy Strana proscribes us from all contact, much less service on your ships. And I am a citizen of Xin Tian—they can extradite. The Treaty bites both ways. Your Bureau would never protect me."

"Galina thinks Kirova might. We can try."

"And if they refuse? What then?"

Yuri looked at her helplessly. "I don't know." He set his jaw. "But I will still ask." He pulled her to him, then looked questioningly into her face. Rinn surrendered to the appeal, though she knew it unwise.

"Yes. You must ask," she said.

He kissed her. "And until then?"

"You can't risk a charge of my 'influence,' Yuri, not and hope to keep your position as captain of this ship."

He frowned. "Another inescapable fact. I'm afraid you're right, dear Rinn." He lifted her hand and pressed it to his lips. "But we will see. I don't accept reality so equably."

"Spoken as a true member of the majority."

He smiled down at her. "Perhaps."

They prudently stepped apart at the sound of footsteps on the ladder. "Perhaps," she echoed, then smiled at him again—and heard the flare of his emotions as he responded. It warmed her, more than she had thought possible.

"What else?" Yuri prompted again the next evening. He looked around the table at faces he knew well, an essential part of the ship he loved: *his* ship, *his* crew. He faced them with a renewed determination, knowing that it showed on his face. "What have we overlooked?"

Zvezda's crew again sat in the conference room, absent one trade officer: however Viktor and Rinn urged, Yuri still would not relent about Tatiana's confinement. Let her stew awhile, he thought. "As Viktor said yesterday, we've considered the biological, the cultural, the primal. What other categories might offer an answer?"

"Technological?" Hara suggested. "Technological imbalance—those laser-weapons of yours, Yuri—can wreak more damage than any biological factors, and here we may have a combination of both plague and revolution. How would technological superiority affect that balance of power?"

"Or is the crucial factor," Galina said slowly, "ownership of technology? If it weren't for the tsetse fly, Africa might have been more advanced and less divided for conquest. Had the Amerindians had another two hundred years to organize a nation-state, the whites might never have advanced to the Pacific. Are the Lily the original masters, or—" Galina hesitated, her blue eyes thoughtful. "Or perhaps a less advanced tribe, a group of barbarians that overcame a more sophisticated society?"

"A stolen technology?" Hara asked. "It might explain much."

"Maybe," Yuri said, still unconvinced.

"But it *is* possible," Khina said. "My Mongol ancestors swept into Europe and wreaked havoc with its horde. The Germanic tribes had an opportunity to succeed the Roman state; Genghis Khan put a stop to that and made everybody in Europe start over. Having picked over Europe, the Great Khan went east and took over China, which just happened to be cycling down into another dynastic flux.'' She spread her hands. ''How often does a steppe culture overcome a city-state society? Do we have a parallel here? Why did the horde succeed on both sides of Eurasia and the Amerindians fail?''

Galina nodded. ''Cultural stability is a defense; weakness can be exploited if the enemy has the luck of coincidence. The change comes from the combination, the contact.''

''And what change will we wreak here, I wonder?'' Viktor said. ''Will we 'crack' their society, too?''

''We haven't always destroyed the counter-society,'' Yuri argued. ''The Arabs managed to keep their culture while taking our technology. The Japanese outsold everyone until they merged into Greater Asia and gave the Chinese the means to handle its population overkill.''

''The Arabs had a technological resource in oil, Japan its societal organization. What does Delta have?''

''Distance,'' Yuri said. ''Unique products we want. And a dominant tribe with massive 'magic.' '' He paused. An idea tantalized at the edge of his mind, and he caught Rinn's look of immediate interest.

''Magic?'' he said to her.

''Yes.'' Her strange dark eyes gleamed. ''Perception, a worldview, a way to enter into their society instead of destroying from without. Magic, Yuri.''

''Whatever are you two talking about?'' Viktor asked, his long face befuddled.

''Something outside your purview, Viktor,'' Yuri told him. ''Magic, power, the ghost-world. But then, maybe not—if anyone understands symbolic reality, it's you.'' His thought leaped through the possibilities. ''Listen, Viktor. What is the one category that binds everything *for the Delteans*? We can study them from without, applying our analogues from our own culture, but how do they see themselves?'' He answered his own question, rapping the table for emphasis. ''Power, magical reality, the spirit-world of demons and the world's magical order. Everything that Rinn has told us has that focus.''

''Magic,'' Galina said thoughtfully. She smiled. ''And what magic might Star-Devils have?''

''Exactly.'' Yuri grinned at her.

Galina glanced at Rinn. ''Well, first off, we have a Starfarer.'' Viktor promptly scowled and she flipped her hand at him. "Stop salivating on cue, my dear, and use that brain of yours. Rinn is an asset: what she can do is 'magic' even to us."

"And we have laser-rifles, too," Hara added.

"And all sorts of other astounding things," Galina said. "The line between science and magic is mainly one of perception, don't you agree?" She smiled again, her plain face lit with interest and approval. "It's a most profitable line of thought, Yuri, perhaps even enough to build a new approach to Delta. Whether biological or cultural, whatever mix of technological and societal change, even if the continents move and the seas rise, all remains a question of magic—to the Delteans. And perhaps that one fact is the key."

Oleg scowled. "I doubt if the commissars will approve of magical approaches, Galina."

"Then let them think up an alternative. We've cudgeled our brains for days—let them cudgel theirs. And don't be so certain about their ossified brains, Second Officer. Kirova has a gift for original thought."

"Maybe." Oleg grunted.

"It's a start," Yuri said. He looked around the table and smiled at all of them, then met Rinn's eyes.

"A beginning," she answered. "For many things."

Chapter 13

SIX DAYS LATER, RINN SAT AT HER COMPUTERMAN station as *Zvezda* lifted off in a blaze of engine exhaust, scoring the basalt floor of the new base. The crew had marked the base with transponders and placed others at the new mine for the next ship due in two months. As *Zvezda* cleared the atmosphere, Yuri launched a message to the waiting satellite, alerting *Nauka*'s captain to the change of site. The ship slipped through the Seguinus system, accelerating along the orbital plane, then launched at a tangent into the strange nothingness of warped space for Mu Bootis.

After the successful entry into warp, the crew settled into its usual routine of transit flight: a round of studies, analysis of the new data gleaned at the last trade-point, and preparation of each crew member's reports for the Trade Bureau. Yuri, earning a slight scowl from Roblev, encouraged Rinn to prepare her own report as both Starfarer and the ship's computerman. The psychologist still worried, unaware of the growing effect of his visits to Tatiana—and the boredom of the trade officer's isolated confinement. Tatiana had had too much time to think. Rinn smiled as she worked at her computerboard, prudently aware of Tatiana's state of mind.

Tatiana Nikolaevna thrived on conflict and the sure barbs she enjoyed inflicting on her crewmates. Deprived of a steady opportunity for such attention, missing Oleg more than she ever expected, Tatiana's feelings had become strangely mixed. Reluctantly, she admitted a certain gratitude about Oleg's accident, whatever her suspicions about its cause. Her choice of Oleg Konstantin had been predatory in its origins, but Tatiana felt a certain fondness for the handsome second officer, both sexual and otherwise. His near-death had upset her assumptions, perhaps even brought a realization of her own attachment.

And Tatiana did not like being a minority of one; she guessed the incident would rob her of her one sure advocate aboard *Zvezda*—at least until she could bring Oleg around again. She paced her small room, irritated with the confinement, and cursed herself as a fool. She had misgauged the depth of Yuri's foolish attachment to Rinn and put her own position at risk. Board hearings were not predictable, even to a trade officer with connections. The situation prompted a change in strategy, though she would not yet admit it to Viktor Fedorovich. Carefully she planned the method of her gradual surrender to his nags, waiting for a better day.

Rinn went calmly about her duties, wondering when Tatiana would comprehend her vulnerabilities to a telepath's awareness. Even now Tatiana's egotism refused to admit the possibility of silent and unknown intrusion, still denying that most basic of her fears. Grimly Rinn doubted Tatiana's similar confidence about Oleg. For all his passion for the beautiful trade officer, Oleg, too, had been thinking.

At midpoint in the warp, Oleg had recovered enough to resume his normal duties, and he began assembling his own reports. Judging from the busy activity aboard the ship, Novy Strana apparently operated by a volume of computer discs, with endless reports up and down the chain. On the third day of warp, Rinn stopped by Oleg's door and saw the second officer struggling to type with one hand, his arm still splinted to his chest. Impulsively, she stepped into the room.

"Need some help?"

Oleg turned awkwardly at the sound of her voice, then shook his head. Rinn smiled uncertainly and took a step toward the door, making her retreat, when Oleg abruptly changed his mind.

"Wait a minute. Maybe I do need some help."

"I would think that's rather obvious," she said dryly.

"The Soviet people are never daunted by obstacles." He shifted to the edge of his seat, then stood, nearly overbalancing. "Or so the Bureau declaims. However, they've never published an exact list of the obstacles that apply. Here, sit down."

Rinn crossed the few steps to his desk and complied. A half-page of text displayed on his screen. "Can you type to dictation?" he asked.

"I suppose so."

"Then commence," he said pompously. Rinn glanced upward to see if he intended some kind of humor, then realized he did not. She bit her lip and looked back at the screen. The tall blond officer leaned uncomfortably against the nearby shelves, his hand cradling his splinted arm.

"I wrote this report earlier," he said as an aside, "but I've decided it needs some editing. I had just described the break in Deltean trade and your astonishing appearance in our midst."

"I see."

"Continuing, then: It is my opinion that the Starfarer, Rinn McCrea, contributed significantly to the ship's safety in extracting *Zvezda* from a difficult situation." Rinn typed as he spoke slowly. "Although some crew members expressed concern about violation of Statute Regulation 1.0872-1, it is my opinion that circumstances required sanctuary, and that Starfarer McCrea has proved herself an asset to the ship. I myself later benefited directly, and I commend her for her prompt and efficient action."

Rinn looked up at him. He smiled shyly, then covered the expression with a pompous scowl.

"Thank you," she said quietly.

"It's merely truth." He leaned forward and keyed the text into memory. "I think that's enough typing for now. Thank you, Rinn."

Rinn hid a smile and rose. "You're welcome."

"I think I'll take a nap."

"A good idea." Rinn walked out, again trying to hide her smile, knowing it would only embarrass Oleg. Pompous as he was, she appreciated the gesture. She allowed a small bubble of hope to form: if the second officer made a favorable recommendation, perhaps the Space Bureau would give more credence to Yuri's "tampered" opinions.

Or perhaps, she worried, they would think she tampered with Oleg, too. She felt a wave of the old disgust, the old frustrations, and stamped up the ladder to the next deck. Would she never be free of this contagion?

Not and remain yourself, she remembered from another time. She nodded to the other crew on the bridge, then took her computer station. I am what I am, she thought defiantly, and called up her own report on the computer screen. Starfarer.

* * *

They had named the world Crystal. It orbited the sixth planet of Mu Bootis, a diamondlike moon as brilliantly white as Venus in Earth skies, its broad ice plains occasionally tinted by shifting pastels reflected from the gas-giant nearby. Beneath ten kilometers of ice lay Crystal's lightless ocean, its currents powered by subterranean volcanic heat and tidal stresses—and, at certain magma vents where heat and chemistry made conditions suitable, a cradle for the first beginnings of bacterial life.

In the biolab, Khina showed Rinn several holograms of the chemosynthetic bacteria that thrived in Crystal's depths. As the microorganisms died, their proteins circulated upward to the rigid ceiling of ice, and then, over centuries, percolated to the surface. FIrst Survey had found their traces there, a new life chemistry created by random evolution in an alien ocean.

"Proteins have nearly unlimited combinations," Khina said. "We can build them in our laboratories, of course, but the process is time-consuming, even when confined to a single variant. It takes time to test hundreds of combinations for a single molecule." She removed the slide from the optical microscope and held it to the light. "These beauties do something different with sulfides than Earth's deep-ocean vent equivalents, though we're not quite sure what. Novy Strana wants more samples to fuss with."

"Terraforming?" Rinn asked in surprise.

Khina looked at her sternly. "Let me reveal my surprises in the accustomed way, Rinn. No peeking."

"Yes, Khina."

"That's a good Starfarer," Khina said, her tone complacent. Rinn laughed, and received the flash of Khina's quick grin in response.

"Just so you remember," Khina said. She replaced the slide in its container, then closed the case. "Anyway, it's that possibility that justified the drill project. *Aryol* brought in the remaining equipment and started the drill; we're here to check progress, feed the little beastie more graphite so its precious gears don't grind to a stop, and collect more samples on the surface."

"I see."

"Then, six weeks from now, *Nauka* will collect the first deep-water samples from the drill—or so goes the plan. The drill-hole is directly over a thermal vent, so they might even catch some living bacteria." Khina's wistful expression showed she would have far preferred *Nauka*'s share of the project.

"How deep does the drill go?" Rinn asked curiously.

"Ten kilometers of ice and another six kilometers of ocean," Khina replied. "A big drill, the best of a very old design—if the ice doesn't shift and break it."

"Can that happen?"

"The experts say no, not at our site, but sometimes such predictions end up a whistle-happy challenge to Allah. 'Don't you dare bother our drill,' and all that." She sniffed disparagingly. "Bureaucrats think they order the universe, so every once in a while Allah stirs His natural forces to remind them differently—not that it has much effect on their assumptions. Bureaucrats are a stubborn breed."

Khina continued repacking the slides, her small hands working with deft competence. Rinn shifted on her lab stool as she watched. "Are you happy on Novy Strana, Khina?" she asked suddenly.

"Yes—though I prefer ship life. The university biologists get all the grant-studies on Novy Strana, and those appointments still follow racial lines; besides, out here everything is new." She glanced at Rinn's face, a bit shy. "Are you happy in the enclave?"

"I suppose—it's certainly better than what I left on Ikanos. And I like the ships, too."

"They suit you," Khina said unexpectedly. "The life suits both of us."

"Thank you," Rinn said softly.

Caution: you care too much. They had warned her, during her first weeks in the enclave: we live carefully here. *If we don't interfere with them, they won't interfere with us.* Or so the enclave hoped—that perhaps in time, Xin Tian might relax its paranoid vigilance and give the Starfarers genuine privacy within the boundaries of the enclave's walled ghetto. The Japanese had that treasured privilege in New Kyoto, the Thai less so in their own district. Perhaps someday telepaths might have security of place and person, a home in a posted district inhabited only by their own kind.

As we possessed on Ikanos, she thought wryly, and wondered if the Xin Tian Starfarers had even noticed the similarity. She had never asked, had not even seen—had merely accepted the ordering of the enclave as the refuge she so desperately needed. *Keep apart, keep your place,* they had counselled her—*the Gifted are pariah.*

Rinn remembered as she watched Khina's delicate face, oval-eyed, smooth-skinned, framed by the complicated braids of her black hair. Khina bent over her boxes of slides—treasures to her.

"Freak!" Mei-lan had shouted, her thoughts distorted with hatred. They had the same beauty, though Mei-lan had hacked off her hair at the jawline and hid her slim body in shapeless quilted cotton—yet in one, hatred and fear; in the other, a lively interest—and proffered friendship.

Why?

Isolation, limits: a constant wariness of outside threat, outside pressure—it was a paranoia common in Xin Tian's wider society, characteristic of the dominant Han Chinese. The Chinese had sought a similar homogeneity for millennia, and so Xin Tian had created comfortable ghettos for the minorities who still survived among them, even on Earth—Hmong, Tibetans, Sikhs, the expatriate whites of Hong Kong, all the outsider peoples of Greater China.

And now Starfarers. We fit in well, so very well, with our Ikanos scars, she reflected. Somehow, she sensed the defeat in the enclave's arrangement, some opportunity missed, some subservience to the majority mind.

Perhaps . . . She hesitated, studying Khina's profile, uncertain if she wished after an illusion of her own designing.

Novy Strana also built its warrens, but in the ships offered a better equality. At least Khina thought so—Rinn sensed her shipmate's deep contentment, interwoven with the joy of her ship tasks, her love for Hara, her liking for everyone in her crew, even Tatiana in certain moods. Still Kazakh in mind and purpose, Khina embraced her ship with all her ardent nature and took service in the deepest sense.

"Rinn?" Khina asked, noticing her silence. "What are you thinking about?"

We might prosper here—but we're more conditioned than we realize. Xin Tian suits us too well.

"Rinn?"

Rinn started slightly, then smiled. "Oh, I was thinking about the enclave—and the choices we make." She touched Khina's hand briefly. "Thank you, Khina."

"For what?"

Rinn's smile deepened. "For thinking I might still be human."

Khina shrugged dramatically. "Oh, that! Rinnushka, it's nothing—even if you *do* peek."

* * *

Zvezda approached the base on Crystal in a controlled glide, a neat trajectory in ballistics that set her down several hundred meters from the drill platform. Yuri studied the configurations of the drill machinery through the ship's exterior monitor, then queried the autonomous computer aboard the drill about conditions since *Aryol*'s departure. Aside from several centimeters of ice creep—a parameter built into the flexibility of the pipe— Crystal's frozen conditions had not affected the steady drilling through the icecap.

The massive drill was a combination of modified oil derrick, a small fusion generator for power, a pump, and the tall shed of the automatic pipe-loader. On the far side of the derrick, a shimmering flat expanse of new ice stretched a hundred meters, made of refrozen water from the ice melted by the drill's action far below and pumped to the surface. As he watched, a new length of pipe shifted smoothly into the derrick; the loader added a small gear-twist to connect it to the pipe below, and the drill continued boring its steady way downward. Were it not for the gradual compaction of graphite under friction, the drill could probably grind away until Doomsday. Sometimes older technology worked amazingly well.

"Everything within parameters," Hara reported.

"Perhaps our luck *has* turned," Yuri said.

"Perhaps so." Hara smiled with satisfaction at the readings on his screen. "It's about time."

Yuri snorted. "You tell me."

The control room was a model of quiet efficiency. He smiled, pleased with his ship, then stretched lazily and glanced around the room once more before leaving to go below. He found Rinn and Khina in the small lab beneath the access bay. As he approached the doorway, he heard Khina's full-throated laugh and a softer delighted response from Rinn. She should laugh more, he thought, and felt grateful to Khina for drawing her out. She still hides too much—not that I blame her.

He stepped into the lab and saw their two heads close together, both dark-haired, one in complicated braids, the other a smooth raven-wing curve to the shoulder.

I like the sound of her laugh, he realized.

"Captain!" Khina called, spotting him in the doorway. Rinn turned and smiled.

"Ready to go outside, Khina?"

"Sure!" Khina jumped off her lab stool and quickly gathered her sampling kit.

"Do you want me to come?" Rinn asked wistfully, as if she expected to be denied the invitation. Perhaps on *Sing Fa*, she usually was—and, in time, had stopped asking. Her tone was another window to Yuri about her existence before *Zvezda*.

"And everywhere they are watched," Galina had said. He wondered if Viktor appreciated that history in his calculations.

"I don't see why not," he said firmly and smiled at her pleased surprise.

"Yes, do!" Khina said enthusiastically. She slung her equipment over her shoulder, waved brightly at Rinn, and left the room in a clatter.

"But surely you know I intended to include you," Yuri said after Khina had gone. He paused uncomfortably. Would he ever become accustomed to her silent knowledge of everything? He felt determined to try.

"Not everything," Rinn answered his thought, her blue-black eyes faintly mocking. He took her hands in semi-apology, then bent to kiss her.

"I'll get used to it," he promised. "Truly."

"It's all right. The *Zvezda* crew has already offered me more than *Sing Fa* ever did—in some respects, even more than the enclave." Her mouth twisted wryly. "Isolation and limits—I've been thinking about the walls I build, that we can all build. I only wish . . . ." She looked down.

"Yes," he said, not quite sure what she wished. He repressed his worry about Novy Strana, knowing she could sense it and add it to her own. Somehow, he did not want her worrying, not about anything. He kissed her again, until she pushed him away.

"We were going outside?" she asked pointedly.

"Uh, yes. You're right."

She chuckled, and he offered her a hand off her stool.

When they arrived in the access bay Khina was already suited up and talking vivaciously to Hara. Tatiana Nikolaevna stood nearby, newly released from isolation. Yuri had resisted that change a while longer but saw the point in the end; already the tensions aboard *Zvezda* had eased markedly. Even so, he had ordered Tatiana confined to the ship and could count on Khina to recheck any suits Tatiana prepared. The trade officer had accepted the restrictions demurely—it might be half-genuine. As Yuri and Rinn stepped into the bay, Tatiana's eyes flicked toward them a moment. Yuri wished for Rinn's Gift to see behind that sullen exterior. He had hoped Tatiana might give up her opposition to Rinn—but if she were melting, the process was moving like a glacier's slow creep.

"All ready?" he asked the others.

"Yes, sir."

"All right. Hara and I will relubricate and check the drill. Rinn, you can assist Khina with the ice samples."

"Yes, sir."

Ten minutes later they stepped into the airlock, all four shrouded in the protective suits needed on Crystal to exclude vacuum and paralyzing cold. The frozen world had no atmosphere, and the glare of Mu Bootis on ice could blind instantly without the dark-light safeguards built into the visor sensors. Even then, the sensor could be that instant too slow; Yuri manually adjusted his helmet controls to their darkest setting, then reminded the others before opening the outer hatch.

The white light burst into the airlock as the door opened, a widening bar of blinding ice-glitter that bathed their suits and the interior lock. Yuri stepped onto the platform, careful of his footing, then picked a gingerly descent down the icy ladder. Before him stretched the ice plains of Crystal, cracked and scarred by the forces that moved the ice. An aurora of colors slowly moved across the icy surface, advancing on the ship—blue, brown, deep purple—as sunlight reflected from the gas giant that filled half the sky. Yuri looked up at the massive world for a moment, half-mesmerized by its vivid color and impression of weight. On the horizon, the diamond-point of Mu Bootis had lifted above the ice peaks to begin the dawn. Crystal was achingly beautiful, even through the filtered dark-light of his helmet. He beckoned to Hara and began the short hike to the drill platform, reminding himself to watch his footing against such lovely distractions.

After a quick inspection of the girders and fusion generator, he and Hara ran system checks on the exterior monitors, repeating the radio checks performed earlier. They took packets of graphite from stores and pumped new lubricant down the pipe through the feeder-tube, then added more graphite to the drill equipment above. According to the computer's sensors, the drill had not yet penetrated the ice cap, but it was nearing the end: within two weeks, the three-lobed drill-bit would pierce the floor of the ice and drop away, allowing the probe to spin its slow progress downward to the sea bottom. Two weeks—Yuri glanced around the horizon, gathering one last look, then closed up the monitor hood.

"It's going faster than the projections," Hara murmured.

"Sometimes there's a disadvantage to machinery that works. If we'd had that extra time at Delta Bootis, Khina might have robbed *Nauka* of the first deep-sea samples."

"I wouldn't tell Khina that right away," Hara said judiciously.

"No, I think not." Yuri smiled and looked toward the two women at the ice-rift near the ship. "Satisfied with the inspection?" he asked formally.

"Yes. Everything's within proper limits."

"Good. Let's go back."

Rinn straightened and held out the sample case at Khina's gesture, then noticed the two men returning. "Are we almost done?" she asked.

"Sadly, yes," Khina said. "Isn't this place beautiful?"

"Yes, beautiful." Rinn watched a swath of vivid purple sweep toward them and flicker overhead. "Lovely, just lovely. I've never seen anything like this." A wave of rose-pink swept by, reflecting itself in the silvery metal of *Zvezda*'s hull.

"Someday a commissar will put up a dacha here, just you wait. They're always looking for some nice place for a new one."

"I'd rather like a house here myself, though central heating might be a problem."

Khina chuckled. "Oh, we could get around that. Otherwise, what's the point of advanced technology?"

"True," Rinn agreed.

She helped Khina gather the last few samples, then waved at Yuri as he walked toward them. The four climbed into the airlock and watched Crystal disappear in a narrowing band of brilliant light. As the airlock door closed, Rinn sighed regretfully.

"We'll come back," Yuri promised her.

"Yes," she answered—though she knew he only half-believed it.

Chapter 14

ZVEZDA LEFT CRYSTAL THE FOLLOWING DAY, heading home. Rinn again sat at her computer station, processing routine systems data as she listened to the final approach to Novy Strana. The ship had emerged from warp to a chatter of radio traffic on the central band, quickly silenced as Khina changed to the Bureau frequency at the out-system base, a monitor ship permanently grounded on a moonlet orbiting in the system's Oort cloud.

A clear dry voice answered her hail.

"Greetings, *Zvezda*. Take orbit six-three-eight, landing station forty-two."

"Thank you, Control," Khina answered. Hara busied himself with the orbit calculations as *Zvezda* descended into the orbital plane of Arcturus, Novy Strana's yellow sun. The tactical display screen winked with markers for several hundred ships, mostly in-system plying the traffic to the rich Arcturan asteroid belts. Novy Strana's fortune still lay in the ores it shipped to the mother-state on Earth, although new products from the Bootean trade routes were building a steady Earth market, particularly the rare crystals created by the tectonics of alien worlds. Rinn had tapped the ship's computers to study *Zvezda*'s home port, preparing herself with information that might be useful in coming battles. From the tension she sensed in Yuri's mind, she knew that the battles were inevitable. A bureaucratic state also reduced many things to one fundamental.

But she also sensed that he did not mind the conformity or the arcane political warfare within Novy Strana's bureaucracy. He still found room to exercise his independence, more than Rinn had ever found in the enclave. Racism was more inflexible than politics, for the Soviets valued results, however achieved. A captain might squeak through anything, provided he brought in the results—and if a commissar chose to champion the practicality of that success and then won the political dustfight with his or her peers. Galina had said that this Kirova might be such a champion. Maybe.

Hope can be a weakness, she reminded herself. Don't expect too much or you may be unprepared.

She sat at her computer station and watched *Zvezda*'s slow approach to the blue-gray world of Novy Strana, now in half-eclipse. On its dark side, an interlinked sparkle of bright light-points marked its busy capital. *Zvezda* descended through night skies to her home port, guided by transponder emissions from the web of navigation satellites circling the planet. The ship entered the lower atmosphere, air molecules screaming off her smooth hull, palpable as a shimmering whine through the thick walls of the ship. Rinn watched the planet turn beneath the ship, a beautiful world still half-occupied, man's new outlet for the bursting cities of Earth, new resource for the raw materials demanded by Earth's industries.

She wondered if the bureaucrats of Novy Strana recognized the inevitable changes forced by a frontier—and how long they would tolerate demands from the mother-state who pretended her interests still matched theirs. Xin Tian competed with Earth in its revolutionary zeal, pretending its goals a continuation of Earth's needs. For a time, that might last—perhaps a long time. But events moved more quickly on Novy Strana; in Yuri's willingness to take risks, to push the system into a new pattern, she sensed a restlessness of spirit that might yield a new pattern, one most uncomfortable to Earth.

"Calling *Zvezda*," the radio said as the ship began her descent to the sprawling port near the capital.

"*Zvezda* here," Khina said.

"Confirming landing at Nexus forty-two."

"Acknowledged. Beginning final approach." Khina turned to Yuri to make her formal report. "We have clearance to land, sir."

Yuri nodded. "Continue program."

Rinn sensed the tension on the control deck, each a subtle

variance. Khina feared for her and doubted a ruling power that still kept its Asian minorities in warrens. Hara met the future with equanimity, guarding his emotions with a fatalistic acceptance of any possibility. Rinn appreciated their empathy and returned it, to both of them. From Tatiana Nikolaevna, confusion and a determination to advance her own interests; from Oleg Konstantin, a complacent and typical assurance that his report would rule the day. From Galina Kirillovna and Roblev, both busy at tasks on a lower deck, she sensed little, as they hid their emotions within efficiency and plans for their debriefing interviews at the Bureau. And from Yuri, a blend of concern, of hope, of muted desire, laced by his habit of worry that he held as a talisman for success.

She glanced at him, less optimistic—yet she, too, had her hopes for a place aboard his ship. Strange, she thought, to wish for a goal controlled by Normals—and perilous. For too long she had looked to the Gift and the Starfarers who shared it; to wish otherwise . . .

But still she did wish, and she watched Yuri's face as *Zvezda* settled to its home port berth.

After the routine landing checks exchanged with the spaceport tower, the *Zvezda* crew prepared to disembark. Rinn retreated to her assigned quarters and prudently packed the few belongings given to her during her limited stay aboard the ship.

"Ready?" Yuri asked from her doorway. She turned and smiled at him, then saw Tatiana behind him. Their eyes met. A brief flare of emotion flashed between them, and the trade officer's expression hardened. What will you do, Trade Officer? Rinn wondered.

"I think she should stay on ship," Tatiana said, "until her status is resolved." Her tone implied that she expected the decision to go only one way.

The captain turned and scowled at her. "Your opinion wasn't asked." Tatiana set her jaw and strode off down the corridor.

"She intends trouble," Rinn warned.

"I don't need your Gift to know that, Rinn." He spread his hands, his smile warm. "Come, Starfarer; let me show you my home."

"Gladly." She joined him at the doorway and felt his fingers slip into hers. His lips brushed her forehead, then lingered a moment before he stepped away.

She followed him to the ladder and downward to the receiving bay. The ship hatch stood open, the decontamination procedure completed. Two technicians had entered the ship with their instruments, their heads bent over dials as they swept through their checks of *Zvezda*'s efficiency. Four others stood outside, as busily intent on their tasks. Yuri brushed past them and descended to a ground-car waiting below. Its twin thrummed alongside, ready to race away toward the distant port buildings surrounding the broad field as soon as the last of *Zvezda*'s crew left the ship. Above the sky glinted a deep mauve as Arcturus sank toward the horizon, ending another day.

Rinn settled herself beside Yuri and Khina in the rear of the ground-car, then glanced hesitatingly at her companions, Galina seated beyond Khina, Hara in the front seat. Galina smiled at her.

"Welcome to Novy Strana, Rinn," she said kindly, nodding her blond head.

"Thank you."

Yuri tapped the driver's shoulder, and they accelerated away from the ship, whispering over the asphalt field.

"It is good to be home," Hara rumbled, as he looked at the wide landing field and the distant huddled shapes of the city. Rinn sensed the engineer's satisfaction in a task completed, his eagerness to see family and friends. The emotion whispered in the others also, a gestalt that shimmered among a crew familiar with each other, each comforted by their shared homeland. She relaxed into the perception with a sigh and thought wistfully of the Xin Tian enclave, her closest equivalent. But an enclave was not the same, only a beachhead on another people's world and one reluctantly granted.

She looked forward through the curving windshield to the low profile of *Zvezda*'s portside and wondered if the Starfarers would ever find a world of their own—and how they might find it.

I'll think of that later, she told herself, and smiled.

Portside approached steadily, finally changing into a row of four-story buildings, grimly efficient in their design and construction. Rinn craned her head near her window to look upward at the blank-eyed windows, shadowed with the deepening gloom of dusk. The car turned at a busy intersection and entered a wide avenue, divided by plantings and neat concrete curbs, then rolled to a stop before a wide building in the plaza at the avenue's end. *Zvezda*'s crew disembarked and mounted the steps to its brightly lit interior.

"Space Bureau," Yuri murmured to her. "We're scheduled for the standard debriefings, so stay by me."

"Yes."

"Don't worry, Rinn," he added, smiling down at her as he squeezed her elbow, but she sensed that he spoke mostly to himself. For all his assurances, the captain was none too sure of her reception.

They followed Khina, Hara, and Galina across the marbled floor to a guard's desk in the center of the wide foyer. The man, dressed in drab uniform, looked up with a scowl, his attitude officious and well accustomed to his authority. Several soldiers armed with laser-rifles stood at easy attention along the curved wall, visible accompaniment to the guard's aplomb. Rinn felt a prickle of apprehension flicker along her spine, a reminding of half-sensed memories she still tried to forget.

"Your names?" the guard said harshly.

"Selenkov, commanding *Zvezda*," the captain answered, then gestured toward the others and herself. "Four of my crew— the others will arrive shortly."

"Names?" The guard's yellow-brown eyes swept over them, then fixed on the ledger before him.

"Termez, Usu, Sakharova, McCrea."

The guard frowned at his ledger. "You haven't any crew listing for McCrea. Where is Tontova?"

"Deceased," Yuri said, his jaw tightening. "That's in my verbal report. What room numbers for our debriefing?"

The guard stared at Yuri unpleasantly, then examined each of them in turn, passing quickly over the two Kazakhs, his eyes flicking between Rinn and Galina. Rinn sensed his attempt to identify the intruder, as well as his irritation at the unexpected problem. This guard did not like departures from routine—no, he *hated* irregularity—and she suspected that quality to be his chief value to the Bureau. An able gatemaster, although unfortunate for the unexpected problem. She set her face impassively, enduring the man's suspicion.

"This must be investigated," he decided. "Wait here." He rose and stamped across the floor to an arched door and disappeared. Two of the nearer soldiers shifted slightly, their attention sharpened on *Zvezda*'s small party.

"It looks like *Nauka* didn't fink on us," Yuri murmured. "I wondered if Shemilkin would preempt us with a warp-capsule." He smiled at Rinn. "I guess he returned us *Aryol*'s old favor."

"Why the arms?" Rinn asked, glancing at the soldiers.

"Procedure," Yuri answered shortly.

"Kazakh rioters, probably," Hara said, stretching, then

smiled affably at Rinn. "We're a dangerous group, and Mother Russia has a long memory."

"Quiet, Hara," Yuri said irritably. "No jokes, please."

"What jokes?" Hara looked at Yuri blandly.

Khina snickered, then bit her lip as Yuri glared at her. Galina Kirillovna toed at the grouted border of a floor tile near her foot. As Hara opened his mouth again, she silenced him with a warning look. It was effective—Hara settled himself to waiting patiently, a quality bred into his race by centuries in the Rodina.

After a few minutes, the guard returned, accompanied by Deputy Minister Zerenkov, a portly official in an ill-fitting uniform. The second man's face was set in an unpleasant irritation, his small eyes flicking incessantly.

"What? What?" he barked as he reached the guard station. "Comrade Captain, your explanation!"

"Comrade Deputy," Yuri said tightly, "It's in my report. We are waiting for our debriefing." He could not control the edge to his voice, and Rinn sensed his quickened heartbeat and sharpened attention as his body tensed to the man's threat. She glanced aside at the armed guards and the wide hall, and felt the closing bars of a trap.

Yuri perhaps hoped to take one issue at a time, but Rinn did not have such luxuries. Concealing her identity now might make matters worse later. She reached into her breast pocket and brought out her Star, then held it up for Zerenkov to see.

"I am Rinn McCrea, Starfarer," she said quietly. "With contract to the Xin Tian ship, *Sing Fa*. I claimed Treaty sanctuary, which *Zvezda* granted. Any fault draws from my request, not *Zvezda*'s acceptance."

Zerenkov stared with widened eyes, then recoiled a step. "Guards!" he shouted, his voice high. He retreated another step, pointing at Rinn. "Put her in detention! Now!"

"Sir!" Yuri protested in despair.

Zerenkov's mouth twisted. "Them, too," he ordered, pointing at each of *Zvezda*'s company. "All of them!"

He turned on his heel and stamped off toward the exit, his footsteps growing more hurried as he crossed the marble floor, as if Rinn carried an airborne taint that diminished with distance—if one escaped. The guards lifted their rifles, keeping their own careful distance. Rinn saw the repressed panic in their eyes; they, too, had witnessed her self-identification. She swallowed uneasily and held herself immobile, offering no excuse for a rash laser-bolt. She had heard of the unthinking prejudice that possessed some Normals, a blind fear that struck to injure and eliminate, satisfied only with the extinction of the threat. She felt that fear stir among the several guards who watched them, each hesitating to be the first to approach her group.

She lowered her eyes to the Star still clutched in her hand. She thought herself immortal, she realized—like all humans. Telepaths had not lost that quality. Would they kill her? Without a chance to defend herself? But what defense could she give them?

She lifted her eyes and stared forward, meeting no one's gaze. I am Rinn, Starfarer . . . After a moment, she heard footsteps behind her as one guard began his approach; the others quickly copied.

"Comrade Captain," a young voice said, copying Zerenkov's harshness, "you will come with me."

"Yes." Yuri sounded defeated, and Rinn repressed all reaction to his despair. Not here, she told herself. Caution. Caution.

The lieutenant beckoned to two of the hall guards, then motioned with his rifle toward the door to the left. "That way."

The guards herded them through a low doorway and into the corridor beyond. They walked quickly, passing through a guardpost at the far end, then descending a riser of stone steps to a dimly lit corridor that stretched the length of the building. The guards' footsteps rang hollowly behind them as they walked deep under the building to another descending stair and another blank-doored corridor, narrower still with another guardpost in a small alcove.

"Halt!" the lieutenant ordered, then saluted the squat officer seated at the desk. "Prisoners, Comrade Sergeant, with this woman"—the laser butt nudged Rinn's side—"to be confined alone. Put the others in a common cell."

"And the charge?" The sergeant lazily opened a ledger book on his desk and picked up his pen.

"Deputy Minister Zerenkov is preparing the charges." The sergeant stiffened slightly at the mention of Zerenkov's name, and he swiftly reappraised the small group of prisoners. "At this point, list them as 'pending.' "

"I see."

Rinn gathered an impression that some "pending" prisoners never received further classification, that action having become irrelevant. Novy Strana still shared that habit with the Soviet mother-state, whatever other changes had developed on the frontier. Her companions looked confused, apparently unaware of the significance—but, then, political prisoners never earned assignment to Novy Strana's precious survey ships.

Only the innocent, she thought. The brave, the ardent, the young with unjaded eyes . . .

Always the disillusioned leaders of humanity's worlds found new youth to exploit. She looked cautiously around the dingy corridor, seeing the inadequate lighting and the scuffed floors. And perhaps I, too, am an innocent.

But she would not doubt the enclave yet. Yet this place invited despair: it seeped from the walls, permeating the air. Nearby she sensed the thoughts of other prisoners, long past hope, each possessed with plans of wild escape to the outland or another colony, unassailable defenses to a silent committee, self-justification, fear, panic, pain. She closed her eyes, blocking out the perceptions, not wishing to listen.

"This way," the sergeant growled. Rinn came to herself with a start and saw their escorts leaving up the stair, her ship companions huddled together. As the sergeant motioned with his sidearm, Khina's eyes flashed with defiance.

No, sister, Rinn thought desperately, *it is not the time* . . . To her surprise, the thought made contact. Khina jerked and looked at Rinn, then nodded. The sergeant led them past several doors, then unlocked one door and motioned to Rinn. As the door shut, Rinn heard the muffled sounds of another door unlocking and more footsteps. Then silence.

She sat down on the narrow cot and examined her cell. Above her head on the low ceiling a naked bulb shed its bluish illumination on rough-plastered walls and a stone floor. The cot took up a third of the space in the narrow cell, a toilet and washstand most of the remainder. The room held nothing else, an able place to remember political sins.

Rinn lay back on the thin mattress and stared upward. It would be so easy to feel angry—and be weakened. Likely anger was the first emotion that blessed these cells—anger at the disappointment of one's plans, at injustice, at one's own fear of such entrapment. On Ikanos, the adepts claimed a superior control of emotions, part of their claim to a superior humanity. Even the enclaves could not restrain a certain smug tolerance of the fears and angers that still gripped Normals, so often directed at the Starfarers themselves.

But without emotions, Ikanos had become a blighted place. Had the enclaves found a better alternative? She had thought so, but even that gave her few defenses against this place.

She counted the tiles in the ceiling, lingering at those nearest the bulb. She glanced away, her vision blurred by light-shocked sparkles and drifting geometry. She followed one of the shapes with her eyes, driving it across the edge of her vision until her eyes again focused on the rough plaster above the cot. The emotions of other prisoners again seeped through the walls of her cell, surrounding her.

With a sigh, she retreated into other-mind. She floated, half-aware, drawing lightly upon the pleasure centers in her mind to enshroud herself in an artificial happiness. She warmed herself at the glowing coil of the Gift and sorted through her memory box like a child with her toys, drifted through dream-veils. She listened to her own breathing and heartbeat, studying their traces within her own mind. *Touch there and you can control . . . see the pattern.* As the hours drifted, she tired of her self-made distractions. She emerged from other-mind with a sullen defiance.

I do not submit, she thought. She had outlasted the adepts of Ikanos for ten years, a child who defied all control. They had won some battles and had inflicted their punishments, but she had outlasted them. Her defiance had accompanied her to the enclave, had created problems in the beginning as she watched all with suspicion, reacting more from interior scars than to new conditions. The enclave had been patient, had waited. And, in time, they had allowed her to take a berth on *Sing Fa*.

And so she had compromised, given loyalty to *Sing Fa* for unequal return. It had not saved her ship. *Zvezda* had offered her equality—perhaps, it was still in promise—and was in danger because of that offering.

She sat up and smiled grimly. I will be the child again, the child I was, she told herself. It was her victory, that escape from Ikanos; compromise had only brought her ambiguity.

I am Rinn, Starfarer . . .

It was time to choose that identity, without equivocation. She reached out with her mind to nearby prisoners and absorbed their despair as the foundation stone to her gestalt of Novy Strana. She must understand her captors, and the Gift would lend the instruction. She reached higher to the levels above where guards processed endless papers—she listened to their obedience, an inattention to wider consequences, a tendency to corruption—and brought it into herself. Then she touched still higher, where bureaucrats pursued their politics, making their secret plans behind socialist deference. She studied Zerenkov in particular detail, sensing that he was oblivious to her intrusion—and taking satisfaction that she realized his worst fears in doing so.

She touched the other high officials of the Trade Bureau, strained for other ministers in distant buildings, and wove all into her gestalt. Some focused only on the internecine battles of their department, seeking a few limited luxuries, a small power over their fellows, perhaps bare survival in difficult times. Others looked to a wider purpose and worried about increasing demands from the Earth mother-state, greedy for the new technological products of Bootean worlds as its own reserves lay exhausted.

Then she found Commissar Kirova as the woman prepared for bed in a distant and comfortable dacha. Kirova longed for new tools to advance knowledge, the welfare of the state, the fortunes of her people, her competent mind weaving all into a pattern of deft influence, subtle threat, a sure knowledge of fatal error and acceptable risk. *There*, and *there*, as a harpist deftly plucked the strings, or a potter guided his spinning wheel. Even then Kirova thought of the startling report of a Starfarer aboard *Zvezda*; her elation laced by a detached worry for her agent Galina, overborne by her automatic sorting and assessment of the current personalities in the Bureau. Deftly, the commissar laid her plans for the morrow, unwittingly baring them to Rinn.

Rinn left Kirova behind and stretched further, seeking more. In the broad pattern of the city, a few secretly dreamed even of independence, of the horizons of a new *Rodina* that would heal the errors of a bloated and lethargic socialism that crushed initiative. Once a twentieth-century premier had sought to open windows to *pereistroika*, seeking change and a new life for his people, only to fall before the juggernaut of the *Pamyat*, those dour-faced conservatives who feared change and refused any diminishment of their personal power. For two centuries, the *Pamyat* had imposed its iron controls of a New Leninism, forcing the state and economy to totter onward until the Soviet star colonies could pour their plenty into the mother-state's coffers, at first a trickle, then a stream, then the river underpinning the mother-state's very existence.

Yet now another current was moving through Novy Strana's echelons of power, impelled by the vibrancy of colonial challenge, of worlds to conquer, of scientific achievements too glittering to fall always before political expediency. Novy Strana still struggled in its set patterns imposed by Earth and its own political convictions, but still it evolved, changed by a prism largely unknown to the managers who had founded it and only vaguely glimpsed by the colonists who acted within it.

Life! The colony glowed with life, the human challenge of the stars. Rinn fell into the gestalt of the world, seeking, knowing, gathering all to herself. She became Novy Strana, straining beyond all she had ever attempted, and bound all into herself.

I am the Rodina, the new motherland . . .

She blinked and wrenched herself from the gestalt, nearly risking the loss of herself. But it was done. She stared at the wall above the washstand, assembling the information in her mind, some only half-perceived and random, some strangely comforting in its familiarity to Ikanos and even the enclave.

Then she smiled. She had no plan as yet, but at least she knew the people who might end the need for any plan—and those who might help. She only hoped that *Zvezda* would not be ended with her, if she failed.

Yes, I will try for that, she promised herself.

Her smile widened. I am Rinn, Starfarer . . .

And I am very dangerous.

Chapter 15

TIME PASSED SLOWLY . . . A DAY, A SECOND DAY, yet a third day . . . without a visitor besides the guard who brought food. Rinn spent most of the time deep in other-mind, gathering her strength, but also studied and listened with the Gift. Her companions from *Zvezda* across the corridor had a less easy time, and now included Tatiana, Oleg, and a doubtful Roblev. Another day passed, and Rinn waited patiently.

A security officer came to interrogate the others but learned little to satisfy him. Neither Tatiana's wild accusations, Yuri's sullen defiance, nor Khina's strange hilarity made sense to a mind bent upon routine and careful behavior. His superior succeeded him, a more artful mind who better understood the twists and turns of political fortunes. Both men carefully avoided Rinn's cell; her smile flickered as she read their unconscious assumption that a metal door and stone walls were defense against the Gift, as if telepathy were a physical assault to be restrained like all other passions.

I am Rinn, Starfarer, she sent playfully at the superior, a crafty man of middle years named Sirov, but he heard nothing. She sat cross-legged on her cot, reexamining her narrow room stone by stone, and waited.

Sirov came to her on the fifth day. As he entered the cell-block, Rinn looked up sharply and thought for the first time of a video-spy set in the ceiling. Somewhere in the building a technician had activated a relay; the action floated through the mélange of thoughts and emotions like a float in a current. Perhaps she had missed the action before and had been observed; perhaps not. Sirov's bootsteps approached her door, accompanied by the heavier tread of the cellblock guard. She heard a metallic click as the guard inserted an electronic key, then passively watched Sirov enter the room.

"I am Colonel Sirov," the stocky man said. He was dressed neatly in a dun-colored uniform, his blue eyes as sharp as his trouser creases. Rinn heard the wariness in his mind, but no fear. A confident man, Sirov.

"Good afternoon," she said, not bothering to shift her position on her cot.

Sirov hesitated, examining her face.

"I sprout my fangs tomorrow," she added, baring her teeth.

"Ah, humor." Sirov was unimpressed. "Good. You keep up your spirits, Starfarer." He leaned against the wall and crossed his arms, both mindful of the shadow of the guard outside the cell. "So where should I begin my interrogation?" he said affably. "I have a report to file—Novy Strana fuels itself on reports. Perhaps you can assist me."

"The charge is already known, and I have no defense to the charge." She shrugged. "Say what you like."

"Ah." Sirov studied her a moment. "Perhaps we can begin with your sabotage of *Sing Fa*."

Rinn bared her teeth again. "Ah," she mocked him.

"Then we can proceed to your mind-control of *Zvezda*'s officers, the induced alien attack upon the ship, and your criminal assault upon Second Officer Konstantin."

"You forgot igniting the volcano."

"Ah, so I did."

"I demand communication with my enclave."

"Noted, but it isn't necessary." Sirov's teeth gleamed. "Xin Tian's ambassador learned of your custody and informed his government. A ship arrived yesterday for your extradition—they, too, call certain things 'capital crimes.' I believe a Starfarer accompanies them."

"Ah. Why aren't you afraid of me?"

Sirov shrugged, his expression hard. "It's a simple test. If I develop any hesitation about your guilt, you have obviously tampered with my mind—and thus given the Bureau further proof of your crimes."

"An interesting jurisprudence."

"Yes, isn't it? Let's begin with your sabotage of *Sing Fa*."

Rinn studied his face, considering her options. Sirov expected denials, protestations of innocence, perhaps pleas for mercy—he met them often in these cells and had learned to discount them. Guilt lay in the fact of imprisonment, not in facts—did he truly believe that? A man accepted his role, learned to live within its restraints and convictions. Sirov had applied his competence as surely as Yuri Selenkov.

"What do you know of Ikanos?" she asked.

"Irrevelant. Stay on my topic, please."

"Not irrelevant. Or, rather, all things can be irrelevant or relevant, your choice. You know your charges exceed reason, but the excess is also irrelevant—a predetermined judgment gives little room for discussion. I am condemned by my Gift; *Zvezda*'s fault lies in my choice to live." She shrugged. "But, to play out your game: my ship was attacked by hostile natives and its crew died. Two survived the initial attack; one survived the trek to *Zvezda*. My fault to be the survivor; Selenkov's fault to be incapable of denying me sanctuary. In our humanity, we are both condemned."

Sirov looked at her impassively. "You induced the natives to attack."

"One fault leads to another; they followed me south and found new prey."

"And Konstantin?"

"I lack the Gift for physical place. Had I not lacked that sense, I could have warned him. My fault again." She smiled thinly. "You see? We are not so far apart as you thought. All we need do is build the logical chain from the first flaw—my Gift. Then all makes sense. A tautology. The Gift is the Gift is the Gift, and you have your neat solution."

"Novy Strana proscribes your kind."

"Novy Strana proscribes Ikanos—with good reason. So do the Starfarers. Again a meeting of the minds. When will I see my enclave representative? I do have political rights guaranteed me by Xin Tian's contract, whatever their angers."

"That will be arranged. As you said, all other matters are disposed."

"Thank you."

Sirov examined her a moment, his lips tight. She sensed his careful review of his own feelings and smiled, amused.

"No change? You are resolute indeed, Comrade Colonel." She smiled more broadly at his flash of anger. Perhaps it was unwise to provoke him, but the man relied on the customary, had too many defenses against his chosen enemies. In his unfamiliarity with telepaths might lie a key—if there was a key, she reminded herself.

Sirov straightened and saluted her casually, then left the cell. The door sighed shut behind him.

She waited another day, aware of the other prisoners on every side. Near midafternoon, the cellblock guard shifted half of *Zvezda*'s crew to another cell, not knowing the reason for the order. Then another presence descended the stairs, and she sat up quickly, her mind suffused with relief and welcome.

Connor!

At attention, Starfarer, Connor answered warmly, his thought abstracted by his focused attention on the Bureau official, a woman, who accompanied him. Rinn heard footsteps approach her cell, and the door slid sideways to reveal her visitor.

"Ten minutes," the woman said harshly, then retreated to her guard station, her heels a sharp sound pattern on the stone floor.

Rinn ran the few steps to Connor and threw her arms around him. *Connor, Connor . . .* she thought raggedly, and then hid her face against his chest. *Safe . . .*

Little one, he replied and stroked her hair. Then he gently disengaged himself and guided her back to the bunk. He looked down at her, his tanned face serious. He looked older, she thought distractedly, much older than she remembered. He was approaching fifty, his hair graying, his face more deeply grooved. *You realize this matter is serious, Rinn,* he said soberly.

Yes. I am already condemned.

Connor's mouth quirked. *By more than Novy Strana and its proscriptive rules. Xin Tian wants your hide. What happened at Delta?*

In a flashing series of images and thought, she told him. Connor looked grave as she finished.

You are the only witness?

Yes.

Connor looked away a moment, weighing options and strategies, then regarded her. *A pickle, little one.*

Rinn smiled. *Definitely. Any ideas?*

I can probably block Xin Tian's protest—the enclave still has influence with the committee, and the delegation here has its own political stew with the Soviets. After all, Captain Hung was poaching. He scowled. *Tell me what you've learned of this world.*

She spread her gestalt in her mind and relaxed. Connor's presence moved in, and together they examined the perceptions.

How did you know I would seek a gestalt? she asked.

You survive, my dear; it would be necessary to understand this place. Your conclusions about Sirov?

He cannot be turned.

I agree. Well, we will see what we can do. Perhaps I can persuade the Xin Tian delegation to care more about its politics than its outrage.

As he turned toward the door, Rinn reached out her hand. *Connor . . .*

He bent forward and pulled her to her feet, then wrapped her in another embrace. *Courage, Rinn. You have the strength, I know it. And I am here.*

Thank you.

Connor tapped on the celldoor, then waited for the guard's approach. As the door opened, he looked back at her a moment, then stepped outside. She sank back onto the bunk and listened to his presence as it left the cellblock like a guttering flame.

She reached out to Yuri in the nearby cell and found him puzzling over the visitor to her cell. He sat on the floor in the wide cell, arms balanced on his knees, hands hanging loosely. Nearby Khina slept, her head on Hara's thigh; against the far wall, Galina stared unfocusedly ahead. Yuri had no idea why the others of his crew had been moved to a nearby cell. He sat patiently, his fear pricking at his mind, not knowing if the future was fair or foul. On Novy Strana, such predictions were too often unavailable to young ship captains who displeased the Trade Bureau. Yuri accepted that, having learned that protest caused even greater displeasure.

Rinn stretched out her hand to the wall of her own cell and laid her palm flat on the stone. *Yurushka.* But he was lost in his own patient waiting, fixed upon the passing of the hours until an answer might be known. Because of her, he sat in this place; she bowed her head and wished it otherwise. Survival for herself—she had thought only of that. But how could she save *Zvezda,* too?

Connor had not even mentioned it. Perhaps, to him, the only concern was survival of one's own breed. The rational choice, she supposed. She let her hand fall and resumed her own waiting, ever aware of her crewmates nearby.

* * *

The next morning Sirov arrived with a busy noise of footsteps and murmured voices. Rinn listened as *Zvezda*'s crew were roused from sleep and shepherded up the stairs, their murmured questions unanswered. A half-hour later, Sirov returned and her own cell door opened, framing Sirov's stocky body. His face held no expression, bland in his unquestioning determination.

"Get up, Starfarer." His tone gave the rank little honor.

"I am ready."

Rinn accompanied Sirov down the narrow corridor, then up the riser of stairs, retracing her steps of five days earlier to the upper level. At the main lobby, Sirov turned left toward a bank of elevators, and they were whisked upward to a higher floor. Sirov preceded her into a high-ceilinged room fronted by tall windows that looked out over the square. Three men and two women sat at a long table beneath the windows, *Zvezda*'s crew in serried chairs to their right. To their left sat a delegation of four Chinese, two men and two women, each dressed in bulky blue cotton tunic and trousers, their expressions petulant. Connor sat next to them, serene and secretly amused. Rinn envied his confidence.

As she entered the room, she caused a stir among the Xin Tian officials, and each fixed her with an outraged glare. She bowed to them, copying Connor's calmness, then followed Sirov to a chair next to Yuri.

"Are you well?" Yuri murmured anxiously as she sat down next to him.

She felt the varying emotions of the others near him, from Khina's glad relief to Tatiana's sullenness, an unconscious greeting none realized they offered. Perhaps in time, she thought, if this unaccountably ends well, they will learn what they offer. She smiled at Yuri. "I am well. And you?"

"Silence!" barked the man at the end of the table. "The prisoners will not speak to each other!"

The woman in the middle rearranged a sheaf of papers beneath her hands, then pushed back a strand of hair that had escaped her smooth chignon. Blond, severe, and authoritative, she wore the brown trade uniform well. Kirova. Rinn glanced at Tatiana—the resemblance was striking.

Connor, look at that.

Connor's eyes flicked from the trade chief to Tatiana. *Hmmm,* he thought, *interesting. Another element for our stew.*

In more ways than you know. She is the woman in the dacha.

Indeed.

Rinn glanced quickly at the Xin Tian delegation. The Chinese still looked petulant, and she sensed their simmering rage. In this blend of political embarrassment and opportunity, would Xin Tian sacrifice her to excuse *Sing Fa*'s own fault? Grimly she sensed that exact plan in their intentions.

"Your attention," Kirova said in a harsh voice. "I am Natalya Mihalovna Kirova, Chief Hearings Officer. I will chair this inquiry. To my right is Pyotr Sergeivich Golovin, Second Trade Deputy, to his right Nikolina Semyonovna Goroskaya, Sub-Minister of Fleet Affairs." The dark-haired man and plain-faced woman stared impassively forward. "To my left is Dmitri Ilarionovich Brodsky, Political Deputy for Trade Affairs," she continued, nodding to the gray-haired man beside her, "and Andrei Arkadyevich Krasin, Second Hearings Officer."

Rinn sensed another title for Krasin behind Kirova's words and caught an echo from Sirov as he stood behind her chair. Secret police, she silently amended, and examined Krasin surreptitiously. His dark eyes were as bland as Sirov's own, but she sensed a complicated mind, with deep secrets and dark memories of interrogations, political triumph, and a complex web of paranoia and race-pride shared by the others. There were currents abroad in the room, a web of political in-fighting among the five—with four sharing a sharp distaste for the imperturbable Krasin—but overlaid by a common purpose. Enemies they might be, but the offworld delegation who waited their justice were the greater enemies. As one, the Board drew together its ranks against their opponents.

With me as the prize, she thought wryly.

Kirova lifted her papers. "We are here to judge the crimes of Delta Ship *Zvezda*. Item One: loss of the Deltean trade base. Item Two: association with a proscribed person, namely, the Starfarer McCrea. Captain Selenkov, you may speak."

Yuri rose to his feet awkwardly, his face a study of apprehension and confusion. "The charges are true, Comrade Chairman." He lifted his chin, staring at her with some defiance. "On the other hand, the First Contact team did not penetrate into the upper peninsula, but established trade only with the southern tribe. Delta Bootis is largely an unknown; it was *Sing Fa*'s misfortune to land in the wrong place." The Xin Tian delegation stirred, their expressions a common mask of suppressed anger and disbelief. Yuri glanced quickly at them, then straightened his shoulders. "As to the sanctuary extended to the

Starfarer, sanctuary is a Treaty right that recognizes mercy to another human, whatever her nature. The Sunstone would not have understood any other choice.''

Tatiana stood up abruptly.

"You have a comment, Trade Officer?" Kirova said, her expression distant and harsh.

"Only to say that the Sunstone value obedience. Apparently they are subservient to this Lily tribe; we defied their tribal taboos by denying them the person they demanded." Tatiana glanced angrily at Rinn. "The argument cuts both ways—"

"And therefore was a command decision," Yuri interrupted. He spread his hands. "I accept this commission and this trial. It is necessary that the Bureau review all decisions by its captains. I protest, however, any political fault. I made the choice for other reasons and found need for an exception."

"Exceptions dilute established policy," Brodsky rumbled, his eyes cold. "I do not accept your argument."

Yuri clenched his hands; Rinn sensed his despair. He lifted his chin again. "Then I ask that the fault be mine alone. My crew either opposed or doubted my decision; they should not be held to blame."

Khina rose to her feet. "I do not accept that exception; I support the captain's decision."

Tatiana stared at the tiny biologist, incredulous, then gawked further as Hara and Galina also rose to their feet. After a moment, Viktor also stood.

"Doctor Roblev?" Commissar Kirova asked, just as astonished.

Roblev shrugged ruefully. "It is a day for pyrrhic actions, Comrade Chairman. Captain Selenkov's heroism has apparently affected us all."

Krasin's eyes hardened. "Or another influence, Doctor." His gaze shifted to Rinn with distaste.

"True," Roblev countered, "the sanctity of one's mind was considered an absolute—until Ikanos. But its possession may be judged against external events. She has earned this loyalty, Comrade Deputy." He grimaced. "I had my doubts, I admit, but now doubt is forced to a resolution, one way or the other. I support Captain Selenkov's choice." His words rang as a challenge, and the Board did not appreciate it.

Rinn looked from face to face, reading opposition and displeasure. They had not expected this—nor, she realized with a swift glance to the side, had Connor. She sensed his rapid rejuggling of advantage and deficit. *See the pattern, Connor,* she told him silently.

"Be seated," Kirova said irritably. "We need no further demonstrations." Her eyes fixed on Rinn. "Starfarer McCrea, you have earned a surprising loyalty from your borrowed ship, but I am not yet persuaded. Novy Strana has ample documentation of your kind's evil. Do not be encouraged."

"As I discussed with Officer Sirov," Rinn said quietly, "I know my fault is assumed. Continue with your hearing, Madame."

"You admit it, then!" one of the Xin Tian deputies exploded.

"Comrade Chien," Rinn said, "you're mistaking the issue in agreement. *Sing Fa* was unexpectedly attacked by the Lily tribe. The ship crew had no time for defense, and I did not understand the threat until it was too late." She struggled to control her expression. "They died—" Her voice broke and she lowered her eyes.

A silence fell in the room for a moment, then she lifted her head again. "My fault," she said harshly. "I failed. But that is not the issue. We are speaking of an earlier fault, my fault to be born. Are we not, Madame Chairman?"

Kirova scowled. "Ikanos degeneracy is well-known to—"

"I am not of Ikanos," Rinn interrupted proudly. "I am a Starfarer of the Xin Tian enclave."

"They're the same thing," Krasin asserted.

"They are not," Rinn declared.

Careful, Connor warned her, his thought tinged with alarm. *Don't argue with him.*

I don't have much to lose, Connor. "Even if they were," she continued, her eyes fixed defiantly on Krasin, "Ikanos exists. You cannot ignore the Gift any longer, for it has become part of humanity, something to be accepted, not ignored or— proscribed," she added ironically. "How can you proscribe a Gift that penetrates all things?"

"Are you done?" Krasin's dark eyes simmered.

"Not yet." Rinn turned to Chien and his companions. "Xin Tian has accepted us, however uneasily. When I fled Ikanos, they gave me sanctuary. I regret that I could not save *Sing Fa*: I tried, and then tried again to save the lone survivor of its crew. But I failed at that, too. I escaped only with my own life, and now that, too, has become yet another failure."

She bowed solemnly to Chien, then to each of his two companions. "I accept my fault," she said earnestly. "I accept your judgment."

Chien glanced aside to Connor, hesitating. "Your opinion?"

My opinion, Rinn? Connor thought at her, somewhat ruefully.

Just be agreeable.

"I agree," Connor said promptly.

"With what?" Chien asked sharply. His black eyes darted to Rinn suspiciously, then returned to Connor. The older Starfarer looked back blandly.

"Some matters, comrade," Connor drawled, "are best left to speculation."

"Such as surreptitious coordination," Chien snapped. "I know you, Connor Matthieu, you and your devious ways. What do you want?"

Connor pointed at Rinn. "Her freedom. Ask Novy Strana to release her from those closed-minded bureaucrats on a world that considers you no friend. All else can be resolved on Xin Tian."

Chien considered, then shrugged. "I demand extradition!" he declared.

"Denied," Kirova said coldly. "She is an enemy of the state."

"She is one of our own," Connor said smoothly. "The enclave considers this matter very serious, a troubling precedent we expect you to resolve."

"Xin Tian also considers this matter very serious," Chien said to Kirova. "We will not accept a refusal."

"You are refused, nonetheless."

Chien rose. "I must report to my government," he said coldly. He stalked out of the room, followed by his aides. Connor slouched in his chair, amused.

"And so you manipulate, Starfarer," Brodsky said angrily, his head jerking.

"As do you, comrade. I'm afraid you have a serious problem, Comrade Chairman, Comrade Minister. I suggest your assumptions might be frustrated." Connor smiled, showing his teeth. "Ah, politics. Aren't they wonderful?"

Kirova banged her gavel on the table before her. "Return the prisoners to their cells. Judgment will follow in two days. And you, Connor, keep to your ship."

"I demand the right to consult with McCrea."

"Denied."

"I protest."

"Your protest is acknowledged. If you leave your ship, you will be shot."

Connor rose lazily and saluted. "Acknowledged," he said dryly. "A good day to you, comrades."

And you said not to argue, Rinn thought at him.

It seems to suit the situation. Be careful, little one.

Yes.

Sirov nudged her roughly, and she moved forward toward the door, followed by the others. She looked around to Yuri and met his eyes. She sensed his bewilderment—but a new hope.

Maybe, she thought. At this point, nothing was sure.

Chapter 16

TWO DAYS PASSED, THEN THREE, AND STILL THE Bureau did not reach a decision. Yuri had given up pacing the narrow cell he shared with three of his crew. Instead, he most often sat against the wall, arms draped loosely on his knees, as he stared at nothing. It was a time of bleak review of his actions.

Again and again, he thought about his choices—and simply did not see the fault attributed to him. The Bureau acted as if he had committed a political crime. Everything in Novy Strana jurisprudence had its political overtones, true, but Yuri customarily avoided thinking about such implications. He wanted only his ship, a series of trade-points, a chance for excellence—was that so demanding?

Until then, he had lived within his world's restrictions, accepting them as the order of things. And the Soviet system had its strengths: Novy Strana had pushed farther in its explorations than any other colony in Bootes/Hercules, certainly more than her sister-world of Rodina at Mu Bootis. *That* Soviet state contented itself with deference to Earth, happy with its role as a mere pipeline of raw materials. He had visited there once during his university training and had come away unimpressed.

He did not understand the bias against the telepaths. Ikanos had made itself a watchword for degeneracy, true, but Rinn . . . The Starfarers were different; he felt that as certainly as he believed in the essential worth of the Bureau. But now the Bureau sought to destroy him, not caring for facts, holding only to its written rules.

Break one rule, he thought, and all successes become irrelevant. He grieved for his ship and his crew. Through his own fault, he had dragged them all down with him. Yet he could not see what else he could have done.

"Yuri," Khina said, then had to repeat his name to get his distracted attention. She, Roblev, and Galina still shared his cell, but the others were being kept somewhere else. Arbitrary choice? Or was there a purpose in the separation? What purpose?

He focused blearily on the tiny Kazakh woman. "What is it?"

"It might still work out. The Xin Tian delegation and that older Starfarer are working on it—and the Board chairman wants Rinn on *Zvezda*. Don't you think that's some cause for hope?"

Yuri smiled slowly. "Do you really believe that?"

Khina brushed back a wisp of black hair. "Well, to be honest, this kind of political trial usually has a predetermined outcome, but I thought I'd offer." She fell silent.

"I appreciate it."

"You're a good captain," she said fiercely. "You made the right decisions."

Galina Kirillovna nodded, then wrapped her fingers in Roblev's hand. The psychologist sat with his head bowed, his other hand slowly stroking his nose. " 'Matters are bleak, but your comrades stand with you,' " she said, quoting an old Russian saying. She glanced aside slyly at Viktor. "Even Viktor Fedorovich."

"At a testing point, Galinka," Viktor rumbled, unperturbed, "we are all forced to a choice—even dialectic psychologists. I see no fault—and no harm in Rinn."

"Why are they taking so long?" Khina asked fretfully. "I hope Hara's all right."

"I'm sure he's fine," Yuri said to comfort her, and hoped it was true. But why the delay? he wondered. Why was the Board taking so long?

If the verdict were truly predetermined, making testimony irrelevant, all defense pointless, why not pronounce their judgment and be done with it? Perhaps the Board considered options less than stripping Yuri of his command, of condemning Rinn. Perhaps. Yuri had heard that politically inconvenient captains often received reassignment to First Survey ship runs, ostensibly a promotion—*join our comrade heroes*!—but all too often the unknown conditions and unlucky accidents of First Contact neatly solved the Bureau's inconvenience. Novy Strana still lost thirty percent of its ship crews in First Survey; the universe was not an easy frontier.

But it preserved the Board's moral stance: *See! we forgave initiative, unhappy choice, restiveness, political mistake. Believe in the motherland, our Rodina! Too bad, an accident—too bad, a lost ship—but the Rodina advances to the stars!*

Rather hard on the inconvenient, he thought glumly. But still . . . He felt his heartbeat quicken in anticipation. First Survey—he might hope for that.

He had heard of a new robot probe to the farther stars of Bootes, even as far as Izar. The First Survey ships would follow soon; Yuri wondered what they would find. Another alien race, perhaps with a technology equivalent to humanity's own? Another Crystal, where aurorae shifted lazily across ice-rifted plains? Or something new, with new dangers, new discovery?

And perhaps the ships might quest a little wider into Chinese space. Novy Strana would not tolerate *Sing Fa*'s poaching without a suitable riposte. He remembered that the two white stars of Nusakan, the beta point of Corona Borealis, showed strong spectroscopic bands of rare earths—lanthanum, hafnium, rhenium—elements Yuri had seen only in minute amounts in the laboratory yet precious to certain new developments in ship technology. Would Nusakan's planets share that overabundance?

And another peril to study: long-distance studies also showed the gravity imprint of a dark protostar within the Nusakan system, a truly massive planet profoundly stressed and torn by the magnetic instability of its primary suns, perhaps as massive as Vega's dark and unapproachable companion. What dangers to his ship in a magnetic field that reversed every eighteen days, in the massive gravity-well of an unignited star? His mind worked rapidly, as if the mission were already his assignment.

Perhaps it will be, he thought, and repressed a renewed impulse to pace the confines of the cell. Perhaps. He fretted with his inactivity and thought of other possibilities. He could be disranked and put to work in a spaceport industry—he had the skills, he might hope for that. More likely, he might be sent to Sirov's labor camps in the hinterland, an ancient Russion solution practiced by tsars and commissars alike. Perhaps, he thought gloomily, they would choose the easiest solution of all and shoot him.

Anything out of ships is only a lesser death, he thought. He would rather be shot than be put to labor away from ships.

Why were they taking so long?

The third day passed slowly, minutes stretching into hours, paced by a slow heartbeat. Yuri dozed, waking himself twice with his own snores. He felt dull and listless, too enervated by his days of confinement to stir his mind. Idly, he thought of *Zvezda*, picturing her corridors and systems in his mind, planning improvements. He thought of Rinn, speculating again about her Gift and her feelings for him. He thought of magic and the Lily tribe: "The line between science and magic is one of perception," Galina had said, and he ached to meet the challenge, to see if the hazarded chance might work. But all thought trailed away into dullness. Drained, he stared at the opposite wall. When would it end?

At dinnertime, the guard did not bring the trays. They waited an hour, wondering about the change in routine. Morbidly, Yuri thought meals might be irrelevant to executed prisoners—but it signalled an end, perhaps. Near midevening, at last, he heard footsteps on the stairs down the corridor, then a murmur of voices at the guardpost. The footsteps then approached his cell and stopped. He stood up, his eyes fixed on the door.

The door sighed open, revealing Sirov. The man looked disgruntled, his face drawn down into deep lines. He beckoned at them, his hand moving abruptly. "Come!"

"Where?" Yuri asked immediately, his voice sharp.

"No arguments! Come!"

Yuri stepped out into the narrow corridor. Three doors away, the guard had opened another cell, and Oleg already stood in the corridor. The second officer blinked at Yuri, his expression dazed. The remaining crewmen filed into the corridor and stood waiting. Then Sirov stepped to the opposite celldoor and opened it.

"Come!" he barked at its occupant.

"Why?" Rinn's tone sounded defiant, and Yuri quickly joined Sirov at her celldoor. She was sitting on the bed in the small cell, her feet drawn up into a comfortable seat. As he appeared in her line of sight, her dark-blue eyes shifted to him alertly. Yuri sighed, seeing that she was all right.

"Come," he said gently and held out his hand. "It's time."

She hesitated a moment, then uncurled herself from her couch and joined him in two strides, brushing past Sirov.

"Yes—it is the time," she said simply.

"But we are together."

"Yes," she said, taking his hand. "We are together."

Yuri smiled down at her, his relief making him careless in front of Sirov. He saw her answering smile—and a small touch of bemusement. I wonder what she hears in me, he thought. I wonder myself. Perhaps love?

Love. The word sighed in his mind, an odd echo that had the timbre of her voice, not his, as if she had spoken in his ear. He felt no alarm, no rough intrusion; the sensation of her thought drifted across his mind like a flicker of emotion, unmistakably hers yet somehow his.

What? He looked down at her, confused. Her presence resonated through his mind, like the drift of Natalya's perfume through the air. She smiled contentedly.

"That's enough," Sirov said harshly. "Move along."

The order jolted him from his odd contact with Rinn; he scowled at Sirov. "Where are we going?"

"No questions! Move!"

Yuri followed Sirov up the corridor, his hand firmly in Rinn's, followed by the rest of *Zvezda*'s crew. He glanced backward as they neared the stairs and saw looks of hope, of bewilderment, of despair. Tatiana seemed strangely subdued; she met his eyes impassively, revealing nothing. He wondered if she knew anything—probably not. For once, Tatiana's political connections might have failed her.

They mounted the stairs and passed through the Bureau lobby, then again climbed the second stairwell to the hearing room. Hearings Officer Kirova again sat at the center table, flanked by the other four members of the Board. She was as impassive as Tatiana; the expressions of her companions were more mixed, two outright unpleasant. The Board had reached a decision, but not all were pleased with it. Yuri glanced at each quickly, trying to read their faces.

"Be seated," Kirova said. Then, after all had taken their seats in the rank of chairs, she added, "Comrade Sirov, you may go."

Sirov looked surprised, his eyes darting to Krasin. He hesitated, then sketched a salute and left.

"That salute lacked a certain respect," Kirova commented dryly, "but, then, Sirov is a disappointed man. Is he not, Comrade Krasin?"

Krasin said nothing, only glowered.

Kirova shrugged, then reached under the table and snapped a

switch. "Let's keep this conversation private in other ways as well." She looked at Rinn. "Rinn McCrea."

Rinn stood up slowly.

"You intrigue me, Starfarer," Kirova said. "Unlike certain members of this Board, I'm willing to look behind policy to reality—but I do so for my own reasons. As I've told my niece, I will not intervene solely on her behalf. Like all crew aboard our ships, she takes her own risks for her actions. Perhaps in time she will understand that."

Yuri glanced at Tatiana and saw her face harden. So Tatiana *had* tried her political strings.

"The same applies to the demands by Xin Tian and your enclave representative," Kirova continued. "They want you back, but we do not take orders from outsiders, treaties and threats notwithstanding. You are a state criminal, and you will remain in that classification until we are done with you."

Nikolina Goroskaya and Deputy Brodsky nodded their concurrence, their faces stern. One facet of a compromise? Yuri wondered. He glanced at the sullen Krasin and wondered also how Kirova had outmaneuvered him—or whether Krasin was playing a game on the others with his expression.

Kirova leaned back in her chair, her eyes narrowed. "So—the first step to a solution is to eliminate irrelevancy. Family ties are irrelevant; Xin Tian and enclave demands are irrelevant. What remains? All politics are ultimately reduced to self-interest, and my only consideration is Novy Strana and the success of its ships. That is the determinant.

"I consider you a tool to be employed, Starfarer—and, like all tools of great value, potentially dangerous. A knife can cut both its bearer and its victim. But Novy Strana wants that tool. Prove yourself too dangerous and we will dispense with you—but, for the moment, we will try the tool."

"You will agree to Contract?" Strangely, Rinn did not sound surprised. I suppose she wouldn't be, Yuri reminded himself. Will I ever get used to what she knows?

"Contract?" Kirova said. "Don't be ridiculous. You are a criminal, but you will work out your sentence as we choose. As for the others of your crew, *Zvezda* is on probation; the ultimate decision about Captain Selenkov's choices will be proved on Delta Bootis." Her cold gaze shifted to Yuri. "Since you made the problem, Comrade Captain, you will solve it—or else."

"I understand, Comrade Commissar," Yuri said. "I appreciate your bluntness."

Kirova's face relaxed slightly, enough to show approval. "Good. Return to us our trade base, Captain, and we will reconsider *Zvezda*'s fate. I understand from my niece that you have a possible plan; we shall discuss it as *Zvezda* prepares for departure. Bring yourself and Tatiana Nikolaevna to the Bureau at eight tomorrow for consultation. In the meantime, we've ordered Captain Shemilkin and *Nauka* to wait at Delta Bootis to assist you."

"Thank you."

"Shemilkin understands the peril of exceeding orders," Krasin growled. "If you feel tempted again, let him enlighten you."

"He will *assist*," Kirova corrected firmly. "What matters is success."

"Why, of course," Krasin said blandly, his face unreadable.

"Good day, *Zvezda*," Kirova concluded. "May you obtain the success we require."

She stepped off the podium and crossed the room with long strides, her blond head carried proudly, then disappeared through the door. Yuri watched the other members of the Board follow her silently, with a look of interest from Goroskaya to Rinn, and a scowl of warning from Brodsky to himself. Warning? he thought. Of what? As the door shut behind them, a buzz of surprise rose from the crewmen behind Yuri, each offering their speculations. Rinn suddenly bent toward Yuri.

"Flipping that switch meant nothing, whatever Kirova thought," she said in a low voice. "Sirov still listens."

"Yes." Yuri stood up and signalled for silence. "To our ship, *Zvezda*. We should not waste time; we have a new mission."

Spoken like a New Leninist hero, he thought sourly, displeased with himself for the playacting. He was surprised and pleased at the reprieve, but he felt a new worry prick at his mind. Wheels within wheels—would he ever be free of them? Kirova was playing a game he did not understand, something against—linked to?—the security police.

Politics! he thought with distaste, though politics had won *Zvezda* a second chance. Why? Did Rinn know Kirova's real intent?

He looked at her and thought that a tool could be employed by more than one hand. Then he wondered if the Board had also thought of that—and already prepared against them.

* * *

The following morning Rinn waited for Connor on *Zvezda*'s exterior landing, her glad welcome open in her thoughts.

Apparently Connor's ship-bound restriction had lifted with the judgment; at least he walked to the ship from the jitney freely and without fear, despite the surreptitious watching of the cab driver, a woman both he and Rinn knew as Sirov's agent.

Connor . . .

He swept her into a hug and smiled down at her. *Greetings, little one.* His gray eyes swept the landing field around them, taking in the agent waiting patiently at the wheel. Beyond them, two other ships prepared for lift-off, with vehicles whistling to and fro in the bright sunshine from the nearby portside. Far in the distance a third ship set down in a flaring backwash of its jets. The driver sat watching them in her mirror through the Plexiglas roof, then quickly looked away when she saw Connor watching back. *Hard to watch a telepath with any efficiency,* Connor remarked, *though that one could still use some practice in the basics. Too bad to disappoint Sirov; that man delights in all sorts of information.*

Yes, too bad. Rinn smiled up at him. *Come in.* She tugged at his sleeve and led him into the ship.

Zvezda also preoccupied herself with preparations, though with a temporarily reduced crew. Galina Kirillovna and Roblev had business at the Bureau, restocking supplies and consulting with their trade department superiors. Tatiana had likewise absented herself with a delayed return from portside, though she had given no specific reason. Hara had taken a day's leave in the nearby Kazakh warren and was due back that evening.

Rinn felt slightly disappointed at Connor's timing; she had hoped he could meet all aboard *Zvezda*, even Tatiana—though those sparks might not be particularly wise. Somehow she felt protective of *Zvezda*, wanting its crew to be put forward in the best light for Connor's meeting. Of all the Starfarers in the Xin Tian enclave, she still felt closest to Connor, the man who had taken her into sanctuary four years before. During her enclave orientation and training, she had seen Connor regularly; after the years apart for her service aboard *Sing Fa*, she realized how much she had missed him.

Connor, she sent to him happily, intertwining his name with her joy, and felt his amused response, warming her.

Little one.

She found Yuri and Khina on the control deck and introduced them. "Captain Yuri Ivanovich Selenkov, Biologist Khina Termez, this is Connor Matthieu of the Xin Tian enclave. Two of the *Zvezda* crew who rescued me on Delta, Connor.''

"Yes, I'm aware of that." Connor bowed slightly to each.

Yuri rose from his chair and shook Connor's hand. "Welcome to *Zvezda*, sir. You've heard of the Bureau's decision?

"Yes, a good fortune to your ship. I really didn't expect that outcome, but, then, our Rinn is a valuable person—apparently even to your Space Bureau." Connor spoke dryly, his tone affable in its diplomacy but curiously distant. Rinn sensed Connor's wariness and saw Yuri stiffen slightly. She looked from one face to the other, perplexed by the sudden tension in the room.

"Thank you," Yuri said, as carefully formal. "*Zvezda* also knows her value. As I said, welcome."

"Thank you. I ask to consult with Rinn—in private, if possible."

"Certainly."

Connor turned to Rinn and raised an eyebrow. *Lead the way, Rinn.*

"We'll be in my room," she said to Yuri. "This way, Connor."

She preceded Connor down the ladder, pointing out the doors to the lab and equipment rooms, then the doors of the crew quarters.

I'm really not interested in a tour, Rinn, Connor commented, bringing her descriptions to a quick stop, *although it's polite of you to offer.*

I just thought you might like to see, Rinn answered. She hurried her steps toward her room, feeling chastened—though she did not know why.

Connor glanced around the corridor and followed her into her room. *A good ship,* he added politely, but she sensed his lack of any real interest. *But temporary, of course. You're contracted with Xin Tian, however you've intrigued Novy Strana for the moment.*

But won't the Starfarers want new contracts with Novy Strana—if it leads to that?

We don't have an enclave here, Connor replied with a shrug. *Even if we asked, Xin Tian would never permit it—the committee doesn't allow independence even to the smaller enclaves on other Chinese colonies. Even there we live on Xin Tian territory.* Connor's mouth twisted wryly.

Oh. Rinn sat down on her bed, deflated. Connor spent a moment examining the room, then studied the building in the picture on the far wall.

I sense your attachment to this ship, Rinn. It's not wise. Gratitude is one thing; alloying one's loyalty is another.

I'm still loyal to Xin Tian.

Connor turned. *Oh? I don't hear that. True, you could not have prevented the loss of* Sing Fa. *A Starfarer is useful only if Normals listen to the advice. Captain Hung chose not to, and the ship was lost as a result. Apparently the ambassador accepts that and may persuade the committee, though it may be a year or more before Xin Tian will assign you to a new ship. Or you might be grounded permanently; the Chinese still prefer simple solutions—and their suspicions.* He shrugged again. *Unfortunate. You have many talents, Rinn; the enclave will do what it can.*

But, Connor . . .

And there is the matter of the marsh-hunter and the compulsion you inflicted on Captain Selenkov on Delta, he continued inexorably. *I didn't speak of it earlier—other affairs had greater temporary importance—but I must report the breach to the enclave. You do realize what you did?*

I didn't intend to kill it, and the other . . . I was very tired and there was need. Rinn looked down at her hands in her lap, trying to repress her emotions at the unexpected sternness in Connor's thoughts. She had thought she had done well—but somehow she had erred badly, despite everything. She remembered her panic and exhaustion in the marsh, her failure to save Mei-lan. She blinked back tears, ashamed of her fault. Somehow even her friendships aboard *Zvezda* had become fault.

I understand your situation, Connor said more gently, *but our position depends on restraint. If you cannot exercise that restraint, you imperil the enclave. It only takes one rogue Starfarer to undermine everything we have built.*

Yes, Connor.

I can understand your feelings, he added, although she sensed he did not, *but the Normals won't. Ultimately, they determine our safety. I realize you entered this ship in a time of great stress; it made certain options necessary. But you cannot look to this ship for what you seek—what you seek, Rinn, is not available to us, and never will be. I thought you understood that from your experience aboard* Sing Fa. *Whatever you think you've found here is an illusion. Don't trust it—and remember that you belong to our enclave, not* Novy Strana.

She lifted her eyes to his. *They saved my life. Doesn't that count for anything?*

Of course it does—and I appreciate their generosity, for whatever motives it was offered. You are valuable to us, Rinn: you have an empathy for others that is quite marked, even unusual. But each part of the Gift has its corresponding weakness. Don't give into yours.

Rinn studied her hands again, saying nothing. She sensed Connor's annoyance at her resistance and set her mouth stubbornly.

I am not Tolan, Connor said irritably. *Don't make those equations.*

I see what I see—it is my strength.

You see delusion.

I don't think so.

"So," Connor said aloud, breaking their mental rapport. "We shall see." The descent into speech was a slap in the face. She jerked up her head and stared at him. He looked back coolly, his thoughts carefully guarded away. She promptly lifted her own shields, throwing back the insult.

"That's not fair," she said angrily. "You offer only your choice, and don't listen to mine."

"I don't have to be 'fair.' You are misguided, Starfarer—consider this a warning."

"I hear you, Connor."

"Good. I suggest you consider it carefully." He took a step toward the door. "When you return from Delta Bootis, assuming matters go well, contact the legate at the Xin Tian embassy. He'll arrange for your transport home."

"Very well."

He looked back at her from the door and his expression softened.

Rinn . . .

She sensed his concern for her, despite his conviction of the right, and yielded him that much. *Good-bye, Connor.*

Good-bye, little one. Be careful.

Yes. She listened to his footsteps retreat down the corridor and followed his mental presence outside the ship to the waiting cab. The driver whisked him away toward portside. She dug her fingernails into her palms, pressing down hard enough to break the skin. She watched as each painful crescent appeared, then worked to widen them.

She heard Yuri approaching her door and sensed his anxiety.

When he knocked at the doorframe of the open door, she did not look up. He hesitated, uncertain, then turned to leave.

"Don't go," she said.

"What did Connor want?"

"It's not important," she said automatically, then glanced up at him. "Or, rather, it is. Please sit down."

Yuri stepped toward the chair on the other side of the room, then elected to sit beside her on the bed. She sensed his awkwardness; in a way, he was as unaccustomed to some things as she. *I wonder why he wants to reach across our differences,* she thought. *Does he know? Is it even possible? And then: Am I human?* She sensed the question in his mind and knew it still troubled him.

"Assuming we succeed on Delta Bootis," she asked, "what will happen to *Zvezda*—and you?"

"You probably know better on that score. The turnings and twistings of the Bureau can be legendary to mortal minds."

She smiled at him wanly. "I'm not an oracle, Yuri; I don't know everything, whatever your assumptions. Krasin's power struggle with Kirova is still in flux, and my precognition ability is largely infant-level." She shrugged. "Or, rather, I know what Kirova wants—me, at any price. And she can always change her mind."

"Oh." He noticed her hands and turned the bleeding palms to the light. "What in the hell? What *happened* between you two?" He stood up and rummaged in her bureau drawer, then returned with a tube of salve. "Will you tell me?" he asked quietly.

She tugged her hands away and got up. She paced a moment, then stopped in front of the picture on the opposite wall. "What is this building?"

"Something in Moscow, on Earth. A museum, I think. Does this relate at all?"

She turned and smiled at him. "You're very patient. You listen to me—I appreciate that. I appreciate many things about you, Yuri. Connor told me not to trust you."

"I see." Yuri scowled.

"It's the standard Starfarer attitude, with some history behind it." She shrugged. "He told me my liking for this ship is a weakness and warned me against any permanent loyalties. He told me I have a choice of two options—only two—and he expects me to choose Xin Tian."

"But I thought . . ."

She smiled ruefully. "So did I. Perhaps we are deluded." She turned back to the picture. "I resisted, though for your sake or resentment of his single-side choice, I don't know. I don't know what I feel anymore. I don't know what future to seek."

He stood and crossed the short distance between them, then slipped his arms around her waist. She turned in his embrace and kissed him lightly. "I need to think, perhaps to remember. I need some time. I'm afraid most of his message was an ultimatum."

"I thought the enclave gave up that kind of pressure."

"Not necessarily. The right is still the right, and Connor feels obligated to assert it."

"But if he's wrong?"

"Yes, if he's wrong. I need to decide that." She laid her cheek against his.

"I've already made my choice," he murmured against her hair. She sensed his affection and admiration, and warmed herself in it. *Love* . . . The word sighed again between them. She closed her eyes and clung to him as he kissed her again. If she chose *Zvezda*, it would be for that offering, Normal or not— and what it might become.

It was her weakness to wish for such things, Connor had said. Then let it be weakness, she thought defiantly.

Chapter 17

WITHIN A FEW DAYS, *ZVEZDA* WAS READIED FOR
flight to Delta Bootis. Galina supervised the loading of supplies;
Hara assisted the port technicians in minor repairs and the delicate task of replacing the ship's fuel load. Yuri and Tatiana spent
considerable time at the Space Bureau, trading information with
Records and consulting with Kirova, while Khina took advantage of the sophisticated university computer to run a cross-and-
compare analysis of the Delta virus. A jitney whisked Oleg off
to hospital for a treatment and a thorough checkup. Confined to
the ship, Rinn watched the crew of *Zvezda* renew their connections to their home port, feeling adrift. Connor had not returned
to visit before his ship left for Xin Tian.

Not fair! she thought angrily, yet she felt apart and alone, an
uncomfortable reprise of *Sing Fa*'s port visits. She occupied
herself with computer studies and a review of ship systems but
spent much time on her bed, staring at the walls. On the fourth
evening, Yuri found her there, doing nothing. He tapped at the
doorframe, then ambled in and sat down in the single chair.

"You look comfortable," he said cheerfully. Already some
of the lines had smoothed from his young face. She sensed his
satisfaction with his ship's preparations, as an ancient knight
might have contentedly admired his newly oiled cuirass and
harness, anticipating the morning's tourney. Once she had found
escape as a child in the Ikanos library, reading such tales. Ar-

thur, Gawain, Launcelot the Brave . . . The heroism was the same, she thought.

"Rinn?"

"How were the battles today?" she asked lazily. He did not answer, and she turned her head to look at him.

"Are you all right?" he asked uncertainly. "Is this some Starfarer, uh, need?"

"What? Laziness?" She laughed.

"Well, you did sleep that time for four days, and sometimes you go away somewhere." He shrugged. "I just wonder about it."

She turned her eyes back to the picture above her bed. "That I'm human?"

"No." he said. "I don't wonder about that anymore—mainly because I don't care one way or the other. You are Rinn; that's all that matters."

Love. She sighed. "Sometimes the world is too much for me and I escape inside myself, into the other-mind. It must be disconcerting to you."

"Just an equivalent, I suppose. We Normals say uh-hum, stare rudely, and then get up and leave. Your method is a bit more gracious." He paused. "*Will* you lie on that bed all evening?"

"I could." She stretched languorously. "Why don't you join me?"

He chuckled. "Now who's bold?"

"So?" she challenged him.

"So nothing. So yes, certainly. So we have a ship's conference to attend right now."

"Ah."

"So 'ah.' " He stood and extended his hand. She swung her feet off the bed and he pulled her to him, kissing her soundly. "So . . ." he murmured against her hair.

"Yes, that."

She laughed up at him as he reluctantly stepped away.

"Ship's business, Starfarer," he said and tugged her toward the door.

Yuri tapped the printouts in front of him and looked around at the faces of his crew, all present except Oleg and Viktor, one visiting the other in the hospital. Tomorrow Oleg could rejoin them and *Zvezda* would depart for Delta Bootis, where *Nauka* waited to assist. He glanced at Rinn beside him, but she was looking elsewhere. He cleared his throat.

"I still think the answer lies in this 'magic' of theirs," he began. "Commissar Kirova agrees, and we've developed a set of ideas to try. First, we'll land at *Sing Fa*'s base, not our own. It puts us closer to the Lily coraal and has its symbolic effect."

"Big brother comes to stomp," Khina suggested.

Yuri grinned at her. "Well, not exactly, but are we agreed on that?"

The several heads around the table nodded, even Tatiana's. At least the trade officer was cooperating that much, though Yuri doubted her motives.

"Second, we have our science to bend into Star-Devil magic. Our laser-armor will deflect their rifle-beams and give us some impressive invulnerability, and a holographic camera might give us an effective ghost. Khina, do you think you could scrounge enough footage from our trade tapes and the autopsy to resurrect Ba-rao-som?"

"To what purpose?" Rinn asked.

"Ghosts are magic creatures. Perhaps the Lily might listen to a shade."

"Hmmm." She looked unconvinced, and Yuri suddenly wondered why.

"You have an objection?" he asked her.

Rinn looked away. "No. Please continue."

Yuri cleared his throat. "Third—and this is the commissar's suggestion—we can use Rinn's Gift to work 'magic' on one of the Lily warriors, perhaps even force the chief to—" He saw Rinn stiffen and stare at him unbelievingly. "There is a problem?"

"That's against the Code. I can't . . ."

"You're our shaman," Tatiana said in a deceptively sweet tone. "You're the key to everything. How can we possibly succeed without you, Rinn?"

"That's enough, Tatiana," Yuri said sharply.

"Yes, quite enough," Galina added, her plain face formidable in its disapproval. Yuri wondered if Tatiana knew about Galina's role in her aunt's coterie. Probably not, not even now.

"This is a primitive society," Tatiana said, flipping her hand at both of them. "To an aboriginal," she continued loftily, "the ghost-world is far more immediate than mere physical force. A laser-rifle too obviously belongs to its operator—kill the operator and the rifle is no longer a threat. Take the rifle and *you* are the threat. But weapons that cannot be seen, a horrible compulsion that cannot be resisted—that is true countermagic.''

"No," Rinn said quietly.

"Then if we fail," Tatiana said archly, springing her trap, "you will be the cause, Starfarer. It's that simple." She smiled and looked around the table at the others, like a cat might preen over her freshly caught meal.

Galina scowled, and Yuri wondered which woman showed the commissar's real intention. Wheels within wheels, he thought. What do they plan against you, my love? Do you know?

Khina leaned forward, her face intense. "Not until after I feed you to the Lily tribe, Trade Officer. They like brains; I'll give them yours. Another simple fact."

Yuri sighed. Why couldn't life be easy? "We will decide on a protocol within Rinn's Starfarer Code," he said firmly, "and nobody is feeding anybody to anybody."

"Not yet," Khina said ominously.

"That's enough, Khina," he said again. "Those are the parameters. Now we need the fine-tuning." Yuri looked around the table, reading their faces—and noted Tatiana's unsubtle satisfaction with the plot she had laid against Rinn. Or had she? Who could tell with Kirova, elder or younger? Magic, he thought. I wish I had a spell for you, Tatiana Nikolaevna. Maybe, eventually, I'll ask the Lily shaman; he could have some interesting suggestions.

"Your ideas, comrades?" he invited formally.

Love, he thought, watching Rinn's face as the crew discussed the possibilities. Where do you go sometimes? Rinn still said little of her life before *Zvezda*, though she had hinted at an escape from unbearable oppression on Ikanos, a life of suspicion and bias on *Sing Fa*. I've been fortunate, he thought, aside from a few political problems, a shrewish trade officer, an alien attack, a volcano . . . He snorted at himself in his majority pretensions. He had solutions, he told himself. Did she?

Love: he struggled to understand. Rinn seemed oddly sad, as if forced to a decision she did not want. He had sensed the bond between Rinn and Connor and guessed at her pain over his ultimatum.

Why can't he just accept us? he thought angrily, offended by the insult to his ship, his people—and guessed the feeling was a premise very familiar to Rinn. Like and like, turned into inexorable division: apparently both sides applied it, both with reason and unreason.

Rinn glanced at him occasionally, giving him smiles, joking with Khina, ignoring Tatiana's gibes. She had again come out of her strange mood—like a crystal might change under polarized light, becoming something new in brilliance and color, yet the same in the essentials. He smiled at his own metaphor. Once a geologist, always a . . .

When we come back to Novy Strana . . . he thought, and realized what the choice might mean to her. What had he to offer her in place of alliance with her own kind? If it came to that, would the enclave enforce that stark a choice? Like and like. Who had the right of it?

Love.

He watched her, knowing she was aware of his attention.

After an hour the conference broke up for dinner, then all participated in the final checks of the ship for lift-off in the morning. Viktor came back late, whirling up in the darkness in a Bureau jitney; to their surprise, Oleg climbed the stair behind him, his face pale but determined. Yuri toasted him with a night-cap vodka in the lounge, then went below to his quarters to sleep. He hesitated in front of Rinn's door, enduring the tramp of Galina's and Oleg's feet as they passed him in the corridor.

Well, there was no better way to announce it, he thought ruefully. He raised his hand to knock on the door.

"Come in," came Rinn's muffled voice in answer.

He pressed the door-control and stepped into her room. Rinn was seated at her desk, a mirror-copy of his own, and smiled as he approached her. The door whispered shut behind him.

"Hello," he said.

"Hello."

Yuri looked down into her strange eyes and felt the gap between them—like and like: What had she told Connor? What had they shared?

What was human?

Hastily he tried to hide that thought, and looked away from her, unable to repress his jealousy.

"I was wondering if you'd follow up on my invitation," she said quietly. "I never slept with Connor, by the way. I had the standard sexual introductions on Ikanos, a brief affair in the early months of enclave to prove I could, no one since. *Sing Fa* practiced abstention, even if someone had been interested."

"I—I didn't mean—"

"Will you stop rocking from one foot to the next and look at me? That's better." She smiled up at him. "I was thinking earlier you remind me of Gawain. He was a brave knight in an ancient English tale, a profoundly heroic type bent on grand deeds, quite like you. That's a perilous development."

"Why?"

"It shows I am losing my mind and reason—and what is a telepath without a mind? There, you say it."

"Human," he complied, grinning.

"See, I still have my reason, enough to follow a thought to its conclusion. No doubt the reason will go next and I'll have no thoughts left at all."

"I'd like to take you beyond thinking," he suggested meaningfully.

"Why do you think I made the invitation?" She took his hand and caressed his palm with her fingers. "Now I'm on the edge, Yuri; I don't know what bright comment comes next. Do I seem doubtful of your skills and make you prove it? Do I drop the pretense and melt into your arms? Or something in between?" She smiled impishly. "You don't know, either. Wonderful."

"Personally, I sleep in the nude. Do you?"

"Clothes are a sign of civilization. I read that somewhere."

"In fact, I also shower in the nude. I do lots of things—"

"In the nude, yes." She stood up and pulled her tunic over her head, then dropped it on the floor. Her bra-halter followed.

"Your turn," she said, then laughed as he pulled her to him. He kissed her, then slowly, tantalizingly, moved his lips lower to her bare breast. She leaned toward him, her hand pressing on his hair.

"Yurushka, love," she murmured to him, "love me now."

"Are you sure?"

"As much as I am of anything. I am tired of my cage, this weighing of every consideration, this endless game . . . I want you."

He kissed her again, and saw the shine of tears in her eyes. "And I want you, Rinn." His finger traced the scar on her cheek and he felt a flare of anger at that cruelty.

She turned her face to kiss his hand. "I have been so alone," she said simply.

Much later, as she rose to her own completion in his arms, he felt the flare within his own mind, a closeness beyond any he thought possible. He tightened his arms around her, shuddering into his own orgasm, and heard her cry out in response.

They lay quietly together for some minutes, not speaking, her hands moving slowly on his skin. He burrowed his face against her neck, smelling her scents.

Love . . . The word whispered through his mind.

"Yes," he said, tightening his arms around her. "I love you, Rinn."

"Love . . . yes, it is that," she murmured. He caught a faint surprise in her tone—and amusement, as if the joke were on herself.

Love . . .

"We are together," she said fiercely. "That's all that's important."

Zvezda emerged from warp outside Delta's cometary plane and angled into the system, sending a radio greeting to *Nauka* as it hurtled sunward. Within four hours, *Nauka* answered, its captain abrupt but curious. By the next ship-day, the ships were close enough for regular radio contact, and Yuri ordered a visual relay through the satellite. The com-screen lighted, revealing Captain Shemilkin's narrow and strong-boned face. Behind him several brown-suited figures worked at stations duplicate to *Zvezda*'s own.

"*Nauka* here. Greetings, *Zvezda*."

"Greetings," Yuri replied. "What's the situation here?"

"Well, we landed at the trade-site," Shemilkin said. "As I told you earlier, nobody came. When we tried to approach the Sunstone, they ran away. Now we're back up here, orbiting endlessly, waiting for you. What in the devil is going on?"

"What you mean, Captain, is how did we get away with it on Novy Strana?"

Shemilkin harrumphed, then looked amused, his blue eyes twinkling. He relaxed slightly, and Yuri remembered how much he liked the senior captain.

"Probably the same way I got out of my difficulty," Shemilkin said, "though I'm still not quite sure how I pulled it off. No doubt you feel the same. I hope you noted my discretion in not sending a message ahead of you."

"Yes, and thank you. How would you like to help us work some magic?"

"Come again?"

"Load yourself aboard an E-frame, Boris Alexandrovich, and

come visit us. We need some coordination. I want to introduce you to someone, too.''

''That telepath of yours?'' Shemilkin's brows contracted.

''Rinn?'' Yuri turned toward Rinn's computer station, where she was surreptitiously watching while she ran her programs. She swung her chair around to face him.

''This is Boris Alexandrovich Shemilkin, the original Russian bear,'' Yuri told her. ''You'll like him.''

''I will?'' She looked back at Shemilkin's image, challenging him.

Shemilkin harrumphed again, then laughed, a rumbling chuckle from deep within his chest. ''I'm a mean old bear,'' he said reflectively.

''That I can see,'' Rinn said.

''Anybody who can walk twenty kilometers through that noxious swamp has my respect, Starfarer. Coming over.'' The screen flared, then blanked.

As *Zvezda* fell into orbit ahead of *Nauka*, a slender needle detached itself from the other ship and edged sideways, three space-suited figures clinging to handholds along the open frame. The E-frame's tiny jet flared again, adding enough foot-pounds to ensure a measured pursuit of *Zvezda*.

''Prepare for E-frame access,'' Yuri ordered, then went below to the lock bay. Within a few minutes, he heard a gentle thump on the ship's hull as the E-frame docked next to the airlock, then monitored the lock controls as *Nauka*'s party cycled through. Shemilkin removed his helmet, then introduced his companions.

''Svetlana Dmitryevna Lyakhovskaya, second officer.'' The glacial blond nodded curtly. ''And Leonid Sergeivich Ryumin, my trade officer—I believe you two know each other.'' The tall dark-haired man smiled and shook Yuri's hand.

''Hello, Lenya,'' Yuri greeted his former classmate. ''Still miss geology?''

''I dabble now and then. Delteans are more interesting—and what *have* you done here, Yurushka? And how are you going to fix it?''

''Come along. We've come up with some dandy ideas.''

''Is that telepath above?'' Svetlana interjected.

Yuri returned her cool glance. ''One problem at a time, comrade. I suggest we table that issue and deal with the other.''

''Telepaths are proscribed,'' Svetlana said.

Yuri scowled. ''We're already long past that particular argument. Rinn is aboard at Commissar Kirova's orders—but I'm sure you'll enjoy sharing impressions with her niece. In the meantime, I'd appreciate having the help of a working trade officer. Mine isn't.'' He glanced at Leonid's noncommittal expression and suddenly felt tired. Do the arguments ever end? he wondered.

When the three had removed their suits, he beckoned them toward the inner door. ''Come along, comrades. Welcome to *Zvezda*.''

Silently, the others followed him to the interior bay door.

''A manufactured virus?'' Shemilkin asked in disbelief. He peered at the microscope screen in the lab, as his two officers craned to look over his shoulder. Yuri and Rinn watched from the lab stools while Khina showed them the slides. Shemilkin shook his head, amazed. ''The Delta natives don't even have settled agriculture!''

Khina shook her braids. ''The university computers confirmed it—even named the parent virus. I'm culturing it now to see if I can duplicate the splicing. Believe me, Captain, we were as surprised as you, but the more closely we look, the more we find to perplex us.''

''Like laser-rifles,'' Svetlana said.

''And the three-finger stones?'' Leonid added.

''We've wondered about those, too,'' Yuri confirmed. ''Tech never has completed the analysis.''

Svetlana straightened and frowned, obviously running through the same questions that had so long puzzled *Zvezda*. ''But what's the answer?'' she asked at last.

''That's what we're hoping Rinn can find out,'' Yuri said. ''She helped tremendously when the Lily warriors attacked with the Sunstone.'' He smiled at Rinn, hoping he did not look entirely besotted. ''With the proper information, we hope we can achieve recontact.''

''Perhaps,'' Svetlana said dubiously. She shook herself slightly, glanced at Captain Shemilkin. ''You were right, Captain. I can see the advantage—and the need.'' Her cool gaze shifted to Rinn. ''Welcome, Starfarer.''

Rinn nodded an acknowledgment, then returned Svetlana's slight smile. Yuri relaxed a little, relieved, and caught Rinn's amused glance.

So laugh, my love, he thought at her, *when I worry about you*. Rinn's smile broadened. *And I probably do look besotted, for all to see. Just like Gawain over his lady*.

"And what role, Yuri," Leonid asked; "will *Nauka* play in your magic show?"

"Well, let's say you'll be useful. We brought some exoskeleton power-suits, borrowed from the Home Police. They use them in riot control, though the worst problems are years past, of course." He glanced at Khina, who chose not to react. "Laser-armor or vacuum-suits would keep off laser-fire but wouldn't be much use against spears or a physical attack. You can be our bodyguard, Lenya." He gestured at the small holographic camera on the sideboard. "Boris can operate our ghost."

"Hmmm." Leonid's dark eyes shifted to Rinn. "After a secret foray for more information?"

"That's the plan."

"And how do you know it'll work?" Svetlana asked.

Yuri shrugged. "We don't. If the plan goes *pfutz*, comrades, we'll have to think of something else."

"Wonderful," Leonid growled.

"But we will see," Shemilkin said.

"Yes, we will see."

Chapter 18

ZVEZDA DRIFTED DOWNWARD ON A BILLOWING
flame and came to rest near *Sing Fa*'s empty hulk. The landing
was easily visible from the coraal two miles to the west; a Lily
party might be expected shortly. Already scouts were heading
for the clearing to investigate. As soon as she finished her landing checks, Rinn left the command deck and went below to her
quarters. Unaccountably, half the others followed her, some
suspicious, others curious.

In her room on the crew deck, Rinn lay back and settled
herself comfortably on the mattress. Captain Shemilkin ambled
into the room and sat down heavily in the only chair, his brows
drawn together in a scowl. Yuri and Galina Kirillovna leaned
against the wall; the others hovered outside in the corridor, Tatiana in front.

"Perhaps we should move me to the conference room," Rinn
said edgily, "so you can *all* watch."

Shemilkin started and looked abashed. "Uh, should we
leave?" he asked, half-rising from his chair.

"I'm surprised you object," Tatiana said with sweet venom.
"Isn't an audience part of being a wonder-girl?"

"Shut up, Tatiana," Yuri ordered.

Rinn sighed. "I could claim that negative thoughts would
dampen my Gift, but that's not true. I've lived among 'negative
thoughts' all my life, Tatiana, some of which would make your
skin peel. I could even claim that doubt removes the psychic

phenomenon, but this isn't a parapsych lab, nor am I a spirit-medium, whatever you think. You are welcome to watch. I will lie here quietly and look rather dead." She closed her eyes.

Yuri stirred uncomfortably. "Can you talk to us while you listen?"

"Not really. It's not a skill I've practiced. I'm sorry." As Tatiana opened her mouth, Rinn added sharply, "And tell that woman to keep her thoughts to herself. She repeats too much."

"Go away, Tatiana," Galina said quietly. "Go away now."

Rinn left them as she sank into other-mind, willing away their suspicions into grayness. Her thoughts looped outward through the closed doors of *Zvezda* into the night to touch the watchers who had stared in surprise and were already hurrying back toward the Lily coraal. She paced with them, then watched from other alien eyes as one reported to an aged chieftain. Beside the chief stood another, resplendent in his shaman's robes, his face unchanging as the scout brought unwelcome news. The shaman exchanged a glance with the chief, then whirled and stalked toward his own hut. Rinn followed him, skipping from mind to mind as he strode through the wide coraal.

You are the one, she thought.

The shaman went inside his hut for a moment, then emerged and settled himself in front of the doorway, incised sticks in his hands. Like a wraith, she leaped the last distance and slipped neatly into his mind.

His name was Lorat, but the people knew him only as Ghost-Walker, three clipped gestures of his own choosing. As shaman, he forebore the protection of a Mouth-Name, the ward against the swamp-demons who quested beneath marshland and water. He was Ghost-Walker, shaman of the Lily tribe, revered to know all things, truth and falsehood, evil and good, the ordering of the world.

So the tribe trusted him, confident in the safety of his magic. Only Ghost-Walker knew the knife-edge of a shaman's knowledge, where the unknown far outweighed the known. Not even the Three-Fingered, the priests in the Mountains of Light, claimed to know all things, though only they had the spear-of-death magic that made the Lily fire-weapons more than useless rods of strange substance. Once a year Ghost-Walker journeyed to the Three-Fingered in their mountain fastness, bearing the weapons whose souls had been devoured by the swamp-demons.

Rinn caught a vague image of a mountain tribe with strange

markings on their faces, each resplendent in fine-crafted strands
of three-finger stones, gesturing briefly with self-mutilated
hands. She sensed that Lorat both admired and dreaded the
Three-Fingered, however competent his own magic. Last year,
the shaman recalled, the Three-Fingered had refused their help,
claiming greater matters for their attention. In the coming journey next season, he might have to beg if they refused again. He
did not like the prospect.

He did not like much at all lately, with the world gone strange.

He sat in front of his hut, glowering at the firelight. A woman
approached him, offering food, but he waved her impatiently
away. He preferred to work his magic on an empty stomach.
Soon Chief Isen-brot-quel would ask his advice about the Star-
Devils, wishing for counsel of blood and strength-for-strength—
an aging chief, particularly a chief with a restless son, yearned
for the greatest of magics, something to stir the blood with a
pretense of youth, to raise the eyes after the joint-stiffness had
long since bent the back into a hobbled curve. As Lorat con-
ferred with Isen-brot-quel, the chief's son would pace the clearing, waiting for the summons to new death-making, a way to
distinguish himself in bloodshed as his gifts in wisdom and patience did not.

Again Ghost-Walker cursed Isen-glov-amar's haste, however
the tribe had honored him for his slaughter of the Star-Devils.
Such decisions were properly given to the chief and his shaman,
not a restless youth who saw a chance and took it, then found
cause to murder warriors more gifted than he. Only Lorat's
sternest of orders had saved Belos from a similar death; once
ignited, the chief's son seemed to have no limits, gifted with a
warrior's madness more suited to ancient times when tribes contended by the fortunes of single combat. The tribes had bred
their beserkers to greater madness, only to have the warriors
turn inward on the people and bring down the world. Of late,
Ghost-Walker felt apprehensive whenever he regarded the son
of the chief. Long before, such a chief had raised the Lily to
dominance; such a chief could now lose all.

And now, chief's son, he thought, the Star-Devils have come
back. For what? he wondered.

He lifted his snout and sniffed, catching the faint reek of
Devil-gases from the east. Their Devil-house sat by the other,
the dead house, as they plotted new evil for the people, new
enticements to steal souls.

What did they want? Souls? Or something else?

He had examined the strange gifts taken from the Sunstone—
cloth that shimmered, pots of a strange hammered stone, odd
gems and other objects—then ordered their sacrifice in the sacred
pools. Those Sunstone who had taken the gifts he had cursed to
death; even now they wasted away to nothing, unable to eat or
sleep, waiting for the swamp-demons to rise to claim them. The
Sunstone chieftain, Ba-rao-som, had eluded his corrective magic,
taken by the Star-Devils into their accursed house.

Why? From the warriors' account, the Star-Devils were weak
and soft-bodied, easily surprised. How could such a people know
the higher magic? And why, if Star-Devils were easily surprised, had this other Devil house escaped?

His six-fingered hands tightened on his spirit-sticks, but still
he did not make the summons-magic. A shaman needed a clear
mind to hear the spirits correctly—and a clear question to ask.
Star-Devils—who could tell with Star-Devils? That the swamp-
demons desired flesh and souls and rose upward to voice sounds
made unwisely, that all knew. That the marsh-hunter attacked
any intruder into its home-space, that also. That the Three-
Fingered rarely deigned to offer counsel beyond the set teach-
ings, only Ghost-Walker knew. And now the Three-Fingered
would not speak at all.

His eyes narrowed, considering the possibilities. Twice before the world-magic had shifted, bringing destruction and
change. The first destruction had ruined the world; the second
had thrown all into flux. A Lily chief had seized the advantage
in that second destruction, driving the Three-Fingered into their
mountain retreat, taking their fire-weapons by force. Perhaps
now the Three-Fingered had begun their revenge, daring the
Lily to enforce their secret tribute as the world decayed into new
change. Perhaps. His neck fur stirred in new apprehension. Perhaps the Lily spirits might tell him if that suspicion had the truth,
though it was a truth he did not want.

Rinn watched as he drew a figure in the dust with his spirit-
stick, casting the first word of the summons-spell. Another figure imposed itself upon the first, then the start of a third, making
the pattern by which a shaman spoke to spirits, those weaker
spirits who guarded the Lily. The good spirits rarely spoke, even
to a shaman, for they saved their strength for the unending struggle with the swamp-demons who sought only destruction.

To distract the Lily spirits risked much. He considered, then
judged again that matters required it. His stick moved.

I make the pattern. Lily spirits, rise . . .

Impulsively, Rinn seized the chance. *Lorat,* she sent to him. *Lorat* . . .

. . . and connected. She sensed Ghost-Walker's start of amazement. Quickly, without moving his head, he linked his first and third minds, at high alert, and glanced around at the darkness. No one. He slashed his spirit-stick through the pattern, disturbing the magic, his third-brain thrumming with alarm. Who? This spirit he had not heard before. He stared down at his sticks with widened eyes, then grew angry. Another change: would the world slide into vagueness, where even mountain rock might shake like ooze-sands?

What was *wrong* with the world? Ghost-Walker quivered with silent rage, his thoughts in turmoil.

Rinn withdrew slightly, belatedly cautious of the alien's third brain. In her eagerness to make contact, she had brushed that instinctive awareness and alerted his defenses. Twice now the aliens had heard her mental sending—she had forgotten the earlier incident with Belos. Did Delteans have a latent psi? She hesitated uneasily, not sure what to do.

She watched as Ghost-Walker again traced part of the summons-pattern, curious despite himself, then scratched it out.

Perhaps if she waited . . .

Ghost-Walker considered, cautiously unlinking his third brain to allow his emotions to cool. A warrior might use the anger-strength to power him; a shaman sought clarity, unmuddied by the frenzied pulse of such compulsions. His first and second minds built new connections as he meditated, steadying him. Who? A new voice—he was certain of it. Though he often heard the spirits move beneath the land, that sending usually required the preparatory herbs and days of fasting. So he had been taught. He stared at the half-made pattern, highly disturbed.

A new voice—whose? He drummed his fingers on the sticks, his neck fur rippling.

What else did he know for certain? That the swamp-demons sought to destroy the world, kept in check by a reed's-breadth. Twice they had nearly succeeded. That he knew, as certainly as he knew the strength of his long body, the joy of wife-coupling, and the ghost-scents of the night breeze. What were their weapons? He numbered them on the end-points of his lines. Uncertainty, stealth, hunting misfortune, limb-paralyzing fear, madness . . . and Star-Devils? His stick froze over the scratches in the hard-tamped soil.

Who *were* these Devils? Who had summoned them? Not the

Lily spirits, who sought only the good, the customary, the alive-ness of things. *Who?* Only one other force contended for the world.

Damn! Rinn thought. She reached out, intending to change, to convert—and hesitated, wary of a skill she had foresworn. What choice did she have? She wavered, caught between the impulse and her memories.

What self survives? a younger voice had asked ages earlier.

Ghost-Walker's jaws snapped decisively. Evil! How clever the demons wove their snares, tempting even a shaman! He rose, treading angrily on the summons-pattern as he stalked forward. Let them entice in vain—Lorat would see that none ventured near them to hear their lies.

He gathered his feathered cloak around his lean body and strode toward the chief's hut. Women and children scattered before him as he approached; even warriors edged away, their eyes widening. At the edge of the coraal enclosure, Isen-glov-amar turned eagerly, his hands clenching his fire-weapon. Ghost-Walker ignored his silent plea for more killing, more death-rages.

You brought this down on us, chief's son, he thought. He ducked under the low door lintel of Isen-brot-quel's hut. You will rue your passions.

See the pattern . . . Rinn wrenched herself away and hovered in other-mind, furious at her own ineptitude. She had thrown away the chance, been careless for only a moment. And when it came to the crux . . . She moaned as she remembered the marsh-hunter's death and Connor's quiet condemnation of her impulsive choice. What would he think of such a choice made deliberately, full-knowing?

"Rinn?"

At the sound of Yuri's voice, she opened her eyes and saw his concerned and loving face above hers.

"Rinn?"

Behind him, she sensed the others. *Different! different!* she cried silently at them. *What can you ever understand of what I do?* She turned away from them all, even Yuri, and hid her face against the pillow.

"What's wrong?" Galina asked, her voice tinged with alarm.

For whom? Rinn thought sadly. Rinn? Or your commissar's tool?

"I don't know," Yuri said. "Vacate the room, please. Captain, if you will?"

She heard the scrape of the chair, retreating footsteps, the sigh of the door. Then, approaching her bed again, his steps. The mattress shifted as he sat beside her, and she felt his hand on her hair, gently drawing it aside from her face.

"Where do you go?" he asked quietly. "And how do I follow you, my love? For I would follow, if I could. I would set aside everything, to be with you."

She turned to him and hid her face against his chest. For a long minute, he held her, his chest rising and falling with his breath. "I'm sorry," she murmured.

"For what?" He tugged gently on her hair to make her look at him. "If I am Gawain, you are my lady love. Isn't that how the tale goes? Or am I Galahad chasing after the Holy Grail, a light forever tantalizing, never truly found?"

"You looked that up," she accused.

"Computers are convenient tools. Whatever is the matter?"

She sighed. "I convinced the Lily shaman that *Zvezda* is a new variety of swamp-demon. He's going to proscribe the ship, make us taboo."

"What?" he asked, startled.

"It's a mess." She grimaced and felt herself flush with embarrassment. "They won't come near us now. Ghost-Walker isn't the type to change his mind."

Yuri shrugged, then considered. "Maybe we can go to the coraal, force the contact." Rinn knew he had always itched to do that, even before Ba-rao-som broke off trade. Yuri found it hard to sit and wait.

She touched his face gently. "Be sensible, Yuri. The Lily coraal has a hundred warriors, all armed with lasers, immensely strong and fast. Even a riot-suit can be knocked to the ground by a determined rush—how effective would we look then, lying on the ground like upended bugs? And if we killed some of them to deter the attack, how would they react then? These people are not easily cowed, and their violence is unpredictable."

"True." Yuri stood up and paced a moment. "But they *have* to talk to us, Rinn."

"Why?"

He stopped and looked at her ruefully. "Exactly." His shoulders sagged.

"I did learn something new, Yuri," she said quickly. "There's another tribe up in the mountains, a people the shaman calls the 'Three-Fingered.' The Lily conquered them some time back, but they still keep the secret of laser-rifle maintenance. Once a year the Lily shaman takes the expended rifles to them for recharging.'' She sensed his immediate interest.

"Three-finger? That's what Ba-rao-som named our stones.''

"They wear garlands of the stones—they might be the source.''

"Hmmm. What else?''

She thought a moment. "They live in caverns of some kind; I picked up a distinct image of enclosing stone. They apparently mutilate their hands to match their tribe's name, maybe as a magic totem. I know it impresses Ghost-Walker. He's not afraid of the Three-Fingered, not exactly, but he respects their magic. And the last time he traveled there, they refused to recharge the rifles.''

"Why?''

"He doesn't know. It bothers him.''

"Maybe we ought to go ask them,'' Yuri said with a grin. "I bet that'll get Ghost-Walker's attention.''

"You *are* determined.''

"Of course. Don't you know? I'm Sir Gawain.''

She laughed. "I love you.''

"That, too.'' He drew her into an embrace and kissed her soundly. "It's all magic, everything is, especially you. And don't worry—I don't intend to fail.'' His mood turned grim. "And they *will* talk to us eventually, whatever Ghost-Walker thinks. It's dialectic.''

"Imperialist.''

"Soviet.'' He kissed her again. "There's a difference.''

Tatiana Nikolaevna scowled as Rinn and Yuri emerged on the command deck. "Are we over our tantrums?'' she asked with an unpleasant smile.

"Shut up,'' Yuri said impatiently. Tatiana only smiled more broadly. Captain Shemilkin and Svetlana looked at her, curious; Khina glared. Galina looked upset, and Roblev's eyes darted from face to face. Rinn did not envy the psychologist; his training only exacerbated his worries, making any conflict, however slight, into a dread possibility. The combination of emotions shifted uneasily across Rinn's perception.

Whatever Tatiana's smug satisfaction, Rinn knew—if Yuri did not—that Kirova had not included her niece in any plans. The real opposition lay elsewhere. She glanced at Leonid Ryumin, *Nauka*'s trade officer and matched his face with an image she had seen in Krasin's mind. Kirova was not the only commissar to place an agent aboard the Delta ships. She wondered if Ryumin's old friendship with Yuri might inhibit his private orders received on the Board's message capsule. Perhaps, perhaps not—not even Ryumin knew for sure. He looked back at her blandly, an eyebrow raised.

"We have a change of plans," Yuri began. "According to Rinn, the Lily shaman had put us off limits. I doubt if a forced meeting at their coraal would be productive."

"I should say not," Shemilkin growled. "Twenty-to-one odds are a bit much even for riot-armor."

"Standing orders prohibit uninvited contact, anyway," Leonid said. "Maybe they'll relent while we wait."

Yuri eyed him. "Wait? Who said wait?"

"I thought that was assumed."

So, Rinn thought, that was what Krasin had up his sleeve. Restrict them enough and they would fail, to Kirova's undoing. Later, naturally, Krasin would retrieve the Delta trade by changing ship orders and allowing *Nauka* to do what *Zvezda* might have done the first time. All of it proper, within procedure. Clever—but not clever enough: in that calculation, Krasin had forgotten *Nauka*'s own captain, another man with independent ideas.

"When necessary," Shemilkin rumbled, throwing his trade officer a quelling glance, "a ship's crew can take initiative."

"With all respect, Captain . . ."

Shemilkin brushed him off. "What did you have in mind, Yuri Ivanovich?"

Yuri quickly explained about the Three-Fingered tribe. "If we can make contact with them, we can stir things up a little, maybe enough to give us another entry into trade. Go directly to the three-finger stone source—and maybe to a tribe with enough influence to let us reestablish trade with the Sunstone, too. The Three-Fingered used to be a power on this world. What do you think, Boris?"

"Hmmm." Shemilkin rubbed his chin and glanced at Svetlana. "A good idea. Are you thinking of a ground expedition? We can hardly land *Zvezda* on a mountain slope, especially if those mountains are as rugged as they look from orbit. We'd need a ground survey for a new base-site, anyway."

"We have two rovers in storage," Yuri said, "one of them

armored. If the Lily follow us, as they probably will, we'll need the protection.''

"Once I get closer," Rinn added, "I'm sure I can find their cavern."

"Convenient," Shemilkin rumbled in amusement. "Kind of a biological radar, aren't you?"

"Something like that." She smiled back at him.

"Sir," Leonid tried again.

"As Yuri is given to say to *his* trade officer, my dear Lenyushka, shut up." Shemilkin winked at Yuri. "I like it. You'll take me, of course. And our trade officers, despite their lack of enthusiasm." He glowered at both Leonid and Tatiana, daring them to say anything. "And McCrea. And—"

"The rover only holds five," Yuri reminded him. "Maybe six if we pass on body-armor."

"Which would be stupid, considering. Svetlana and your engineer can monitor communications. Has Termez finished making her ghost?"

Khina nodded. "I've loaded fifteen minutes of general movement and speech into the camera, sir. I can give you a schematic of the sequence."

"Then we'll take him, too. Maybe we can use our magic scenario after all, if developments develop. I hate to waste a good plan. You agree, Yuri?"

Yuri bowed slightly, yielding to the older captain's expertise.

Shemilkin harrumphed. "We'll see if it works. And if it doesn't . . ."

Yuri grinned. "Then we'll think of something else."

Shemilkin shook himself like an old bear rousing from its winter sleep. "In the meantime, let's not get ourselves killed. Riot-armor will help, but even its invulnerability might be limited. The Lily tribe may have other things we don't know about—and the Three-Fingered even more so, if they're the source of the technology we've seen."

"And they're probably virus-infected, too," Yuri agreed. "Unpredictable."

"Life is unpredictable, comrade. We'll just keep everything in mind when we go."

Chapter 19

THEY LEFT AT DAWN THE NEXT MORNING ABOARD the armored rover, a squat semiamphibious all-terrain vehicle capable of rapid land travel and occasional jet-assisted hops over obstacles. Yuri took the controls, rapidly reacquiring his easy handling of the machine from prior surveys, and headed northeast. Captain Shemilkin sat in the second command seat at Yuri's right, ready to handle the comset and laser-cannon; Rinn sat behind Shemilkin on the middle bench seat, her head turned toward the Lily coraal, expecting trouble. Yuri could see the tension in her face whenever he glanced at her. Leonid and Tatiana sat together on the third rearmost seat, hanging onto sidestraps as the rover lurched and swayed across the mud-pans.

All five wore suits of riot-armor, powered exoskeletons of lightweight titanium, mobile, strength-enhanced, and surmounted by sophisticated sight and communication gear set into the helmets. A half-dozen laser-rifles rode in the storage racks near the ceiling, and a week's supply of food and medicines were stored in the rear compartment. On the rear seat between the two trade officers sat three boxes of trade goods that had especially attracted the Sunstone. Yuri intended to remain optimistic.

"We were seen leaving the clearing," Rinn said to him, her voice slightly tinny in his earphones. "The watcher informs Chief Isen-brot-quel."

"What d'you think they'll do?" he asked.

197

"Do? Follow us, I expect. When Ghost-Walker realizes we're heading toward the Three-Fingered, he could be capable of anything. The Three-Fingered control the highest magic, Yuri, and Ghost-Walker thinks you're a swamp-demon."

"That's why we have biological radar." Yuri turned and grinned at her, trying to lighten her mood. Last night they had come closer than ever before, a space of several pleasant hours spent in lovemaking, tale-telling, and speculation about the Delteans. Yet, even then, he had sensed her disturbance. Something was bothering her, more than the tension of the expedition—but what?

Would she tell me if I asked? he wondered.

"Your radar thanks you," Rinn murmured, her blue-black eyes shadowed in the close confines of the rover.

Yuri bent his head sideways, trying to see more of her face, then nearly had the rover controls yanked out of his hands as the vehicle lurched into a mudhole. He heard Tatiana's squawk as a heavy box of trade goods tipped off the rear seat onto her foot.

"Want me to drive, Yuri?" Leonid taunted from the back.

"No, thanks. Uh, sorry, Tatiana."

Tatiana snapped a rude word, unappeased. Yuri tried to drive flawlessly for the several moments until matters cooled, then glanced back at Rinn again.

"Eyes on the road, Captain," Rinn said, smiling.

Love . . . Her mental voice was the first touch of the cool evening breeze after a hot day, the pale gleam of crystal in a shadowed cove, a flowing spring-water of a rippling laughter. He sighed despite himself, remembering the touch of her hands on his body. He was getting to understand Oleg's attitude. *Love* . . .

I can't think when you do that, he told her. *And I have to drive this rover now.* He heard her answering chuckle as she obediently vanished from his mind.

A kilometer farther, the rover splashed through another pool onto a wide mud-pan, then bumped onto a hard-packed trail that led upward toward the foothills. Yuri geared down to a stop and glanced inquiringly at Shemilkin.

"Better footing, and it goes generally northeast," the other rumbled, looking at the narrow track out the rover window. He leaned forward to key the orbital stereoscan map on the console viewer and studied it. "You said it takes Ghost-Walker a two-day walk, Rinn?"

"About that."

"Hmmm. Say thirty to forty kilometers, probably up those stepped plateaus." He pointed to the map's winding contour lines where the marshland merged into the foothills of an ascending mountain range, then tapped his finger on a computer-enhanced yellowish blur nearby. "See: there's that forest on the slope up ahead. This trail leads right into it."

Yuri turned the rover onto the track, then accelerated the pace as he felt the balloon wheels bite into the soil. The agile little craft hummed along the trail at twenty klicks an hour, safe enough on the even terrain. They climbed a gentle rocky slope and reached a widely set grove of trees, several thirty meters high and vaguely reminiscent of Earth's ancient cycads and horsetail ferns. Shemilkin craned to look upward at the clustered fruit beneath the wide crown of leaves adorning each tree.

"Strange," he said, half to himself. "An evolution that develops sentience but never improves trees past a basic primitive form. I doubt if this world has any angiosperms at all. Even the marsh-lilies are a variety of club-moss."

"Tania found an angiosperm weed on the coast," Leonid said.

"She *thinks* it's a flower," Shemilkin commented. "Here taxonomy begins all over again."

Yuri steered through the boles and underbrush as the trail wound itself up the slope, detoured around a rocky outcrop, then emerged on a kilometer-wide grassy plateau spotted with open-water pools. The silvery grass rippled in the morning breeze, an unending chevron pattern repeated in the still water. The sun glinted.

"Pretty," Shemilkin grunted, "but poor drainage. Watch out for bogs—two tons of metal sinks fast in a quagmire."

"It might be better to skirt the whole plateau," Yuri agreed. He pointed to the left at the trail winding along the rocky edge of the meadow. "Apparently the natives do."

Shemilkin again grunted his assent. The rover rolled briskly along the trail, the border of long grass swishing its sides. Twenty minutes later, as they rounded the far edge of the plateau and began to climb again, Shemilkin checked in with *Zvezda*.

Hara reported all quiet at the ship, but several intrusions on the ship wards a few minutes before.

"A Lily party passing us, most likely," Svetlana added. "We tried to get a count, but they moved too fast through heavy cover."

"Rinn?" Yuri asked.

"I hear them," Rinn said after a moment. "About thirty warriors led by Isen-glov-amar. And Belos, though he keeps a careful distance from Isen-glov-amar. Ghost-Walker is with them, too, and two of his aides. I expected he would come; he can guess exactly where we're going—though, of course, he thinks it's demon-inspired." She paused. "They have reached the track beneath the forest, moving very fast. At this speed, we'll just stay ahead of them."

"Until we slow down," Tatiana pointed out, her voice tinged with apprehension. "Do you hear the Three-Fingered, Rinn?"

"Not yet. But something . . . something ahead." She hissed at herself, exasperated. "I can't catch it. I have to be closer."

"When *Sing Fa* was attacked, you heard *Zvezda* at twenty kilometers," Tatiana said snidely, "or so you said. Why the difference now?"

"I had similar arguments with Captain Hung about my Gift, Trade Officer, and I'd rather not repeat them with you. Maybe when the Lily catch up and I have the stress of recent deaths among my crewmates, I'll repeat the preconditions. Care to volunteer as a victim?" Rinn's voice was edged.

"Just do your best, Rinn," Yuri said encouragingly.

"You comment too much," Shemilkin rumbled to Tatiana. Tatiana shut up. For a moment, Yuri wished he could borrow Shemilkin as part of *Zvezda*'s permanent ship equipment—the older captain seemed to have a marked dampening effect on trade officers, his and Yuri's both.

At the next cliffside, they passed through another grove of trees, each topped by bulbous fruit and palmlike leaves, then followed the trail as it turned true northeast. The path narrowed through a massive split rock, heading upward. Yuri touched the rover jets and jumped their craft over the barrier, then shifted to sixth gear as the grade increased on the far side. The rover climbed the slope, its heavy wheels gouging deeply into the soil, slowing as it reached the top.

Before them lay the grasses of another plateau, here in broad patterns of iridescent purple and deep blue-green, spotted by isolated patches of marsh-lilies. A kilometer away, ringing the plateau on three sides, massive bluffs of yellowish stone rose several dozen meters high. The trail led directly forward, skirting a series of small pools. The rover hummed along the dirt path as it led them onward through the grass.

"Stop, Yuri," Shemilkin said suddenly.

"Why?"

"Back up a bit."

Yuri obliged and peered along the line-of-sight that attracted the other's attention. Shemilkin pointed to the right. "I see regular shapes, too regular to be natural. See? There at the base of that cliff."

"I see them. Shall we investigate? Rinn?"

"Isen-glov-amar's reached the first plateau; we might have a half-hour."

"Only a half-hour?" Yuri swivelled in his seat to look at her. "We've been making twenty klicks consistently."

She wrinkled her nose at him. "I told you they were fast, and even Ghost-Walker comes from a warrior breed."

"Hmmm. Let's chance it." Yuri swerved the rover off the path and bumped across the uneven grassland, then accelerated. Shemilkin held on with both hands as the rover lurched and swayed with the rough ride. Yuri bounced the rover across a stream and then another as they made a quick pace toward the cliff and what lay beneath it.

"Ruins?" Tatiana's question came half-gasped as the rover bounced hard over a rocky outcrop.

"Might be," Leonid muttered, also bending forward to peer through the front window. "Looks like you were right, Yuri—there was a higher culture here once. That's definitely quarried stone."

The rover rolled up to the formation, a jumbled group of stone cubes half-concealed by vegetation. At that vantage, Yuri could see that the ruins extended into a hollow in the cliff, steadily rising in height to a broad two-story building beneath the cliffside. A guard outpost? he wondered. Perhaps a dacha—he could see the outlines of a garden wall, and a number of small structures that might be outlying storage units near the main house. The stones were badly eroded by weather, most tumbled from their original positions. Yuri rolled up to one of the outer walls and stopped, then cracked the rover doors. Shemilkin levered out his long body, followed by Leonid and Tatiana.

"Rinn?" Yuri prompted, lending her a hand. She emerged, her face a puzzle of expressions behind the faceplate of her helmet. "What is it?" he asked.

"Pardon?"

"You look so strange."

The other walked hurriedly toward the ruins, talking excitedly. Rinn looked up at him, her lips quirked upward in a half-smile.

"Oh, this is quite new to me, this exploring. I never did get out of *Sing Fa* much." She looked around the meadow and cliffside with wonder. Then she glanced southward toward the pursuing Lily warriors and frowned. "I only wish I could spare all my mind for the looking. Look at that!" She pointed to a tri-lobed flower nestled in the grasses nearby, then took an exploratory step toward it. The flower shivered slightly, then delicately lifted its leaves and stalked off to a safer grass clump a meter away. Rinn smiled in delight. "It's an animal!"

"How can you tell?" Yuri said in a mock growl. "It still looks like a plant to me."

"Oh, it knows what it is. What a lovely creature!"

"As are you, my love. Come, let's look at the ruins." He tugged at her sleeve and led her toward the cliff. The others had walked up to the cliff-face and were peering into the shadowed building. As Rinn and Yuri approached, Leonid turned toward them.

"Ceramics!" He held up a twisted pinkish shape, rough-edged at one end of the break, a delicate convoluted curve to a cup-bowl at the other. "I think this was a drain spout—look at the technique, Yuri. It's something entirely new!"

Yuri took the broken bowl and hefted it, then examined the glaze. "That explains the lack of steel in the orbit surveys." He ran his eyes over the crumbling building. "I wonder how high a culture they had."

"And how much still survives among the Three-Fingered," Leonid said, taking the bowl back from him. "Let's mark the site and go see."

Yuri studied him a moment. "I thought you said standard ops ruled forever."

Leonid shrugged. "I had an obligation," he said shortly, confirming another of Yuri's suspicions. "I'd much rather trade with high-culture aliens than mud-wattle marsh-dwellers."

"The Sunstone are a gentle and dignified people," Yuri corrected quietly.

"That's beside the point. Let's go." Leonid matched words to action and strode off toward the rover.

"A good idea," Rinn murmured, again glancing southeast.

"I want to see a little more first," Yuri said as Shemilkin gestured to them from the building doorway. Tatiana had disappeared inside. At the doorway, Yuri paused to run his glove over the carving on the stone door lintel. Even long weathering had not erased the flowing curves of the abstract design. He bent forward, examining the ceramic intaglio in the grooves. "Amazing. How did they bind it to the stone?"

"There's more inside," Shemilkin called. His voice rang with a kind of triumph, even elation, impelling Yuri through the doorway.

Several stones had fallen from the roof, allowing sunlight to enter the shadowed foyer. Shemilkin and Tatiana stood in the center of the room, their heads turning in a vain attempt to encompass the rampant sweep of ceramic mosaics across the interior walls. Blue, green, a deep crimson, a pale yellow—the colors swirled in intricate pattern across every wall, interrupted only by the monotone blue inlay of lamp brackets and several stone benches ringing the ovoid chamber. At the far end, another door led inward to other rooms. At their feet, a floor of small colored tiles, none larger than a few centimeters, repeated the swirling geometry on the walls. It was a dizzying display of color and simulated movement, half-seen in the gloom of the broken roof.

"The physical senses," Rinn said in awe. "They've caught that in their stonework."

"All abstract patterns," Shemilkin murmured, his dark eyes moving as he turned in place. "Similar to the mosaics I saw in ancient Arab mosques on Earth. Theirs was a delight in geometry as the visible sign of God's unknowable and palpable thought. Did the Delteans seek the same artistic idea, I wonder?" He stepped forward to bend over a delicate bench of blue inlay. "It looks like it was cast in a single piece. How do you do that without magnetic field controls? Platinum catalyst? How did they reach the necessary temperatures?" He straightened and looked solemnly at Yuri. "This is a major find, comrade. We could spend a year studying this place and still have questions."

"Wonderful," Tatiana breathed as she turned through a complete circle yet again. "Oh, wonderful."

"I suggest we not delay," Leonid said impatiently, his voice crackling over the suit-radio band. "If you please, Captain."

"Coming, Lenya." Yuri gestured reluctantly to Shemilkin.

Five minutes later the rover was again hurtling across the grass, making up for lost time. As they crashed back onto the path, Yuri heard a muffled hooting behind them and accelerated recklessly. The path plunged again between high rocks, a narrow squeeze for the rover, then began climbing the next cliff. He glanced in his rearview mirrors and saw a pack of pounding alien shapes rushing after them barely a half-kilometer behind. A new burst of speed up the slope increased the distance; the rover climbed, spinning its balloon wheels in the packed dirt of the trail, once nearly slewing off the edge. On the plateau above, Yuri accelerated still more and added more distance between the rover and their pursuers.

"Close," Shemilkin said.

"I'd rather not confront them now," Yuri agreed. "I wish we'd had more time at the ruins."

"An alien archeological site will get its own attention, believe me." Shemilkin leaned forward and activated the satellite link to *Zvezda* to report their find.

"Excellent, Captain," came Svetlana's cool voice. "For your information, *Nauka* reports an incoming messenger capsule from Novy Strana with your designator. Shall *Nauka* leave orbit to meet it?"

"Yes, have Ivan bring it aboard—but tell him whatever the Bureau wants can wait awhile. I'm busy." Shemilkin snapped off the com and glanced at Yuri. "Nag, nag, nag—does it ever stop?"

"Bureau orders have the highest priority," Leonid said pompously.

"Your opinion wasn't requested, Trade Officer." Shemilkin cocked an eyebrow, his blue eyes twinkling. "Sometimes, Yuri, I think the Bureau would make a good collective wife, complete with G.U.M. shopping bag and formidable scowl. 'Do this, Boris, do that,' until one can hardly move in any direction without a warning reproof." Yuri heard a stifled gasp from Leonid at the heresy and grinned. Shemilkin had not liked being dragged away from the ruins, either.

The rover whirled across another grassy plateau, then wound back and forth along a narrow trail through a gentle slope of broken stone. As they reached the top of the slope and rolled onto yet another grassy plateau, Yuri glanced in his side mirror. The Lily warriors had kept the pace easily.

"Good stamina," he muttered.

"They are a warrior breed," Rinn said. "They can run all day and into the night, when necessary. It is part of their honor." Yuri picked up their speed a little more. "I can hear others ahead," Rinn added a moment later. "A watcher at a stair and a city beyond. And—" She stopped. "Something else I can't catch, something in a chamber under the stair. Asleep? Drugged? Odd."

She pointed to the right at a distant cliff edging the far side of the wide meadow. "Bear in that direction, toward the cliff stair— it's the endpoint of the city road."

Yuri turned the rover off the trail in the indicated direction. Beyond the cliffside they could see the crags of a distant peak, the first of the interior range of mountains. The noon sun glinted off pale stone tinted by the greenish glow of a light cloud cover, a hue repeated in the shimmering movement of the grass. To the left rose the featureless jumble of another eroded cliff; to the right a sweep of forest edge to the southeast ringing the far rim of the shelf plateau.

"There," Rinn said, pointing straight ahead at the cliff. "The road begins in that gap in the rock."

"What gap?" Yuri peered at the cliff as the rover bumped slowly forward.

"The Sacred Stair," she said obscurely. After a moment she added, "We are seen from above, Yuri. A Watcher, a servant of the Three-Fingered. He runs to tell the Children of the Stair, other servants—berserkers who have the Madness." Yuri turned to look at her and saw her looking upward, her expression abstracted and shadowed. She shivered then and looked at him. "I hear a larger community in a city of caverns a kilometer beyond him. Another messenger is leaving to inform the Elders of the Three-Fingered. The first is awakening the Captain of the Stair." Her eyes widened, and he saw her expression change to sudden horror. "Oh!" She raised her hands involuntarily, her breath exploding with the exclamation.

"Rinn!"

Rinn's eyes rolled upward in their sockets, and she sagged sidewise like a loose-jointed doll.

"Rinn!" he shouted again. Cursing, he unbuckled his seat restraint to reach her.

"What's the matter?" Tatiana asked in alarm.

"She's fainted. Boris, keep a lookout." He clambered around his seat and checked Rinn's suit controls, then tugged her into a more comfortable position lengthwise, her feet propped across the narrow aisle. He bled in more oxygen into her suit from her tank, then shook her slightly. Her head lolled, eyes closed, face deathly pale. Involuntarily, his eyes lifted to Tatiana.

"I didn't!" she squawked, recoiling backward. Yuri felt inclined to believe her.

"Didn't what?" Leonid asked, confused.

"It's a long story," Yuri said. "She's out—I don't know how

long. If you will, Tatiana," he added forcefully, "watch over her. And you'd better put your heart in it, too, Tatiana. No more games, I'm warning you." His eyes met hers for a long moment.

"Yes, *sir*," Tatiana said, tossing her head.

"Exactly."

"We are running out of time," Shemilkin said tightly, one hand gripping Yuri's shoulder.

"From both directions, I'd say," Yuri levered himself back to the controls. "She made contact with somebody."

"The Children of the Stair, berserkers," Shemilkin concurred. He looked up to study the high cliff-edge. "The rover-jets might get us up there."

"Would waste a lot of jet-fuel—we wouldn't have much lift capacity afterward."

"True. Just keep enough to get down again, I'd say."

"Right." Yuri gunned the engine toward the cliff-face, then activated the chemical jump-jets. The rover lurched upward, veering dangerously close to the rocks with its forward momentum; Yuri corrected with a blast of the forward jets. As the rover lifted, laser-fire glanced off the windows from below, suffusing them in a diffused reddish light. Yuri spared a hand to adjust the polarization controls, blocking out the distraction. The rover struggled another two dozen meters, then swayed uncertainly as it met the air-currents near the top of the bluff. He touched the side jets, fighting for control, and nudged them past the edge to land jarringly on the nearby shelf of rock.

"Keep alert, comrades!" he said. A half-dozen laser-bolts shot by the cliff-edge, and Yuri could hear the frenzied hooting of their pursuers below. Ahead of them stretched a bleak terrain of broken rock, crevices, and boulders, the talus of a higher bluff straight ahead. The rover bumped forward at a slow crawl for several meters to the edge of the break. Yuri scanned the ground ahead and to the sides, searching for a better route, then shut down the engine.

"Impossible," he muttered, wishing again that the rover had more flight capability. The jet-dial showed their reserve fuel almost gone in the profligate blast that had lifted them to the clifftop. The small atomic engine gave them nearly unlimited power for ground travel, but the rover was not designed for more than hopping an occasional obstacle. "I guess this is as far as we go."

"I agree," Shemilkin said, looking around alertly. "At least we're out of range."

"For now," Leonid warned. Yuri heard the snap as the *Nauka*'s trade officer unclipped a laser-rifle from its brackets.

Yuri turned in his seat to check Rinn's status and saw Tatiana seated beside her limp body, the Starfarer's helmet cradled in her lap. Tatiana lifted her eyes to his, her face pale with apprehension.

"Anything?" he asked.

"She's still unconscious, but vital signs are steady. Why did she pass out?"

"I don't know," he said. "And no snide questions about why I don't know all her secrets."

Tatiana stared at him coolly. "You said 'no games,' Captain. I agree that the situation requires the essentials. What do we do now?"

"You watch over her, make her comfortable. Hand me another rifle, Lenya. I want to see what's happening below."

Leonid passed a laser-rifle forward, and Yuri unsnapped his belt. Shemilkin reached for the com and called *Zvezda* for support.

"Coming, sir," Svetlana's voice crackled. "Preflight check will take ten minutes."

"Take the minutes," Shemilkin said. "Make a safe landing, not a hasty one, in the meadow. Do you have a fix on our position?"

"Triangulating now. *Nauka* is still out-orbit after the capsule, sir. Shall I recall them?"

"No. Let me talk to Usu."

"Yes, sir." As Svetlana gave the com to Hara, Yuri nodded at Leonid and climbed out of the rover, then waited for Leonid to join him. He took a quick glance around, checking conditions.

"Keep a watch on my back, Lenya. I don't trust them to not have a way up those cracks."

Leonid nodded soberly and flexed his hands on his rifle. "You got it, Yuri."

"Let's go."

Cautiously, keeping an eye on all directions, the two men advanced toward the cliff-edge.

Chapter 20

AS LEONID KEPT A WATCH TO THE REAR, YURI crouched and peered over the cliff-edge at the meadow below. A large group of aliens clustered together a dozen meters from the cliff, laser-armed, a shaman in his feathered collar standing arrogantly in their midst. He had a few seconds of observation before Ghost-Walker spotted him and stabbed an arm upward; a dozen lasers swung in instant response. Yuri jerked back reflexively, then flinched as concentrated laser-fire glanced off the stone inches from his helmet. A chorus of hooting filtered upward.

"Angry bunch, aren't they?" Leonid said.

"I'd be, too." Then he heard the Lily warriors' hooting stop as neatly as a snapped control on a tape recorder, and hazarded another look over the edge. Beneath him to the left he could see a shadowed crevice with the faint regular box-shapes of a winding stair—something moved on the stair, descending slowly, something big. Yuri squinted, trying to see better, careless of the Lily's laser-fire. But their attention was not on him.

As one, the Lily warriors edged nervously backward. Ghost-Walker raised his arms and begin gesticulating, a close counterpoint to the Sunstone's cursing of *Zvezda*. The bulky shadow moved ponderously downward, then emerged into the sunlight. Yuri gasped.

The alien stood half again as tall as the warriors who confronted it, two meters tall and nearly as long, his arm and leg muscles shifting smoothly as he moved, with a massive head that turned slowly from side to side, great eyes blinking in the sunlight. He held a long spear, wickedly barbed, in his many-fingered hands. As Yuri watched, the berserker crouched low, legs splayed, and snapped his jaws with an audible clack, then again and yet again, shuddering more violently with each snap of his jaws. The Lily warriors wailed their defiance.

In answer, the berserker leaped forward, rushing at them with blinding speed. A dozen laser-bolts arced toward him, burning into flesh, igniting his shaggy mane, but still he moved, oblivious to the burns. His spear ripped through the belly of a Lily warrior, then swung to the side into the neck of another. With a roar, he pounced again on a third, stamping and crushing with his powerful limbs, his mane flaming. The Lily retreated, still blasting with their rifles, as a second berserker emerged from the shadows of the stair.

"Yuri!" Leonid shouted behind him.

Yuri turned quickly. With horror, he saw a massive head rise from the crevice near the rover, its eyes fixed on the two humans near the cliff-edge. A powerful hand swung upward, grasping for a handhold. The alien levered itself out of the rift, slipped backward, and caught himself on the broken stone. Leonid broke first and ran for the rover, shouting a warning.

"Lenya!" Yuri cried. The berserker rushed and caught Leonid in two long strides, knocking him to the ground with a blow of his fist. Leonid bounced hard on the broken stone, his rifle skittering out of his hands. He screamed as the alien pounced again and lifted him high in the air, then dashed him downward onto the rocks.

"Kill him, Boris! Kill him!" Leonid shouted as he rolled desperately aside. Yuri saw the gunmounts on the rover swivel backward, but the alien was too fast. In a blur of motion, it leaped on its victim again, planted a massive foot on Leonid's back, then reached downward to yank backward on his helmet. Yuri heard the sickening crack as Leonid's spine snapped. So did Shemilkin; the rover's guns ignited with a flash, blasting the alien and Leonid's body to a common ruin.

"Damn! Damn!" Yuri sagged, his useless rifle cradled in his arms, staring at what was left of the smoking corpses. It had happened too fast, in an instant. Dazedly, he tried to shake off his shock, then stared in renewed horror as another alien's head lifted above the edge of the crevice.

"Move, Yuri!" Shemilkin's voice crackled in his headphones, impelling him into action. The rover guns swivelled, followed almost immediately by another blast. Under its protecting fire, he ran for the rover. The door opened as he reached it, and he flung himself into safety. As the door hissed shut behind him, another berserker crashed into the metal skin of the rover.

He heard Tatiana sob brokenly as he gunned the engine into roaring life, then reversed gears. "We're backing up!" he warned. The rover hurtled over the cliff-edge, tipped, and began to slide backward. Tatiana screamed in fright, and Yuri caught a glimpse of her terrified face in his mirror, her mouth distorted, eyes wide. "It's all right, Tatya," Yuri said gently. "Take it easy. Take it easy now."

"But Yuri—" she began, then visibly struggled for control. "All right," she said after a moment. "I'm all right."

As the rover tipped past forty-five degrees, Yuri activated the belly-jets for lift, then touched on the nose-jets, propelling them into open air for a controlled fall. They landed a few seconds later with a jarring thud. He promptly gunned the motor, quickly backing farther, then whirled the rover around to face the meadow.

The Lily warriors had taken a stand two hundred meters from the cliff, their massed group menaced by a half-dozen berserkers smoldering with laser-burns but still moving forward. The Lily kept up a steady laser-fire, but the beams visibly flickered as the power-charges waned. Yuri saw one Lily warrior throw down his laser-rifle in despair and reach for the spear on his back. He heard a faint shout as Ghost-Walker, still alive in their midst, raised his arms. A berserker feinted toward him, then crouched, jaws snapping.

"Target practice, Boris," Yuri ordered coldly.

The rover guns spoke again, crisping the alien who menaced the shaman, then swung toward two others and blasted them to ashes. Yuri rolled the rover forward to give Shemilkin a better angle, and the older captain picked off the three circling the Lily to attack from behind. The lone survivor turned toward the interlopers and ran at the rover. Shemilkin waited until he was a dozen meters away, blasted, then swung the gunmount away from the blackened corpse toward the stair, waiting for any other guardians who might dare a renewed attack.

Yuri waited a moment, then drove slowly toward the Lily warriors. Laser-rifles lifted in defense, and he promptly stopped. He waited, watching them, and saw Ghost-Walker shake himself dazedly. A moment passed, then another. Still the shaman hesitated. Yuri gripped his hands tighter on the controls as he watched Ghost-Walker. Behind him, Tatiana talked urgently to Rinn, trying to wake her.

"Come on, come on," Yuri muttered at the shaman. "Do something." A moment later, Ghost-Walker drew himself up proudly and began to stride toward the rover. "You brave bastard," Yuri said admiringly.

He saw a warrior drag at Ghost-Walker's arm. Hands flashed—the warrior's protest, the shaman's angry response. The warrior raised his rifle warningly, then aimed it directly at Ghost-Walker as he continued to gesture with his other hand. The shaman stiffened, his neck crest flaring. The other warriors stirred nervously, sharing glances.

"Hmmph," Shemilkin said. "And who are you, Isen-glov-amar?"

"It has to be. And I can just bet what's he arguing, too."

"No takers on that," Shemilkin said. He reached for the comset. "Calling *Zvezda*."

"*Zvezda* here," Svetlana responded immediately.

"Status, please."

"Preflight almost completed, Captain. Lift in ninety seconds."

"Land in the meadow near us, attack alert. We have trouble here."

"Yes, sir," Svetlana said calmly. "Sixty seconds to lift."

Yuri swivelled in his seat toward Rinn. "Is she awake?"

"No." Tatiana looked frustrated. "What's wrong with her?"

"I don't know. Rinn!" Yuri shouted and saw the other two wince as the shout reverberated in their own headphones. "Wake up, Rinn!" He reached back and shook her violently.

"Rinn!"

Rinn curled near the glowing spark of the Gift-coil, blocking out all sound and sight, all other consciousness, save this innermost essential of her self. The Gift-coil spun idly like a bright weathercock on its pivot, amusing itself with its own random movement. Playfully it invited her to dance to Infinity, an endless play and counterplay without end.

Gift . . . She reached out and touched the glowing coil, warming herself at its fire. Only here had she found safety when the Guardian awoke in his chamber, sensed her presence within his mind, and attacked viciously. The assault had staggered her, leaving just enough control to change pattern and escape. She had plunged back within herself, panicked, then waited within the winnowed curtains of her subconscious mind for a pursuit that did not come. She grayed into other-mind, seeking its healing, and now waited as she had once waited aboard *Sing Fa*, safe in her deepest self as danger stalked nearby.

Gift . . . She smiled, watching her toy.

She had ignored a disturbance behind her, as someone prodded for attention, demanding, pushing, wanting. *Go away! I will not listen,* she thought. *I deny your evil, refuse your sending.* She shuddered at the memory of the darkness in the Guardian's mind, a darkness that never ended, had no reason, had no control. *No!*

Rinn! Another's thought sounded dimly in the gray distance, a known voice, a safe voice. Involuntarily she half-turned toward it, then shook herself from her fog. *What?* She fought upward away from the Gift-oblivion, remembering other needs.

"Rinn!" As if stepping through a curtain, she was abruptly aware of her body, of a rough shaking. "Rinn!" Yuri called to her. She opened her eyes.

"What?" she asked faintly.

"Wake up, Rinn," he said, relief suffusing his mind.

Love. She saw his face through the faceplate of his helmet, then matched his armor to the seamed ceiling overhead, the sense of enclosed space, Tatiana's physical presence next to her. "What?" she repeated, still dazed.

"You passed out," Tatiana said, her voice reverberating unpleasantly in Rinn's headphones. Rinn changed pattern and took the knowledge she needed, careless of courtesies—the cliff, Leonid's death, the battle with the Guardians—then touched the anger of Isen-glov-amar in the clearing and expanded still outward, deep into the Mountains of Light. Cautiously, she walked invisibly among the minds of the Three-Fingered, wary of the Guardians who slept beneath every stair.

"Rinn!" Yuri called.

In a distant cavern, a breath-heavy messenger reported the death of six Guardians, of strangers at the Stair, more than Lorat and his Lily hooligans. Heads lifted and turned toward others, questioning.

[It is prophesied], the Second Elder said.

[But not in this formulation], another protested, one junior and still bound to certainties. [The cusp has not yet moved into the ninth pattern. It is too soon].

[Nevertheless, we shall see]. The First Elder, who spoke rarely in Councils, moved his three-fingered hands in solemn dignity. All hands stilled as dark eyes fixed anxiously on his aged face. [Prepare my carry-chair], the Elder said. [Saphanet shall speak for me].

Near the doorway, Saphanet bowed low, the sacred stones of his Circlet of Honor thumping against his chest. [Your Wisdom], he motioned reverently, then bowed still lower as the First Elder rose stiffly from his stone chair.

"Rinn!"

Rinn shook her head violently and sat up, returning to the here-and-now. "The Three-Fingered are coming to the Stair," she said. "Isen-glov-amar argues for our deaths."

"The second we can see," Captain Shemilkin rumbled.

"I must go out," Rinn said. She reached around Yuri and cracked open the rover door, then levered herself out between his seat and the door-stanchion. She emerged from the rover into the afternoon sunlight, a greenish glow reflected in shimmering waves across the meadow grass. As she came into view, the Lily warriors stiffened. She paused a moment, then walked several paces away from the rover and lifted her hands.

[I am the shaman of the Star-Devils], she announced. Behind her, Yuri and Tatiana emerged from the rover, each armed with a laser-rifle, and quietly took position behind her to the left and right. A distant thunder waxed as *Zvezda* descended from the sky, counterpointing Rinn's words. As the ship landed several hundred meters up-meadow, Rinn waited, listening to Captain Shemilkin's hurried report to the ship, and used the extra seconds to clear herself of her fogs.

I am Rinn, Starfarer . . .

"Easy now," Yuri warned softly.

"Magic," she assented. She raised her hands again. [Greetings, O Lily], she signed.

Ghost-Walker lifted his upper arms in response, then hesitated, torn between two impulses. Who? he wondered, sensing the Change in the world and not wanting that Change. At his movement, his two aides drifted to left and right, setting the pattern for Meeting.

Isen-glov-amar promptly stamped his foot.

[No! No]! he gestured angrily. [There is no talking]!

[Talking has begun], Ghost-Walker chided him, conceding the point in the action of his own aides. [Take your place, son of the chief]. Behind him, Belos and two others shifted quietly toward Isen-glov-amar. Belos has waited for this chance, Rinn realized. He still mourns—and now hates.

[I do not permit]! Isen-glov-amar declared. His hands moved on his laser-rifle, the bore pointed dangerously in Ghost-Walker's direction. Rinn sensed Isen-glov-amar's anger as his arrogance led him to new excesses, new daring. As the tension grew, Rinn saw his jaws snap in response to the prompting of his third brain.

She promptly stamped her foot, distracting Isen-glov-amar from that dangerous temptation. He half-turned toward her, his rifle centering on a new target.

"Watch out," Yuri warned behind her.

"Yes. Hold your fire," she told the others, wary of Shemilkin at the rover's guns, and of a keen-eyed Hara at *Zvezda*'s weapon controls. She swallowed painfully, guessing what she might have to do. He cannot be turned, she thought, her eyes on Isen-glov-amar, knowing that the arrogant warrior was the crux. Give him a show of victory and all could be lost with the violent Lily, even their crafty shaman; defeat him with her "magic" and the watching humans behind her would see everything they accused of the Starfarers. What choice?

How do I choose?

She sensed Yuri's tension, his concern for her, for his ship, his success in all he tried. If he failed—if *they* failed here . . . What is the cost? she wondered. She trembled in her agitation, unable to know the right of it.

I am Rinn, Starfarer.

I am Rinn . . .

She lifted her hands. [Son of the chief]! she motioned forcefully. [Why do you feed on your own people]?

[You are Star-Devils]! Isen-glov-amar's hand swept toward the ground in furious denial. [You know nothing]!

[I am a Lily spirit], Rinn declared.

Heads lifted in surprise, dark eyes widening. She felt a suppressed thrum from the Lily, a many-colored emotion—of startlement from Ghost-Walker, a stab of superstitious awe from his aides, of sudden fierce hope from Belos. She responded to that hope, based in lingering grief and hatred for this violent leader, and blended it with her own grief for *Sing Fa*, and the new hope of *Zvezda*.

[I am a Lily spirit[, she repeated, staring at Isen-glov-amar, then reached out with the Gift.

Death, she wished him. She made her hand into a claw, palm upward, and reversed it, matching intention with the Deltean gesture for a death-curse. Isen-glov-amar crouched, his jaw snapping. [Die], she signed.

Isen-glov-amar howled his defiance and charged across the grass, his rifle raised as a club.

Rinn heard the shriek of grinding metal as Shemilkin swivelled the gunmount toward him. "Hold your fire!" she ordered furiously.

She spread her arms wide and began the staccato dance of death-exultation, spinning, jerking, using her movement to pace her plunge into Isen-glov-amar's mind. As she encompassed his first brain, he faltered and staggered drunkenly to the side, his rifle dropping from nerveless fingers. She took the second brain and tore its mind to shreds, then bored inward to the third brain and ruthlessly crushed the *aliveness* that powered heart and breath. Like a marionette with broken strings, Isen-glov-amar sank slowly forward, limbs loose, eyes emptied, jaws still open in a last silent scream.

Rinn shuddered as she felt Isen-glov-amar's remaining mind drift into isolated strands, a torn spiderweb that vanished into nothingness, taking all anger, all need, all self with it. Behind her, she sensed the shock of her human companions.

Have I lost all, truly all? she grieved, tempted to follow Isen-glov-amar into that vast darkness.

She shuddered again, then raised her hands and spoke directly to Belos. [Shield-brother], she said, adding the graceful over-gesture of sorrow. [I was there when he killed another for his own fault. I was there when you grieved. Take this death for your brother's honor].

[I will, O Lily spirit], Belos answered, his dark eyes shimmering with emotion.

[I haven't decided that], Ghost-Walker said irritably.

"Boris," Rinn called. "Activate the camera *now*."

A ghostly image materialized beside Rinn, an ancient chief with laser-rent body. Rinn raised her hands and borrowed the memorized sequence from Shemilkin's mind, moving her hands in tandem with Ba-rao-som's image. Ghost-Walker's eyes narrowed, his glance flicking between Rinn and the hologram.

[What trick is this]? he demanded suspiciously.

Rinn pointed at Ba-rao-som. [Listen to him], she replied. [He brings important words].

[No]. Ghost-Walker matched deed to word by turning his

back to her. Yuri watched as he elevated his backside and twitched it disdainfully.

"What the hell?" Yuri asked.

Rinn lowered her hands. "He doesn't believe in the ghost. Nor in me." She sighed as half the Lily warriors turned and lifted their own backsides in insult, until only Belos faced them, looking around uncertainly. The array of twitching behinds was a ridiculous anticlimax.

Rinn looked down at Isen-glov-amar's body. It didn't work, she thought. Do you win after all, son of the chief? Ba-rao-som continued his speech to an oblivious audience, then flickered into nothingness as Shemilkin switched him off.

In the distance, at the base of the Stair, Saphanet strode into the meadow, followed by the First Elder's chair swaying on the backs of four servants. He paused, taking in the gleaming bulk of *Zvezda*, the corpses half-hidden in the grass, the massed posture of the Lily warriors, the three strange gleaming creatures with bulbous heads, two with weapon-sticks in five-fingered hands. He noticed their hands, wondering. Only five fingers, not six—did they understand part of the truth?

He signalled to the lead servant, halting the Elder's progress for safety, then bravely walked toward the strangers in a loose-limbed stride, signalling his intention for talk.

As he approached the strangers, he cautiously watched the Lily party from his side vision, ready for anything from their tumultuous breed. Their shaman had some sense—at times, he amended irritably—but knew little beyond his rituals and rude demands. Even now, he demanded by holding the Posture of Contempt as Saphanet approached, placing his own choosing over proper deference of greeting to the Three-Fingered. By custom, Saphanet would now do insult to one party or the other, with no middle ground.

Saphanet decided he did not like being pushed.

He stopped and glanced back at the First Elder. A hand lifted and gestured briefly. [Ignore his rudeness].

Saphanet turned back to the strangers and arranged his stance into a comfortable posture, then lifted his three-fingered hands and made the gesture of talk-invited. The stranger to the left, the one without a weapon, immediately responded.

[Greetings, O Three-Fingered], it said. Saphanet peered forward and saw a face within the transparent head. Did they live within shells like a reed-snail? [My courtesy to the First Elder], the other added and bent forward as if gripped by sudden pain. Curious: was it ill?

[Thank you], he said, judging the response suited any possibility.

Ghost-Walker stamped forward, gesturing angrily at Saphanet. [You insult us! How dare you speak to those we proscribe]?

[You were born insulted], Saphanet replied coolly. [Have a care, shaman, or our magic will remain unshared]. Ghost-Walker halted abruptly, quivering in his rage at the threat—but halted nonetheless. [You may listen], Saphanet instructed him. [You may not interrupt].

[I am the shaman of—]

[The Lily People. That I know well]. He glanced beyond him at the array of Ghost-Walker's warriors and decided to ignore them. Change was on the world; if the Lily attacked the First Elder, even a conservative Council would see the wisdom of loosing the new cadre of berserkers, long bred in secret from the few survivors of the last destruction. Saphanet would be well revenged if Ghost-Walker decided to be a fool.

He turned back to the strangers. [Who are you]?

Another stepped forward, its weapon cradled in his single pair of arms. It bent forward and laid the weapon on the grass. An offering? Or was this one also abruptly ill and forced to disarm itself? Saphanet watched intensely as the stranger straightened.

[We are Star-men], it said haltingly. [We come to trade. We come in peace, defending only when attacked]. It paused and glanced at the other on the left, the first one. Saphanet saw its mouth working inside its head-shell, saw the other's flap in return. Mouth-sounds? He heard nothing audible and wondered about it: truly these creatures had strange ways. Perhaps they signalled each other with their mouths, too, being encased in shells that limited posture. The taller one looked back and raised his hands again. [We wish you well], it said, adding a gesture of deep respect—not quite appropriate to Saphanet's Council rank but close enough. [Will you trade with us]?

Saphanet considered, glancing at the First Elder for guidance. The Elder ruffled his neck fur, signing prudence. [We will consider the offer, Five-Fingered], Saphanet said to the strangers. [Welcome].

[No]! Ghost-Walker's gesture was a plea of despair. [They are swamp-demons]! His hand stabbed at a Lily corpse nearby;

Saphanet noted for the first time that it bore no visible wounds.
Disease? It had no interest for him.

[They have killed the son of the Lily chief]! Ghost-Walker
declared.

[That is not our affair], Saphanet gestured, irritated by the
irrelevancy. [Now we will depart for our city], he said courte-
ously to the strangers. [We will await your return].

[When]? asked the third stranger, small-bodied like the first.

[In a span of days, one less finger than your hand, one more
than ours], Saphanet decided, liking the neatness of the choice.
He turned, omitting after-greetings to the furious Lily shaman,
and stalked slowly back to the First Elder.

[Well done, my Saphanet], the Elder said to him.

[Your Wisdom], Saphanet acknowledged modestly, although
he quite agreed.

The First Elder raised his old eyes and looked beyond him at
the Star-man house. [It is too soon, but much was lost in the
Cataclysm, still more in the last Change. Perhaps even Truth
has a different shading than we believed].

[Yes], Saphanet said, greatly daring.

[And perhaps not], the Elder amended, reproving him. At his
signal, the servants swayed his chair to their broad backs and
bore him toward the Stair. Saphanet followed obediently, denying himself a look backward at the Star-men and their strangeness. Better that, than to find that the Change they promised
might be illusion.

If it was.

As the Elder was borne into the Stair, Saphanet could not
repress one last glance, hoping it was not.

Chapter 21

YURI WATCHED THE THREE-FINGERED DISAPPEAR into the cliffside stair, then took a deep breath, still not quite able to believe they had agreed to contact. Ghost-Walker hissed at him, his neck fur ruffling.

[You will not win, Star-Devil], the shaman said malevolently.

[That's that you think], Yuri signed back.

Ghost-Walker spat and stalked back to his warriors, then signalled them to gather up the Lily bodies. The rover's gun-turret followed the Lily warriors as they circled wide around *Zvezda*. Yuri saw Belos glance backward at Rinn.

[Go in peace], she gestured after him. Belos shuddered, then followed after the others, not daring another glance.

"Peace?" Tatiana asked with a snort. "After you killed Isenglov-amar?"

"It was necessary." A wash of fatigue swept across Rinn's face.

Tatiana tossed her head. "That will be discussed, I assure you. The Bureau will be very interested in your Code now, Starfarer."

Rinn looked at her coolly. "Why the protest, Tatiana? Didn't you get what you wanted? A 'magic' display with overt use of the Gift against others? Surely you understand revenge, Trade Officer. I welcome you to try to take yours, for whatever fault you think I've done you. Strange, to turn something on its ear

219

like that, but Normals always seem to manage. I could say other reasons, quite rational, all trade-oriented, a smart debate of choices in an uncertain situation, but mostly revenge. He killed my crew." She smiled thinly. "As I would now kill for you, Tatiana Nikolaevna, if any caused your death." She shrugged. "Wise or not, I've made my choice." She gestured at the cliff-side stair. "You have your trade back. Now leave me alone." She turned away and trudged toward *Zvezda*.

"Rinn," Yuri called after her.

"It's nothing," she said tiredly. "Just forget it."

The lock-stair unfolded itself as she approached the ship. The lock bay door opened a moment later, and Khina bounded down the stair to throw her arms around Rinn.

"You were wonderful, Rinn," she said, then glared past her at Tatiana. "Russki bitch," she hissed.

Yuri groaned. "Not now, Khina. That goes for you, too, Tatiana." He pointed at her warningly. "Everything goes on hold, especially your mouth."

"How dare you!"

"I locked you up before; I can do it again."

Tatiana's mouth shut with a snap.

"Good," Yuri said. "We've had quite enough today, and we have our own dead to mourn. Or have you forgotten Lenya?"

"No, sir," she mumbled rebelliously.

Yuri abruptly lost all remaining patience with her.

"I'm surprised," he said violently. "But, then, it wasn't Oleg, was it? Maybe if it had been, you might get off this orbit of yours about Rinn. But then, maybe not. Maybe you can only care about one thing at a time, Tatiana."

Tatiana whirled to stamp away, and he grabbed her arm, yanking her around to face him.

"Listen to me. I love Rinn. I love her! Do you hear that? Bureau or not, your aunt or not, Delta or not, I won't let you harm her. So give it up, Tatiana." He shook her roughly, hard enough to snap her helmet back and forth against the bindings.

"Let me go!" Tatiana screamed, hitting at him.

"Give it up!"

"Yuri!" Shemilkin called and hurried toward them. "Yuri!" He dragged them apart. "What's wrong with you? Have you lost all sense?"

"Look at her," Yuri yelled at him. "We succeed, we get the trade back—and all she sees is some new accusation, some new threat, to throw at Rinn. I've had it with you, Tatiana! You'd better watch out!'' Trembling with rage, Yuri stalked toward the ship.

As he reached Khina and Rinn, he looked up to scowl at them both. ''My, my!'' Khina said with awe. ''Remind me never to cross you, Captain.''

Rinn laughed softly. ''Sir Gawain,'' she said, her dark eyes shining with tears.

He smiled at her ruefully. ''I've screwed up the crew dynamics something awful now; Viktor'll have my hide. And you *are* wonderful, my lovely love.''

''If you think so,'' she said.

''I know so. Come; we've work to do.''

Three hours later, *Zvezda* caught up with *Nauka* in orbit high above Delta's atmosphere. ''Return home?'' Yuri stared at the impassive face in the viewscreen.

''That's what it said.'' *Nauka*'s engineer shrugged. '' '*Zvezda* will return home immediately, with Captain Shemilkin to assume full authority here.' '' He glanced at his captain standing beside Yuri's chair. ''Orders, sir?''

''Politics!'' Shemilkin snorted. ''It has to be that.'' He turned toward Rinn's computerman station. ''And *Nauka* continues alone, to trade with the Three-Fingered. I'll miss your able service, Starfarer.''

''Perhaps we will return soon, Captain,'' Rinn said quietly.

''In political matters, return is uncertain, my dear. Blast and fire! We're coming back to *Nauka*, Ivan. Prepare for E-frame recovery.''

''Yes, sir.''

Shemilkin turned to Yuri. ''I give you my Lenya to take home, Yuri Ivanovich. See that they bury him well. And I do hope you—both of you—return quickly.''

''But you don't believe it.''

Shemilkin shrugged. ''Something has happened, something political. Perhaps Kirova pushed too far and upset the power balance with Krasin. He's quick to exploit any weakness, that one. Or perhaps Earth is pressuring the Bureau; I doubt if Xin Tian has given up so easily on getting Rinn back. Who knows? But best of luck to you.'' He extended his hand, and Yuri took it, rising from his chair. Boris drew him into a quick embrace, then signed to Svetlana. ''We must be going. Good fortune, comrades.''

"And to you on Delta Bootis."

"Yes."

As *Zvezda* moved out to warp-point, Rinn remained at her computer station, watching the faces of her crew, matching sight to the emotions that flickered from them. She saw Khina wink at her and roll her eyes, then met Roblev's calm gaze: his expression was accepting and intrigued. Galina was troubled, Oleg more aware of Tatiana's anger than any fears of his own. Hara proceeded stoutly with his duties, accepting her magics as he might accept the cleverness of his machines. She relaxed into the gestalt of their acceptance, for which Tatiana's lingering opposition was only a savor.

Strange how easy it is for them, yet not easy, she reflected. If I were faced with the same choice, would I be as generous?

She felt a weight of years shift from her shoulders and looked around the deck again. This was home.

She reached into her breast pocket and brought out her Star, then propped it in the small recess above her computer station. It glinted in the muted light of the control room, catching the multicolored gleams of control lights on metal panels. Rinn's star, she thought, admiring it wistfully. One star as emblem, another as ship, neither guaranteed, neither yet lost. Which will survive, I wonder?

"I've seen that only twice, both in crisis," Yuri said at her elbow. "Why do you bring it out now?"

"A ceremony, love. Only that. What do you think has happened on Novy Strana?"

"Lenin only knows."

Tatiana turned in her chair and glared at Rinn. "And when the Bureau finds you can *kill* with your Gift?"

"Tatya . . ."

Tatiana's head jerked. "Don't call me that!"

"But I will, Tatya. Are we not sisters?" She forestalled Yuri's angry reproof with a raised hand. "You press her too hard, Yuri. Let it be." Her eyes flicked to Tatiana. "As much as I love your demonstrations for me, telepaths *are* to be feared, if they come from Ikanos. I grew up with them, and everything that Novy Strana fears happened to me—except the loss of ultimate self. How I avoided that, not even the enclave knows. We never know why the Group-Mind lets us go. Yet when I boarded the Xin Tian freighter, they were trying to dominate me, even then, at the last. The malice is real; don't underestimate it.''

All eyes had turned to her, some confused, some noncommittal, some concerned. She spread her hands, addressing all of them. "I was born with the Gift; I cannot escape it. But I mean no harm—I only make the choices I feel compelled to make. As I have chosen you, comrades. You may not yet realize it, but I have thrown away the enclave by my murder of Isen-glov-amar.''

She looked at her Star sadly. "Connor warned me not to care too deeply, to walk a narrow line that denied full commitment. But I chose, and it was *murder*: he had no defense against me. But for your sake, I chose—and I sense your choice in return. There is a binding among us, into *Zvezda*—and that is a thing to be guarded.'' She met Roblev's eyes and felt their accord, at last.

We guard this ship, he and I, each in our own way, she thought.

"All my life I have been denied the binding you find so easily among your friends and family. I fled Ikanos, which murdered my parents. I found the enclave, and found division even there within our walls. On *Sing Fa* I was hated and distrusted. I am different, far more profoundly than you are different from each other, but you have given me a place to stand.'' She curled her fingers into Yuri's hand and smiled up at him. "And so, I say to all of you: don't press Tatiana, as I have been pressed all my life. Don't drive her to a choice of yes or no.''

Tatiana was silent, her dark eyes flicking from Rinn to the others as she again weighed advantage, wheels within wheels. Oleg bit his lip, caught in his own choices.

"In some things,'' Rinn said, answering their doubt, "there are no wheels. I guard this ship, Tatya,'' she continued. "I guard you, despite your doubts about me. In time, perhaps I'll earn your trust; perhaps not. Like Novy Strana and the Three-Fingered, perhaps even the Lily tribe, in everything there can be a binding.''

Or so we hope, she thought, looking around at the faces—and finding some proof of it.

"But they have recalled us,'' Tatiana said uncertainly. "Everything might change.''

"Perhaps,'' she agreed, and sensed that Tatiana would bide her time. Even in a Change of the world, many would be cautious. She smiled at them all, content.

* * *

On the following day, *Zvezda* reached warp-point and launched for Novy Strana. During the days of warp, Rinn worked and played with the crew of *Zvezda*, sharing each night with Yuri, spending most of the day with Khina when Yuri was busy, and, to her surprise, with Viktor Roblev, who approached almost shyly. She treasured each day, imagining it might last forever, knowing that time likely was running out. At its end, the ship entered the Arcturus system and passed through inbound and outbound traffic, then settled on its landing square near the capital. The Bureau summons came immediately.

As she settled beside Yuri in the backseat of a jitney, he took her hand and pressed her fingers affectionately. Another ground-car bearing Tatiana Nikolaevna and Roblev whisked away into the distance; the others were still waiting at the ship. Yuri watched Tatiana's ground-car a moment, then tapped the driver's shoulder.

"Space Bureau, please."

"Yes, Captain." The car rolled forward and accelerated, Sirov's agent at the wheel. Rinn dipped lightly into his thoughts, then decided he knew nothing. Another advantage of men content with naked orders; Sirov must value them.

"This time I sent our report ahead of us," Yuri said, his eyes also on the driver's back. He shrugged, dismissing the man's presence, and turned to her. "What do you think Kirova will do?"

"It depends on her problem." Rinn lifted her chin slightly and tried to find the commissar in the squat buildings ahead. "Perhaps our report scrambled things again."

"I'm sorry about all this," he said awkwardly. "It's not fair."

She nodded, understanding him. "It's your world, your people."

"And yours, if they allow it. I can accept losing *Zvezda*, if I do. I don't know what I'd do if I lose you—or had to choose. Do you understand why?"

"Yes."

"Is that treachery?" he wondered aloud, troubled.

"No, love. Only another choice, as difficult as mine; I understand." She moved her fingers in his.

He looked out the window, still fretting. "You did well," he said, more to himself than to her, as if he were practicing arguments for an unseen listener. "You're an asset to the ship.

The mission would have succeeded . . . Where will you go if they won't agree?''

"I will survive. I'm a good survivor."

"Yes," he murmured as they rolled into the plaza before the Bureau. Rinn smiled at his averted face.

Love, she thought.

"Yes," he said. "It is that."

He offered her a hand out of the jitney, and they walked up the broad steps to the open door, then followed the guard's directions to an upper floor. At the end of a corridor, they turned into a small office, well lit by wide windows and crowded with the heavy furniture favored by Novy Strana bureaucrats. Kirova sat behind a desk, her blond hair neatly coiled, the picture of competent authority. To one side sat the Xin Tian delegate, his lips pursed with satisfaction, and, beside him, Connor, his expression cold, his mind rigorously concealed from her.

"Ah, Captain Selenkov," Kirova said. "And McCrea. Welcome." She stood and motioned them to chairs in front of her desk, entirely affable. Both the delegate and Connor stared at Rinn, offering nothing. Kirova ignored them. "I've been reviewing your report again, Captain, and I must say the Bureau is pleased. Your performance especially, Starfarer, led to the success. It was more than I expected."

Rinn sensed the tension ease from Yuri's muscles as he guessed what she saw clearly in Kirova's mind. The body in question was not Yuri's ship, only herself. And that surrender was not as certain as Xin Tian thought. Kirova busied herself with her papers a moment, then lifted her serene face. Behind that serenity, Rinn sensed steel and determination, a hint of recent arguments with others, a tentative victory.

"I will accept custody now," Chien said brusquely. "Starfarer McCrea, you will accompany us to—"

"Not so fast, comrade," Kirova checked him. "We have reconsidered our position. We have decided this is first a local matter, not a Treaty problem; our legate is informing the Earth council now for its review. After all, McCrea is still classified as a state criminal; you may have her back when she completes her sentence."

"But—but—" Chien sputtered. "What sentence? She hasn't had any trial!"

"An oversight we shall correct—in due course." Kirova smiled slightly. "Perhaps in a year or two," she added, twisting the knife. "Our law permits indefinite detention. I choose to detain her aboard *Zvezda*."

"I protest!" the Xin Tian legate snapped.

"Noted," Kirova said coolly. "As I said, the decision is changed. We will keep her."

"You can't do that!" Chien shouted. "Earth has ordered you to surrender her!"

Kirova turned to Connor with a half-smile. "And you, Starfarer?"

Connor looked back coldly. "As I informed you earlier, the enclave has no further interest in this woman. Xin Tian's intention is strictly punitive." His eyes shifted to Rinn. "When Xin Tian has corrected your precipitate decision and reacquires custody, McCrea will be repatriated to Ikanos."

Connor . . . she pleaded, but he refused to hear. She looked away from him.

"*If* it corrects; we shall see. Thank you, comrades," Kirova said, dismissing them. Chien hesitated, half-minded to protest again at the cavalier treatment, then rose and stomped out in a huff, Connor following. The three listened to their footsteps recede down the corridor.

"Now," Kirova continued equably. "To more important business. Captain Selenkov, we are sending you on temporary assignment back to Delta, to complete the reestablishment of trade you have begun."

"Temporary?" Yuri asked sharply. "*Zvezda* is a Delta run ship."

"We have need of *Zvezda*'s collective talents in more challenging tasks. Your first stop after Delta will be Nusakan. The specifics are on your instruction tape." She handed a computer disc to Yuri.

Yuri took the disc and read its label, his fingers moving in a subtle caress across the surface. "Nusakan is in Xin Tian space," he said slowly.

"Exactly. Do you expect us to accept *Sing Fa*'s poaching so equably? I give you the opportunity to right the affair." It was a dismissal.

"I see." Yuri hesitated, glanced at Rinn, and then rose.

Rinn remained seated, her eyes fixed on Kirova. "I'd like to talk to the commissar alone, Yuri." She saw an involuntary flash of alarm in Kirova's eyes, then the smooth functioning of self-control. *So you aren't quite that certain about me,* she thought. *Interesting.*

Kirova considered. "Will you excuse us for a few minutes, Comrade Captain?"

Yuri bowed slightly, reached a hand to brush Rinn's cheek, then left the room.

"You have something to say?" Kirova asked.

"Why choose *Zvezda* for the poaching? Yuri has corrected his error, and Krasin no longer uses the incident against you. Why demote us to First Survey?"

"First Survey is an honorable—"

"Let's be honest, Madame. You know exactly how the Bureau uses First Survey—to put your rebels into danger, where their restive talents are more useful—and far away from Novy Strana. Why *Zvezda*?"

Kirova shrugged. "It is an available ship."

"I asked for honesty—you'll gain more from me by giving it. But no matter. You are trapping me into action against Xin Tian—and perhaps my own enclave. If a Xin Tian ship catches me in their space . . ."

"All the more reason to be cautious, Starfarer." Kirova smiled benignly.

Rinn studied her face. "Krasin's doing?"

"In part. He has his concerns, as do I. The rest is mine. I intend to keep you, Starfarer, far longer than I pretended to Comrade Chien. How better to cement your loyalty than to arrange a single choice?"

"And how do you know I wouldn't have chosen your choice without the prompting?"

"I have learned to avoid ambiguity."

"I see. I have a small price for you to pay in return."

"Indeed? Since when must I give terms at all?"

"The Gift is a *conscious* talent," Rinn reminded her.

Kirova shrugged and leaned back in her chair, her face relaxing into amusement. She waved a negligent hand for Rinn to continue.

"You say I am a state criminal; does that prohibit my posting as Captain Selenkov's ship wife?"

Kirova frowned. "I admit there are few precedents. You wish this?"

"Yes. You intend to post another woman to *Zvezda* for him; cancel that plan, please."

Kirova's eyes flickered, then stilled. "As I've said, an interesting Gift, Starfarer. What else do you know?"

"Enough to ask another question: does my criminal status prohibit my rank as computerman on *Zvezda*?"

"I prefer assistant trade officer. So you know that, too."

"I know many things, Commissar. I suggest you be more gentle with your niece. She might accept me as crewmate, but never as rival. In return, I'll ask Yuri to drop the sabotage charge you've tried to finesse with Krasin, not exactly with success. Or is it your intention that I never make peace with Tatiana?"

Kirova stared at her, surprised again. "You wish peace?"

"Someday we might discuss what I wish, Commissar, when you are truly interested. I have one more request."

"State your request."

"Give me a Contract. Make me Starfarer on *Zvezda*— sanctioned as criminal, with whatever initial restrictions you wish—but give me room to build a new corps for you. Give me a place a begin, a place to defend—and if *Zvezda* survives the risks of First Survey, I will deliver a people to you."

The promise lay on the air for a moment.

"Indeed," Kirova said softly. She paused, considering. "And can you do this?"

"Perhaps not. But I have found another option to Ikanos, one that some of the enclave might prefer to Xin Tian's restrictions. Connor guesses that and considers it threat enough to proscribe me." She smiled thinly. "I am very dangerous."

"As am I, Starfarer."

"Do we have an understanding then?"

"Perhaps. You may have the ship wife rank you wish—and the computerman posting. The other I will think about. Return to your ship, Starfarer. We will talk again—when you have returned from Nusakan."

"Thank you." Rinn rose and bowed formally, then left the room. Yuri was waiting down the hall, pretending to read a bulletin board. As she emerged from the room, he turned and looked at her worriedly.

"What was that all about?" he asked as she reached him.

She slipped her hand into his. "I'll tell you later."

"Well," he said, squeezing her hand, "I kept my ship—and you—for now, at least."

"Yes, for now. Politics, Yuri. She's tried to solve us both. You are restive and 'inconvenient.' I am a tool one wants and another disputes."

Yuri scowled at Kirova's door. "That's what *she* thinks. Like Ghost-Walker may discover, events can be otherwise." He looked down at her, and his expression softened. "It might have been easier to let you go, my love. We have a double-edged sword over us—you, me, both inconvenient—assuming we return from Nusakan."

"Yes, assuming." She shrugged, pretending a careless bravado, and heard his answering chuckle.

He raised her hand to his lips. "Ah, but they've miscalculated," he said. "Together, Starfarer, not even the universe can defeat us."

"Yes." She smiled at him. "Let us try for that, my Comrade Captain."

ABOUT THE AUTHOR

Born in Portland, Oregon, Paula E. Downing received a B.A. in History from Whitman College in 1973. During law school, she clerked for a federal judge and served as Articles Editor for the *Oregon Law Review*. She is now a personal-injury lawyer and municipal judge in Medford, Oregon, and is married to fellow SF writer T. Jackson King. Paula and Tom (carefully supervised by four cat-persons) live in a large house on eighteen acres of wooded property south of Medford. Besides managing her law practice and writing novels, Paula writes an ongoing column for the SF & Fantasy Workshop, has published two juvenile stories, and edits for *Pandora*, a small-press SF magazine based in Michigan. She is currently working on her fourth novel.